Peter Smith was a newspaper crime reporter for 37 years in England and Canada, where he turned up at hundreds of crime scenes and worked closely with homicide detectives and pathologists. As the crime reporter for the Calgary Sun, Alberta, Canada, he won awards for covering the Columbine School massacre in Littleton, Colorado, and was sent back to England to cover the case of a doctor who murdered 216 patients. He has written two true-crime murder books featuring Canadian cases he covered. Now retired, he lives on a remote tiny island off the west coast of British Columbia, Canada.

To Joan,
with best wishes
Pet Smith
Quadra Island
2023

To all my secret sources everywhere.

Peter Smith

Hitting Deadline

AUSTIN MACAULEY PUBLISHERS™
LONDON • CAMBRIDGE • NEW YORK • SHARJAH

Copyright © Peter Smith 2023

All rights reserved. No part of this publication may be reproduced, distributed, or transmitted in any form or by any means, including photocopying, recording, or other electronic or mechanical methods, without the prior written permission of the publisher, except in the case of brief quotations embodied in critical reviews and certain other non-commercial uses permitted by copyright law. For permission requests, write to the publisher.

Any person who commits any unauthorized act in relation to this publication may be liable to criminal prosecution and civil claims for damages.

This is a work of fiction. Names, characters, businesses, places, events, locales, and incidents are either the products of the author's imagination or used in a fictitious manner. Any resemblance to actual persons, living or dead, or actual events is purely coincidental.

Ordering Information
Quantity sales: Special discounts are available on quantity purchases by corporations, associations, and others. For details, contact the publisher at the address below.

Publisher's Cataloging-in-Publication data
Smith, Peter
Hitting Deadline

ISBN 9781685628963 (Paperback)
ISBN 9781685628970 (ePub e-book)

Library of Congress Control Number: 2023901848

www.austinmacauley.com/us

First Published 2023
Austin Macauley Publishers LLC
40 Wall Street, 33rd Floor, Suite 3302
New York, NY 10005
USA

mail-usa@austinmacauley.com
+1 (646) 5125767

I would like to thank all those detectives in various CID offices and homicide units who shared their knowledge with me and the coroner's officers in England and the medical examiner's office staff in Canada who gave me their valuable time over the years, which helped to inspire me to write this book.

Thanks, as always, to my wife, Amanda, who has listened to me talking about murders and skeletons, blood, and bodies all the time I was writing this book. And she's never complained about the piles of crime books, newspaper cuttings, notebooks, and murder files filling the house from office to attic. Add to that, her computer skills have saved me many times when my writings were in danger of flying off into cyber-space.

Table of Contents

Chapter 1	11
Chapter 2	26
Chapter 3	59
Chapter 4	79
Chapter 5	106
Chapter 6	128
Chapter 7	137
Chapter 8	153
Chapter 9	174
Chapter 10	219
Chapter 11	229
Chapter 12	240
Chapter 13	244
Chapter 14	251
Chapter 15	261
Chapter 16	279
Chapter 17	292
Chapter 18	299
Chapter 19	302
Epilogue	306

Chapter 1

"**A woman's body, dismembered by a chainsaw, was found buried in the backyard...**" The comfortable clicking of the computer keyboard was music to his ears. It had been a busy day and night, driving 300 kilometers to the scene in southern Alberta and digging out the story. Driving back, he was pumped with adrenaline in that nervous zone a few clicks over the speed limit, making the judgement call where if a cop saw you, he couldn't pull you over, but still giving yourself a chance to get back to the office in time for deadline.

On the way back, he'd even smiled to himself at the thought of digging out the story of a dismembered body buried in a yard. It would be a slick sick joke he'd probably repeat in the office where his overtly macabre reputation already mystified his colleagues. This was a reporter who wrote with such sensitivity as to sometimes bring tears; a man who treated traumatized real-life victims with such compassion as to move them to write letters of appreciation to the editor. So how could he be such a ghoulish weirdo who relished death and murder with a gleeful smile and with a black-humor joke for everybody?

He'd pulled his maroon Chevy van into the Calgary Mail's parking lot, feeling smug that no one had dared park in his spot under its designated "Police Reporter" sign. Well, he deserved to feel smug. For years, when he was younger with a mop of black hair and definitive black beard, he'd had to park wherever he could find a spot. Now 54, with most of that hair gone and the remainder greying fast, and with that beard now a salt-and-pepper grey fast turning white and with a whole life-time of experience under his belt, he'd finally warranted having his own parking spot.

He was soon inside the glass front door of the modern, still antiseptically clean, office. The three-story flat-roofed modern commercial building was uninspiring, similar to many others on this northeast Calgary industrial site. It lay directly under the flight path of commercial airliners making their approach to Calgary International from the south. On daytime flights into Calgary, Ben couldn't resist looking down as the aircraft would fly first almost directly over the flat-roofed uninspiring oblong building of the Calgary Echo—the Mail's great rival newspaper a few flying seconds further south on the flight path—and then a few moments later the Mail's oblong building would slide under the wing. Its modern glass and stucco exterior could never rival the allure of Ben's first newspaper office where his career had begun more than 30 years earlier.

It had red brick walls which hadn't seen jet airliners overhead—instead, it had swastika-covered aircraft in the sky above. It had survived a rain of high explosives from Hitler's Luftwaffe bombers during the Blitz on southern England. Ben still recalled how its old wooden staircase, with treads bowed with wear, smelled with a lifetime of printers ink ground into every step. Now, inside this fresh clean building, he stopped and swore. Across the foyer with its welcoming potted-plants under the framed faces on the wall of editorial staff members who'd won managerial approval for deeds well done, a hallowed place from which his face had never smiled down in 11 years, the interior glass security door was locked against him.

"Fuck," he muttered as the cardboard sign proclaiming "Security guard on rounds, please wait. Back in 10 minutes," mocked him from where it hung inside the office, where he wasn't. What pissed him off was the number of arguments he'd had with the city editor over tiny matters like this. All day he'd been working under pressure to get this story and bring it back halfway across Alberta on time. He'd driven on the edge all the way back, enduring those nasty knots twitching in the pit of his stomach when he took bends so fast he knew it would be his stupid fault if the van had come unstuck, because he was really overdoing it. And he'd shaved those minutes down, and got this close at 9:45 p. m., still 45 minutes to deadline, and now he was locked out.

"Put a fucking system in where your reporters have got keys to avoid this crap," he'd argued last time it happened. But his years of experience had taught him that screaming in the boss's face never brought results, it just made him feel better. First, the management would never trust reporters to have keys. Come on. And secondly, such a simple scheme would cost. Not a lot, but any scheme that cost money was as frowned on as the typo in yesterday's late edition. It was just another aggravation in his routine, another pressure. He snatched the internal foyer phone off its hook, hit 122 to the city desk and yelled, "come and let me in, I'm locked out down here." At this time of night, Frank, the lone guy manning the desk one floor up, now had to leave the police scanners, every phone in the newsroom and whatever story he was writing, no matter how near he was to deadline, to waste time coming down to let Ben in.

"Could be solved if reporters had keys," Ben was thinking as Frank reached the door. And wouldn't you know it, didn't it always happen, just as the night guy reached the door, so did the night security guard. Inside at last, heading up the stairs, busting for a piss after the three-hour drive fueled by two cans of Diet Coke, Ben knew he'd have to wait for that luxury until after the story was in—after deadline.

"Excuse me, sir," called the security guard up the stairs politely. "Could you come down and sign in? You haven't signed in."

"No time, mate," Ben called back, knowing this was another aggravating thorn that would come back to stick him. The management had issued simple and unbreakable instructions to security staff that EVERY employee would sign in every time they came into the building. Ben hadn't signed the book in 11 years, not once. So security guards regularly reported him to the management, and some executive from the third floor had kicked the city editor for the failings of one of his reporters, and the city editor had lashed out at Ben. And he'd screamed back. "If you want a story in on time, I haven't got time to fucking sign in."

Ben knew his latest refusal to waste time signing in was going to trigger this security guard, rightfully doing his job in his crisp white shirt and immaculate tie, to make a report that would go to management, and the chains would rattle down through the system until Ben and the city editor would be in each other's faces again.

A woman's body, dismembered by a chainsaw, was found buried in the backyard of a home where a man's body had been discovered by police 24 hours earlier…

For Ben, the only thing in life better that one dead body was two dead bodies. He never hid it. His whole life was straightforward, black-or-white, "tell-it-like-it-is" open simplicity, and the office knew where he stood on dead bodies. They would hear his unwavering Brit accent proclaiming his favorite exclamation, "right on" and they'd know someone, somewhere, was dead, usually the more horribly the better, and he'd been given the story. Many reporters hated stories about death and destruction. Their professionalism meant they coped with them, covered them, but if they never had to write another one that would be fine with them. Ben seemed to relish the thought.

Back in England, where he'd spent 21 years doing this same job, hadn't his best friend been Art, the city's his coroner's officer? Many's the day he'd spent a lunch-time coffee break in Art's office, turning the conversation round to Art's archive of photographs of the dead. He'd seen grossly deformed bodies torn to pieces by trains. Others had been taken from the sea with glistening shiny bones picked clean by sea creatures, mostly crabs. And always Ben was learning macabre details that those who deal with death professionally keep to themselves, because no one else needs to know, and even fewer would want to know.

Ben stored the knowledge away. Once, here in Canada, he'd been sent to a suspicious body in a field—"right on." Arriving in the field before the RCMP had found time to cordon off the area by the square mile as was their practice, Ben had seen the main trunk of the body before it was covered in a yellow tarp for the sake of decency. It was in the field at the bottom of the embankment where a raised railway line skirted the boundary, and it didn't look suspicious to him. It was decapitated.

In the few moments they had been there, the RCMP had found time to place one tarp a few yards along the line over where the head and the arms had come to rest. This was a "lay-your-head-on-the-railway-line" suicide, Ben reckoned, and he hadn't spoken to anyone yet. Once, in Art's office in England, his coroner friend had shown him pictures of three separate suicide-by-train decapitations, and had asked him what he noticed odd about them.

Disappointed that he wasn't alert enough to observe what he was being shown, Ben gave up.

"Well, all their heads are off," said Art in his deep sonorous voice which Ben reckoned must have been excellent for expressing sympathy to grieving relatives.

"Yea, I see that much," said Ben.

"See, all their arms are off at the elbows," said Art.

And he was right, now he came to mention it, Ben could see that.

"Why?" asked Art.

Again Ben was disappointed he couldn't see the answer.

"I'll tell you," said Art, always pleased to regale his keen student with a gory detail.

"They can't bear to hear the train coming, so they cover their ears with their hands," he said, covering his own ears with his hands, which automatically brought his arms up level with his head, crooked at the elbows. And then it was obvious. Ben could see, as the victims lay with their heads on the railway tracks, with hands over ears and arms crooked level with their heads, the crunching train wheels would have to take both arms and the head, exactly as in the photographs. And here it was in real life. The glimpse Ben had of the body showed him it was headless and its arms were ripped off, and the tarp along the track was widely enough spread to cover a head and two arms.

He was soon on the radio to his city desk with the update. "This is a zero-seven—I'm on my way back to the office." He couldn't disguise the element of disappointment in his voice. "Zero-seven" was the police code for "suicide" and it meant no story as far as the Mail was concerned. From on high one day an executive decision had come down, decreeing the paper wouldn't run suicide stories—none, ever, almost no exceptions. Ben had many an eyeball-to-eyeball screaming match with his city editor over that one. Some great news stories had never seen the light of day because of the rule.

It had been the harder for Ben to accept as he'd spent all those 21 years in England reporting every suicide. Over there, every suicide warranted a coroner's inquest which was a public hearing covered by the press and Ben hardly ever missed one. Over here, a suicide death seldom if ever warranted a fatality inquiry, and as the police also practiced a policy of almost total silence on suicides, Ben's frustration was complete. It surprised him that even his fellow reporters didn't share his view on suicides.

Ben's straight-down-the-line reporter mentality was to report the facts, all facts, get the facts damn right and tell the readers what happened. He could never see the nuance of nicety which permitted him to write about some drug-runner in the basement of a southeast home blowing out the brains of some other drug-peddling rival because it was a murder, but which prevented him writing about some otherwise upstanding member of society blowing his own brains out because it was a suicide. The victim was just as dead. He'd be missing from his daily routine next day, and people would wonder where the hell he was. It wasn't Ben's fault the guy had chosen suicide. The guy had shown no nuances of nicety, leaving his brains in a pink arc across the wallpaper of his dining room for his wife, or worse, his kids to find, why should Ben?

Ben saw it on a greater scale. Why should he, a reporter, have the right to censor from the public things happening in their midst. What peculiar set of rules accepted on the one hand making the life of a murder victim fair game, yet a suicide's history must remain a secret between the victim and Ben. Society must never know. The argument was, so executive editors explained every time Ben banged heads with them on the subject, that writing about one suicide would sway some other depressed soul over the edge and promote another. The paper could be blamed for being the catalyst to a string of suicides. Ben would shake his head and leave it. Like some guy who's just gone bankrupt and discovered his wife's having it off with the boss and is thinking about ending it all, is suddenly going to see a story in the Mail, and decide, "that's the final straw, where's my shotgun?"

Strangely, there were a couple of exceptions. The paper lifted the blanket ban on suicides when it involved multiple suicides linked to underworld cults. Ben had covered two of these, and both had been front-page stuff. He'd traveled south through Alberta to where kids were hanging themselves one by one while heavy metal music blared from their ghetto-blasters in the background amid tales of bizarre Satanic-cult behavior. And he'd gone back north of Calgary where kids started hanging themselves one by one amid speculation a witch-like girl was influencing them. The paper didn't mind these stories on the front page.

For Ben, the only other saving grace in all this was if the suicidal guy hell bent on killing himself took someone else with him, Ben was back in the running. Murder-suicides were fair game. As by their very nature they must mean two dead and often more, they were nearly always front page, high priority, where everything Ben could find out would get into the edition. Like this chainsaw horror on his screen right now.

There was a lot Ben knew that wouldn't appear in his story. He was frustrated that the combination of legal restraints, the paper's respect for human decency, and his reporter's choice to respect the sanctity of "off-the-record" information, meant he invariably knew more than would appear in print in his story.

On a global scale, Ben was always saddened by how little of any murder story ever got out to the public despite his best efforts. The moment of murder, the plunge of the knife, the tightening of the hands round the throat, was a moment of intimacy between two people. Almost always it was secret, private, a climax of emotion between the two. And only one ever survived to know exactly what happened.

Getting as near to that knowledge as possible was a fascination for everyone. There was an undying morbid curiosity among all society to know as many sordid details as possible of every murder. But many links existed in the chain of knowledge between the exact facts known only by the killer and the version of what happened that was ultimately accepted as the true story by society. Ben knew his readers were always the last link in the chain—never knowing the whole story. Often, unfortunately, only Ben knew just how surprised and disappointed they would be to know how little of the whole picture ever got through. The truth had been through an obstacle course of filters before it ever reached the front page.

At its heart was the killer who always knew everything. Secondly, there would possibly be a close circle of people near to the killer who may have sometimes been taken into his confidence when he felt his secret could be kept safe. But that didn't always happen, and if not, and the killer stayed insular and secret, society had no access to this second link. Invariably the close friend or relative of the killer, the person chosen as his confidant, would only receive a version of the slaying biased and twisted to suit and favor the killer. The truth had been filtered for the first time.

Next in the chain came peripheral witnesses who may not even have realized how close they came to the action. The shopper who saw a guy running, the home-owner who heard what sounded like a shot at midnight in the house next door. These people each separately knew a little, but had no idea where their piece of the puzzle slotted into the overall scene.

Whichever police force then became involved, brought in without doubt the biggest single filter of all. An enormous flood of information poured into the police on every homicide inquiry. That was their purpose—find everything of the remotest relevance to the killing, and its solution will be in there, waiting to be extracted. But how much of the information which poured in filtered down through the chain? Only as much as police wanted to let slip, and it was often tantalizingly little.

Next in the chain came the hungry sharks in the media who needed every drop of blood that fell through the police net. This was where Ben came in.

While wily detectives worked hard to keep their innermost workings hidden from the media, Ben had learned early on that getting these guys to open up to him would be the cornerstone of his work. It was a matter of building trust. They had to trust that if they wanted secrets kept, he would keep them. And he did. But when snippets came out, Ben could expect they would come to him first. And they did too. There were steps along this difficult pathway to trust.

Ben recalled one breakthrough day in an English police station detective office when he was given access to the unit's tuck box. Cops don't get regular meal breaks. They grab a bite when they can. Their tuck box worked on a trust system. You took food, you left money in the box. It soon became evident Ben was around. The tuck box takings swelled. The numbers of Tunnocks milk chocolate tea cakes decreased daily. They were Ben's favorite. And he displayed good choice. Years after he gorged on these marshmallow delights, a top executive from the makers—from the tiny town called Uddingston south east of Glasgow in Scotland—was knighted by the Queen. It turned out Sir Boyd Tunnock had hit on the Queen's favorite marshmallow tea-cake!

Ben's sweet tooth helped him further cement ties with these detectives. Ben and a certain bunch of detectives were all well overweight. Marshmallow tea cakes will do that to you. They decided, between them, to go on a "sponsored slim" for charity. With tape measures round their rotund bellies, they were photographed at the start and again weeks later, all displayed in Ben's paper. The police widows and orphans fund benefited handsomely, and the men looked good. That was until the lure of the marshmallows took over and to a man the very same team took part in a "sponsored fat-up" for charity in which they were even more successful and raised even more money!

Of course, while Ben's "yo-yo" dieting worked wonders for building trust with the cops, it helped turn him into a diabetic later in life. After sharing many a pint of Horndean Special Brew beer in a pub with detectives playing cribbage in those early days in England, Ben spent his later life in Canada supping diet Coke and Pepsi after diabetes set in.

It was important Ben became trusted. Without the media, society had no access to any details. But even at this stage, when investigators like Ben had harried people close to any murder, extracted crumbs of knowledge from the peripheral witnesses and squeezed their police contacts, and got to know something of what happened, there were still more filters between that knowledge and what society would ultimately be told.

Once suspects got arrested the legal system encased the whole matter in a labyrinth of regulations governing what could and could not be revealed. Courts would rule seemingly vital tracts of evidence—gathered at great effort by skilled professionals—inadmissible, never to be heard at trial, and never to filter through to the public. Publication bans thrust upon the media by legislation stifled more details, and woe betides the likes of Ben or any reporter or editor who breached the net. Ben could then take whatever small fraction that remained after all that and present it to the reader, who warmed himself or herself in the smug feeling that at last he or she knew the secret behind the case.

Ben spent his life trying to beat these restrictions and tell it like it really was. He had talked to killers, heard their twisted truths, and interviewed peripheral witnesses even before police reached them. And police had filled his mind with secret knowledge they knew the regulations would ban him from repeating in print. Ben had sat through murder trials and heard the details that would have brought convictions if only they'd ever reached the ears of jurors. His whole life was spent getting the truth about murders out into the light.

So what was the murder ingredient in this case today? Basically, the bones of it were that this guy had murdered his wife, used his chainsaw in the backyard to reduce her to manageable pieces, and then buried her here and there under an apple tree's spreading roots. And the suicide element came next day when he locked himself in the garage and gassed himself with the fumes of a heater. Of course, as is always the case, everything unfolded in the opposite order. Police first found the man's body, and only later found the wife's remains.

Ben enjoyed this natural reverse order of things murderous. Murders nearly always begin with the finding of the body, then the establishing of the corpse's identity, then the revelation of his or her lifestyle, acquaintances, secrets, and last known activities. Between them, these components usually throw up a motive for the investigators, and probably a suspect, an arrest and a charge, and a court case and a conviction—and by then the whole story was known. But during each of these stages, pieces of the puzzle land maybe months apart, never necessarily in sequence, and even if each development made copy in Ben's paper, they were fragmentary stories, just snippets along the way.

Ben's greatest enjoyment was taking the whole story when it was all known at the end and letting it unfold. He loved how the beautiful dove-tailing of all the snippets and all the fragments usually produced a story of true-life intrigue far more shocking and dramatic than any fictional writer could invent.

Look at this case.

Ben had gone to the next door neighbor, who was happy to talk to him out of sheer incredulity. "Come in, come in," he said—a welcome Ben seldom received at any door. When you're a crime reporter digging into dead people's pasts and meeting grieving relatives left behind, few people want to know you. He'd spent a lifetime having doors slammed in his face. But now, he was in here. The elderly gentleman with his welcoming smile, soft voice, and his comfortable house slippers, led Ben through a narrow house into his neatly manicured back yard, carefully tended, with pleasant patio deck and a sturdy wooden fence all round.

"See that apple tree over there," said the man, pointing next door to where it had happened, "see the branches sawn off, well, I was watching him."

I heard this chainsaw, so I watched.

"He never does any yard work. All the years I've lived here, I've never seen him out there. His wife even mows the lawn. I saw him take those high branches off."

Ben saw the fresh, light brown dead-end stumps high on the tree.

"Of course, once he had them on the ground, I could hear him cutting them into smaller logs, but I couldn't see him doing that because it was behind the fence," said the neighbor.

That was his snippet, his fragment of the story, pretty much all he knew. His non-gardening neighbor had suddenly taken to pruning the apple tree.

Ben had got a bigger fragment from the police chief himself. And this was a stroke of luck. Getting the scoop on these stories was mostly through plain hard work by covering all the bases, but luck played a role. Sometimes, a passer-by to some crime drama would be a Mail reader and call in, and Ben would be half a day ahead of the rival Echo paper down the road. His scoop would let him bask in the limelight in the office as the blue-eyed boy for the day. And the next day, the passer-by would be an Echo reader, and call it in to them, and they'd be so far ahead, Ben would be floundering, wondering how come today the shit was landing on his shoulders, when it was just down to the stroke of bad luck.

Like the day Ben drove an hour west of the city where overnight, the Mounties had found an elderly couple burned to death in their charred minivan, both having been butchered long before the killers incinerated what was left. In the spacious gently rolling foothills with glorious snow-tipped Rockies as a backcloth, Ben searched for several hours for the scene, using all his reporter guile, before stumbling on it before any other media. Nothing more than a scorched stretch of grass in the ditch alongside a culvert with four patches of blackened steel wire to show where all four tires had burned almost to nothing. Painted on the roadway were short orange and green lines at odd angles, clearly where investigators had plotted the last tracks of the minivan and the first tracks of the killers' getaway car.

Ben was alone with not a soul for miles. Standing there, with no sign of another human save for a jet-liner's vapor trail straight-lining across the huge Alberta sky, Ben's smug satisfaction at finding the scene of death soon melted as it took him nowhere. He had no witnesses, not even a nearby farmer in a field, not even a farmhouse from horizon to horizon. Damn Alberta for being so empty.

It had taken him so long to find the spot he could only stay a short while, gathering every descriptive detail he could before he had to leave to make it back for deadline. And with no information coming from the Mounties as none ever did, Ben's story was very threadbare. The details of the butchery and the scene description were fine, but he had no names of victims or background. So it was a disaster next day when the Echo blasted the names and the life history of the murdered couple together with their picture right across its front page. More shit landed on Ben in the office than he could remember.

Later, he learned his dogged determination at finding the scene before anyone was his undoing. Long after he'd left, the pedestrian reporters at the Echo eventually got there, but they found some guy looking at the scene, didn't they. Some guy who was there because it was his friends who'd been murdered, some guy willing to talk about them, willing to put the Echo in touch with everyone who knew them. Some damn guy who hadn't been there when Ben needed him.

But today, the luck of timing had been with Ben. The Echo had heard about this death half a day ahead of him, had traveled the 300 km south and got there when an impenetrable wall of yellow police tape had the whole place sealed off.

Yellow police tape had a magical power. Ben, who had spent many an hour standing behind yellow police tape dying to cross it and never daring to do so, had seen a seminar put on by Ed Stone, the staff sergeant in charge of the Calgary city homicide unit, in which he showed a slide to illustrate the power of yellow tape. It was a murder case where a terribly decomposed body had been found in a field. In the middle of nowhere, the first officer at the scene found himself with only a three-foot remnant of a roll of yellow police tape in the trunk of his cruiser. That was all he had.

Halfway across the field from the corpse, he stuck two sticks in the grass and tied his three-foot length of yellow police tape between them. Stone's slide was a distant overview of the field, taken from the police helicopter. It showed row upon row of police cruisers and television trucks, and reporters' cars all parked in the field, the front bumper of the nearest cruiser being hard up against the three-foot length of yellow police tape. No one had dared go round it or approach any nearer than an imaginary line extending it in both directions across the field, such was its power.

And today, the Echo had arrived when most of the street had been cordoned off behind the yellow police tape. Their reporters had done their best with neighbors at the far end of the street beyond the tape and others on this side, and left almost empty-handed. But being so late, half a day behind, Ben and the Mail's photographer Max Greywood, weren't arriving until dusk, and by then, police had narrowed down the vital areas requiring yellow tape, and had lifted most of it, leaving just the death house with its tell-tale back yard inside the cordon.

As Ben and Max arrived, they saw a strange sight in the near-dark gloom. This character in baggy shorts and knobby knees intercepted them on the sidewalk in front of the house. Having established Ben and Max were from the media, he led them down the side driveway through a gate and into the very yard where the deadly dismemberment had taken place. Who was this apparition? None other, Ben discovered, than the city's police chief himself. Now this was luck. Imagine being so late at a story the police had done their work and lifted the yellow tape to let you near the scene, where earlier media were excluded, and then being so late, the police chief himself—God only knows why in baggy shorts—takes you right into the heart of the drama.

And it was a dramatic scene, though thoroughly eerie. Throwing long shadows from the floodlights they'd erected, forensic experts in ghostly white overalls were kneeling over a grid pattern of tapes punctuated by little flag markers. The flags denoted nuggets of evidence and here and there in the gloom on the ground lay the deepest of black, oblong shadows, obviously little pits from where human limbs had been recovered. Max's atmospheric photograph of this scene of death was destined for the front page from the time his flash froze it in a blinding white millisecond.

"Acting on information received," began the chief in the marvelously stilted language all police officers reserve for media, "officers undertook a grid search of the yard of this dwelling and recovered human remains, which are being transported to the office of the chief medical examiner for examination and analysis."

Then, as in the early stages of every murder, came the almost compulsory sparring between the reporter and the cop, this time between Ben who wanted more, much more, and the chief, who'd given what he was going to give, and wasn't giving another word.

"Was it a woman?" asked Ben.

"That will be up to the medical examiner to decide," said the chief.

"Was it an adult, was it a child?"

"That's up to the medical examiner."

"Was the body dismembered with a chainsaw?"

"The medical examiner…" and so on.

But Ben's persistence earned him one vital extra answer in that spooky yard with the white ghosts busy under their floodlights and the chunky man in shorts all standing under the apple tree with its abruptly ending freshly-sawn branch stumps.

"We did recover a chainsaw from the garage, and it's been sent away to the crime lab for analysis," said the chief.

This was the fragment of fact Ben needed.

Now, the story was almost complete. He had the neighbor seeing the man wielding the chainsaw, he had police forensic experts studying the very same chainsaw, and separate bits of human body being extracted from all over the back yard. He could have put it together himself, but, when you're a reporter, and your words are about to end up in black and white for all time, you have to have every fact confirmed and right. Ben knew he couldn't allow himself the luxury of guessing a single element of his story.

He turned to his last resource. Every reporter has inside sources, people inside every organization, committee, and group, who'll tell him what's going on, whose name will never appear in print, and who, if the reporter is worth his salt, will remain undetected by those around him at all times. This was another police force outside Calgary, but Ben's years of work had earned him a network of sources pretty far and wide, who'd learned to trust his commitment to keep them secret. He called on a source, well, a couple actually, and with the combined knowledge of what they revealed, he could construct the whole story.

Ben could put together in a coherent story in the right order of events all the fragments that had unfolded for police in the reverse order—finding the man's body, then the chainsaw, then the human remains in his back yard. The home-owner here had killed his wife in a domestic fight in the house and had decided the way to dispose of her body was by taking her apart with the chainsaw and burying her in the back yard. Fearing neighbors would be inquisitive to a chainsaw whirring in the yard apparently without reason he began sawing off the highest branches of the apple tree, knowing neighbors could see this innocent activity from over the fence.

But on the ground in the yard where the apple tree limbs landed, were other limbs, in fact the entire body of his wife. With a whir here to shorten a tree limb, and a whir there to shorten the tibia and fibula, his wife was reduced to manageable pieces among the apple tree boughs and no neighbor could see what was taking place down low because the fence was so high. And when his wife was ready for planting, this man who hated gardening so, dug the necessary plots and put the pieces in the ground until his gruesome task was complete.

But the overpowering enormity of taking a human life was too much and the killer chose to end his own life, adding one odd twist. Before he sealed his garage airtight shut so the furnace fumes would suffocate him, he sat before his own video-camera and made a full confession of what he'd done and where he'd done it—and left the tape prominently visible alongside his chair. The officers who found him still sitting there, dead, didn't disappoint him. They found his tape and played it, instantly receiving precise instructions on where to find his missing wife, and how to recover her.

As Ben's inside sources revealed all this, he smiled quietly to himself. Hours earlier, when the chief had started with, "acting on information received..." this was what he had meant. The chief knew all about this tape, and the confession, and the directions to the body, and had turned all this fascinating and newsworthy detail that Ben would have killed for then, into that bland and empty phrase that Ben just hated to hear. Cops had similar meaningless phrases to disguise every juicy circumstance when presenting them to the media.

Ben remembered one miserable rain-sodden day in England when he'd stood in a downpour for more than an hour outside a south-coast home where the frantic police activity could only mean there had been a murder. Only when the rain driving in off the English Channel had soaked the gathered media through to their skins, did the detective chief superintendent, the head of the county C.I.D. himself, emerge from the home with his prepared statement.

"We have here an elderly woman who has died of injuries which are other than accidental," he said, without elaborating another word despite a barrage of questions.

Ben later sat through the trial of the killer and learned this frail elderly victim had suffered 32 stab wounds before the frenzied maniac in an orgasm of blood-lust had ejaculated over her butchered body. Only a cop's lifetime of training in keeping information from the media while still actually smiling at them face-to-face and talking to them, could come from the scene of such savagery and conjure up the phrase "injuries other than accidental."

Ben finished his chainsaw horror story, with every detail. He attributed the vital ingredient of the chainsaw to the police chief, the vital wielding of the chainsaw to the neighbor who watched it being wielded, and the suicide video tape tying all the threads together to "anonymous Mail sources," whoever they may be. And it was in on deadline. By three minutes. He'd been doing this now for well over 30 years and he still couldn't resist wandering over to the sub-editors' section of the newsroom to see his story in print. Here, sub-editors were building pages, trying to hit their deadline with stories arriving late from reporters. He looked at that front page, with white words across Max's eerie dark photograph of the backyard scene of carnage. "TWO DEAD IN CHAINSAW HORROR" Right on!

Chapter 2

The phone call came next day.

Ben almost missed it. He had two phones on his cluttered desk. One, on its busted stand making it lean sideways, was for incoming calls on the "145" number he gave everyone. On the other, "146" his tape recorder was always plugged in and ready. When "145" rang, he'd pick up "146," hit the necessary code and it would automatically transfer the caller to the tape recorder phone, leaving the in-coming phone free for the next call. Except the cheap system the Mail paid for could hardly handle this basic requirement.

When Ben smacked the necessary code, the system would pick up another call, it's true—but not necessarily the one Ben wanted. Many's the time, his stupid "145" sat there still ringing while his tape recorder line had picked up someone in the far corner of the newsroom trying to send in school basketball results or some budding starlet wanting to display her navel, cleavage and thighs as one of the Mail's "Male Delight" pin-ups. Ben's screaming at management over this failing never brought results either.

So "145" rang, and Ben punched the code, and politely got rid of the guy calling from a film studio in Hollywood who wanted the film critic instead, before punching the code again just in time to catch his "145" caller.

"Mail newsroom, Ben Ludlow," he said.

"Look, you don't know me, but I'm told I can talk to you, and you might do right by me," said a voice Ben didn't recognize. "Look, I'm in the pokey for something I ain't done, do you want to hear about it?"

Oh God, what a start to the day thought Ben, inwardly groaning. He'd get nutcases like this two or three times a year. They were losers who were always in jail for crimes they never committed, or who were being savagely beaten by brutal cops all over Calgary. They always called repeatedly, believing, if they'd talked to him once, he was their salvation on the outside, available at all times. And miraculously, he was going to perform some sleight of hand to spirit them out of jail, where their lawyers and all the mercies of the Canadian legal system had failed.

"Right on, what happened," said Ben in his most listening voice, all apparent eager anticipation. Even Ben was surprised how deeply he could inwardly groan and outwardly encourage all at the same time, "start at the beginning, what's your name?"

"Ron, Ron Lincoln, I don't expect you remember."

That name did ring a bell. Ben had this magic filing system of his own for every murder case he'd ever written about. He had these grandiose plans for writing a series of documentary classic murder books based on all his cases one day, whenever he found time. So he salted away every cutting, every article, even those from the enemy Echo down the road, all his notes and phone numbers and contact names in a separate file for every separate case. They now sat in the office in eight grey metal filing cabinets, four high and two wide, numbered one to eight, stacked alongside the window. Other reporters relied on the Mail's library for their back references, but not Ben. He had done a nice little deal with the guy down in maintenance, who "found" these filing cabinets going to waste in some remote corner of a basement storeroom, and wheeled them up on a dolly for him, much to the envy of the newsroom. It had cost Ben half a salmon. His summer holidays spent sea fishing off the west coast of British Columbia often left him with enough salmon for all kinds of bartering. Every file in the eight drawers was numbered, and the names of every killer and every victim were cross referenced in Ben's "murder list" index in his computer It now held more than 7,800 names. His files were almost legendary. The custodians of the Mail's own library room turned to them occasionally. Even Ed Stone, down at the Calgary city police homicide unit had used statistics from Ben's meticulous files in seminars he used to lay on for the media. And the remarkable thing about the files was Ben had this uncanny sixth-sense of remembering who was in there. Cops would issue a press release about some pedophile about to be released from prison into some unsuspecting Calgary community. Ben would tell the city desk "hang on," he'd visit "Drawer 2" go to the "pedophile" file, and find "pedophile 35"—and it would be this guy. And Ben's story that day would include all his sordid and scary background, so an unsuspecting community would be well forewarned. No, Ben's files didn't stop at killers and victims. Pedophiles, bikers, major drug-runners, international fugitives, they were all in there.

And now the name Ron Lincoln rang a bell.

"Look, I got done for topping this woman, but it's all bullshit, man. Fucking cops stitched me up for it. I don't know how you can help, but I want fucking out of here. This is wrong, man."

Ben heard a commotion on the other end of the phone, like a voice over a public address system in the background behind Ron.

"Oh shit, I got to go, man. Look, I'll call you back same time tomorrow, right?" said Ron.

"Yea, you do that, no problem."

Ben was already punching "murder list" into his computer. Ron Lincoln was going to be in here somewhere.

"LIGHT TREADER Mervin—killer (stabbed Native in downtown bar)"

"LILLINGTON Jason—killer (beat guy to death in southwest apartment)"

"LINCOLN Ronald—killer (tortured woman to death in Red Deer)" Drawer 1, File 185

"Right on!"

A lot of guys phoned Ben from prison. Mostly they were whining losers, like a guy with festering sores between his toes who called once moaning that the guards wouldn't give him the huge doses of medication he reckoned he needed. What kind of headline did he think that would make in the Mail.

"Festering Toes Shocker in City Jail." Yea, right.

Then there was one regular. Soon after Ben arrived in Canada in the late 1980s this guy called for the first time and from then on until the early 90s he called damn nearly every day. He started like all the rest, in jail facing a murder rap which he reckoned he hadn't done. Ben's skepticism was reinforced one day when he heard that this guy, Garry Chartreuse—Ben's own version of "Deep Throat"—had been taken from his cell and charged with another murder. Get out of that one. But the calls kept coming in, only now Garry reckoned he'd been framed for two murders. The reporters in Ben's office couldn't understand why Ben didn't tell him to piss off, but every day he phoned, Ben chatted. After all, it had to help your contacts to know a two-time murderer. The day came when Garry went to his preliminary hearing for the first murder, and on the second day, the judge brought the whole thing to a halt, throwing the case out for lack of evidence. Exactly what Garry had predicted would happen. Of course, he was still inside on the second rap, and still kept calling daily. When the second murder actually went to trial, it took a jury only three hours to find Garry not guilty, and after 19 months in prison for two murders he told Ben he didn't do, early in 1990 he came out. And he still called damn nearly daily, except for occasional breaks when two or three weeks would pass with no word. Seemed to Ben, this guy was as deeply sunk in the underworld as you could get. One day there was a homicide in Calgary, and next morning Garry called, asking Ben for some information. He wanted to know if anyone had been arrested yet.

"No, not yet, don't think they've got a clue," said Ben.

"See if a homeless guy named Barney's in the frame," Garry said.

Next day Stone of homicide put out a release on the slaying, updating it with the news that Barney Dempster, 23, had been charged with first-degree murder.

When Garry called next day, Ben asked him how the hell he'd known about Barney.

"That cocksucker came to my house, his brain fried on some shit, desperate for a place to crash. Said he couldn't go back where he was shacked up. I told him to fuck off. But I knew why he couldn't go back to his place. There was a cocksucking body in there," he said. Garry had the foulest mouth Ben had ever come across. But, as usual, he was on the money. His information was always right. He was always in touch with ongoing crime. When $100,000 worth of frozen meat was stolen, didn't it turn up in a garage which Garry owned?

"I sub-let that garage to this cocksucker, and he does that with it and the shit lands on me again. I had nothing to do with it," he told Ben, on a call one day that was followed by three weeks of silence. But the familiar voice was there again, calling in on 145 three weeks later.

Ben asked, "Where you been?"

"Colombia," he said.

"What, you mean Vancouver or Victoria?" asked Ben with idle curiosity.

"No, you fucking nut-case, not British Columbia—Colombia, you know, Bogota, you know, South America."

Ben cringed. What the hell would this guy have been doing in Bogota, Colombia for three weeks? Drug trafficking, gun-running, smuggling illegal immigrants, or all three—Ben bet for sure it wouldn't be sight-seeing. Ben played Garry well. He used the man's inside information to lever confirmations and verifications out of other people, so their names appeared in the stories, and no one ever knew who the original source was. Garry only once made it into a story and it was a cracker.

Early in 1990, not long after Garry had come out from his 19 months inside, he wanted to meet Ben, arranging the rendezvous in the plush and sumptuous surroundings of a top quality Calgary hotel foyer. Ben went, and they sat beneath Turner oil paintings on the walls, in sinky comfortable leather armchairs with copies of "Vogue" and "Cosmopolitan" on the ornate coffee table. Ben had no idea if they were supposed to be blending in here, but he felt damn conspicuous, with this craggy faced, white-haired, roughly-dressed foul-mouthed man, clutching bundles of well-thumbed and crumpled documents, which Ben just knew heralded a long session. Ben clicked on his tape-recorder, and Garry nodded his approval.

"I want to go public on this," he said.

"I'm telling you things now you can put in the paper if you think you have to. I'm not bull-shitting you. All the times I've called you, I've never bull-shitted you, now have I," and he rambled off on what Ben guessed was the background pre-amble to the main story. But, to be honest, this was pretty good stuff in itself. Garry owned up to some heavy-duty underworld activities. He'd done bank robberies in his day, been inside for stuff he did do, and had survived some scary horrors in war-torn back-streets in Africa. He said he'd been a gun-runner mercenary, living on his double-crossing skills, making sure he was being paid by whichever side was winning the war at the time—and paying most. He had a scar across his throat, the damage inside leading to his cancer and rough and gruff voice. This was after some disgruntled African modern-day warrior got pissed off at being double-crossed, and shot at him with one of the guns he'd just sold him!

"It wasn't the only fucking time I was shot at—but it was the only time I got fucking hit," he said. "Once they started firing at us as we took off in an old DC-3, and put a row of bullet holes down the fuselage, the cocksuckers."

Garry, who seemed to be happy to drift off reminiscing about these highlights of his earlier days, snapped back to business.

"What I'm going to tell you is no bullshit. This is about the bombing of the oil plane," he said.

Ben kept a deadpan poker face, but inwardly his emotions suddenly churned. *Oh shit, he's going to tell me he did the oil plane bombing,* he thought to himself. *What the hell am I going to do with that?*

Ben's mind raced through what he knew already of the oil plane bombing, the worst single act of terrorism ever carried out against Canadians, with 109 dead including damn nearly every senior oil executive in Alberta, together with two leading oil sector politicians. It was a United Airways of Canada Boeing 737-300 which had taken off from Edmonton International Airport bound for Houston, Texas, on June 1, 1985.

These were the days when the Athabasca Oil Sands of Alberta were being opened up, and this delegation of oil executives and politicians had just finished visiting new facilities coming on line at Fort McMurray. From there, they traveled down to Edmonton and boarded flight UA 731 for their monumental trip to Houston. There they were attending the final in a series of conferences which would cement new agreements between Canadian and American oil industry bosses. These agreements would see a massive increase in American purchases of Canadian oil.

This conference would have global implications in the oil world. Until that date, Saudi Arabia was the world's top producer of oil, and the USA was partially dependent on its Middle Eastern oil supplies. But if this colossal Canada deal went through, Saudi would be relegated to a secondary supplier with enormously adverse consequences to its economy.

As Flight UA 731 was over the Gulf of Mexico on its final approach into Houston it was ripped apart by a massive explosion. All 109 people on board perished and not all the bodies were even recovered from the waters of the Gulf.

Ben snapped his mind back to listening to Garry.

"This all started early in 1985," Garry said.

"Oh shit," thought Ben, "he's going tell me he did it."

"I'd been wheeling and dealing all over western Canada, Alberta mainly, and I'd been involved with some heavy-duty violent bastards that you don't need to know about," said Garry.

"Anyway, this day, a couple of Arab guys I never heard of want to see me. They've done some background on me, and they want me, and I'm told there's a fucking bundle of money in it for me. So I meet them, and they bring out this fucking suitcase, and open it up, and there's $250,000 dollars in it, right there in my fucking hand. All they want me to do is put a bomb on a fucking United Airways of Canada plane out of Edmonton. They make the bomb. I make sure it gets on board. I'm away with 250 big ones, and no one even knows it's down to them. Dogshit cocksuckers."

"I done some fucking bad things in my time, but putting a fucking bomb on a plane full of innocent people's fucking beyond me. I wasn't touching that. No fucking way. Who did they think I was, Carlos the Jackal, no way? I might be a bad bastard, but I'm no international terrorist."

"So, for the only time in my whole life I went to the cops. I went to Edmonton city police and told 'em. I gave 'em the names of these two guys. I told 'em what they were planning. I told 'em it would be a United Airways of Canada plane. I told 'em they had the bomb ready. But this was Garry telling 'em, wasn't it. Fucking jailbird Garry, fucking armed robbery Garry, fucking lying-through-his-teeth Garry."

"They didn't do nothing. And just a few weeks later, on June 1, I'll never forget the date, the oil plane got fucking blown up. More than 100 people murdered, and I'd warned the cops, I'd told 'em who was going to do it, how they were going to do it, and they fucking dropped the ball and let it happen."

Ben was riveted. This wasn't your run-of-the-mill whiner. If this lot was right, this was bigger than Watergate.

"And that was what started it all for me," Garry went on. "Once that bomb went off, the fucking cops knew they'd cocked it all up. They knew if I went public telling people I warned them and they ignored the warning, which is what happened, the shit would hit the fan. They had to discredit me. Suddenly, one day, out of the fucking blue, a bunch of cops turn up and right on my front lawn, right in front of my kids, they fucking arrest me for a murder in Calgary on a day when I wasn't even in Alberta."

"Then, when I'm inside waiting for that trial, they come in and tell me I'm fucking arrested for another murder. Somewhere right in there is when I started phoning you from in the remand center."

"See, after that, it don't matter what I say about warning the cops about the bombing. Who's going to believe a man charged with two murders? Since I been out, they fucking pull me over all the time, they run the checks on me and it comes up with me charged with two murders. It don't fucking say one charge was dropped and I was cleared of the other one. Fucking no way, I'm down for a double murderer all the time. They fucking framed me for those two murders, so no one would ever believe my word when I tell them about my bomb warning to the cops."

Ben was sitting as far forward in his plush armchair as he could listening to all this.

"Jesus Christ," he said. "How can I check this lot out?"

"Easy. I got the names of the cops I told. I got the names of the Arabs who offered me the cash. You can check it all." It was all in his crumpled documents, all hand-written in a large scrawl, and horribly misspelled.

Ben took the documents, and over the next few weeks he did check. He struggled with the hand-writing, non-existent punctuation and damn nearly illiterate spelling until he made sense of it all, then he checked. Yes, the Edmonton city police did know of Garry, and yes, they had passed his information to the RCMP in Edmonton who were handling the bombing of the oil plane. Ben checked further with the RCMP. Yes, Garry's name was contained in the files on the oil plane bombing investigation. From various sources, Ben established several other authorities knew the police had been warned in advance about the bombing. Incredibly, one of the Arab names Garry had given Ben was a man later blown up and killed in a car-bombing in Riyadh, Saudi Arabia. Garry had given Ben the man's name, and after he was killed, police confirmed he had been a prime suspect in the bombing. Ben already had chapter and verse of the arrests and charges Garry faced and how both murder raps had evaporated under the glare of legal scrutiny. Every damn word he told him checked out.

So he wrote the feature—very carefully.

Maintaining a skepticism and suspicion which his crime reporter life had ingrained in his acceptance of anything told him, he couched the story in this way. He explained that reporters are told some amazing tales in their travels, and this was one of them. And he ran through Garry's almost unbelievable account—his murky underworld background; being chosen by Middle Eastern terrorists as a plane bomber; ducking out of it; warning police; watching them ignore his warning; how that led to 109 innocent people being blasted out of the sky; and then being framed for two murders to discredit him, so no one would believe him when he went public with the scandal of the incompetent police. Of course, Ben's version left out Garry's blistering language, so it could be published in the Mail. It was a hell of a read. The Sunday editor was delighted. Ben acceded to Garry's one request, that he not use a photo of him. As Garry starkly summed it up, if this group had no qualms about bombing a plane load of passengers, they'd hardly blink twice at taking him out of the picture.

Along these same lines, there was a sequel to all this. Just over two years further into the police investigation of the bombing, in April 1992, Ben got another of his regular calls from Garry, back in his "Deep Throat" mode.

The call came in on 145 as usual. Ben switched it to his taped line.

"Ben Ludlow, newsroom."

"You busy? We gotta meet...." By the time Ben had heard the first five syllables, he'd recognized the cancerous growl.

"What's the problem? Got something new for me?" asked Ben.

"Not on the phone. I'm coming to you. I'll be out there in your parking lot in 10 minutes. You'll know me. I'm the only one out there in a fucking stretched limo," growled the voice.

"I'll be there," said Ben, trying to imagine what the hell Garry was doing in a stretched limo. Ben spent 10 minutes putting some of the mountain of files on his desk back in their right cabinet drawers. Why was it, the files he used most often always had to go back in the bottom drawers? Ben's rotten knees meant he couldn't squat. He had to kneel very gingerly to get files back in the bottom drawers at floor level. He cursed every time. He'd lost one knee-cap, shattered into several pieces in a yacht-racing accident in England. He'd ended up yelling in agony on a beach clutching his knee. They'd carted him off to hospital by ambulance still wearing his life-jacket and strands of seaweed tangled round his leg. He'd had ligaments and cartilages removed from the other knee after a soccer collision as a schoolboy. For years, he'd saved his ripped knee ligament preserved in formaldehyde in a transparent plastic vial as a weird memento. Now age had added the pain of arthritis. No wonder Ben let files pile up on his desk.

Ten minutes later he walked out into the parking lot. Ben always admired the view from the lot with half of Calgary's sprawling city spread out in the foreground and the snow-capped Rocky Mountains as a backdrop far out to the west. There, sure enough, at the far end of the parking lot, a gleaming white stretched limo dominated the lines of boring cars. Ben faced a double dilemma. Garry must have stolen this one—no other explanation. So if Ben got in and they were stopped, he'd be a passenger in a stolen car. Secondly, if he was out driving with Garry and heard an urgent news story on the scanner in his pocket, he'd either have to miss the story or take Garry to a scene swarming with cops.

"Fuck me rigid," said Ben to himself, walking up to the limo. He went to get in the back, where he envisioned himself sinking into the deep leather seats, where the champagne would be on ice waiting for him.

"No, come in the front with me," said Garry.

"What the hell is this thing, Garry? What are you doing in one of these?" asked Ben, climbing in the front passenger seat. Garry's weather-beaten face cracked into a crinkly smile. "It's my new job, man. I'm a fucking limo driver. I get to drive it around between calls. It's all on the fucking level," and he swung the wheel, and the limo purred its way out of the parking lot.

Ben buckled up—force of habit, and was still fiddling with the belt in the unfamiliar latch, when he recoiled in pain. The latch had a sharp metal burr which ripped two of his fingers.

"Shit. You in charge of maintenance on this thing? You oughta get this seat belt fixed, it's lethal," said Ben.

"Fuck. No one ever sits there. The customers always enjoy the real comfort in the back. Sorry. Hang on, here's some paper," said Garry, and Ben wrapped it round his fingers. Ben was always surprised how much finger-tips bled when you cut them. Finger-tips and ear-lobes were the two bloodiest parts of the human body. He didn't want to get blood on the limo's leather. He could see he'd already dropped dog hairs off his clothing on the floor—that was bad enough.

"What's this all about?" asked Ben.

"It's the fucking oil plane bombing thing again," said Garry. Ben's dilemma dissolved. He listened intently.

The RCMP had been back to interview him again, said Garry. And this time they did want to hear every detail he could remember about the Arabs and the $250,000 and the names and the plots. They'd made it clear they would eventually want him to testify when arrests were made. And the RCMP investigators were deadly serious. They were thinking along the lines Garry's mind had traveled. They agreed that he was going to have to disappear into the witness protection program. The RCMP wanted him "disappeared" where they could find him when the day came, not disappeared off the face of the earth at the hands of bomb-plot terrorists.

"You can't write nuffink about this bit, but I thought you ought to know. When it gets to trial, you could be looking at the star fucking witness. Just thought you ought to have the heads up," said Garry.

"Christ, that's all a bit heavy duty. Have they told you when the trial might start?" asked Ben.

"Nah, but they reckon I might be hidden away for a fucking long time. Suits me," said Garry.

The stretched limo had swished almost silently through the back-streets of north-east Calgary, and with a leisurely spin of the wheel, Garry turned back to the Mail and drove Ben right to the front door of the paper. Ben went to get out, unwrapped the bloody paper off his fingers and stuffed it into the ash-tray.

"Thanks for the call. When you give your star evidence, I'll be there. You'll be the hero on our front page," said Ben. "And get that bloody seat belt fixed, you maniac."

Garry grinned like a Cheshire cat, and gunned the stretched limo out into the street.

And the witness protection program must have worked. Not long after this encounter, toward the end of 1992, Deep Throat's calls dried up completely. Wherever Garry was hidden, he wasn't risking blowing his cover by calling Ben. It crossed Ben's mind perhaps the Arab bombers' skill at finding Garry was better than the RCMP's ability to hide him. Perhaps they had taken him out. Whatever, Ben never heard from him again.

And strangely enough, the only other time Ben wrote a story based on another of these calls from inside the prison bars, that inmate definitely ended up dead.

Once, a Native phoned Ben complaining the prison guards had taken away his prayer beads, discriminating against him because of his race, oppressing him because he was a Native. Ben followed it up, and discovered the man's prayer beads that he needed for meditation in his cell included pipes which could have been used for smoking anything you could imagine, enough materials to make a small arsenal of home-made weapons, and enough nooses to have half the block hanged overnight. But Ben ran with the story, and was later amazed to discover that the inmate had won his battle, and had his prayer beads reinstated. He was serving time for manslaughter when he first phoned Ben. He hadn't been released more than a few years, when he turned up in Ben's files again. This time he was charged with manslaughter again. He beat a homeless man to death in a downtown Calgary alley. He was so out of his brains on alcohol he was still kicking the victim when cops arrived on the scene. He did a few more years inside, then, mystifyingly to Ben, won an early parole. The last entry on this man who'd killed twice appeared in Ben's files fairly recently after he snuffed out another life. The prayer bead Native had hanged himself.

Ben opened his Ron Lincoln file. It was a case he didn't recall in great detail. It was up in Red Deer and he'd written about it, but he hadn't been there. In fact, this one had almost ended up in his "minor murders" file. He always chuckled sickly at the thought—a "minor" murder. Bet it wasn't minor to the guy who got murdered, but it made sense to Ben. These were murders with some vague Calgary connection that he'd write about for one day and then forget. Like a horrific shocker in New York, where the killer had physically held his victim against the propeller of a light aircraft until it had splashed most of him across the airport tarmac. The aircraft had been leased from a Calgary company, so it made a headline for the day—"CALGARY PLANE IN MURDER HORROR"—but as none of the players were from Calgary, it never warranted any more stories. It became a minor murder—Drawer 2, File 14A (MM86).

Or what about the file numbered Drawer 2, File 14A (MM 85)? This one almost sounded like the start of a sick joke, but it happened. A one-legged, one-armed, deaf teenager in Saskatchewan had taken a shotgun to his grandparents on a farm, and was convicted of two counts of first-degree murder.

But Lincoln had produced slightly more copy and had escaped landing up in the "minor murders" file. Here were the first headlines "WOMAN SLAIN IN RED DEER" and "GRISLY DISCOVERY IN SNOW" together with a photograph of an RCMP tent erected over the body while scenes-of-crime forensic experts worked as shadows inside—all very dramatic. Thumbing through, Ben reread the details. The victim was Gillian Warnoski, a 25-year-old bank teller who'd worked at the Toronto Dominion bank in Red Deer. Calgary's RCMP major crimes unit detectives had taken over the case and all they'd say was this dump site where Warnoski was found wasn't the crime scene. She'd been murdered somewhere else and thrown out here from a car. And clearly by someone who wanted the world to know he'd committed a murder. With all central Alberta to choose from, this killer left her body on a stretch of grass beside a busy road leading south out of Red Deer's Gasoline Alley just before the main turn-off to Calgary. Very nearly everyone travelling south through Alberta stopped off at any one of the fast food outlets or restaurants on Gasoline Alley in Red Deer before continuing south. Not surprisingly her very exposed body was soon seen. From the follow-up story on the second day, it was clear the dumping ground was so busy that someone had obviously seen a suspicious vehicle leaving there at about the time police reckoned the killer was dumping the body. They issued a description of a rust-bucket pale blue Ford truck with the offside front wing a distinctive dark blue that didn't match.

Now Ben remembered why there wasn't much in this file. It had all happened so quickly. Several people remembered seeing this truck. Investigators soon traced it, found its owner living in Penhold just south of Red Deer, and it was soon all over. Ronald James Lincoln, 30, of Penhold, was arrested and charged with first-degree murder, and that effectively stopped the stories until the trial. It was January 20, 1992 when they found Warnoski's body and inside 14 months, in March 1993, Lincoln had been convicted and sentenced to life with no parole for 18 years. That was the high end of the punishment scale. In his file, Ben found the story written the day Calgary's chief medical examiner, Dr. Keith Parker, had given his testimony at the trial. Warnoski had been hideously tortured by a sexual sadist. Her nipples had been bitten off, her body, bound at the wrists and ankles had been mutilated, both when she was alive suffering in agony, and after death. While she was alive, a cigarette had been used to burn small ragged-edged round holes in the skin on her forearms. Different knives had been used to slash and carve her body, but the similarity in the wounds led Parker to say the same man had used the different knives. There was only one killer. But the slashings, burnings and mutilations hadn't killed her. As this sadist slaked his lust on her body during this prolonged attack, at some point he'd strangled her manually. That was the cause of death.

Ben read this page and regretted he'd sounded so sympathetic to Lincoln on the phone. What a bastard. In the file, Ben read again the Crown's closing speech. The forensic scientists had found Warnoski's blood in the trunk of Lincoln's pale blue Ford truck with its one dark blue front wing. Lincoln was a regular customer in Warnoski's branch of the TD bank, where he held his account, and knew her well. The clincher was they found Lincoln's DNA on a cigarette butt stuffed high inside her vagina—indisputable DNA. This was a perverted sexual sadist. God knows why any defense lawyer even bothered trying to defend him. No wonder he got life with no chance of parole for 18 years. And now this fucker was going to be calling Ben back again tomorrow claiming he was framed, and wanting Ben's help in getting out of jail.

Ben threw the file on the new pile growing on his desk. Murder files were always piled up there. Brendan, the Mail's court reporter, the only guy in the newsroom who'd been at the paper longer than Ben, would call.

"You got a file on MacKenzie, Jason Robert MacKenzie?" he'd phone and ask from the media room at the Court of Queen's Bench.

"Yea, hang on."

Into the computer, "murder list," File 200, over to the eight cabinets, find the file, back to the phone.

"What do you need?"

"What's it about, the trial starts tomorrow?" Brendan would ask.

"He's that young guy who beat that older guy to death in that downtown hotel. You remember—he hit him with a cistern lid because he made sexual advances to him. Hang on, I'll fax you a couple of pages."

"Cheers, Ben. I tried the library, and they didn't have him."

And instead of taking the file back to the eight cabinets, Ben would throw MacKenzie on the pile. And this would happen every day until the pile threatened to topple over. But before there was ever a disastrous toppling, Ben would wait for a quiet Saturday, when he'd have a "file" day, and be busy all day, putting all his beloved files back in the cabinets until his knees ached.

Lincoln still topped the pile, available for handy reference, when Ron called in at the appointed time next day. One thing about these callers from prison, they were punctual. Perhaps it was to do with their lives being regimented, or something.

"You worked out who I am yet," said Ron.

"Yea, got the file in front of me right now," said Ben, hoping the disgust he felt for this piece of shit didn't sound in his voice.

"Look, I know it sounded like they had me fucking nailed down, but it wasn't me. I've done some bad stuff in my time, I've been inside, but this wasn't down to me. All I want you to do is listen to me, and we can't do this over the phone. We gotta meet in here. What d'ya think?" he said.

"Yea," said Ben, one of those totally non-committal "yeas" that fill in a gap in the conversation, but don't mean anything.

"Alright. Look, I'll get you on my visitor's list, it'll take a few days, but when it's sorted I'll call you back, okay."

"Yea," said Ben, fairly confident this guy wouldn't take the trouble and nothing would come of it. Ben really wanted this guy to stay behind bars forever, hopefully until some con with the right sense of prison justice might take a tire iron to him in a workshop.

"Yea, call me back when you got your end tied up," said Ben.

It wasn't every day Ben got a one-on-one interview with a convicted killer. He would turn it to his own advantage. First, he'd ignore the feeling of being manipulated by this pervert. Secondly, Ben inwardly resolved never to actually help him. And best of all, Ben started looking for the story he could get out of it. To start with, Ben wanted to be armed with every fact he could find about the Warnoski murder. He had one contact he needed to visit for more information, but before that he'd read through the file of cuttings again—well, as carefully as he could, with the scanner running full blast in his ear, and an office full of phones needing answering.

No other reporter had to pay attention to the scanner like Ben did. It was his job. It blared out every message from police dispatch to every unit, from fire dispatch to every fire truck and from EMS dispatch to every ambulance and paramedic. All Ben had to do was discern from the incessant chatter which transmissions meant a story was breaking which the newsroom needed to react to right now. Thirteen years of constant attention had taught him the codes. The most vital was "10-32" on the police channel which meant "dead body" and which pricked his ears no matter how deeply engrossed he was in a telephone conversation, or talking with someone in the office. He knew them all right down to the most boring and routine messages, like fire trucks telling their dispatcher they were "2 station A-I-Q" which meant the rigs down on 17 Avenue S. W. were "available in quarters," back in the station, off the radio. Often Ben's trained ear had given the Mail a useful lead when he'd hear some momentary snippet. "1601 to dispatch, you got an ETA for the ME," which hardly anyone in the room even heard let alone understood. This was the sergeant in the south end of the city sounding like he needed the medical examiner's investigator in a hurry, like there was some urgency about whatever dead body he was dealing with. Ben would check with a phone call, discover there was a suspicious body in a southwest apartment block, and make sure the newsroom reacted now. He'd alert Chuck, the photo editor. Chuck would radio a photographer out on the road and tell him to get to the scene, and Ben would grab his overcoat, stuff his tape recorder and notebook in the sagging pockets, grab the mobile scanner, and portable radio, and head out. Half the newsroom would have no clue what was going on as Ben raced down the corridor on his way out.

"What you got Ben?" the city editor would shout.

"Dunno, a body in the southwest, I'll let you know when I get there, photo's on the way. Right on!" For Ben this was the routine of death.

Of course, most of the time, hours of incessant scanner chatter produced nothing. But Ben had to listen just as carefully in case the next message was the big one. It was a particular skill to isolate the voice on the scanner from amid the bedlam of a busy newsroom. At the Mail, the newsroom was a vast open-plan room with each reporter's desk hived off on three sides by a low partition covered in blue felt. Visually, each reporter had some small degree of privacy but audibly the room was one large melting pot of ringing phones amid a constant buzz of conversation. Ben's desk was the first one in the newsroom and on the other side of his low partition was the city desk, the hub of the little empire, where his boss planned the look of the day's paper. Ben settled in to read this Warnoski file again, while in the background fire department hazard materials specialists were checking out a nasty odor in the southeast—no story there—and paramedics were responding to an elderly woman suffering a seizure—no story there.

When he'd finished reading, he put the file back on the pile. Now at least he knew as much as was released to the public and was revealed in court. He rang a certain contact who'd know more, and was soon on his way out of the office, fully equipped—tape recorder, notebook, mobile scanner, portable radio, cell-phone and cell-phone charger.

Every time he stuffed his bulging pockets with the essentials of modern communications in the year 2000 he remembered fondly the simple days when he started in journalism 35 years earlier in England when all you ever needed was just a pencil and a notebook. In those days, you needed good shorthand skills which meant you could keep up with anyone no matter how fast he spoke. Hell, you needed 120 words a minute of impeccable Pitman's shorthand before you could even apply for a reporter's job on Ben's first newspaper. And you also needed a pocket full of coins so you could phone in a story from the nearest phone box. And that was in the days when iconic red English phone boxes revolved around the "push button A" and "push button B" system. After you'd inserted your coins and dialed the number, you waited. If your caller answered, you'd push button "A" on the phone's cash box and you'd be connected. If there was no reply, you'd push button "B" and the machine would automatically refund you your money. This all made Ben chuckle to himself, being a newspaper dinosaur like he was. To begin with, when he first started, his newspaper in England still used hot metal. Many young cub reporters coming into the Calgary Mail's newsroom in 2000 had never even heard of hot metal. They'd stare in disbelief when Ben would describe how the old original system used to work. Ben used to love to go down into the very heart of his old newspaper where banks of linotype machines were ranged like rows of monsters towering over the men who operated them. On each machine was a huge cauldron of molten lead. The operator sat at a keyboard with 90 characters on it, working with the reporter's story on a sheet of copy paper clipped to his machine. Every time he'd type an individual letter, an "a," the machine would produce a separate lead slug with the required letter engraved on it in reverse—a backward "a." He would type a line of type and the machine would produce a whole line of separate lead slugs, making the line of backward facing type—hence the machine's name. The machine would deposit this row of lead slugs into the right place in a steel contraption which formed part of the whole page of type. This became damn heavy—too heavy for a man to lift, so the steel form sat on a trolley and was wheeled around. Ben recalled this was atmospherically noisy and metallically smelly. Down there, in the very engine room of the newspaper, Ben would hold one group of men in awe. These were the proof readers. It was their responsibility to ensure no steel form ever left that room with a typo on it. Ben would watch as they studied the fresh lead slugs in the forms. They read every paragraph, every sentence and every word in lead slugs that were *upside down* and *back-to-front* to them. And they could read a page as fast as Ben could read the final product in its normal form. Ben used to shake his head in wonder. Ben immersed himself down there so often he learned some of the tricks of their trade. If a typo was discovered quickly enough, the individual offending lead slug could be removed and the right replacement slug inserted. But occasionally there wasn't the luxury of that much time. Instead a quick tap with a metal chisel would deform a lead slug and that page would be printed, not with a glaring typo of a word spelled wrongly, but instead with a smudgy mark visible. A small smudge was less damaging to the paper's reputation than a glaring spelling mistake.

And at the end of every day, every page of type was disassembled and every lead slug was removed from the steel forms, and placed back into the big bubbling cauldrons at the back of each machine where the slugs disintegrated once again into molten lead, filling the cauldron ready for the next day.

Ben was proud to be part of that hot metal system. It would be his story, his words, on those sheets of copy paper clipped to each linotype machine each day. And each of these was a very important and carefully prepared piece of paper. This was in the heyday of typewriters, mechanical typewriters, nothing electronic when Ben started. These were wonderful, clattering typewriters whose individual letters would tangle together when Ben got all excited about some murder and typed so fast the retreating arm carrying one character couldn't get out of the way before the next metal arm carrying the next character hit it and jammed it—and what music when a whole newsroom of typewriters were clattering together near deadline time. Stories were written with one paragraph to one piece of copy paper—wind the sheet of paper in, type one paragraph, and wind it out again. Wind in the next sheet, type a paragraph and wind it out. Why? Ben first worked that way because he was trained that way, though he didn't know exactly why. But later he learned. The first paragraph would end up in the paper in larger and bolder print than the other paragraphs. This was no accident. When Ben's first sheet of copy paper left him, it went to a sub-editor who would write instructions right on the sheet to the linotype operator telling him what size print it must be. Separate following paragraphs might be in italics or bold print and would need separate instructions written right on the sheet. This could only work if each paragraph appeared on a separate sheet. It was another source of amazement to Ben that everyone could translate these instructions, written, as they were, in a marvelous mixture of hieroglyphics, brackets, letters and numbers, like a complicated algebraic formula beyond Ben's understanding.

On some rare dramatic day when a large story was breaking right on deadline, Ben had experienced the stressful trauma of sitting at his typewriter with a sub-editor hovering over him waiting to rip the first sheet out of his machine so he could start covering it in hieroglyphics as Ben got on with the next paragraph. They couldn't wait for Ben to finish the whole story, they had to have the sheets right now—one at a time for speed. Ben remembered it wasn't the easiest of tasks to write a coherent story when someone kept taking away the very words he'd just written. But he mastered it.

Of course, when things weren't quite so frantic, when there was a little more time, Ben enjoyed using the pneumatic pipe system which linked every department in the building to distribute his precious stories. Ben would finish writing today's story, roll the sheets into a tube and insert them into a plastic cylinder. He'd place the cylinder into the pipe and close the end. Powered by a vacuum suction system, the cylinder would ascend inside the pipe, run around the ceiling and drop down a downpipe, landing on the sub-editor's desk. He would cover the sheets in the necessary pattern of hieroglyphics before re-rolling them, replacing them in the cylinder, and send the cylinder up the pipe to land moments later in the linotype operator's tray.

That was all another world—pencil written shorthand notes, clackety typewriters, cauldrons of molten lead, plastic cylinders flying about inside metal pipes round the ceiling—no wonder the kids of 2000 looked at Ben as if he was the ancient mariner of the newspaper industry.

Getting the story in those days was one thing. Getting it back to the paper presented its own difficulties. Finding a phone box was the first problem. Finding one that hadn't been vandalized by some moron was even harder. Ben's old English paper had a bank of brilliant fast, accurate typists sitting in the office waiting to take his copy if only he could reach a phone, wherever he was. Ben recalled this one occasion when he had travelled to Edinburgh, Scotland on his day off to see the Commonwealth Games. While there, to his amazement, it happened an athlete from his home town only won a gold medal. Sensing a scoop, Ben wheedled his way into the athletes' village, snatched an interview with the local-town hero, quickly scribbled a story in his notebook, and searched around for that elusive phone box.

With time fast approaching his deadline, and with his story burning a hole in his notebook, he dodged into a totally deserted gymnasium in the village, and there, on the wall, was a phone—a God send. In no time, he was connected to the typists and his scoop was in full flow when two tall men, immaculately dressed in impeccable suits, strode up to him.

"You can't be here, you have to get out now," said one.

"Hang on," said Ben, "I'm on the phone putting over my story."

"I don't care what you're doing, you can't be here," and they approached Ben menacingly, as if they were about to physically remove him.

"What's your problem, I'll only be a minute," said Ben.

In the next few seconds amid a flurry of movement, Ben was disconnected from the office, physically removed and placed unceremoniously outside the gymnasium, bewildered and angry.

Only then did he discover what this was all about. It only turned out the Queen herself was about to walk through that very gymnasium on her way to meet medal-winning athletes for a royal photo-op. The two tall guys were special branch security officers with orders to clear the gymnasium of everyone before the Queen entered. And that definitely included Ben.

"Stand there and do not move," said the special agent, and Ben obeyed, standing behind a neat row of athletes as they waited in line to be introduced to her majesty. So it was that in all the pictures taken during that royal session Ben appeared as this single mysterious bystander apparently hiding surreptitiously alone in the background.

It was while Ben was still a crime reporter in England that his ancient world of journalism underwent its first earth-shattering life-change. It plummeted into the chaos of modern technology. Computers arrived. Faithful old worn-out typewriters were discarded and these new bulky cube-like boxes with cramped screens appeared. These were the very embryonic days of the computer when they crashed for no apparent reason more often than they worked. The computer technician might just as well have moved his bed and belongings into the newsroom, he was there so regularly. Ben remembered computer training as very basic. He, like all reporters, had to learn the fundamentals. One of the first lessons was the "double click." Apparently if you spaced the two clicks of a double click a split-second too far apart, the machine wouldn't work. If you hit the double click too quickly, it wouldn't work either. Getting such a basic step as the timing of the double click right took one whole session of the training. Who knew?

And then Ben's whole world changed for the second time. After 21 years in the comfortable surroundings of his contacts and knowledge of the inner-workings of his settled way of life, he and his wife upped everything, flew out of England and nine-hours later had dropped into Calgary, Alberta, Canada. Here he was about to start a new life as a newspaper reporter in a bustling western prairie city. They had landed on a Friday night and he was slated to be at his desk on the Monday morning.

But before that even happened Ben had experienced the first language shock which took him by surprise. Ben only got into Canada because, in advance, he had been offered and had accepted a job on the Calgary Mail. The newly arrived couple were met off the plane by two high-ranking editorial members of the Mail, who whisked them straight off to the nearest bar a few minutes ride outside the international airport.

"What'll you have," asked the managing editor.

"I'd like a pint 'a' bidder and my wife'll have 'an 'alf," said Ben, already picturing in his mind a pint glass of dark beer sporting a frothy head on it.

"You'd like what?" said the managing editor.

Ben repeated his request, a little more slowly.

"I'd like a pint of bitter and my wife would like a half."

The managing editor looked very perplexed and went off to the bar, returning shortly with nothing Ben had ever seen before—a huge pitcher of at least a gallon of light-colored beer and four glasses.

Ben had experienced first-hand that there was a language barrier between this fresh-off-the-boat Brit, speaking his native English, and Canadians, who clearly didn't understand the nuances of the mother tongue.

This same problem raised its ugly head in the early days of Ben's new career in a far more serious example which nearly cost him his job right away. Not many weeks after arriving it happened Ben was the lone night guy manning the city desk for the final hours before the paper shut down for the night. Nearly at the end of his shift there was an almighty traffic accident almost outside the window of the office. One large vehicle was upside down and the whole highway was full of emergency vehicles with blue and red flashers lighting up the night sky. Ben decided it was so bad he'd have to write a short story to catch the late edition. A few phone calls filled in the details and he captured it all in two short pithy paragraphs.

The shit hit the fan first thing next day when all of Calgary read Ben's words. "Two people were critically injured last night when an articulated lorry rolled over onto the central reservation on Deerfoot Trail…"

"What the fuck's an articulated lorry and where in hell's name is the central reservation?" screamed the city editor, throwing the paper at Ben. It was then that Ben learned that what had always been an "articulated lorry" in England was, in fact, a "semi-trailer truck" in Calgary, and what had always been a "central reservation" dividing a highway in England was, in fact, a "median" in Canada. Over here, a "central reservation" would be somewhere where indigenous First Nation people lived. Who knew? Ben didn't—but he soon learned the hard way.

Mostly, doing his job was pretty much the same in Calgary as it had been in England—knocking on the doors of grieving families trying to extract the life histories of their recently departed loved ones. But Ben discovered Canada had one useful innovation which England lacked. The whole genre of the Canadian school yearbook was a God-send for investigative journalists like Ben. Every school in every city kept yearbooks with individual professional quality mug-shots of every pupil, and often their thoughts and ambitions included somewhere in the text.

Many times Ben had a mug-shot and half the life history of some guy found dead at some murder scene within minutes of the guy's name being released. Ben would have found him in his school's yearbook. It was a strategy for Ben that every time he had any reason to visit any school he'd pick up the yearbook, and any previous yearbooks if he could find them. It all started in a haphazard manner with a yearbook here, and another there until Ben realized what a useful resource they truly were. Then he organized the system. He stacked them away, school by school, year by year until they were a great catalogue of thousands of names and faces that had been through the city's education system. At the time they left school, the students' achievements were quite rightly and proudly recorded. But a few years later when their young adult lives brought them into Ben's focus, usually for all the wrong reasons, he'd know all about their earlier lives, spelled out there in black and white in the yearbooks. It came to a point after years of Ben's careful book gathering that schools became leery of letting their yearbooks fall into the hands of the media. They worked out what Ben was using them for, and tried their best to thwart him.

Now, 20 minutes after setting out for his certain contact, Ben, still needing this one more piece of information, was pulling up outside the office of the chief medical examiner. Ben was careful to ensure no one knew who it was in that big complex who talked to him, and nothing he ever learned in there appeared directly in print. But the background information he knew about many a murder case would have surprised cops, lawyers and even murderers themselves. He was ushered into the familiar office where he sat down and started another of his regular conversations in there that never took place.

"Do you remember the case of Warnoski, Gillian Warnoski, Red Deer, 1992?" he started.

"The torture case?" asked Ben's contact who remembered it vividly despite the eight years that had passed.

"Yea, the same. Can you tell me about it?"

Ben sat fidgeting for a few minutes while his contact went out and returned a moment later with a thick manila folder holding documents and photographs. He kept it on his side of the desk away from Ben until he decided how many of these secrets he could reveal. Ben felt it was only right he should show the contact he'd researched the case as best he could before coming here to ask for more.

"I know the torture with the cigarette ends was carried out while she was still alive, her nipples were bitten off and there was mutilation after she was dead, and she was strangled, and the killer used two knives, all that came out in court," said Ben.

"Yes, but some strange things didn't come out," said his contact.

From the folder, he took out the plastic album of autopsy photographs marked "Gillian Warnoski" and slid it, open at page one, to Ben. Whatever pictures the words "torture" and "mutilation" had conjured up in Ben's imagination, they weren't nearly as grisly as the truth shown here. The pictures here on page one were of the body at a stage only two detectives and medical examiner staff ever see in each case. At the murder scene, for those unfortunate enough to have to look—witnesses who discover the body, the first police officers called, the body removal team, and investigating detectives—everything is covered in blood. It's horrible to look at but, after all, it's only a red liquid. The true story of pain and suffering is most starkly revealed at the next stage, in the medical examiner's office, when the blood's been washed away, and the wounds are revealed. After the blood is washed off and before the pathologist's knife makes its probing incisions, the body is seen only by the pathologist and his team and the two prime investigators who are there to be taught what secrets the body can be made to reveal. Ben wanted to learn all he could here, too. Two cigarette burns on each forearm showed the torture must have lasted a frightening long time. He could see most of Warnoski's body was covered in long deep slashes that all gaped open. Long parallel slashes down the front of her thighs, across her abdomen, all seemingly uniformly long, each about six or seven inches.

"See these slashes, clean edged and neat at each end, these were made by a two-edged knife blade," said the contact.

"But see these here, a bit torn at the ends and more like they've been ripped, well these were done with a serrated kitchen knife. But see the regular series of five parallel slashes across the abdomen. The two on either side are made with the two-edged knife and the one in the middle with the serrated knife. All made by the same killer using both the knives."

Ben's contact drew the plastic album back across the table, shuffled on a couple of pages and slid it back to Ben.

"Look at that. That never came out in court. What do you make of it?" he said, pointing to a strange shape seemingly carved into the woman's flesh with three short strokes of the double-edged knife.

"Well, it kind of resembles a mountain peak with a straight line of cloud running from one side to the other across the top," Ben ventured, thinking of the Rockies.

It was high on the woman's left thigh and the knife slashes which carved it were much shorter than the other mutilations.

"Couldn't it just be random slashes near each other, Christ, there are enough slashes all over the place."

"Yes, that's what was finally decided," said Ben's contact. "They discounted them meaning anything and just added them as three more slashes making up the 30-odd separate wounds noted on the body," and he took the album back and turned to some photographs at the back.

"This is her clothing, well, what was ever found of it. Not a lot. But this is strange. As you could see in those first pictures the killer left her panties on, at least that's what it looked like at first, but when the autopsy started, and her panties were taken off, the center crotch piece had been cut out, probably with the double-edged knife, quite carefully, so he had access to her vagina, but there was no sign of rape, well, in fact, no sign of sexual intercourse at all."

"So what about the guy's DNA on the cigarette end in her vagina?" asked Ben, remembering what the pervert did.

"It's all about humiliation and how the killer viewed his victim," said the contact. "Some of these sadistic sexual killers see all women as garbage. That's why bodies are often found dumped on landfill sites, thrown away like so much disposable rubbish. It's a classic profile. He used the tortured victim's body as the garbage can for the cigarette end with which he tortured her. Look at this," he said, turning back to the autopsy pictures.

"See these rope burn marks and reddening of her wrists and ankles as well as the cigarette burns, well they were made when she was tied up still alive. The burns and reddening are the beginning of bruising. This was proof of her being tortured."

"Now," he said turning the page, "look at these linear marks round her knees which were bound together and raised when the body was found. No hint of reddening, see how they look quite different, cutting into the skin. Her knees were tied together after death. And it looks like there was a simple reason. After her death, he'd stuffed the cigarette end into her vagina, and to make sure it stayed in there, he'd tied her legs tightly together and lifted them above the level of her body so it wouldn't fall out. That's unusual. Most sadistic killers like this leave their victims with legs splayed wide open as a final gesture of humiliation. This was just the opposite, probably because of the cigarette end."

Ben didn't take any notes. He never did in these conversations that never took place. He always felt it would somehow take away the implicit trust he'd built up with his contact over the years if the contact could see there was a written record of their meeting. But Ben wanted things absolutely clear in this mind. Leaving the medical examiner's office, he drove for two minutes then swung over into the turn out alongside the Bow River, where he could see one of his best fly-fishing spots on the far bank, and parked up. Here, he jotted down everything he'd seen and been told in the last few minutes, so he had the best possible record of what he'd learned. This time, he even drew himself some amateur thumbnail sketches of what he'd seen. Then, secretly wishing he could turn right and swing over the Crowchild Bridge and drop down the bank into his fishing spot, he instead pulled out into the eastbound traffic which led away from the fish, away from the Bow and back to the office.

At his computer, Ben opened a file, not in the "news" section where he wrote all his stories, but in an obscure "supplements" section, which few people had access to, even if they knew how to access it. He wrote up his notes, printed them out, deleted the file, tucked the page of notes in his "File 185—Ron Lincoln" and no prying eyes in the newsroom were any the wiser.

It was only four days later when Ron rang again. It was fixed. Ben was on his visitor's list. As soon as Ben contacted the prison, they could meet.

"Christ, this guy's gotta be keen," thought Ben, wondering how the hell he'd cut through the prison red tape that quickly.

"Right on, leave it with me, and I'll set it up with the prison," said Ben, still inwardly hoping someone would kill this evil pervert in there before he'd have to go and listen to his whining.

"Look, when you come, bring in some smokes and a copy of the Mail. The ones in here get lost right away," said Ron.

"Shit, here we go," thought Ben, "haven't even got there yet and he's after smokes and the paper, then it'll be money, then fucking pot or cocaine, these bastards are all the same."

"Right on, I'll see what I can do," he said, performing the old "think-one-thing, say-the-other" trick, inwardly vowing not to take Ron anything. But after he'd put the phone down, and made a couple of calls of his own, he discovered in this case Ron was as good as his word. Ben had phoned to ask the prison authorities if he could visit the following Tuesday at 2 o'clock. They demanded the request be put in writing, Ben faxed it in writing, and two hours later, presumable after they'd checked into Ben's background, permission was granted. There was a bunch more paperwork, like faxing them the details and license plate of the van he would be driving, but finally it was a go. Now Ben had to sell it to his city editor. Driving to the Drumheller Penitentiary, doing the interview and getting back would take the whole day. He wouldn't be listening to the scanner, he wouldn't be answering the office phones, and there wasn't any guarantee of copy, but if things went well, there could a feature in it for the following Sunday's paper. This was always the juiciest carrot to dangle in front of the city editor. The Sunday editor was always screaming for features, and if the city editor could go to one of the never-ending tangle of afternoon planning meetings and announce he had a feature lined up for Sunday, his afternoon would run very much more smoothly.

"Yup," said Frank, seduced by the carrot. "Go Tuesday, you better get a feature, and have it in by Friday for Sunday's paper. Are you taking a photographer?"

"No, I'm not, think about it," said Ben, inwardly groaning at having to explain to Frank that interviews in jail with convicted murderers weren't conducted in a blaze of publicity. They were half-secret little affairs everyone tried to hide up. Prisons don't like reporters snooping around, they don't like them talking to inmates at great lengths, and even prisoners don't like seeing other inmates blabbing their mouths off to reporters, even if the writer is trying to look as inconspicuous as possible. The whole thing's a horrible sordid undertaking, which wouldn't be helped one bit by having a photographer, festooned with cameras and 500 mm lenses all over his person, firing flashes in people's faces.

"No, I suppose not," said Frank, who's thoughts were already full of the following Sunday paper's headlines—"SEX SLAYER SHOCKER—Mail Exclusive" with hidden camera pictures from inside the Pen.

The following Tuesday, Ben was on the road north out of Calgary, heading for Drumheller well before 2 o'clock. He took the familiar right turn on the Beiseker road, remembering to slow down very deliberately at Beiseker itself, where the RCMP detachment was right on the main drag. The 50 km/h sign was precisely located so if you were even a few seconds late slowing down, you found yourself going right past the front window of the Mounties while still breaking the speed limit. Not a wise move. Ben remembered braking suddenly down to the speed limit when he went to Beiseker one time when the town's hotel had burned to the ground on an icy, perishingly cold winter's day. Ben had got some remarkable home video that day. He had this thing about filming big fires, which he used to edit into two hour films and sell through fire magazines across North America.

What was outstanding about this blaze was how the tiny Beiseker volunteer fire department had overcome the problem of having no aerial ladder, no means of firing water down into the hotel from above. It was brilliant. They commandeered a crane. They suspended a metal cage from the jib and put firefighters in the cage with a hose. By having four heavy ropes leading from the four corners of the cage to the ground, each pulled by teams of firefighters, they could guide the cage backward and forward over the face of the blazing hotel knocking down fiery hot spots. That became part of Ben's "Fires—Volume Three" video tape which sold nicely at $14.95.

On another day, Ben was going to Hanna and clean forgot about the Mounties at Beiseker. He sailed past their office going too fast—but they weren't looking and he arrived at Hanna without a hitch. It really was his lucky day. Not only did he dodge a bullet back there in Beiseker but he had been sent out to one fatality and ended up with two bodies. Right on! Just outside Hanna is a tiny airport used frequently by sky-divers and parachutists. On this day, a student parachutist on his first jump had suffered some malfunction and smacked into a farmer's dusty ploughed field nearby. By the time Ben reached the scene, it was crowded. Firefighters, paramedics, RCMP and passers-by were mostly huddled round a car and an ambulance well away from the scene in the field where the parachutist had been killed. Ben discovered a doctor had been driving past and had witnessed the parachutist hit the ground. Instantly realizing his professional skills might save a life, the doctor drove across the ploughed field to help the man crumpled on the ground. As his car raced across the dirt, it lifted a large dust cloud behind it, until he screeched to a halt alongside the contorted body.

In seconds, as he knelt at the man's side, the drifting dust cloud enveloped them both and the whole scene before it blew past on its way downwind. Incredible as it sounded to Ben, the doctor suffered chronically from asthma, and the dust cloud and the nervous stress of the scene brought on an instant and quite deadly asthma attack. The sky-diver's body was still covered by a tarp in the field, and the doctor's body was still in the ambulance, where paramedics had been unable to revive him. There was an unusual sequel to Ben writing the story about the doctor who laid down his life trying to save someone else. Many months later, he received from somewhere out in eastern Canada a letter from the doctor's parents, thanking him for portraying the death of their son in such a sensitive way. Ben didn't get many letters like that. He got plenty accusing him of being a vulture, and gloating over other people's misfortunes, and sensationalizing tragedies, but not a lot saying thank you.

Then he was pulling into the prison. He was always amazed how crowded the parking lots were—probably 50 or 60 cars here. What were that many visitors doing at a prison, anyway? Just as he got out of the van, a woman came staggering across the parking lot, carrying a giant cuddly panda toy, a set of bright green plastic steps and a child's plastic slide, and trying to push a stroller with a toddler in it, who was squirming and who'd almost succeeded in falling out. Ben helped her, taking the panda and the slide.

"Hey, thanks, this is a struggle," said the woman, sexily dressed, as Ben could now see with the panda out of the way. She had a great deal of cleavage with freckles going a long way down—and leopard skin-tight pants—very tight pants. "Hold still, you little monkey," she said, catching the squirming child before it could escape. They all stopped at a station wagon, and the women lifted the hatch, piling in the steps, and slide and panda and stroller and heaving the little one up, clutched in the crook of one arm.

"He likes to see the little one," she said, nodding toward the prison to indicate where "he" was, as if some kind of explanation was necessary.

"Yea," thought Ben, "I bet he prefers to see the skin-tight pants and the freckles."

"Right on, have a nice day," he said lamely, as he walked off toward the main gate, knowing she was hardly likely to have many nice days, struggling to bring up a squirmy kid on her own while her old man was in the slammer. And he felt genuinely sorry for the kid. Every time Ben visited prisons for news stories he felt sorry for the gaggle of kids wasting their childhoods sitting in jail holding-areas, staring glumly at dirty whitewashed walls so struggling moms could visit selfish dads. Ben had spent all his childhood days in England playing on the local south coast beach with his sister, swimming in the sea, hunting through rock pools, until the day's total enjoyment left them crashed out for a secure sleep at home, five minutes' walk back from the beach, where Mom and Dad were always there.

No kid should ever be made to see the inside of this miserable place, thought Ben as he walked to the steel cage wicket containing an overweight guard. The fat man checked Ben's driver's license, his Mail identity card and his Canadian Citizenship Card (you have to have three pieces of picture ID to get this far). Then he checked Ben was on the permitted visitors list for prisoner 06716 Lincoln. Finally, Ben was inside.

"Sit there and wait. He'll be out," said another guard, and Ben sat on a metal bench with a small shelf just big enough for him to balance his notebook and tape recorder. A sheet of heavy glass separated him from what looked like a similar tiny space on the inside. Ben was mentally psyching himself up to extract the most from this interview when he was suddenly there—Ronald Lincoln, looking pretty much like the file photograph Ben had studied a lot in the past few days, but a little thinner and more drawn in the face. Lincoln picked up the telephone on his side of the glass. Ben lifted his receiver.

"Hiya Ben. Recognize you from your logo in the Mail," said Lincoln, working to ingratiate himself from the first moment by appearing to be a Mail reader and follower of Ben's stories.

"Yea, I recognize you from the pictures in your file from the trial," said Ben. "I don't know if what you're going to tell me will make a story, or whether we'll use it or what. Just so long as you don't expect big headlines in tomorrow's paper campaigning for your release, or anything."

"Look, I know. I don't expect nothing. But this is how it is. This is a fucking stitch-up. They got programs in here, where you have to first cough to the crime, be remorseful and all that, you know, and then you can get on the program. Well, fuck that. I didn't kill that fucking woman, so I ain't coughing to it, and fuck being remorseful for something I didn't do. So I ain't on any programs, so they take me for a bad ass…"

"Hang on," said Ben, who could see this turning into a long whining session with not much useful information coming out. "Let me run through what happened, according to what came out at the trial and what I know, and you give me your version. That'll give us some facts to start with."

"Okay," said Lincoln.

"First of all they said you knew this woman. Did you?" asked Ben.

"Yea, well, not really. Look, she was one of the women at the TD bank where I banked in Red Deer. I been going there years, and she'd been there a few years. You know, sometimes you get one teller, sometimes another. She was called Jill. Once my Master Card got fucked up and she sorted it, and told me if it went wrong, call the bank and ask for Jill, for her, that's how I knew her name."

"Did you ever meet her or see her other than working in the bank?" asked Ben.

"No. Never. She was just one of the women in there."

"Alright. What about your truck?" Ben asked. "It wasn't any old truck. It was distinctive, wasn't it? How do you explain witnesses seeing it driving away from where the body was dumped? I mean that must have been your truck, mustn't it?"

"Yea, I don't think there's no doubt. That was my truck. I don't have any fucking clue how it was seen there. I been over this fucking hundreds of times in my mind. The night before, when I got home I parked it in the alley at the back of my house in Penhold, like I always do. Next morning, when I went out to work, it was there in the back alley. Then later, when I got fucking arrested, the cops tell me half of Red Deer saw my truck at a murder scene in the middle of the night. Fuck me. I know every night I park it at home. I park on a slight angle to the wall at the back of my yard. That following morning it was square to the wall, but I suppose that night I'd parked it straighter than usual. I never loaned it to no one and I don't know what was fucking going on."

"Well," thought Ben to himself. "One explanation could just possibly be that your truck was out there at a murder scene in Red Deer because you were behind the wheel," but he put his next question, looking Lincoln in the eyes, as well as he could through very thick glass.

"What about them finding that woman's blood in the trunk of your truck, then? Do you think it was her blood?" he asked.

"Yea, their forensic guys said it was. Who the hell am I to know any different? But I don't know how it got in there. Just imagine it was you. You park your car at the back of your house tonight, and in a week's time, cops find blood in the trunk from somebody what's been whacked. You can't argue about whose blood it is, but you don't know how it got there. How can you, if you didn't have nothing to do with it?"

Ben thought, "You smooth bastard, you know how the blood got there, because you put her body in there to carry it to the end of the Red Deer road that night. No wonder the cops had you, mate," but he kept sticking to the questions.

"Alright," he said, "I've got to ask you this. Even if there was some explanation for how come your truck was seen where the body was dumped, and some explanation, which didn't involve you, for how her blood got in the trunk, how can you explain your DNA on the cigarette end inside her body. I mean, I want to help if I can, but you've got to see it from my point of view. That's the whole case, right there, isn't it?"

"Look, I can't explain that either. That is straight forward impossible. I thought it had to be a mistake, some cock-up with DNA, but they said there wasn't no balls-up, no one got nothing wrong. Soon as they said they had that, I knew I'd had it. What can I think? Only me and fucking God know I didn't do it. But I can't explain to you what did happen, 'cos I don't know."

Ben's innermost sensibility blanched at the juxtaposition of Ron Lincoln's foul mouth and God. He was fairly convinced now Lincoln was the sadistic sexual pervert who'd tortured and butchered an innocent Red Deer bank teller. Apart from 20 minutes of denials, he hadn't given him a shred of anything new to go on. But Ben persevered.

"Was there anything strange or unusual happening to you at that time that might be kind of related to it or did this lot come out of the blue?" he asked.

"Nah, nothing I can think of related to it. It was just one fucking disaster after another that year. My fucking house in Penhold got broken into, though whoever done it didn't get my money and didn't hardly make any mess. I think he must have got disturbed before he got started. Then, a couple of weeks later, my truck got dinged by some fucking hit-and-run merchant, and I had to put a new wing on it. I got that out the 'pick-your-part' yard up there in Red Deer. Then I got lifted for this lot, and that was the end of it. I been inside ever since."

Ben was now more convinced than ever Lincoln had murdered Warnoski. He was just a man in denial, there wasn't any revelation of any alibi police have ignored for Ben to crusade with. There was nothing. So Ben decided to think about what story he could screw out of him instead. Maybe Ben could gain some insight into his perverted character for a feature for next Sunday.

"Is it right," Ben started, just a little wary of dragging up some of the more secret information about Lincoln's background which Lincoln probably didn't realize he knew, "Is it right you were convicted in the late 1980s of living off the avails of a prostitute?" he asked.

"Got convicted of it, yea," said Lincoln. "We was just living common-law, and it was her way of contributing, you know. It all ended in a load of fighting, and she turned the fucking law on me, and I got done. I'd been inside before that, and she told 'em how I hammered her around, but that wasn't no more than any other couple, but they put it all together and I got done for being her pimp."

"Look, when I was inside before all that, I done things and I got caught. With her, she was working the street, and I beat the crap out of her a few times, and I got done for that. All that happened. I'm levelling with you. I ain't denying any of it. But I ain't bullshitting you when I'm telling you I'm fucking in here for this lot, and I never done it."

Ben clicked off his tape recorder. Another 20 minutes of flat out denial wouldn't add to the tape full of denials he'd already got. This man had been in here eight years, and hadn't been able to come up with anything better than repeating over and over that he didn't do it.

"Okay. I'm going back to the office, I'm going to talk to my editor, and see what story we can print, and I'll know by tomorrow. Can you call me around the same time as usual, and I'll know by then," he said.

"Did you bring any smokes," said Lincoln, who in a flash had picked up the "I'm-not-wasting-my-time-on-this-any-longer" inflection in Ben's voice. Lincoln had mentally switched off the interview in his mind, and switched back to being the old lag in prison thinking no further ahead than his next cigarette.

"Yea, I brought them. You know how it works. They've got the packet out there in holding and they'll get them to you. Don't forget to call me tomorrow."

For a while on the drive back to Calgary, Ben ran over the interview in his head. He was disappointed really. He'd hoped Lincoln was going to reveal something he could get his teeth into, but there was nothing. It had been about as useful as an RCMP press release. So he gave up thinking about it, pushed his favorite tape into the slot in the dashboard and cranked up Chris Barber's trad jazz band full volume all the way back to the office. It was as he reached his desk and saw the pile of murder files there that something registered in the back of his mind. Even as Lincoln had been talking back there in the prison, something had flickered in Ben's thoughts, but before he'd had time to pursue it, they'd moved on. Now, he needed to think about it again. He ran his tape recorder back a few times until he found the words he wanted again.

"*My fucking house in Penhold got broken into, though whoever done it didn't get my money, and didn't hardly make any mess. I think he must have got disturbed before he got started. Then, a couple of weeks later, my truck got dinged by some fucking hit-and-run merchant, and I had to put a new wing on it."*

That was it. Now it clicked. Years ago, when another loser in jail had called Ben with the same old sob story about being innocent and in jail for a crime he didn't commit, that guy had run through the same scenario. That first guy had been burgled, and had his car tampered with just before he got arrested for murder, something like that. Who the hell was it? In the office Ben wasted 15 minutes of his life waiting for the Mail's appalling, obsolete computer system to log on so he could turn to his "murder list" and start hunting. You didn't have to wait 15 minutes for a clackety old typewriter to warm up, thought Ben. But once he was "in," he soon found it. His impeccable files and his sixth sense knowledge of finding his way around them soon turned it up.

Chapter 3

It was file 137. Darren Sunderland, sentenced to life for the first-degree murder of Jill Bereson. Ben remembered this one well. This was a Calgary murder. This was another sex pervert who'd murdered this waitress from a restaurant and dumped her body on a golf course in what was then the far south of Calgary, where the city was running into the prairies. Since then, the city's flourishing urban sprawl had pushed the city boundary miles further south. This golf course had now become an oasis of green in a jungle of asphalt roads and grey roofed houses. This was another part of the city Ben associated with death. Not being a golfer, he'd only ever had two links with this course—and they both involved death. There was this murder. And the only time he'd been there before was to one of its large water hazards for a drowning. A line of shoulder-to-shoulder adults were shuffling through the water until with an anguished cry, one man stumbled, bent down beneath the surface, and came up clutching the lifeless body of a girl who'd been missing under water for half-an-hour.

Harrowing scenes of anguish followed while people tried the kiss-of-life on the little girl in vain. Her mother, hysterical with terror, watched as it became clear it wasn't working. Ben was warding off bullying golfers who decided the best way to display their frustration at not being able to help the little girl was to push the media around—these reporters they saw as vultures, who were after all, only doing their job.

That water hazard was alongside the ninth fairway. And that was where early morning golfers had found the body of Jill Bereson, a 23-year-old brunette on November 5, 1990, a crisp day at the tail end of an Indian summer of seemingly never-ending warmth. A day later, when Ben picked up a photograph of the victim from her shocked parents, he discovered a tiny detail which added a sense of sadness to his background story on the victim. Just two days before being murdered she had become engaged to her childhood sweetheart called Jason Briscoe. She had joked happily with her parents that although she'd be changing her name she'd end up with the same initials.

Ben clearly remembered this case as one of the few times when he'd covered a murder funeral that the family weren't distressed at his being there. It was an integral part of Ben's work that he attend the funerals of murder victims. It was human nature for family and friends to remember the very best of their recently departed, no matter what circumstances had surrounded them being killed. So each time Ben was there, the Mail used the opportunity to record the fondest memories of each victim in his compassionate stories. But most families never saw it that way on the traumatic day of their funeral. Here was that damn vulture from the media again, who'd already pestered them since the day it happened. This time Jill Bereson's family was different. Ben's sympathetic approach from the minute he had been hunting for a photograph struck a chord with them. Now they even nodded to him when they saw him at the service.

It wasn't always that way. Ben recalled one family funeral when he and another Mail reporter were there under double death threats. Ben was there with Ray Ludlow—would you believe, another Ludlow but not related—who was Ben's mentor, an older guy who'd seen far more than Ben would ever see. Ray had worked on the National Enquirer. He'd won his spurs at the time of Elvis Presley's funeral. Photographs of Elvis lying in state were strictly forbidden, so typically, the Enquirer sent Ray to get one. Knowing he'd never get in the door, let alone get close to Elvis's coffin, Ray had a plan. He bought himself a bunch of cheap point-and-shoot cameras, gave them to various people in the line-up with instructions for them to sneak a photo when no-one was looking.

"Get me a picture and you're in for big bucks," Ray promised.

One guy had strapped his camera to his ankle, then, near Elvis's coffin, suddenly had to bend down to tie his shoe lace. In a second, he had the photo and no one saw. Not until, that is, the picture appeared on the front page of the National Enquirer where everyone saw. Ray had scored his greatest triumph.

But the National Enquirer worked in mysterious ways. When it decided to get rid of a reporter it no longer wanted, it had a unique system of operating. It would give the poor unfortunate an impossible task and when he failed to get the story, because in truth it never existed in the first place, he was fired. Ray had one such an assignment, failed and was fired.

On this death threat occasion, he had worked on a multiple murder with Ben involving a hard-bitten family living in Trochu northeast of Calgary. One brother was already serving life for having taken a shotgun to the family's grandmother, and now another brother was charged with murdering his own young bride and her young toddler. When Ben and Ray had been poking around the family getting the initial stories, they'd seen shotguns and rifles in each of the family's vehicles. The death threats were quite simple.

"You come near the funerals and you're dead," was what the caller on the phone had said. "We got shotguns and if we don't get you that way we've got two Doberman Pinschers and we keep them hungry."

Ben told the city desk what was at stake.

"Ah, that's only words, go anyway and don't come back without the story," was the reply.

The two Ludlows went, survived and came back with the story. Ray totally outshone Ben. He even found a relative who confided in him the very secret the family didn't want revealed, that the young bride had been buried wearing her wedding dress.

That wasn't the only time Ben had been honestly scared at a funeral. He'd had to cover the funeral of a member of a biker-gang, and biker-gangs hated media. His one clear memory of the service was that in the middle of the hushed eulogy one biker had let out the loudest fart Ben had ever heard. Afterward more than 20 bikers had revved up their Harley Davidson machines into a box formation four across and five deep and had performed a mass ceremonial wheelie past the church—intimidating but impressive.

Ben had been to so many funerals he knew by heart the words of what he soon discovered became the most often used music at such services—Eric Clapton's "Tears in Heaven." Ben had watched many parents dissolve into floods of tears at the opening line, "Would you know my name if I saw you in heaven?" Composed in despair while Clapton was grieving for his four-year-old son who'd fallen to his death from a high-rise window, this one song would break the resolve of entire congregations who would heave and sob with the distraught family. For these suffering mourners may have been hearing these sad words for the first time, seemingly referring personally to their loss. Poignant they may have been, but they hardly affected Ben any more, after all, in one year he'd heard the lyrics 19 times. This was that exceptional year when Calgary suffered more than 30 homicides. It was obvious to Ben that heaven was on everyone's minds at these somber occasions. The second favorite music was the song "Holes in the Floor of Heaven" and Ben had lost count of how many times he'd heard that one too. But funerals weren't only about loss. Ben was always intrigued by the depth of additional emotions funerals created on top of the obvious intense sadness. He'd covered one when a family feud was present, with hatred on both sides. One side of the family issued tickets in advance and members of the other side of the family, without tickets, weren't allowed inside. Bouncers even guarded the door of the church to keep out the unwanted.

The ghastliest funeral Ben ever saw was after ten members of one family were all killed when their minivan was in a terrible road crash and burst into flames. There is a scale of proceedings at most gravesites. Usually, a single black hearse followed by a small convoy of black funeral cars arriving signals the service will start shortly. On this grim day in a rural burial site with wide open prairie spaces all round and no buildings nearby, Ben watched in amazement as a flatbed truck arrived, dominating the landscape, with ten draped caskets lined up side-by-side filling the flatbed. Later Ben watched, almost in disbelief, as a crew of grave diggers was employed to lower the coffins into the communal grave. They put in one layer of caskets, then covered them with a structure of wooden beams to support the second layer of coffins, with more beams on top to take the third deck of coffins—a triple-decker of death. Even Ben had never seen anything like that.

But maybe the saddest one Ben ever encountered was a funeral for a murdered homeless man. No one went—no friends, no family. On a day fittingly pouring in rain, there was the somber representative of a funeral home, an obligatory member of the Salvation Army and Ben.

In contrast, Jill Bereson's funeral was quite the opposite. The church had been packed. Her family was large, her fellow workers at the restaurant where she worked turned out in force and she had a huge circle of friends. The church was decked out with happy pictures of her.

From the photographs, it was clear she had been a beautiful girl with sleek black shoulder-length hair. But the golfers who found her that dreadful day never knew that. All they saw was a sickening matting of blood where face, head, hair and grass had clumped into a dark red, almost black shadow in the early morning light.

Ben flicked quickly through the headlines in his file. "GOLFERS FIND MURDERED WOMAN" on day one, "MANHUNT FOR KILLER" on day two, and "TEARS FOR FAVOURITE WAITRESS" on the coverage of the funeral, which Ben attended. But not until February 1991, nearly four months later, was there a headline, "MAN CHARGED IN GOLF COURSE MURDER." There was copious trial coverage nearly a year later culminating in the headline on January 10, 1992, "KILLER JAILED FOR LIFE—No Parole for 20 Years," with a background piece from Ben. For now, Ben just glanced at the headlines. He turned to the section he reserved at the back of every file.

"Background notes." This is what he wanted. Here were his photographs of Bereson, several different shots, including ones that didn't run in the Mail, and a mug-shot of Sunderland, the killer, and all the police press releases. These which ran from day one which said only "foul play was suspected" right through to the last release which announced "Darren Sunderland, 39, of Calgary, has been charged with first-degree murder." There were scribble pad notes with relevant phone numbers, and then the pages he was seeking, his interview with Sunderland.

The murderer had already been inside for 14 months at the time. His appeal against conviction had been rejected by a higher court, and this time Ben did the whole thing by phone. Sunderland had been a kind of gentleman killer compared to the usual bad-ass convicts who went down. He'd been a textile salesman. Sometimes he was driving around Alberta and B.C. Sometimes he was jet-setting to Toronto and Quebec, meeting fellow salesmen, attending seminars, and perfecting his persuasive smooth-talking of customers. In his background notes, Ben also found the transcript he'd written up of his interview with Calgary's homicide cops. When Ben was preparing a background feature on Sunderland to be run after sentencing, he discovered the man's lifestyle played a major factor in the five-month hunt before homicide detectives ran him down. Det. Barry Gray in homicide, the primary on Bereson's murder, spent a long time in the homicide office going over the case with Ben.

Ben would hardly forget that day. At least, six of the homicide cops were in the main office, when Gray drew up a chair for Ben to sit on as he pulled out the file. They'd hardly started talking when Ben farted, audibly. At least, the chair on which he was sitting farted audibly. Ben ignored this terrible moment and carried on talking as bravely as he could, hoping they probably hadn't noticed. But one of the six detectives shuffled his chair away from Ben in response. And a few minutes later Ben definitely farted out loud. Several of the cops sniggered. One asked, "You alright, Ben?"

Ben carried on talking with Gray, but now the other guys sidled away to the far end of the room, wrinkling their noses as if retreating from a nasty smell. This left Ben conspicuously alone in the middle, with only Gray tucked against the wall anywhere near him. Then Ben led out a revolting bubbly fart, looked up and saw, through the glass in his separate office, the head of homicide convulsed in hysterical laughter with something in his hand. Ben's coolness under this intense pressure had earned him the respect of the office, and they relented. Gray, the bastard, had rigged a trick farting device under the seat of the chair, and the boss in his side office had operated the remote, letting off the farts at the opportune moments to cause Ben the greatest possible embarrassment. The whole office had thoroughly enjoyed having the Mail's crime reporter as their squirming victim. God help any poor secretary who suffered at their hands! So it wasn't surprising Ben remembered this interview. Still muttering about "you miserable bastards" he had drawn his chair nearer to Gray, now it was safe to do so, and concentrated on Sunderland.

"When we first found Bereson's body, it didn't take long to identify her and find out she was a waitress at the White Spot Restaurant, you know, the one down south there," said Gray. "So we had two teams hived off to find out all the other employees who worked there, and from going through the restaurant receipts, we worked up a list of all the regular customers there who might have known her."

"This gave us a list of about 40 people we needed to interview, who might have known her and her habits."

"And one of the regular customers there was Darren Sunderland."

"The restaurant employees knew him well as some flash salesman who entertained potential customers there, and who tipped big. You want to get noticed by restaurant staff—go regularly and tip big."

"We interviewed him early on, and he admitted being a regular there, knowing Bereson as Jill, as he knew three or four of the other waitresses. He accounted for his actions on the night of the murder, and he just went into the index system with all the other regular customers at the restaurant."

"But at this stage he wasn't a suspect?" Ben had asked.

"No, no more than everybody's a suspect in the early days," said Gray. "But then, just before Christmas we had quite a break."

"As Bereson's body had been dumped on the golf course, and her skull had been caved in with a golf club, we had another team looking at every member of the golf club. It's well known that killers sometimes dump bodies in places where they're comfortable, you know—where they're used to moving around. Well, there were 570 members on the list, and it was some time before we realized one of the members was none other than Darren Sunderland."

"That's neat, we thought. That was the first—and only—name to come up on both lists. He knew our murder victim from talking with her at the restaurant, and he was a member of the golf club where her body was dumped."

"Put him right in the frame. Elementary, my dear Watson," Ben had said.

"Well, hang on. It was a start. You can't go around arresting people just because they know a victim and move in the same circles," said Gray.

"We ran him through the computer, and came up with an old charge of rape from years before, but he'd been acquitted, so that didn't help much, but anyway, we interviewed him again, and he consented to us searching his car. Remember, by now, this was January of 1991, and if it was him, he'd had since November the previous year to make sure nothing was left for us to find in his car—and always presuming he'd used his own car to carry her body. There were a lot of 'ifs' at this stage."

"But it was his car that broke the case for us. The scenes-of-crime guys found traces of blood in the trunk. The samples went off to the RCMP crime laboratories in Edmonton, and when the results came back in the middle of February, they were positive."

"Jill Bereson's blood in Sunderland's trunk," Ben had underlined in his background notes.

The noose was quickly tightening round Sunderland's neck when more lab results came back. These showed that the murder weapon, a golf club, a 7 iron, found thrown into long undergrowth off the fatal ninth fairway was identical to the set owned by Sunderland. While it bore no useful fingerprints, its hand grip had two fibers embedded in it matching the fibers in Sunderland's golf bag. Other golfers had similar sets of clubs in similar bags, including similar 7 irons, so this wasn't totally damning, but excellent additional circumstantial evidence.

Gray told Ben that the final clincher, the last nail in Sunderland's coffin, came on February 23, 1991, soon after all those results had come back from the crime laboratory. The medical examiner's office came up with their laboratory test results on a cigarette end found in the victim's vagina. The DNA on the cigarette end was Sunderland's DNA. That did it. Next day, February 24, 1991, he was arrested and charged with first-degree murder. "Sunderland's DNA on a cigarette end inside Bereson's vagina" Ben had underlined that in his background notes as well. Ben's background piece on the "Golf Course Killer" ran the day after he was sentenced to life on January 10, 1992.

Now Ben studied again the notes of his interview with Sunderland. Sunderland had rung him only a month after his appeal had been turned down, protesting his innocence, what else! There were the usual things these killers always pointed out. Sunderland had explained to Ben how he'd allowed homicide investigators to have his car for examination because he knew he had nothing to hide. Did Ben think he would have given it to the cops if it was full of incriminating evidence? Sunderland had been stunned when they came up with blood in the trunk. "I bet he was," mused Ben. Sunderland had no idea how it got there. *Well, being the killer would be one logical explanation,* Ben thought to himself. On the phone, Sunderland told Ben, yes, he knew the girl, Jill, the waitress; and yes, he was a member of the golf course; and yes, he knew the particular stretch of rough where the body had been found very well. The major fault in his golfing game was slicing his drives to the right, and many a time he'd ended up in that very rough alongside the fairway on the ninth.

Sunderland pointed out some more "illogicals" in the case against him. Why, he'd asked, would he kill a woman, using his own golf club, leaving it to be found nearby, and dump her body on a golf course everybody knew he played on, bringing suspicion right down on him? And why would he pick a woman lots of people knew he knew from his favorite restaurant? Sunderland added up all these illogical elements for Ben. He kills a woman who can easily be linked to him. He dumps her body on a golf course half of Calgary knows he plays on. He leaves her blood in his car for four months. Then he offers the car to the police for them to find it. Then he allows police to take bodily fluid samples from him, so they can check his DNA against the killer's DNA which the killer knows the police must have.

As Ben read over these notes again, he could still remember how exasperated Sunderland had become on the phone all those years ago. Not only at facing a life sentence for this murder he reckoned he didn't commit, but because he'd been portrayed as just about the most stupid and bungling killer ever born to have left so many clues. And then Ben came to the passage he thought he remembered.

"Yes, I was right, here it is," Ben muttered to himself.

When Sunderland was at his most angry and frustrated, he'd told Ben a bunch of bad things had happened to him around that time. On Halloween Night that year, a few days before the murder, someone, under the guise of "trick-or-treat" had broken into his home in Calgary and stolen one of his most expensive golf clubs. His whole set of clubs were available, but the thief had chosen one and left the rest, though the others were damn expensive, too. That was very mysterious. And, although it wasn't important, but it just showed what a bad run of luck he was suffering, around that same time his car which was parked outside his Calgary home had been broken into. Nothing had been stolen. In fact, his dashboard, which was usually untidy and dusty, had been tidied up and cleaned. Sunderland was ranting at this point. What kind of idiot breaks into a car just to clean it and tidy it for its owner? He'd parked it up the night before and next morning there it was, tidied and clean.

"Right on," said Ben, happy his beloved files hadn't failed him.

"What's your problem, muttering to yourself," said Frank, sitting across from Ben.

"Oh nothing," said Ben. "Not yet anyway."

"Is it going to make copy for tomorrow's paper?" asked Frank.

"No, forget it," said Ben, as he compared these two interviews. He had no idea what it all meant, but it was amazing. Here was Sunderland's interview in 1992, and Ron Lincoln's interview today, eight years apart, yet they were relating damn nearly identical stories.

Both men, one from Penhold and the other from Calgary, were inside doing life for murders of young women. Both of them talked about having their homes and vehicles broken into around the time of the murders they were charged with, yet nothing was really stolen. And there was something else less tangible but similar about the accounts given by both of them. Ben finally put his finger on it. Neither man denied any of the details of the case against them. That was it. Every other inmate who'd ever called Ben claiming he was innocent had called the cops liars, called witnesses liars, or offered far flung excuses why they'd been at crime scenes.

Ben recalled one killer who'd rung him up, claiming he was innocent, and who had an explanation for how his semen, proved by DNA, ended up inside a young girl's body, even though he swore he hadn't murdered her. He had told this story to Ben, and later used it as his defense in court. He said that day he'd masturbated, and then, without washing his hands, had gone out for a walk in the woods near his home. There, to his amazement, he stumbled on the body of a young girl who'd been murdered and dumped in the woods by somebody else. Then, he confessed, he did do something wicked. He admitted putting his finger inside her vagina because he couldn't control himself as the opportunity was there, and accidentally, the semen left on his finger from his earlier masturbating had got inside the girl, but he hadn't killed her! The court hadn't believed him either, and he was now doing life.

But neither Sunderland nor Lincoln had come up with any outrageous story like that to explain essentially a similar scenario. Both of them agreed with everything the prosecution had found. They both told Ben they did know the victims, agreed it had obviously been their vehicles used to transport the bodies, but they had no idea how that happened, and they had no idea how their respective DNA was found on cigarette ends inside the women. For each man, that was impossible. But they didn't blame anyone, didn't accuse anyone of being liars, didn't offer crazy excuses, both agreed all the facts were right—except they didn't do the murders. What the hell did it all mean? Ben was convinced they were the two killers, the DNA left no doubt about that, but what were all these similarities in their stories. Ben had an idea that might at least provide half the answer. Maybe Lincoln was a straight-forward copy-cat killer. The details of Lincoln's murderous attack in Red Deer with the two knives were still fresh in Ben's mind. Now he needed to know the details of how Sunderland had butchered his victim in Calgary all those years back.

Ben knew about DNA. There was no mistake about it. He'd written a full-length feature on DNA for the Mail, even going to the extreme of giving the cops saliva and hair specimens so they could provide his DNA profile. This was used as the art for the feature. For privacy reason, the cops had been nervous about providing any other person's DNA profile to the Mail just to provide art for the story. So they used Ben's profile. Knowing how indisputable DNA evidence was, confirmed Ben's believe these guys had been rightfully convicted of the murders. But he still needed to check out Sunderland.

It was three days before his contact in the medical examiner's office had a spare moment for one of their conversations that wouldn't take place. Ben parked up, and went inside, past the soothing indoor fountain and profusion of rich dark-green tropical plants in the foyer. These were all presumably aimed at calming the grieving and the bereaved, those who were the true customers of this office, apart from the dead, of course. Inside his contact's office, there was a slightly longer than usual delay this time when Ben asked to look into the case of Jill Bereson murdered by Darren Sunderland on Nov. 5, 1990. This case had been dealt with by the previous deputy chief medical examiner of Alberta, Dr. James Keen, who had since moved on to Nova Scotia or New Brunswick or somewhere out east the year after this murder in April 1991. But the files on murders from 10 years ago remained here, and Ben's contact brought Bereson in and spread her out on the table.

"What was it you're after," he asked.

"Well, you remember a little while ago I was asking about the Warnoski murder from 1992, because the killer was bugging me about being innocent and needing publicity. Well, I don't believe him for a minute, but I'm checking it all out, and I think his murder of Warnoski was a copy-cat of this Bereson murder in 1990. It's not very important, but I wonder if you think I could be on the right lines," said Ben.

"Well, if you are right, it'll be the first time," said his contact, who enjoyed winding him up.

He went straight to the photo album, full body shots, victim wearing nothing but her panties, and excessive mutilation. Even he was immediately struck by the similarity of some of the injuries on this body to those Ben and he had seen on the Warnoski photographs. Bereson's body had also been burned with a cigarette end—just once—and mutilated with long slashes which gaped open. Not so many as with Warnoski, and according to Keen's autopsy notes, all with the same knife. So with Bereson there were fewer wounds, and only one knife, and with Warnoski there were many more wounds caused by two knives.

"Look at this," said Ben's contact, turning the photo album to a close up of the young woman's breasts. "Bereson had one nipple badly bitten, but it's still attached. Warnoski, if you remember, had both her nipples bitten off—similar, but not the same."

"What do you make of that?" asked Ben, pointing to a small group of slashes on a photograph of the woman's abdomen.

His contact looked at the wound, and consulted Keen's autopsy notes again.

"At the time, Keen referred to them as a small grouping of three slashes shaped rather like a wooden chair with a high back, made with the same knife after death," he said.

"Yea, I can see that," said Ben, understanding these wounds looked like a side view of a wooden chair, "but why would someone do that?"

"God knows why they do any of this. In a mad frenzy, they slash and hack and I doubt if there's any sense to any individual blow," said the contact, who so far had found enough dissimilarities between the two to think Ben really was on the wrong lines.

Then his eyes caught a paragraph in Keen's autopsy notes which made him furrow his brows deeply and stare at Ben. What was going on here? Should he keep this secret from Ben, or point it out to him? He'd already gone this far down the line letting Ben have access to things he ought not to, so he might as well go the whole way.

"Listen to this," he said.

"I removed from inside the vagina, one cigarette end entirely unseen from exterior. It was sent for laboratory analysis and DNA testing."

The results were recorded later in the report.

"DNA results match saliva on cigarette end to that of suspect Darren Sunderland."

"Right on!" said Ben, feeling damn smug his copy-cat theory had suddenly become a good possibility. Maybe even a probability.

Here was this first pervert, Sunderland, using a cigarette to torture and burn his victim, then stuffing the cigarette end in her vagina after she was dead, then slicing her up and biting her breasts.

And then there was Lincoln, the copy-cat, having no doubt studied the trial coverage of the first murder, where all those details came out, and carrying out his murder to produce a similar end result. He'd even tied his victim's legs together and raised them up so the cigarette end wouldn't fall out. He'd sliced up his victim, and bitten her nipples off.

Ben's contact must have read his thoughts.

"You could be right you know. That Warnoski could be a copy-cat of this one. The pathologists wouldn't have seen any link, because Dr. Keen did the first one, and Dr. Parker did the second one, and neither of them would have known about the other," he said.

"But it doesn't make a lot of sense for Lincoln to copy-cat Sunderland's murder, though. Why would he do that? Sunderland was already serving time by the time Lincoln did his murder, so it's not as if he could suggest Sunderland had done them both. But if you're right and Lincoln did copy-cat that first murder, it would explain the similarities."

Ben drove away from the medical examiner's office, and parked up in his usual turn-out and scribbled hard the salient points of what he'd seen, complete with a quick sketch of the wooden chair wound, before driving back to the office. He didn't play his Chris Barber tape this time. He was trying to understand what he may have stumbled on, and was trying to concentrate. He started with the basic facts. These were two totally unrelated murders, the first in Calgary, with a guy convicted on solid DNA evidence, and in the slammer doing life. Then, along comes another murder, totally unrelated, in Red Deer, 150 km away, with another guy, banged to rights because of DNA evidence, and he's doing life. Quite right, thought Ben, always an avid advocate of heavy punishments and the death penalty. Both of them are squealing they didn't do it, and now it looks for all the world as if the second guy had actually carried out a very good copy-cat murder of the first one. That was about the sum total of all Ben had discovered. It didn't go one inch toward suggesting the second guy Ron Lincoln was innocent—which after all was what Ben was checking out. He wasn't any less confused by the time he reached the office and parked up.

"When the hell are you going to do some work that's going to appear in the paper?" asked Frank, who's staff of reporters was so small, he couldn't afford the luxury of them working on airy-fairy backgrounders which might, one day, if they were lucky, produce copy, but which didn't do anything for tomorrow's edition.

"There's a fatal road crash out at Strathmore with a guy killed whose wife's pregnant, see if you can harass her, and in today's obits there's another Native dead up on the Siksika Reserve, see if that's not another suicide, will you."

It was the office norm to save the day's dead people for Ben. This was about average any time he came in the room. There would be a deader or two for him to work on. They'd be flippant about him harassing the relatives of the dead, only because he'd come up with the story nine times out of ten. Of course, he didn't really harass them. Sure, he'd contact them, but in a thoroughly understanding and sympathetic manner, being as unobtrusive as a reporter could be, considering he was trying to persuade these people to talk to him at a time when they were so distraught they could hardly talk to their fellow family members. It was the hardest part of Ben's job, and he confronted it daily, often hiding his discomfort at it in the office with a giant show of bravado. Many times after a particularly harrowing interview where he had just persuaded a widow in floods of tears to part with a photograph of her beloved husband, he'd put the phone down, punch the air in triumph, and yell, "Right on, another one in tears." Other reporters would tell him he was sick. His "harasser" reputation would go up a notch, and he would have hidden his real sadness for the family behind his bravado again.

It had occurred to Ben after one busy day when he'd had a triple fatal road crash out on an otherwise picturesque road in the foothills west of Calgary heading to the Morley native reserve, that he ought to keep a tally of all these deaths day after day. It was an awful but honest truth that each death was ultimately reduced just to a story in the next day's paper. Ben was too well aware that each one had been a devastating life-changing tragedy for someone left behind. For the survivor, be it a wife, husband, mother or father, life as they knew it would never be repairable, but for Ben, well for the whole newspaper industry really, that personal tragedy was no more than so many column inches in the next edition. For Ben, all these deaths were crowding in on his memory and he decided, yes, he would record them in a single book.

This wasn't for consumption by anyone else. It wouldn't mean anything to anyone, but it was an impersonal, if rather sad accounting of this part of Ben's life. Someone else's personal tragedy had already been reduced to tomorrow's front page story for the paper, but now it was now further reduced to a one-line mention in Ben's "death book." It was a simple and telling entry—date of death, name, where killed, how killed, comments—just the bare bones, as it were. Ben laid down rules before a name could be entered. It had to be a death Ben had covered and it had to have appeared in the paper. It was all encompassing and simply chronological. None was any more important than any other. Major stories which ran on the front page for days on end like sensational murder cases would get their one line (Feb.28, 1991—Angela Braithwaite—Pincher Creek—murdered—maybe linked to others). Little one paragraph stories tucked in on an away page would get the same one line if they included a death.

Ben kept his record meticulously day after day for years. With 25 lines per page in his spiral-bound death book, it was surprising how quickly a page would fill, and surprising how varied were the ways people could die or be killed. The "how killed" column contained "murdered, explosion, fire, road crash, train crash, plane crash, electrocution, avalanche, drowning, boating mishap, school massacre, parachute failure, trapped in machinery, landslide, bear attack, cougar attack"—very nearly something different every day. It came as a small shock one day that Ben finally filled his death book—and with 70 pages that totaled 1,750 people whose deaths he had covered individually. To his amazement he found he needed to start a new book and years later he found he had completely filled three "death books"—more than 5,200 people. Other reporters, who went through entire careers without ever having to encounter any topic even approaching death, would see Ben's "death books" on his desk and shake their heads, pitying the sick mind that had produced them. But Ben saw the books as useful tools in his arsenal of research material for his stories. They gave him an instant insight into whether some strange or unusual death had ever occurred before, and he could map trends if strings of similar deaths took place over time.

Only once was Ben bested in this macabre enterprise. Not surprisingly it was Ray Ludlow, the old hack who'd seen things even Ben couldn't imagine. He reckoned Ben's death book was child's play. He had been in Mexico when an earthquake had struck, and he's sent back stories on the deaths of 10,000 victims at once. Ben said that didn't count as he didn't have their names. That was one disaster that never appeared in Ben's death book. He'd never covered a fatal earthquake. He'd been sent to one in the States, but fortuitously for San Diego no-one had died. Unfortunately for Ben's book, no new lines were added.

Now he had a road crash at Strathmore and a mystery death at Gleichen. He started with the Native first. Here was one of those amazing exceptions when the Mail this time was looking for a suicide story because there had recently been a major commission report talking about this very reserve at

Gleichen east of Calgary, and its appalling suicide rate. He was just putting his first call in when a shout went up from the rim.

On the far side of the newsroom was a circular highly-polished table, hence the "rim," where sat the copy editors who planned the day's pages, concocted the headlines, and when necessary, mercilessly cut Ben's hard-won copy to size when his 30 line story had to fit into a 20 line space. Ben will have spent an entire day persuading, threatening, cajoling, pleading, and even tricking some person vital to his story to come up with a comment—only to have a copy editor chop out that very quote to make his 30 lines fit the 20 line space. And all that when Ben had been told, probably ordered in the first place, to produce 30 lines. Most reporters—who lived in blissful ignorance of the pressures of trying to fit ridiculously over-written stories into too tight spaces—called most copy editors "rim-pigs" because of this endless battle. One guy on the rim had the daily task of monitoring every wire, every minute, making sure the Mail never missed anything vital anywhere locally, or across the nation or elsewhere in the world.

"Plane crash in Fort McMurray—five dead—Calgary family," he shouted. The news had just moved as an "urgent" on one of the wires.

"That's you, Ben. On your way," said Frank. "Get yourself sorted, and we'll start making reservations."

And that was it. Whether the 25-year-old Native east of Calgary was or wasn't a suicide, and whether the widow of the guy killed in the car crash at Strathmore would ever talk to the Mail, were no longer Ben's immediate problems. And when he'd next be able to spend time trying to look into the pervert Ron Lincoln and all that, God alone knew. This was a scenario where the Mail excelled. When something big broke, the Mail moved. Ben had been on so many of these breaking stories out of town, out of province, sometimes in the States, or even England, the first steps were a well-orchestrated routine of chaos. Phone home. "Pack me a bag, love, I'm off to an avalanche in BC, or floods in Manitoba, or a serial killer in Vancouver, or, this time, a plane crash in Fort McMurray." Grab the lap-top computer, cell-phone, extra notebooks and pens, then drive home, pick up the bag—always perfectly packed with everything he could possible need—drive to the airport, pick up the tickets which the office will have phoned ahead to reserve, and onto the plane, this time a little Dash 8 propeller job. Once they were airborne Ben always had a moment's reflection on probably the main reason why he loved this life. It was its total unpredictability. He'd started the day pondering what Ron Lincoln, a perverted murderer, was really trying to do. For a few minutes, he was about to intrude on the grief of a widow and study the social problems leading to suicides on a Native reserve, and now here he was, circling away from Calgary International Airport on one plane headed for someone else's plane crash.

The secret of working well on these away assignments was trying to prepare your plan of action while in the air. Ben had been the Mail's reporter at the Columbine school massacre in Littleton, Colorado. It had been the same chaotic routine that day. In the newsroom, they'd seen the first television pictures with news of eight students wounded at some time around noon. Ben was on a plane by 2:30 p. m. and was touching down at Denver International Airport by 5 o' clock. But he was working, preparing, even before he hit the ground. He talked to as many passengers on the plane as possible and discovered the guy sitting next to him lived right near the school in Littleton. The man's wife had already phoned him, scared and in tears, not knowing if their son was among the wounded. By the time they touched down, Ben had the interview written up as a column ready to be filed to the office. But even Ben's preparations didn't prepare him for what happened that day when they landed at Denver. First priority, always call the office, find out the latest. Ben called, wondering how the eight wounded were getting on.

"Ben, it's 25 dead," said Frank.

"Fuck me rigid," said Ben, and went into action.

Get a hire car, get from Denver to Littleton, find the school, interview survivors, find a hotel to transmit copy, and get stories filed, all in those first few frantic hours before deadline. Over the next few days, it was later established the death toll was 15 not 25, but that was enough to keep Ben finding stories and pumping out copy day after day, working non-stop from 7 a. m. to 11 p. m.

One important basic ingredient of working for the Mail was that it was a newspaper which believed in having its own man on the spot. Most newspapers were content to take in syndicated Associated Press or Reuters reports, but not the Mail. Executives believed its readership felt a closer rapport with any story if the Mail's own man was on the scene. And more often than not this was Ben. His stories were the Mail's own "exclusives."

Ben later reflected that this Columbine massacre illustrated perfectly what life was like for a crime reporter. For most people, survivors and family members who were there amid the bullets and the bombs at Columbine, life stood still from that moment onward. And make no mistake, Ben was there. He was in time to hear the last of the pipe bombs explode. He interviewed a survivor who showed him blood on his shoes. "He shot my best friend right next to me—that's his blood on my shoes," the shaken teen had told Ben. But after five frantic days of pouring out copy from Littleton, Colorado, Ben was called back to the office. Next day he was in the grounds of a Calgary high school where a kid had been stabbed to death. And while he was there his city desk yelled at him on his hand-held radio to leave right away and get his butt down to Taber in southern Alberta where there had been a "Columbine school copy-cat fatal shooting." While other people closest to the Columbine tragedy would never move on with their lives, Ben had already been catapulted onward through a fatal city school stabbing and a Canadian school shooting half a province away—and he'd only been away from Littleton for 48 hours!

And now, as the Dash 8 droned northward, Ben was working out the plan of attack for this one. He'd probably have two hours after touching down before he'd need to be filing copy. In that time, he'd have to organize a hire car, find the one family in Fort McMurray where the Calgarians killed in the crash were headed, persuade that family to talk to him, write his exclusive story and get it back.

There were two nasty moments on the flight in. First, as the Dash 8 was on final approach, Ben could see down below, the wreckage of the Calgarians' ill-fated plane, half burned out, half split in two, a crumpled mess at the end of a long groove carved in the ground to the left of the runway. Thoughts of crashing are somewhere in the consciousness of every plane passenger, even those who won't admit it, and seeing that wreck down there didn't help Ben's consciousness too much. It was raining hard as they came in, and Ben's seat was alongside the undercarriage leg, which on a Dash 8 is right there alongside the window. As they touched down, a mighty spray of water fountained up from the wheels like the bow-wave from a speed-boat. That, too, did wonders for Ben's consciousness. As it happened on this trip, getting the story and getting it back wasn't the problem. Ben got a hire car, found the family, got his story, used the offices of the local newspaper to get it back, together with photographs of the family members who'd been killed, and all in time for deadline. Just.

So now, it was approaching 11 o'clock at night and he pulled into the nearest motel to get a room. He ignored the red illuminated "No Vacancy" sign which someone had obviously just forgotten to turn off, and carried his hold-all and laptop purposefully into the foyer.

"No, we don't have any rooms at all, didn't you see the sign?" asked the receptionist.

"Okay, no problem, thanks," said Ben turning round and heading back out to the car.

This motel was the first in a line along the street. He quickly swung the car toward the next, this time heeding the "No Vacancy" warning, driving straight past and heading for the third. It suddenly dawned on him that red illuminated "No Vacancy" signs were visible as far as the eye could see. Trying his luck well down the line, he pulled into another, drove under the compulsory "No Vacancy" sign and walked into the foyer, not bothering this time to carry his hold-all and laptop with him.

"Do you think there's a room anywhere in Fort McMurray?" he asked, a lot less confidently than when he started at the first motel.

"Not a chance, sir, no way," was the reply.

"The oilmen are in. If you haven't booked in advance, you've got no hope. Surely your office didn't send you here at this time of year without booking in advance."

Ben felt a little pang of panic. What the heck was this?

"I'll phone around for you, but I'm sure it'll be no good," said the receptionist, already dialing one of a list of numbers on a sheet hanging on the wall. She was as helpful as she could be, dialing the first four on the list, learning, not to her surprise, they were all completely full.

"Your best bet," she said, obviously having encountered this problem with ill-prepared out-of-towners before, "is to drive to the next town, it's only 45 minutes, and you could possibly have a chance there, but even then I couldn't promise you."

And that was that. Ben moved the hire car to a distant corner of the packed parking lot of the Morning Light Motel, parked up, reclined the passenger seat of the hire car, and endured a miserable, uncomfortable, freezing night trying to cat nap as best he could. He wasn't too impressed with Fort McMurray.

Ben got back in the office two days later, long enough for the other guys to have piled 48 hours' worth of rubbish on his desk. It was a dreaded sickness afflicting all reporters. If there's a vacant desk where no one's sitting, they suffer a compulsion to put their garbage down there. As the first guy finishes reading his newspaper, he drops it there. That's the unwritten signal to the rest of the room. Now the first rubbish has landed, everyone knows it's fair game. Discarded faxes, unwanted memos and empty envelopes rain down from every passing reporter. Ben groaned, heaved the barrel-sized garbage bin over from across the room and swept the whole damn mess inside making sure none of the murder files on his holy pile went in with it. Then he saw the tiny pink message pad slip in his pigeon hole.

"Ben. Call the M. E.'s office. 2:30 p. m. Wednesday. They wouldn't say why."

That was when Ben was flying back from up north. He phoned his contact, who reckoned if Ben brought one of the new "Male Delight" pin-up calendars over there, with this year's array of buxom wenches bursting from their bikinis, he might learn something of interest. As it happened, the Mail's promotion department was temporarily out of sexy calendars, Ben discovered, so he drove across the city and went into his contact's office with only the promise of one to come.

Chapter 4

Ben's contact seemed genuinely excited about something.

"You know you had me look at that Bereson murder, you know, the woman on the golf course, the one with the autopsy done by old Jim Keen, and you know you were going on about your theory about one up in Red Deer being a copy-cat," he started. "Well, that set me thinking. I recalled old Keen had mentioned there being a possible copy-cat to the Bereson killing, but it wasn't Red Deer. No, he'd done the autopsy on a woman murdered in Pincher Creek. He mentioned there were some similarities as if it was a copy-cat."

"Of course, if you'd brought me a calendar, I could have shown you the file, but as you didn't, I'm afraid that becomes privileged information no longer for your eyes."

He was bull-shitting again. He had the file on his desk all the time.

This was Angela Jill Braithwaite, 33, found murdered in a field off Highway 3, where a little slip road leaves the main drag heading south to Pincher Creek in southern Alberta. Her body was found on February 28, 1991.

Ben always thought of people with their ages attached, between commas, as if it was part of the name itself. This wasn't Angela Jill Braithwaite; this was Angela Jill Braithwaite—comma 33 comma. Ben's friends outside the newspaper would ask him why the hell the Calgary Mail always put ages alongside every name. It was a lesson Ben had learned in the first week at the Mail. That age between commas was the best single adjective ever invented.

So John Nobody gets killed in a car crash. If the reader is presented with "John Nobody, 11, was killed" they have an immediate picture of a young lad with his life ahead of him. If they were to read "John Nobody, 73, was killed" they instantly have a picture of an old white-haired man who'd already enjoyed a full life. All Ben would have added to the story was the age in commas and a vital part of the picture was filled in. And Ben well remembered all the times this tiny detail had caused him untold pain. Interviewing people suffering mental trauma—as everyone was if Ben was interviewing them—they would talk about whatever tragedy had befallen their loved ones, and include all kinds of personal, revealing and often shocking details, but ask them for their age and the shutters would come down. "What do you want to know that for?" they'd snap. Ben could hardly tell them it was the directive from the boss that every person whose name appeared in a story had to have an "age in commas" or they, and their interesting information, would not appear at all. Of course, when someone was dead this problem didn't arise. Even the notoriously uninformative RCMP press releases would include a victim's age—like Angela Jill Braithwaite, 33.

Ben remembered this one. Well, he remembered what happened when he was on his way down there. It had been snowing hard for days, and Highway 2 south was covered in solid compacted snow, and very slick that day. He'd set off in his Chevy van while Dennis the photographer was up ahead in his sports utility. This was another day when the usual chaotic routine had kicked in. One minute Ben was in the office checking out the story of a very strange robber and the next he was in the van heading to Pincher Creek for a murder. The robber Ben left on his desk was a guy who disguised himself by wearing women's black panties pulled over his face for every heist—"they are always black ones" was the official description. That was as far as Ben got with that story that day.

Within minutes, he was south of Nanton, stupidly doing 120 km/h on the ice and snow in the southbound lanes when he lost the back end. It was definitely happening at 120 km/h, but it registered to him in agonizingly slow motion. The van slid slickly sideways still southbound in his lane. He remembered his thought processes. "Wedge my foot and lower leg against the central consul and hang on tight to the wheel, ready for when it rolls." But it didn't roll. It seemed to accelerate, though his foot was off the pedal, and all too deliberately it slid diagonally forward into the median, with its flat grass hidden by a deep layer of snow. Now he was travelling at sickening speed, perfectly sideways over the snow in the median, still not slowing down, still surely about to roll at any moment. The gut fear in Ben's stomach had held him for several seconds now on this appalling slide.

And then it happened. The wheels must have gripped a fraction of traction. They propelled the van forward and sideways across the width of the grass median and up into the fast lane of the northbound section of Highway 2. The pile of ploughed snow at the median's edge slowed the van a little, but now it careened sideways, still going south in the outside northbound lane. Frozen in abject terror, Ben saw two semi-trailer trucks in convoy, line astern, coming north, probably doing 100 km/h as they were entitled to, and hurtling toward the side of his van. Ben remembered thinking, "Oh fuck, I'm going to die," as the first semi swept across the windshield, a bow wave of slush hitting the van, followed by a second wave a split-second later from the second truck, and they were gone. And the van had stopped sliding. Ben threw it in reverse and let it roll slowly back down the slope into the snow of the median. He switched off the engine, got out and vomited into the snow, feeling the trembling in his legs and seeing his hands shaking beyond his control.

It had been a pretty bad moment for Dennis, up ahead. He'd happened to glance back in his mirror and watched Ben's slide right from the beginning. He'd seen him go sideways down the outside lane, then sideways across the median. Then, just as the first semi-trailer truck got to where Ben was sliding south in the northbound lane, Dennis saw a huge plume of snow and slush go up, and knew Ben was under the semi. He was shaking as he turned round and went back, not knowing what he was going to find. He arrived at Ben's side, amazed to find the van intact, and Ben, head down puking in the snow.

Pincher Creek was out for a while. For Ben, whose whole life was spent dealing with other people's violent deaths, this was the nearest he'd ever been to dying. He couldn't believe how helpless he felt, and how he couldn't get rid of this nausea. It was many minutes before any strength came back in his legs and he could stop shaking. He and Dennis looked at the marks in the snow and could see the front of the van had pushed out to the dotted white line separating the outside lane of the road from the middle lane, where the two semis had passed. He had missed certain death, absolute obliteration, by the width of the white line. Dennis drove Ben northward back to Nanton where they sat in a gas station coffee shop, and Ben drank coffee until the nausea finally passed. Then they drove back to Ben's van, and they carried on to Pincher Creek, Ben trundling along slowly in the inside lane. Oh yes, Ben remembered this murder. After this one, he never drove fast on slick roads again, and he went right out and spent $400 on new snow tires with monster treads. He could still remember getting home that night, and dissolving into tears with his wife, mostly in the knowledge she came within inches of having a police officer knock at her door to tell her he'd been killed—and all because of his stupidity.

Ben's contact took Angela Jill Braithwaite out of her file. He spent a short while re-reading a few pages of Keen's notes before sharing the information with Ben.

"Well, it's not as clear cut as the one you're looking at in Red Deer, but you can see why Keen thought there were similarities," he said.

"I like that—clear cut—ha, ha, mutilated bodies—right on," joked Ben out loud, immediately wishing he hadn't said it. "Ah, wash my mouth out with soap," and he lowered his head in mock contrition.

Before looking at the file, Ben was racking his brains trying to think of any reason why this murdered woman in Pincher Creek should be linked to the tortured woman on the Calgary golf course. On the golf course, Bereson had been mutilated with a knife, and from what he remembered of this one, Braithwaite in Pincher Creek, it was a whip. He certainly remembered a headline "Whip Torture Terror" on one of the stories he wrote about this case. He was hardly likely to forget it. It was a sport in the office to take outrageously tabloid headlines off Ben's more sensational cases, and pin them on the notice board behind city desk, where, taken utterly out of context, they appeared as the work of a continually sick mind. There, among garish Mail front page headlines in stark black print, proclaiming, "Sex Slave Death Ships," "Tales of Terror," and "Hideous Hacksaw Horror" was the infamous "Whip Torture Terror," the whole wall staring down at Ben every day to remind him other people's most traumatic and personal disasters were his life's bread-and-butter.

Ben's contact ignored the horrible "clear cut" pun, and carried on.

"This victim was tortured before death with a whip, suffering numerous whip lashes over a prolonged period, probably hours," he said. "Many of these lashes produced bruising, visible on the skin which was found to be pronounced at autopsy in the soft tissue under the skin."

The contact was reading from Keen's autopsy report.

"Other lashes were inflicted nearer to the time of death, causing visible skin abrasions only. The whip had been wound round the victim's neck to produce ligature strangulation." Ah, Ben was right.

"After death, the victim's body was mutilated with a knife."

And, almost knowing what they expected the knife wounds to look like, Ben and his contact turned to the plastic album pages containing the autopsy photographs.

"This is what Keen was thinking about," said the contact. "Look at this."

Long gaping slashes, showing bright yellow fat under the skin, stretched across her abdomen, down her thighs, and in the photographs of her back, each buttock had been slashed open. Ben was the layman in all this, but his contact was the true professional.

"Do all slashing knife wounds look alike?" Ben asked. "I mean, if you looked at 10 different bodies which had been slashed with a knife, would they all look alike, and you'd therefore deduce the same man did them all, or are some knife wounds different? Know what I mean?"

"Yes. There is some similarity with any knife wound. But they are all different. Some are just on the surface, or just under. Some are with the knife in up to the hilt. Some are penetrating stab wounds. Some are long drawn slashes," said the contact.

"I think that's what Keen was getting at. There is a similarity here between the slashes we saw on Bereson, and the slashes on this victim—a similarity in depth and length and some similarity in pattern across the body."

"But if Keen did notice it at the time, it's not surprising he didn't mention it. You see, up in Calgary, their woman had been murdered, they'd caught the guy, he'd been convicted and was doing life before this murder happened in Pincher Creek. He could hardly tell them he'd found the handiwork of the same killer, when he knew the killer was inside, could he."

"No, he never told anyone officially. He just mentioned it in passing to me once, that he'd seen these maybe similar wounds on two murdered women and wondered if whoever had done the second killing had been a copy-cat of the first."

Ben asked to look at the photographs again, and he turned to the photograph of the back. There, above where the slash had dissected the right buttock was a group of smaller slashes in another strange pattern. To Ben, it looked like an open human eye from the side, one slash forming eye-lashes flicking up, another adjoining slash forming eye-lashes flicking down, and the two slashes joined by a short cut where the eye ball would have been, looking grotesquely at the remnants of the buttock ripped apart by the mutilator.

"What about how she was found? Were her legs together? Was there a cigarette end?"

"I wondered when you'd ask," interrupted Ben's contact.

"No. There was nothing like that. She was found on her back, her legs splayed wide open, the classic tell-tale of a sex-killer who's left his victim in the most exposed and humiliating position possible for whoever discovers the body. But this guy must have been really twisted. He left her like that, but he'd put her panties back on her after cutting out the crotch-piece, as if he was drawing the finder's attention right to her vagina. But there was no cigarette end in her, no DNA, not even similar to the Calgary woman, except for the knife wounds. As Keen saw it, it was just a possible copy-cat and not even a perfect one, at that."

This time, as Ben pulled away from the M. E.'s office into his turn-out to scribble out the Braithwaite notes, he didn't feel half so confident this was a copy-cat murder. When he'd started all this, when Ron Lincoln insisted he hadn't killed Warnoski, the bank teller in Red Deer, Ben had nothing to go on. But when Ben had discovered the links to Sunderland's murder of the waitress Bereson in Calgary a couple of years earlier, he was sure Lincoln had carried out a copy-cat murder. It was all there. He'd copied leaving a cigarette end in the victim's vagina as Sunderland had, he'd manipulated the body so the butt stayed there, though he used a slightly different method, but the result was the same. After all, the DNA from the cigarette ends had trapped both the killers. Lincoln had copied the slashing knife wounds which Sunderland had made before him, and he dumped his victim where she'd easily be found, just as Sunderland had. Ben was pretty confident about all that. But now this Braithwaite case down in Pincher Creek which the M. E.'s office was saying was a copy-cat didn't really fit. It was after Bereson in Calgary and before Warnoski in Red Deer. But this one was all about torture and murder with a whip, totally different. There was nothing to do with torture by burning with cigarette ends, which was after all the hallmark of the two really similar murders. This was all wrong. And there was no DNA in this case. It was completely different. The only similarity was slashing knife wounds, and hadn't his contact told him there were always some similar elements in all knife mutilations. No. Ben would have to read his files on the Braithwaite case through all over again, but he didn't really think it had anything to do with anything. After all, he finally convinced himself with one last piece of logic, what were the chances of two separate killers each choosing Sunderland's murder of Bereson in Calgary to copy? That was absurd. One copy-cat killer—Lincoln—was plausible, but two would be unheard of, even in the often stranger-than-fiction world of murders. No. Braithwaite was a non-starter.

Back at the office, Ben walked in to loud applause and clapping. It wasn't aimed at him, naturally, but over in the lifestyle section the whole newsroom was gathered in a cheering semi-circle around Lorraine. She'd been the popular lifestyle editor for the past five years and was leaving to have a baby and was being presented with her communal gift from all the reporters in the room.

Ben was glad he'd put his $10 in the envelope and signed the giant card which accompanied every such farewell presentation. Lorraine had played a big part in one of his most exciting and fascinating trips—the only time the Mail had ever sent Ben back to England for an incredible serial killer. It had started when the guy reading the wires on the rim mentioned there was a story out of Greater Manchester in England about some doctor who was reckoned to have murdered 45 patients.

"It would make a hell of a Sunday feature, perhaps we ought to go," was the first clue of what was coming.

"D'you fancy going to England, Ben?" Frank asked.

"Is the Pope Catholic?" Ben asked. "Right on!"

And as fast as that, it was settled. Well, almost. The Mail had a reputation earned over years of careful practice of getting the maximum mileage out of the minimum expenditure. Management called this sound business sense. Others called it being tight-fisted. It soon showed itself that day as a half-question, half-suggestion which filtered down from the Mail's management, through Ben's city editor to Ben. The inquiry was whether he had any relatives in Manchester who might, at very short notice, like about two hours, put him up for a week while he pursued the story of this murderous Dr. Harold Shipman.

Ben was clean out of relatives in Manchester in the far northern reaches of England, about as far away as you could get from his relatives in Portsmouth on the south coast. Ben could see his England trip foundering on the rocks of expenditure. Without relatives over there to put him up on the cheap, the Mail would have to fork out for a week's hotel bills, and that would be a killer more deadly than any doctor. It was at this moment of crisis in Ben's life that Lorraine came to the rescue, and earned her $10 in the farewell envelope.

"I've got an aunt in Macclesfield," she offered.

A lifeline had been thrown and Ben grasped it. He dashed into the library, came out with an atlas, turned to the England page, and could instantly show his city editor that Manchester and Macclesfield were no more than half a centimeter apart on the map.

"That'll work," said Frank.

There then followed a touching scene at Lorraine's desk, as Ben implored her to contact her aunt and ask if she could accommodate this stranger for a week. Ben lied desperately to Lorraine.

"Tell her I'm neat and tidy, won't mess up my room, I don't drink, I don't smoke, and I'll be out working nearly all hours of the day and night, so I won't be any trouble," he said.

Lorraine, the little darling, a petite short-haired blond with a skittish happy little laugh, relayed all this to Aunt Gertie, who said she'd be delighted, and asked when would this stranger be arriving?

"His plane leaves in two hours," said Lorraine, and there seemed to be a long silence on the other end of the line. But it was agreed. Aunt Gertie would take Ben in. Now the picture changed. With Ben's accommodation fixed on the cheap, for next to nothing hopefully, everything fell into place, and he was on the plane in two hours headed for Manchester, England.

Actually, it stopped first at Heathrow, London, where, in the terminal, Ben saw, to his amazement, a Fleet Street tabloid headline proclaiming "Doctor May Have Killed 77 Patients."

"Right on," thought Ben. "It was only 45 when I took off, now it's 77, and I've only reached Heathrow!"

Thanks to Lorraine's Aunt Gertie, that entire trip was amazing. By the time it was all over, Ben had produced at least three full pages of stories a day every day he was there, and the man dubbed "Dr. Death" was reckoned to have murdered 146 patients. Years later the British justice system officially listed the names of 215 people as being murdered by Shipman. Lorraine's Aunt Gertie was an absolute sweetie who pampered Ben like a long-lost son, laundering his clothes, cooking him sumptuous meals, and overlooking his failings. "Neat and tidy" Lorraine had said. It happened that the only electrical socket in Aunt Gertie's house which would take Ben's lap-top computer cords was at the top of the stairs, while the only telephone outlet in range was on the landing halfway down. So for the hours Ben was transmitting stories he was squatted on the stairs festooned with cables and leads up and down so no one could pass his obstacle course without difficulty, no matter how urgently they needed the upstairs washroom.

Then on the second day of his stay, the row house next door caught fire.

Ben, who'd worked for 21 years covering fires in England before he moved to Canada, was soon in his element, out there in the street chatting with firemen, while their colleagues clambered up ladders and over the neighbor's roof confining the blaze to the area around the chimney.

"We've been here 35 years and there's never been a fire in this street," said Gertie. Ben had only been there two days and one had broken out already.

In the news room, Ben joined the clapping semi-circle and when it had died down and reporters starting drifting back to their desks, he went over and hugged Lorraine, wishing her all the best.

"Give my best regards to your Aunt Gertie when you're next in touch with her," he said, and he went back to his computer to find Braithwaite on his "murder list."

She was "File 143," between "BRADLEY Bradley—killer (stabbed a guy in a wheelchair 36 times)" and "BRANDLE Kenneth—killer (mummified his victim in a closet.)" Ben often wondered what would possess some parent with the last name of Bradley to give their son the first name of Bradley. Who knows?

Ben recalled the Braithwaite case the moment he opened the file. There had been just the tiniest possibility he'd met this woman on his travels to Pincher Creek. He'd worked on some major cases down there—an unsolved double murder of a local firefighter and his lover; a guy beaten to death and left where his blood turned the snow-laden pathway alongside the town's museum crimson red; a woman who was last seen leaving a bar, and whose body turned up months later, battered on rocks in a river, but was never classified as a homicide; and even a guy shot dead inside the local police cells—quite an impressive list for so small a town. And then there was this case of Braithwaite, the librarian. On nearly all these earlier cases, Ben had resorted to studying a pile of background in the town's library. He'd sat there, under the children's paintings on one wall, studying back copies of the town's newspaper, and found all kinds of snippets about some of the players involved. He got to know the women librarians well enough, and they eventually let him sit in their private office. They let him pound out some of his stories on their computer and fax them to the Mail office—provided, of course, he let them read the stories first, so they were at least one day ahead of the gossip in the town.

Angela Jill Braithwaite had been 33 when she was murdered. Ben remembered the women he dealt with seemed to be slightly older, so perhaps he hadn't actually met Angela. Well, Angela was her name, but everyone in town called her by her middle name, Jill, so said the backgrounder Ben had written on her which he found in his file. "Jill" was on the wooden name-tag standing neatly on the corner of her information desk where she worked. Ben's backgrounder showed Jill was a career woman, single, and happily devoted to making her library an important part of the community. But Jill was more than just a librarian. Her name appeared in the acknowledgements page of a book "*Horsemen of the West*" by Randy Steadman which wasn't a John Wayne western, but a historical documentary of famous ranchers, cattlemen, horsemen and pioneers who settled Saskatchewan and Alberta. In the acknowledgements, she was thanked for the assistance she'd given in researching through the library the ranching history of southern Alberta, especially around Pincher Creek. Ben mentioned this fact in his murder backgrounder about Braithwaite for a very special reason. A little detective work on his part revealed that on the line preceding hers in the acknowledgements was a tribute to the help given to the author by Pincher Creek rancher and historian Paul Andres.

So who was he? What did he have to do with anything?

Only that Paul Louie Andres, 37, of Pincher Creek was Braithwaite's murderer—the same man. Now convicted and doing life with no parole for 20 years.

Braithwaite's body was discovered on February 28, 1991, and Andres was arrested almost four months later to the day, on June 29, 1991. Ben covered his trial at Lethbridge Court of Queen's Bench the following year. There he met and interviewed Steadman, the author of the "horsemen" book, who'd worked with both a murder victim and her murderer. Steadman's story made a great little sidebar to the main "Whip Torture Terror" feature. Ben read it again in the file. And saw, stuck to the page, one of the Mail's little yellow message stickies with a scribbled note on it. "Paul Andres called, says he's innocent, call back, Kingston, Ontario, 2:30 pm Tuesday." That was in the original handwriting. Ben, keeping notes meticulously, as usual, had added 24/8/95. Scribbled in tiny scrawl on the bottom of the sticky, he'd later added "tried 25/8, 26/8 and 27/8. No luck." So this guy, too, convicted in 1992, was still trying, three years later, to interest someone in listening to his story that he was innocent. But Ben hadn't been able to reach him, so he'd obviously taken the view Ben wasn't interested, and never pursued it further.

"Yea, good riddance anyway," thought Ben reading the file again. What this guy did was worse than Ron Lincoln. Andres was a respected and fairly wealthy rancher, with a farmhouse, barns, and horses set on the hill stretching south out of Pincher Creek down toward the U. S. border. Being a man of the saddle, always in a cowboy hat, and a man of history, he soon cemented close ties with the rodeo circuit in southern Alberta. That took him and his famous cowboy hat to the rodeo capital, Calgary. And that put him in with the Calgary Exhibition and Stampede, where he became the unofficial historian. Calgary Stampede annual posters over the years looked damned authentic because Andre had researched their olden day cowboy riding gear, so they were spot on. He did a lot of this research in the Pincher Creek library. And he did a lot of it with Jill Braithwaite. So, it was no surprise to anyone when Steadman wrote his "horsemen" book that Jill and Paul were top of the list of those people he thanked most for help with the research.

But it was a surprise. Well, a shock. Let's face it, a bombshell, when Paul was arrested and charged with Jill's murder. Ben had interviewed ranchers all round Pincher Creek. They couldn't believe him capable of any murder. Not the man they knew. Let alone a sadistic, sexually-perverted sex-torture slaying—never. And of Jill Braithwaite, who he'd worked with so closely? Not in a million years.

Ben's files contained his blow-by-blow account of the trial as he saw it in Lethbridge. He recalled how lacking in atmosphere it had been, as all Canadian trials are, compared to the electricity he'd felt when covering murder trials in England. He remembered fondly the giant mahogany docks and desks and podiums at the Hampshire Assizes in Winchester, Hampshire, and even at the Old Bailey in London where he had once covered the trial of a Lord Mayor of Portsmouth charged with massive frauds. He imagined again the Queen's Counsels and barristers all in black flowing robes and curly white wigs, some in half-moon glasses over which they would peer and glare theatrically. There was even one with a monocle, who would let it fall from his face on its lanyard in an expression of incredulity when the accused, cowering in the dock, told some outrageous lie. And all these pompous legal giants were ranged in order of seniority before the bewigged judge enthroned in his commanding position atop his mahogany bench. Even the defendants were larger than life on this dramatic stage. Ben recalled one murderer convicted of shooting dead a customs officer who'd intercepted his narcotics, being sentenced to life.

"Take him below," thundered the judge.

"I hope you die of cancer screaming in agony," growled back the surly killer, as guards dragged him from the dock. Spine-tingling, some of those moments had been for Ben.

But there in Lethbridge he remembered, the court was not much more than a glorified office. Damned uncomfortable wooden seats, a bit like church pews, with lawyers in simple suits and ties. These lawyers, supposedly central figures in each case, didn't look much different even from the newspaper reporters present—if it wasn't for the notebooks and scraps of paper bulging from the pockets of members of the press. No wigs, no robes for these legal advocates, and each lawyer with a stick microphone to pick up his every word. Whatever happened to the thundering voices that struck fear into the hearts of trembling villains when they knew the prosecution had just ripped their carefully constructed alibi to shreds.

Ben read again the Andres trial. There had never been any doubt. One eye-witness put him, with his memorable cowboy hat, sitting in his truck, at the site where the body was dumped—a cast-iron witness. Forensic scientists from the RCMP crime laboratory in Edmonton had nailed it down even tighter. Andres' truck had an oil leak and had leaked oil where it sat parked for the few minutes he spent dumping Braithwaite's body. They had chemically tested the oil composition and could state categorically that that particular oil came from that particular pickup truck and none other. And the forensic experts put another nail in Andres' coffin. They identified blood in the box of his pickup as coming from the victim. They had enough blood for DNA analysis, and it was Braithwaite's blood. But the icing on the cake for the Crown was the whip. Under Braithwaite's tortured body in the grass, detectives found the end of a bull whip, a few inches of leather, splayed out, probably during the thrashing of Braithwaite's flesh as she was tortured. If they could find the owner of the whip, they'd have themselves a murderer.

It took them nearly four months, and by a tortuous route.

Investigators from the Calgary major crimes unit, the Lethbridge criminal investigation division, and Pincher Creek itself, were men and women well versed in the rural horse and cattle heritage of southern Alberta. But even they were astounded to discover how many people owned whips. Every rancher, every cattleman, the children of every rural homesteader, every horse-owner, very nearly everyone in southern Alberta owned a whip. If there had been only scores of whips or even merely hundreds, teams of officers could have checked each one. But there were thousands of whips and the task was impossible. Week after week, officers were checking whips as part of all their other tasks, but none was found with its tell-tale tail missing. And in the meantime, a huge breakthrough early in the case threw them up a prime suspect, so it looked as if it was all over.

Two weeks after the murder, a Lethbridge police K-9 dog handler was exercising his dog Kobie near where they were billeted halfway between Pincher Creek and Cowley to the west. Suddenly he saw his dog go into its "blood" routine, indicating a human body. Intrigued, the handler went over to where the dog was agitated by something in the hay in a section of a field. He saw what looked like bloodied stalks, not a great deal, but enough to activate Kobie's senses.

He pulled the dog away, called for backup, and waited until officers arrived to cordon off the field, photograph and record the find, and remove the hay for forensic examination.

It was human blood on the hay. More importantly, it was proved to be Braithwaite's blood. Kobie had probably discovered the killing field where she'd been murdered before being taken to the dump site.

The investigators rode this wave. Land checks soon turned up the owner of the field who was very interesting. He had a previous conviction for sexual assault. On the strength of the finding of a sex-slaying victim's blood in the field of a convicted sex-offender, the man was arrested and brought in for questioning. He quickly came up with an alibi—playing cards in a room in the back of a Pincher Creek motel with three truckers for the whole of the evening of the murder. He knew the date was February 28. He always drew out cash on the last day of the month for their regular night of gambling and booze.

"You go ask them. They'll tell you. I was there into the early hours. I was totally smashed, brainless when I left," he said. And he came up with three names. Tracking down truckers in southern Alberta was about as easy as photographing snowy owls in winter, but weeks of work turned them up. And all three of them reckoned they were losing their hard-earned cash at the card table, just like the suspect said they would. So how did he account for the blood-stained hay in his field, the investigators asked? That wasn't so easy to dodge. The ground underneath the hay had no blood on it. It was just the hay.

"Who put it there?" they asked.

"I did. It was still perishing cold in February, and I put out the hay for my cattle. No, not my ranch-hands, I put it down."

"So where did you get the hay?" they persisted.

"Here and there, I don't know, from various ranchers."

Again the suspect came up with names, and the investigators treated each of them as suspects themselves, checking out whether they remembered selling this man hay and when. One of them was Paul Andres. He answered the routine questions, even had some paperwork to help him check it out.

"Yes, I sold him hay. Well, 'sold' is a bit strong, it was just beer money really—he only wanted four square bales. I threw them in the back of my pickup and drove them out to his place," he said, looking at the paperwork. "March 1. No problem," he said.

The investigator hoped Andres didn't notice his ears flushing red and glowing as the blood rushed through his veins. Here was a guy selling bales of hay to their suspect the day after the murder. And carrying them in his pickup truck where they would have soaked up any liquid in the truck—like very fresh blood perhaps.

"Can we look at your truck, sir," he asked, trying to make it sound absolutely routine and boring, when he knew it could be the whole case, right there.

"Be my guest, it's down the drive by the gate where it's always parked. It saves me driving up the slope when the ice is on the ground. Hang on, I'll come and open it up."

Pickup trucks used on farms and ranches are hard-working machines. Caked on slush and mud mask original colors, dents and dings give them their character, and if you don't carry 50 different leaking drums and cans and tanks of fertilizers and chemicals in a year, you aren't any kind of rancher. Andres' pickup had character. It was stained and dirty, bore war-wounds and didn't smell too good. Some of the staining was inside the floor of the box. Those stains needed examining properly.

Andres' truck was put on the back of a flat-bed and driven away, and as Ben recalled from the trial, it was in the truck that the forensic scientists found enough of a stain to test it for DNA and find it was Braithwaite's lifeblood.

The convicted sex-offender was fast falling out of the suspect's frame, the spot being taken over by this Andres guy. Clearly, the blood had been on the floor of Andres' truck. It only contaminated the hay when he carried the bales in the truck to the sex-offender, earning a few dollars beer money. The tortuous route to Andres was almost complete. With enough suspicion to earn a search warrant, officers went back to his ranch, and its stables and barns and sheds. First, they went through his stables, and found riding whips, all intact. But in his barn, in a corner, not hidden but casually thrown down as if not to attract anyone's attention, was a bull whip, a dirty, much-stained whip with a tattered end. A whip with its tail missing!

Andres was arrested, and as more evidence came in he was charged. Investigators discovered the full extent of his historical work with Jill at the library, and how they were close acquaintances. They had him knowing the victim well. They had her blood in his truck so fresh on the day after the murder it rubbed off on hay he was carrying. They had the hay as evidence. And they had his whip. The medical examiner matched the pattern on the whip to some of the welts on Braithwaite's body.

As Ben pored over these details it struck him that the reading of whip impressions on human skin might at first seem rather unlikely. But Ben knew it had happened famously in a classic murder case back in England. Ben had studied it in one of the true-crime murder documentaries he owned in his extensive library of such books littering one room in his house. The notorious murderer was Neville Heath in a case from 1946, when one of his two victims was found bound, and sexually mutilated with whip lash markings across her body. The world's foremost forensic pathologist at the time, Dr. Keith Simpson matched the impressions of the whip on the woman's body to a whip found in Heath's possession, and that crucial whip evidence helped send Heath to the gallows.

Here, in Braithwaite's murder, the medical examiner was also certain. Andres' whip caused Braithwaite's exact injuries, he could say without question. And by the way, the stains on the whip were more of Braithwaite's blood. The tip of the whip was forensically matched to the one in his barn. It was actually quite a famous whip, one which Andres had used in his performances as a star bull-whip attraction at the Calgary Stampede a few years earlier. He couldn't argue it wasn't his.

And then came the clincher, late in the day, after Andres was already charged. As if the police needed it. An eye-witness came forward to say he'd seen Andres sitting in his pickup truck on the night of the murder at the dump site of the body. The witness was categorical. It was Andres. He'd recognize that cowboy hat anywhere. It was Andres' truck—none other was quite as dirty. The witness hadn't come forward earlier because Andres was such a respectable man in the town, it just couldn't be him. But when the witness heard Andres had been charged, he felt he just had to tell what he'd seen in case it was important.

Ben finished reading the file. Two things were clear. Andres deserved every day of his life with no parole for 20 years, and this was mostly a whip murder. Despite all the slashing with the knife, and the mutilations afterward, they didn't make it a copy-cat killing. Ben was taking this one off his list.

For a while back there, he really thought he was onto something interesting. Here were three apparently unrelated murderers, in Calgary, Red Deer and Pincher Creek, all convicted of killing women they'd met casually, all with some similarities in the slayings, and all three protesting their innocence from inside their prison cells years after being convicted. Ben's gut instinct was to be wary of the two he'd spoken to at length, Ron Lincoln and Darren Sunderland, as being tricky liars. Yet there was still some nagging doubt gnawing at the back of his consciousness they may be different from the run-of-the-mill killers who usually bugged him from inside. Could they be telling the truth? then there was Andres, who'd tried to contact Ben in—half-hearted effort to protest his innocence. Ben was dismissing him because the similarities in his murder and the other two weren't strong enough, which left him with next to nothing. It wasn't the first time one of Ben's planned murder features had fallen flat. He'd had great expectations for this one. He'd envisioned the gaudy headlines already pinned up on the wall behind the city desk…"STRING OF COPY-CAT KILLINGS" or even better…"COPY-CAT KILLINGS SHOCKER"

This "over-the-top" headline thing started one weekend when Ben wasn't even in the office, but it was his Sunday feature that sparked it. He'd been out in Vancouver, trolling through the sleaziest back streets and alleys around East Hastings where it was reckoned a serial killer had murdered 31 hookers—and never a trace of a single body had been found. All kinds of news media had been there and done their "serial killer stalks the city" stuff. But the second night Ben was there, he felt he'd stumbled onto something he hadn't read anywhere else. From the part of the hookers' stroll he was cruising, one large wharf jutted out into Vancouver harbor. The dirty, sludge-laden, oily water lapping the shoreline showed it was busy with shipping which left this scum on the surface. Used condoms, needles and smashed cigarette lighters littering the few miserable stones at the water's edge showed the place wasn't only busy with shipping.

For Ben, the story started with something one of the working girls mentioned in passing. She didn't mind wasting her valuable time talking to Ben at the curbside, as long as Ben didn't mind her trying to entice every passing motorist over his shoulder. And after all, he had given her a full pack of smokes to start with. She lit up before Ben said a word. Ben had been on a few ride-alongs with the vice unit back in Calgary, where the girls on Calgary's strolls were at least half sexy. Here, in the bleakest depths of death alley for hookers in the grimiest hell-hole on East Hastings, the women were grim. This girl looked bloody ill, the cigarette rubbing against an angry-looking lip sore, haggard in the face and skinny. She wore a threadbare ugly green dress with a foul and unmistakable once-white, now very off-white, stain down the front near the hem. She didn't mind talking about the threat of murder hanging over her head. She'd known two of the missing 31 girls.

"Everyone says they're missing. They're dead, you know that, don't you," she volunteered.

"Yea," Ben nodded. After all, that was why he was here.

"It's the ships," she said, "that's where they went. Them Orientals come off the ships, they've got heroin back on board, loads of it and we're all users to some degree. I touch it just now and again, but I'm not hooked."

Ben recognized the self-denial. Every junkie he'd ever spoken to only touched drugs now and again, but weren't addicted. Yea, right.

"But some of the girls," she went on, shaking her head and blowing out to clear the cloud of smoke obscuring her face, "they've gotta get fixed every few hours. Some of them go back on board with the Asians. Another ship sails out and another girl disappears," and she shrugged her shoulder, her scrawny skin wrinkling over her collar-bone.

"Me. I ain't never going on a ship. I don't care how much heroin there is, you won't catch me out on a ship. Asking for trouble, that is."

She suddenly stepped forward, out into the road, where a scruffy rusty station-wagon had slowed and was pulling up. God knows how this woman had attracted this John's attention over Ben's shoulder. He hadn't seen any visible signal. But she'd pulled a punter, and after only three or four sentences of conversation, she got in, and they drove off. Ben shuddered at the thought of paying $20 to get a blow-job from those sore-infected lips, or paying the extra to get inside that stained dress. Not a lot extra. By the time these desperate addicts were hiring out their over-abused bodies out here in this God-forsaken place, they weren't worth a lot. In some of the most crowded back alleys in East Hastings, up against a wall among the dumpsters, and sometimes inside the dumpsters, a man could catch syphilis or AIDS for no more than $10. And while Ben's imagination was picturing it, it crossed his mind, just imagine, if this woman disappeared into the night and never came back to her spot on this sidewalk alongside the sagging chain fence, what would that mean? If she became the 32nd missing Vancouver hooker, would Ben have just witnessed a serial killer at work?

But what was this about the ships? Was it just the phobia of one woman? Could she be right? Ben had already touched base with several of the women's shelters and hard-pressed agencies trying to provide havens-in-hell for street-workers. These were places out there on the front lines where women could escape from their frequent violent encounters. One was in a church, another, in a bus which literally provided mobile escape out on the streets. Ben went back to the women running these retreats, and asked, seemingly out of idle curiosity, about a rumor he'd heard about Orientals taking girls out to the ships.

"Come in here," said Ruth, an alias of one of the helpers in a shelter, where, living under aliases was a very sensible part of survival. Ben found Ruth tucking clean sheeting over some couches, where, likely in the dead of night, some prostitute would seek refuge from a beating, or rape, and be glad of a few hours respite from the outside horrors. Ruth led Ben into a small side office.

"I was talking with a prostitute..." he started.

"Just a minute," Ruth interrupted sharply. "They're street workers. We don't call them hookers and we don't call them prostitutes. In here, they're street workers."

Chastened, Ben continued, "She told me she was scared to go out on the ships. She was saying that's where the missing women went. They went out for the heroin and the men on the ships, then the ship would sail, and presumably, somewhere out to sea the woman would be lost overboard forever."

"A lot of us believe that," said Ruth. "I've talked to street workers who believe that. I've talked to one woman who only escaped off a ship when her pimp went on board and took her off. It would explain everything. All the other serial killers anyone's ever heard of leave bodies lying around. Officially there are 31 women missing here. Between you and me, we think it's more like 80 to 100. And they haven't found one body. No remains, no hint, no clue, nothing." Ruth was one of the women that really knew what was going on.

Ben soon came head-to-head with the reality that there's a bad political taste in the mouth for any city to have to admit some unknown number of its citizens—at least 30 and maybe up to 100—have disappeared without a trace. Could it be that Vancouver, jewel of British Columbia's tourist trade, had a dirty, sleazy drug-addict hooker serial killer problem? Ben knew he wouldn't hear that confirmed in the polished and glazed corridors of city hall. Hell, if it hadn't been for a growing groundswell of anxiety and table-thumping by a few determined friends of the missing women, the police wouldn't have begrudgingly admitted there was a problem at all. Nearly 30 of these women had mysteriously disappeared before the police would entertain the thought they ought to investigate possible links in the gaps appearing in the ranks of the prostitutes of East Hastings.

Ben discovered the same two-faced attitude to prostitutes existed here, as everywhere. Vancouver society and the smug establishment keeping its wheels turning smoothly really didn't care about whatever deadly ingredients hookers brought into the mix of their daily lives. After all, these women didn't have to be there. No one was holding a gun to their head to put them there on the streets. Whatever came down on their heads was their own fault.

And in contrast, out on the street itself, Ben found the opposite view—that these women were human beings, where Ruth applied the sensitivity of calling them street workers. Ben found that out there, fellow street workers knew the personal horror stories each had suffered before ending up on the stroll, just about as near the end of their tether as they could get and still be alive. So now, Ben had discovered that his story that sex-slave death ships were behind the ever-growing list of missing women had been confirmed among the women who knew. Women who'd experienced the fear, women who didn't care for the crap and bullshit platitudes used by the politicians. Out here on East Hastings, the ships meant death.

Now, Ben had the uphill task of getting anyone in authority to confirm the theory. No one conceded there was even a problem officially. It is much easier to point out that by their very nature prostitutes are transient. They are mostly homeless, rootless drifters just as likely to sell their bodies next week in Toronto, or Winnipeg, Edmonton or Calgary, as stay here. So if they aren't seen alongside their usual run of litter-laden sagging wire fence, it doesn't mean they've been murdered. It means they've moved on. And no family has ever heard from them again. Hell, that means nothing either. It was probably escaping some disastrous gone-to-hell family nightmare which drove them out here in the first place. Society certainly can't trouble itself with every street worker who doesn't appear alongside her parking meter for her regular middle-of-the-night catch-the-drunks-coming-out-of-the-bars shift. And the police can't launch a murder inquiry every time a girl disappears. Don't be stupid. When she comes off her booze binge or comes down off whatever high she's on, she'll be back. They always are.

Except on East Hastings, they didn't come back—ever.

Intent on getting his confirmation, Ben took his "sex-slaves death ships" theory to the police through all the proper channels and received a bland enough reply.

"That is something we have looked at, but at this time there is no evidence to substantiate it," he was told.

Of course there's no evidence, thought Ben, that's the point of taking them out on the ships. But he read the official quote again, and realized straight away it was just what he needed. The police would obviously hope he'd be dissuaded by "no evidence" and forget the whole thing. Instead, he emphasized "something we have looked at." Here it was. Vancouver police had investigated the "sex-slaves death ships" theory. Ben had learned a long time ago to take notice of every word an official spokesman said.

Once, a post office official had told him proudly that 97% of all mail handled arrived safely and within two days—which was pretty impressive as it handled 40 million pieces of mail a day. The spokesman wanted Ben to write about the 38,800,000 letters arriving safely. Instead, Ben did the mathematics and wrote about the scandal of the post office failing to deliver 1,200,000 items of mail every single day. It was what the spokesman said. It was on the record. It was the story. And now he had this one.

He filed it, it ran to four pages, and it ran under the huge headline on Sunday's front page, "SEX SLAVE DEATH SHIPS." By the time he returned to the office days later, the headline was up on the wall behind the city desk, and a new tabloid art genre was formed with Ben as its founder.

This wasn't the only time Ben had trolled the dimly-lit back streets of a big city among hookers living in fear of a serial killer. A sadistic murderer had been ghosting through the darkness hunting down victims in Spokane, Washington's red-light district in the late-1990s. Ben wasn't far behind him, hunting down copy for another good Sunday read.

By the time the Mail sent Ben down into the dirtiest back-streets of Spokane, the deadly sadist had already amassed a three-column scorecard which Ben saw in the police serial killer task force headquarters in downtown Spokane.

In the "definite" column were the names of eight dead prostitutes.

In the "probable" column were three more.

The third list, of "possibles," totaled 28 women. And that was only among the bodies police had found. A lot more women were missing. It was like deja vu for Ben. Perhaps this was the end-of-the-road common denominator of depravity lurking in the blackest recess of every big city. Every metropolis had its prostitutes. Every prostitute population had its heroin addicts. Maybe every big city had its sadistic killer who preyed on these wrecked women. Ben discovered that the most depressing cesspits of Vancouver and Spokane were identical. The final picture was the same. Here in Spokane, among the dirt on stretches of wasteland where other people discarded their garbage, this serial killer was dumping his bodies. In Vancouver at that time, no one had yet physically found the dumping ground, whether it be at sea or on the land. But in both cities, Ben found the very bottom line of all this misery wasn't the pitiful existence of the desperate women victims, or the merciless brutality of the psychopathic killer, but the human suffering of the families the women left behind.

Ben found them all over Spokane. One grieving woman, Kate, had lost her younger sister. Kate still remembered her sister in the happiest of times, on her wedding day. Kate loaned Ben the happiest photograph, when her sister's cascading brown hair was crowned with a perfect white lace bow, and whose silver-painted fingernails were immaculately manicured for the day. The serial killer task force found the sister in a landfill with her hair matted brown with mud and caked black with blood where she'd been slaughtered and sliced open. Her fingers were only good now for providing the prints through which they identified her.

Kate still hadn't understood any of it since that first bombshell of discovering her young sibling was a heroin addict already ashamed of the life her addiction was dragging her into, ashamed of having to sell her body over and over again every night to pay for the next fix. When the task force found her sister's body on Boxing Day, it was like Kate's whole world has crashed. She knew what the killer's legacy would mean for her family. Not only had her dearly-loved sister been taken away. But now no-one would remember her as the beautiful bride with cascading hair. From now on, she would always be just a nameless, faceless, heroin-addict hooker and the serial killer's sixth victim.

Another grieving sister, Lynn, had lost an elder sister. Lost her just when it seemed possible she might be about to get her back from the dead end of heroin addiction. Just a few days before the serial killer had slaked his thirst for sadism on her sister's drug-ravaged body, Lynn received a good news birthday card from her. Her sister never forgot Lynn's birthday. In it, she'd written, "I've never been so lonely. I'm still using heroin daily and prostituting to pay for it. The good news is in one week's time I stop the heroin. The nightmare is nearly over." Lynn's sister had been accepted into an addict treatment program after waiting for months, and was clearly confident it would wean her off her drug addiction.

For Lynn, it meant Christmas was going to be good. She had her sister's present wrapped and sitting on the Christmas tree ready for when she'd come through the door. But she didn't show. And when the phone rang next day, it still wasn't her sister. It was a woman from the serial killer task force. Minutes later, it wasn't her sister coming through the door, it was the task force. Her sister had been stabbed and they'd found her body dumped on a landfill site, they told her. That she'd been horribly mutilated and sliced up they didn't tell her. Nor did they tell her the killer had left his personal signature on her. He had put three plastic bags over her head. Police found plastic bags fitted over the heads of all his victims. For her sister, the nightmare was over. For Lynn, it had only just started.

Ben discovered again that there in Spokane, as in Vancouver, serial killers were only one small part of the violence hookers endured nightly. In both cities, the women tried protecting themselves with an instant intelligence system. They circulated a list of the most dangerous Johns trolling their strolls, adding to the list as soon as they could after they'd endured the latest bout of violence. They were uncomplicated lists:-

"…knife, likes to cut, green truck with rusty fenders."

"…knocks out, drags into car, rapes, two-tone blue truck."

"…violent, hacksaw, has a truck with fancy chrome wheels."

Here in Spokane, some entries were more detailed. Like one John who liked to play religious music real loud while strangling the prostitute, telling her he was sending her to her maker. And another sadist who whispered in one prostitute's ear how his greatest fantasy was to butcher a hooker.

The serial killer task force studied the list every day. Maybe the serial killer was already on it. The whole list scheme was coordinated by a single outreach worker who Ben interviewed. She once organized a memorial vigil for the victims in the park by the river. As the name of each murdered woman was read out, a handful of rose petals were thrown onto the water. Through tears, the woman told Ben how residents of Spokane living downstream were surprised to find their river carpeted in rose petals. It all went in the feature.

Ben walked the dump sites where the killer paid his victims their final humiliation, and where he had enjoyed heaping scorn on the task force. One deadly night, he had discarded two bodies alongside each other in the same landfill. After forensic scientists has scoured every part of the dump until they were certain it contained no more clues, the killer had revisited the site to taunt police by throwing out another body right where the officers had concentrated their search. This he did on April Fools' Day.

Ben's three-page Sunday spread was the good read he'd promised Frank it would be—framed by mug-shots of a dozen of the dead women, each with their whole lives reduced to the same painfully short caption "name, age, found stabbed to death, and date the body was found." The feature had it all. Scared women working the strolls, the serial killer still on the loose, frustrated cops always a step behind, and a disturbing message for the future. The day Ben arrived in Spokane, another woman was reported missing. The task force still didn't know if they'd even found all the killer's existing dump sites. They didn't know if they had found all his bodies. They were dealing with the end of the line for those women. And every day, more women were disappearing, beginning the circle again.

All Ben's work put two more headlines on the wall behind city desk. "TRAIL OF MISERY" was in the bigger letters, with "UNIMAGINABLE TERROR" just beneath.

From what he'd seen, Ben better understood what these women suffered day after day. But he could never imagine what mental anguishes they must have endured which would lead them to resort to this as the only way of life left open to them. And many of them were so frighteningly young. Ben recalled years before as cops built their trust in him, he'd been invited to ride along with the Calgary vice unit as its members worked tirelessly to get these women off the streets. He'd sat in the back of the undercover police car as it trolled the city's downtown stroll. They'd picked up a scantily dressed woman who'd beckoned them alluringly, leaning into the car to make sure the guys could see down her cleavage to her belly button. Under arrest, they sat her next to Ben in the back seat. Only later, after he'd had to admit to himself she did look mature and sexy, did Ben discover she was a 15-year-old runaway from Winnipeg! The vice squad got her off the streets and on her way back east next day.

Ride-alongs were a major step in building trust for Ben. Strict rules applied. No matter what he saw, only what was agreed between him and the cops ever got into print. He went ride-along with the "bait car" squad. A spectacular silver Mustang would be parked in a busy shopping mall parking lot, and the careless driver would hop out, slam the door and go shopping. This at a time when the area was plagued with car thefts. Here was an open invitation for every opportunist car thief. In various vehicles dotted through the lot were squad members, their eyes trained on the car. Ben sat with one team. When a suspect idled up, slipped into the car and turned the key, all hell broke loose. The car travelled a few yards, then the engine cut out and all the doors locked automatically. Cops appeared like magic from all corners of the lot and another car thief was in the bag.

It wasn't only cops that Ben worked with. He'd had to foster trust with all first responders—firefighters, paramedics, emergency room staff—to do his job and he'd been ride-along and shared personal time with them all.

It had started in England with his city's fire brigade. After years of earning their trust, they'd call him out on big fires in the middle of the night. They'd turn out the fire engines, alert the senior officers, then phone Ben. He promised them, if they'd take the trouble to call, he would go—no matter what. He knew he was thoroughly trusted when one night they called him at 3 a. m. to a big fire in the city's dockyard. In seconds, he was out of bed, dressed and just leaving the house when the phone rang again. "Hey, we were just kidding, there's no fire, just testing you," said a familiar voice! Ben knew if they could treat him that way, he'd been accepted as one of them. Firefighters even took him into fires. He was photographed inside one blazing ship's chandlery factory, but he wasn't in there very long. When he heard a large gas cylinder hissing behind him, he quickly got out. Firemen had to stay and deal with it, risking an explosion amid the flames and heat, but Ben was out of there.

In England, "Bonfire Night" every November 5 is a nightmare for fire brigades. Every household in the land has a bonfire in every yard on which families burn a "guy," an effigy of Guy Fawkes, who had tried to blow up their Houses of Parliament in 1605. Party-goers stand round lighting fireworks and enjoying their mighty celebrations. Thousands of bonfires go out of control every year destroying homes and buildings, and hundreds of people get injured by fireworks. Ben was trusted to go ride-along with the fire brigade on those nights. He had to admit to some excitement riding in the back of a fire-engine hurtling through the night with lights flashing and sirens blaring. One night they had 12 runs on Ben's fire engine and came under attack from kids throwing stones as they worked to put out a ridiculously dangerous huge bonfire alongside two houses.

Ben reckoned it was up to him to build a rapport with the people he was writing about—like the firemen—if his stories were to be accurate. As it happened, Ben was a good union man. He wasn't into politics or ideologies, he was into the union if it could help him get paid better. When the journalists on his paper were called out on strike, Ben was there every day. His job, heavily bundled up standing on the picket line, was to keep the brazier fire going all through weeks of a bitter winter strike. One day one of the city's fire engines suddenly pulled up at the picket line. Several firemen who recognized Ben came over and gave the striking journalists a large box full of food.

"You did it for us, we're doing it for you," said the sub-officer in charge. Ben knew what he meant. A year earlier, when the city's firefighters were on strike, Ben spent many hours on their picket lines and organized boxes of food for them in their time of hardship. As the fire engine pulled away, Ben knew his rapport with the firemen had been cemented.

Riding along with paramedics was a different kind of eye-opener for Ben. He saw first-hand the amount of abuse and physical violence paramedics went through, even from those people they were working to help. Ben wondered why drunk men, bleeding from all kinds of wounds, still had the energy to treat paramedics as the enemy when they're only trying to save their lives. And when Ben spent many night shifts in a hospital emergency room he was surprised to see the same mindless violence offered up to nurses, doctors and staff. What the hell was wrong with some people?

Ben believed he could only write accurately about these professionals if he'd experienced their lives first hand. He'd won awards for his coverage of a terrible tragedy in 1979 when 15 men had perished when a storm hit the famous Fastnet yacht race. He'd been there in the western extremities of England when helicopters were flying in survivors. Hell, Ben had even picked up one of the world's most famous racing yacht designers from the helicopter base after he'd been plucked off his storm-wrecked yacht, and driven him for several hours back to the finish line at Plymouth in his humble Vauxhall Chevette company car. Here, in the crowded media center, the international press were trying to reach the man by phone for interviews, while, all the time Ben had been getting the world scoop first-hand from the man himself. In those days, technology didn't exist to get photographs back to the office. Ben decided there and then to drive the 170 miles back along the south coast to his office in Portsmouth with his exclusive rescue photographs, deliver them, then drive the 170 miles back through the night to Plymouth for the rest of the story. And to discover just how difficult it was for rescuers to see tiny life rafts in the storm tossed Atlantic Ocean, Ben was invited to go fly-along in a Nimrod search aircraft. It was an incredible experience for Ben. The crew dropped a smoke canister into the heaving white-streaked waves, flew away and returned over the spot. They told Ben the canister represented a survivor in the sea. If Ben missed seeing it, the "man" would drown, and it would be Ben's fault for not spotting him. Ben concentrated harder than he'd ever done before, and he never once saw the canister or the smoke. When Ben wrote his feature praising the work of the yacht race search-and-rescue crews, his admiration for them came from his authentic experience of what they had gone through.

Now, two more days passed which brought Ben no nearer his hoped-for "copy-cat killer" dream headline. He was kept busy though. He got some great video footage of a northwest city house fire where two firefighters were bowled over backward by a gas blast inside a kitchen. The explosion had them tumbling through his viewfinder as if it was staged. Then he spent nearly an hour in a northeast industrial site watching cops trying to round up an exceedingly ugly mother moose intent on running through traffic with her ungainly backward-bent legs flailing every time they approached her.

Back at the office, the next phone call was vital.

Chapter 5

"You got my girlie calendar yet," said a familiar voice.

"Sitting right here on my desk," Ben lied.

"Well, you'd better bring it right over," said his contact in the M. E.'s office, and thank God, this time, when Ben went down to promotions, they had a calendar, with January's buxom wench showing sun-tanned breasts bubbling over her bikini top on the front cover.

Ben strode into the medical examiner's building with his calendar very properly concealed in a plain brown envelope, ever sensitive to offending anyone who might guess what the anonymous package might contain.

"Oh, you've got his girlie calendar then," said the receptionist, nodding to the huge envelope under his arm.

"How do you know it's not X-ray plates?" asked Ben, aware he'd been found out.

"Yea, chest X-rays, I expect. Go on in, he's waiting for you," she smiled knowingly.

Ben went in to where his contact was waiting, slid the calendar out of the envelope and pushed it across the desk.

"Look at January," he said "she looks like a dead heat in a zeppelin race."

"Wow, you don't get many of those to the pound," said his contact, and in a flash, calendar and envelope disappeared into his desk drawer.

"These cases you've been bringing to me," said the contact, and it was immediately obvious the joking was over. "We might have to see the authorities about them, something strange is going on. I don't know yet what it is, but I'm going to show you something. I want you to do some more checking in your files, and when we've discussed it a lot more, someone's going to have to look at it all."

"Right on," thought Ben. "What's this all about?"

Ben's contact pulled out another file.

"This is another homicide with similarities to the other three. This killer's inside doing life for murdering this woman, but I can't believe the similarities," said the contact. "There are four killers doing life for these murders, yet all the cases have something in common and I can't understand it."

He slid the file across the desk.

Ben read the name on the manila folder. "Angel Shepherd." What the hell? Ben knew this case really well. Just the thought of it made his mouth water. This one was huge. This was the Taber vicar who murdered a young woman in his congregation. This one attracted national headlines. The vicar had pleaded guilty. It threw shock waves throughout western Canada, it being Bible-punching country, where the church plays a welcome stabilizing role in the lives of millions of people. A vicar committing murder, and a sensational sex-slaying at that, and confessing, was monstrous. The media was in a feeding-frenzy for this one, and Ben played his role as a great white shark as fiercely as any of the scavengers.

"Broadbent, that was his name, The Rev. Jacob Broadbent," said Ben. "This one can't have anything to do with the others. He pleaded guilty. Don't you remember, he refused to allow any defense. Said God was the only entity who could judge man, and all but refused to recognize the court existed." Ben was gushing now. "You must remember, this was the guy with the nose-bleed problem, who bled all over the crime-scene. They had enough DNA to sink a battleship. That's why he pleaded guilty, he knew they had him by the ecclesiastical short-and-curlies, God was just an excuse." Ben became rather irreverent when he got excited.

"How can he be linked with these others?"

Ben's contact waited patiently through all this exuberance and slowly pulled out the plastic album from inside the folder, like a magician drawing a rabbit from his black top hat.

"No," said Ben, knowing, even before looking at the photographs, what he was probably about to see. And his contact was right.

"Where have you seen these before," asked his contact, turning to the first page of a full-length body shot of a woman naked but for her panties. Then he showed Ben the third page where he pointed to a series of wicked slashes that had ripped open Angel Shepherd's abdomen and thighs. Ben saw the parallel cuts down the inside of her thighs were gaping open so there was more interior flesh visible than skin holding the horrific wounds together.

"These knife wounds are so similar to the other three, I'm afraid we've got to show our findings to somebody. Something's going on here that doesn't make sense. This guy pleaded guilty to doing this. Did he do the others? I know he couldn't have done. He couldn't have been in all those other places. That doesn't work. Could they all be copy-cats? That's so incredible, it's just impossible."

Ben's contact hadn't finished. He turned the page again, and Ben had also seen this ghastly savagery before. This victim's left nipple had been bitten off. Ben recalled the autopsy photographs of Gillian Warnoski, where Ron Lincoln had bitten off both her nipples. They were gruesomely similar. Except this sadist perverted man-of-the-cloth had added a grisly touch by underscoring the shape of his victim's breast with a deep mutilation, a curving slash, like a crescent moon. Ben's contact shut the photo album and slid it back inside the folder.

"I'm not going to do anything about all this until we have some clue as to what's going on. Look back in your files about this vicar, and come up with an answer, you know, see if you can't do something useful for a change," he said, half a challenge, half a tease.

When Ben got back in the office, he was dying to immerse himself in this old Taber classic again. Just imagine, he might have the chance to resurrect the sexiest, juiciest scandal of the decade, the sex-slayer vicar. But first he had to finish his "Crime in your Community" feature. God, he hated it. It was a two-page feature which ran every week, consisting of crime prevention tips from cops to help each of the city's separate communities combat crime in their area. Even the cops couldn't be bothered to provide copy for the damn thing. So every week Ben trudged round the district cop shops trying to draw out snippets for the feature. It was like pulling teeth. It wasn't as if anybody ever read it. One highlight of the two-pager was a table of weekly statistics of how many homes were burgled and how many vehicles stolen. By mistake, one week, the Mail's practice template of statistics which bore no resemblance to any real figures was published. This included a table showing the tiny south Calgary community of Midnapore suddenly suffering 833 armed robberies instead of their average one or two. Not a soul noticed. No one in the Mail's newsroom realized the error, no cop complained about the shattering crime wave suddenly sweeping this little community, and not a single resident in the new war zone of armed robberies phoned in. Ben was the only one who saw the blunder and he kept quiet, completely reassured in his conviction no one ever read the damn thing.

"I hate 'Crime in Your Community'," he sang out loud in the office, this chant having become one of his catch-phrases. On the Mail's health beat was a reporter, Phil, a small, wiry young reporter who had a brilliant knack for imitating people's voices. He really ought to have been on the stage. If you had your back to him when he did Preston Manning, you'd think the politician had walked into the newsroom. His Prime Minister Chretien was so damn good you'd think his mouth would have to be crooked, and he could win an "Oscar" with his Kathryn Hepburn. Whenever Ben was slogging away on this blasted community feature, Phil, a very astute judge of what was going on around him, would sometimes chant "I hate 'Crime in Your Community'," mimicking Ben perfectly, exaggerating his English enunciation.

Not mentioning he'd noticed the blunder in the Crime in Your Community feature wasn't the only time Ben had ever kept quiet about something not quite right in the newspaper. And the other time he'd kept silent very deliberately.

It so happened Ben had run a weekly column for stamp collectors in the Mail—not technical, but generally light-hearted and varied, so much so that the editorial bosses were happy to let it run for more than 600 editions. One week he matched a story about cattle creating major greenhouse gas problems by flatulating all over the world with a stamp showing cattle for his column. For a laugh, Ben started the first paragraph with the letter "F," the second paragraph with the letter "A," the third paragraph with the letter "R" and the fourth paragraph with the letter "T." He then continued this all through the column and it was completely unnoticeable unless you knew to look for it. No one in the whole newspaper saw it and so it appeared, seemingly innocuously, in all 50,000 copies of the Mail that week, "FART," "FART," "FART," "FART"—all the way through the flatulating cattle column.

It took Ben several hours to finish his hated "community" chore, and it was well into the evening before he could even think about the Rev. Jacob Broadbent of Taber. This was going to be a night when he'd be there in the office until 1 a.m. That was the magic hour for the Mail. That was when the world stopped. Once 1 a.m. was reached, and the lone night guy manning city side and the lone guy on the rim went home, nothing happened anywhere on earth for the next seven hours. The whole of the Mail's computer systems shut down, so even if a reporter wanted to work later he couldn't. When the early morning guy came in at 8 a. m., the Mail was reconnected to the world, and could begin catching up with the lost night. Well, tonight, Danny, the night guy would have company until 1 a. m.

Ben punched "murder list" into the computer and scrolled down through the letter Bs.

"BROADBENT Alan—victim (transvestite male hooker found beaten to death under railway bridge at Indus) No."

"BROADBENT Chris—killer (pounded ex-wife with a cricket bat) No."

"BROADBENT Jason—killer (Taber vicar in sex-slaying shocker, confessed to murder, doing life.) That will do nicely. File 152."

Quite interesting murders produced medium thick files in Ben's cabinet drawers. Better murders were sometimes so thick, he separated them from the rest and they earned a hanging folder of their own. The Rev. Jason Broadbent had a full and bulging hanging folder to himself. He needed it. Ben read the files and remembered. It all started on July 4, 1991, when a woman's body was discovered on a gravel road leading to a small oil installation. Here, a bunch of ugly pipes and metalwork spoiled the rolling prairie of southern Alberta just north of the township of Taber. The discovery of oil under Alberta brought the province wealth but left it with a legacy of metalwork protruding above the surface here and there. And workers in the oil patch serviced these installations, reaching them along little gravel tracks across the wheat fields. Getting to the body was easy for the RCMP. An oil patch worker who'd driven up this one particular track had serviced the oil installation and was driving back out when he saw the body half in the ditch. He drove into town and brought the local Taber police out to it. Taber is one of the very few towns in southern Alberta with its own police force in addition to an RCMP detachment.

On this morning, one glance at the bloodbath-body on the gravel track told the Taber police officers this was a job for the RCMP, and they soon had the Mounties on scene. But what was easy for the RCMP was a nightmare for Ben. Hours later after a ferocious 300 km drive from Calgary into the general area, Ben's problems began. He then had to find one body on one gravel track near one oil installation somewhere "north of Taber." The local police played dumb and pretended they didn't know what he was talking about. The RCMP plain refused to say where it was. Ben kicked up plenty of dust hopelessly driving up and down gravel tracks north of Taber, until suddenly, a low-flying blue-and-white helicopter caught his eye. "Ah-ha, gotcha," he said, swinging his van hard right at the next gravel cross-roads to follow the chopper. This was obviously the police going to the scene. Ben inwardly gave thanks to the rural planner who had divided southern Alberta's flat plains into one section square plots and made all country roads neatly square to each other, running straight and strictly east-west or north-south. He saw the chopper a bit southeast of him, and knew if he headed south two rural blocks and then east two rural blocks, he'd be there. He saw the helicopter hovering. "Playing into my hands, they are," he enthused. He blessed the perfect flatness of the land with its far distant perfectly visible horizons. It worked like a charm. A few more minutes of foot-down driving, dragging up a dust cloud, and he was at the helicopter. The wrong helicopter!

It was an oil company helicopter with executives making some top management inspection of an oil installation!

"Fuck me rigid," Ben muttered to himself, turning the van round and heading north again. By stopping every pickup truck, he saw on every gravel track north of Taber, he finally found someone who'd seen police cars, and he eventually arrived at the right scene. And there, sitting snugly in the corner of a field alongside the RCMP road block was the blue-and-white RCMP helicopter, a different model to the one he'd chased, this one with "POLICE" in giant blue letters across its paintwork. Of course, he wasn't actually at the body. The RCMP had put this road block in where the gravel track joined the township road and the body was still out of sight. It was the way they always worked.

That first day Ben could do no more than research the victim in his files. Angel Shepherd, 21, and still single, was a very much respected Taber resident. Pretty with long black hair, she was employed as a receptionist in the more popular of the town's two photographic studios. There she worked surrounded by framed portraits of smiling brides, impeccably dressed smiling children, smiling graduates in perfect black gowns, all smiling down from their framed positions round the walls—wall-to-wall smiles. She was a very active member of the Taber Tabernacle Church, helped run the Sunday school for the children, and seemed to spend most of her time at the church, arranging flowers, or preparing for next Sunday's services. Over the next few days, Ben learned more. It seemed Angel had thought it rather presumptuous to have such a "Holy" name and called herself Jill instead, so no one in the church could be offended. It appeared she was on her way home from the church when she'd disappeared on the night of July 3, and her body was found next day. Ben recalled while he was in Taber and not making much progress, as the RCMP apparently had no suspects, something strange happened. His first day story had appeared under the headline "CHURCH ANGEL SLAIN" with his picture by-line inside. Next day he was approached by two men who asked him "Are you Ben Ludlow with the Mail, saw your picture in there today?"

"Yea," said Ben.

"We've got something for you. Come and have a coffee."

And inside Tim Horton's, Ben found he was talking to two members of an RCMP detachment down by the Canada-USA border. He never discovered their names. He didn't need to know. What they gave him was good enough without him needing their names. They stayed just long enough to tell him that the sheet of paper they'd given him was completely authentic, and they were gone. They each ate their doughnuts—police really do eat doughnuts in Tim Horton's shops, Ben discovered—and left. Ben read the document. It was a confidential memorandum from the detachment's senior officer to his lower ranks. It ordered them, each one individually, to carry out a strict traffic ticket quota system. It outlined how the RCMP there were strapped for cash, and how each officer was to hit a quota of $80 a day in tickets. What's more, failure to bring in $80 a day would seriously hinder any officer's hopes of promotion, and if an officer fell far short of his quota he would suffer disciplinary problems. And there it was, dated and signed by the boss himself. There had been a huge and never-ending battle between police and the public over the numbers of speeding and other traffic tickets issued by cops. Senior police spokesmen always insisted there were no quotas, and every ticket issued was aimed at improving road safety. But every motorist who'd ever got caught and coughed up the fine reckoned he'd been bitten by the police cash-cow, and knew in his heart another officer had met his quota. And now here, in Ben's hand, was a memo, signed by one of the top police brass, spelling out the quota his officers had to meet. It was huge. It splashed across the Mail's front page next day, and inside, the Mail carried a rag-out picture of the memo itself, to prove it existed.

Not many weeks later, while Ben was still working on Angel Jill Shepherd's murder, he heard of a strange follow up to the doughnut shop story. The boss at the RCMP detachment down south had suddenly been transferred out of province. In Ben's eyes, that meant he'd effectively been fired. Wow!

He never knew whether his expose of the quota system and the firing were related, but Ben also remembered suffering a nervous and very uncomfortable sequel.

Many months later, Ben was ordered to attend an extremely posh and stuffy official police function at the prestigious Palliser Hotel in downtown Calgary. This was one of those affairs he hated, having to wear, not only a tie, but a bow-tie at that. This Fairmont Palliser, the city's most luxurious and historic landmark was not Ben's scene. He shook his head at the unnecessary top-hatted valet who ushered him through the plush front entrance like he couldn't manage it himself. Ben knew all about the glittering Palliser history, knew about the grey Tennessee marble floors beneath his feet in the grand lobby with its marble columns stretching up to the ornate ceilings overhead. Ben would have been much more at home just one block north at the York Hotel, with its rough and cramped main doorway, having scruffy pan-handlers trying to crowd and fleece him for a quarter rather than have valets bowing before him.

Ben had once covered a murder outside the front door of the York Hotel on a day when no less an international dignitary than the Queen herself was being bowed to by valets at the Palliser. He wrote a heart-felt editorial column about these two different worlds just one block apart. Police at one scene were on their knees in the gutter where a murder victim's blood had spilled, seeking evidence. And a block away top brass from the senior echelon of the force strode in immaculate dress uniforms being presented to Her Majesty in the sumptuous setting of the Palliser's luxurious interior.

On this day, feeling uncomfortable in his choking tie, Ben took his seat at a circular mahogany table, where the organizers, for social reasons, had mixed its guests to encourage conversation. Little immaculately printed cards instructed each guest where he should take his seat. Ben found his card, printed ornately in gold, after all this was the Palliser, and on his table to his right was relieved to see the name of a Calgary police superintendent he knew well. And then he glanced to his left, and saw, in horror, who would be sitting next to him for the evening.

There, as if placed by some mischievous and sadistic hand of fate, was an immaculate and ornately scrolled card for the senior officer of a certain RCMP detachment, the former senior officer, that is, the former, recently transferred out of province senior officer. For three hours that night, from appetizers at 8 p. m., through the entree at 8:30 p. m., the dessert at 9:15 p. m., and speeches for hours, not a word passed between the two of them—an officer likely deposed by a newspaper story, and the reporter who wrote the story. Memories of that night still made Ben squirm as he sat reading the file again.

What happened to put the major crimes detectives onto The Rev. Jacob Broadbent was almost like something out of a crime thriller, except no fictional author would ever have invented such an outrageous twist in any murder plot. It had all taken place quickly. The oil patch worker who'd found the body at the side of the gravel road had seen a brown station wagon pulling away on the township road as he was arriving. Detectives soon tracked down the eight brown station wagons registered to motorists in and around Taber, and with each owner's consent, searched each one. Forensic scientists very soon found traces of human blood on the floor of one, and soon matched it by DNA to the body, and though the detectives themselves could hardly believe it, they found themselves face to face with the good Reverend. It was his car. And the officers had an ace up their sleeves. They knew something from the crime scene that would trap their killer. A lot of blood had been spilled at the scene, and forensic blood-spatter specialists had been called in. Ben always loved it when these guys became part of a murder inquiry. The media loved to call them "blood-splatter" experts, when their official title was "blood-spatter" investigators. Ben loved how much more blood-curdling "splatter" was than "spatter" even if the price paid was a small sacrifice to accuracy. For a long time, their examination of Angel's body at the scene centered on the blood on the body.

They deduced one vital fact. She'd been murdered and mutilated somewhere else and her blood had dried before she was dumped there. But there was fresh blood on the corpse. Droplets and splashes, which had landed on her body, and a few dribbles (probably not the terminology they used) had even landed on the tiny stones making up the gravel of the track. Someone, either the killer or someone else who'd come across the body later, had bled onto the corpse. Only when the specialists were satisfied they'd extracted every possible detail from the scene so far was Angel's body rolled over. And there they found the vital clue.

On the hard ground under her body were droplets of the fresh blood. It could only have been the killer. He'd obviously cut himself during the earlier blood-lust mutilation, had bled a few drops onto the ground here, then placed his victim's corpse down, and moments later bled on her body, as well. He probably wasn't worried, expecting police to assume all the blood at the scene came from the body. This couldn't have been blood from any later passer-by. The killer had bled under the body.

Once the detectives had found the victim's blood in Broadbent's station wagon, he was called in for questioning. In the interview room at Lethbridge police headquarters, officers stared and searched, letting their eyes start the investigation before they ever asked him any questions. Where was the cut that had bled so profusely? They examined his hands. Soft, a little sweaty, but only to be expected in a man who's car's just been found with blood inside it, but no cuts, not even a scratch, not so much as a healing scar. They looked at his face, his head, forearms, every inch of skin that would be exposed, but they could find nothing. Their interrogation ranged from the general to the specific. Yes, of course he knew Angel Shepherd. Well, he knew her as Jill, and she was a stalwart of his church, a pillar of strength in his congregation. He was shattered by her death. Yes, he knew pretty well when she would be at the church, and when she would be leaving, and what route she took going home. But no, he had no idea her blood was in his station wagon, and he had no idea how it could have got there. Yes, she'd been in his car before, he'd given her many a lift, but no, as far as he knew, she had never bled in the car.

And then it happened.

Broadbent suddenly clasped his right hand to his face, and it came away covered in blood. He was having a nose-bleed, a violent nose-bleed that was depositing droplets and splashes and dribbles on the interview room table. Some even landed on the interrogation tape-recorder. The questioning stopped in mid-sentence. The two lead investigators stared incredulously at each other for a split-second.

"Don't worry," mumbled Broadbent, clutching a handkerchief to his nose with his head thrown acutely back so he was looking at the ceiling, "I get this all the time, it's very inconvenient."

"Inconvenient" wasn't the word the investigators had in mind. "Fortuitous," "a God-send," "Manna from Heaven"—any of those would do, especially with a God-damn vicar—a God-damn murdering-bastard vicar, whose nose had just landed him as the prime number-one suspect right in the frame for a hideous sex-slaying.

Things happened very quickly after that. The crime laboratory soon confirmed through DNA matching that the vital droplets of blood under Angel's body were from the vicar. They already had Angel's blood smeared in the vicar's car. And his car was seen leaving the area where the body had been dumped. He knew her well, and he knew her routine. He knew where she would be at all times of the day. She'd been murdered on July 4 and just seven days later, Broadbent was charged.

Church life in Taber would never be the same again.

Come to that, headline writing at the Mail was never the same after that. Ben looked again at the giant headlines in the file. "VICAR CHARGED IN SEX SLAYING SHOCKER." That one was on the city desk wall. Two more shockers followed.

"VICAR SAYS 'I DID IT.'"—and then the strangest headline of all "NOSE BLEED SHOCKER TRAPS KILLER VICAR." Not long after Broadbent was charged, the legal proceedings against him accelerated through the courts when he let it be known he was pleading guilty. He was waiving his rights to a preliminary hearing, and wasn't looking for any lawyer to delay the outcome. It turned out this wasn't any admirable expression of remorse or contrition, but what many took to be an over-zealous and misguided application of religious beliefs by the vicar. Before the trial, he prepared and circulated an odd statement which was widely publicized. Ben had a copy in his file, of course.

"To whom it may concern," it began.

"Before all else, I wish to express my deepest sympathies to the family of Angel Shepherd, and it is my fervent prayer that they are constantly strengthened by the power of God which I know is enveloping them in their hour of greatest need since their loved one was taken from them."

"Those among us who choose to sit in judgment on their fellow man, have placed upon me the burden of accepting the guilt of man's inhumanity to man, illustrated by the destruction of this life. There is but one who sits in judgment on the efforts of man, and I am comforted in the deep knowledge He will accept my soul into the Kingdom of heaven. I am at one with Him, and He with me. Jesus Christ was crucified when those among men who sat in judgment on him, assessed him as having broken the laws of man. Jesus' crucifixion has shown for all eternity man has not the right to sit in judgment on his fellow man. One only can be our judge, and I am prepared to leave my life here on earth and my soul for eternity in his everlasting care."

"For it is written in the Scriptures in many places, man shall not judge his fellow man. The actions of man are for the judgment of Jesus Christ alone. There are those among you who will say I did this thing. Now I will say I did this thing for the sole purpose of removing from you the sin of judgment which the Bible forbids. I commend you to read Deuteronomy Chapter 1, verse 17:-

'You shall not fear man, for the judgment is God's. The case that is too hard for you, you shall bring to me, and I will hear it'."

"The Bible even tells us judges have no right to judge their fellow man. It is written at 2 Chronicles, Chapter 19, verse 6:-

He said to the judges, 'consider what you are doing, for you do not judge for man but for the LORD'."

Ben turned the page. There were chunks of the Bible from Exodus, Leviticus, the Psalms, Isaiah, the Romans, all over. All apparently condemning man for judging his fellow man, and all explaining how God himself would pronounce judgment on sinners.

The deeper into this ecclesiastical debate Broadbent delved, the more rambling became his statement, explaining seemingly why he was admitting to the crime, why he wasn't going to contest the charge in court, and why no lawyer would be fighting to keep him out of prison. Reading the statement again, Ben noted what had struck him the first time he read it. There was not a single mention of what Broadbent had actually done. No mention of the killing itself. And there certainly wasn't a single word of rebuttal against the heap of evidence, both forensic and circumstantial, which the Crown was going to present against him.

Sending the statement to the media had the desired effect for Broadbent. The Mail's headline, SUSPECT KILLER CONFESSES—VICAR SAYS 'I DID IT', pretty well summed up what he was saying, even if it stripped away the religious qualifications with which he'd confused the issue. Headlines have a way of doing that. And so it came to pass, on March 19, 1992 that the Rev. Jacob Broadbent took his place in the dock at Lethbridge Court of Queen's Bench where Ben listened to him plead guilty to the first-degree murder of Angel Shepherd. A vicar pleading guilty to the sex-slaying of an innocent in his congregation—wow! Ben remembered looking into his eyes and seeing a religious fervor burning there, as if there was a pride in what he was going through. Ben had covered hundreds of major trials in England and Canada but he'd never seen such strange intensity in the face of an accused man. Perhaps this one really did believe he was cleansing the sins of all mankind.

For the law to take its rightful path, the law of man, that is, the Crown still had to present its case, even though Broadbent had pleaded guilty. And so the court, the media and a stunned society heard from the mouth of the prosecutor the gruesome story of Angel's murder. He told them how Broadbent had snatched her away, had murdered her, mutilated her body in a blood-lust and dumped her like so much rubbish. And how, during the dumping of the corpse he had suffered a nose bleed, and had bled under and onto the body. The prosecutor told the court how, at first, the investigators couldn't understand where his blood had come from until that dramatic and incredible moment in the interview room when another sudden nose-bleed showed them everything in a blinding flash of revelation. The Crown prosecutor dotted every "i" and crossed every "t." He covered the eye-witness who saw the vicar's car leaving the area, the DNA match of Angel Shepherd's blood in the vicar's car and the damning match of his blood on the victim's body. That just about sewed it up.

But what happened next was fantastic.

Ben had chosen that split-second to look at Broadbent, sensing the prosecution was winding it all up, just to see his reaction, when Broadbent suddenly grabbed his face and flung his head back almost in one move, nearly cracking his skull on the back of the dock.

He was having a nose-bleed—right there and then.

Seconds earlier, some skeptics in the court had found difficulty in believing the Crown's amazing story that the investigators had received this miraculous break when their suspect had bled for them, almost on cue.

Now, he was doing it again, right before the very eyes of everyone in the courtroom. It was proof positive.

The court went into recess for a few minutes so guards could get Broadbent's nose to stop dripping evidence all over the dock. When he returned with a splattering of blood down his shirt, he suffered the ignominy of listening to his fate with a wad of cotton wool stuffed up one nostril.

It led to that cracker of a headline, "NOSE BLEED SHOCKER TRAPS KILLER VICAR." The purpose of headlines, well, front page headlines, at least, is to attract attention, so the pedestrian passing by the Mail box on the street just has to stop and buy one. Better still, if you can catch a motorist's eye, and get him to screech to a halt in his car and buy one, it's a good headline.

I bet this one attracted a few screechers, thought Ben. The judge sentenced Broadbent to life in prison with no parole for 20 years, and Ben remembered watching him put his hands together, very oddly, as if in prayer and lifting his head to the heavens. It was possibly an after effect of the nose-bleed, but to Ben it looked as if the vicar was making a gesture of thanking God, as if, somehow, being punished on earth by his fellow man was what he wanted. All in all, it was as strange a finale to a murder trial as Ben had ever seen.

Ben was pretty well through the file now. Most of his other murder files went on a great deal after the sentencing. Nearly every murderer appealed his conviction, trying desperately to find some legal technicality to unlock the cell door which the weight of evidence against him had swung shut. They usually generated more stories—"killer to appeal," "killer appeals," "killer's appeal rejected"—some rarely taking their perceived technicalities as far as the Supreme Court—"killer appeals to Supreme Court," "killer's appeal rejected by Supreme Court"—and that was usually the end. Broadbent's cuttings file was much shorter. He had a ton of background in there, but no more stories. Broadbent had ordered his lawyer not to appeal at all. He wasn't interested in the judgment of mankind, whether it was right, wrong, peppered with legal technicalities, or as sound as a rock, because only God could judge him, and all else was irrelevant. He'd been inside for eight years, and never made a murmur. Ben had received no whining phone-calls from him, moaning about injustice and declaring his innocence. Ben closed the file, trying to think whether anything he'd read helped with this peculiar problem of the four totally unrelated murders which seemed vaguely similar to each other. It was 12.50 p. m. It was as much as he could do that night. He picked up his coat, and was just passing Danny who still had 10 minutes left on his shift, when his ears instantly caught a heightened voice on the scanner.

"One command to dispatch, we need a second alarm in here," yelled a fire captain.

"Where the hell's that?" asked Ben.

"Some motor-bike shop downtown," said Danny.

"I'm going videoing," said Ben. "We got a photog down there?"

"No, not at 1 o'clock in the morning," said Danny. "And the rim won't replate this late for a fire. Just go and enjoy your videoing. You're mad, this time of night."

Mad he might be, but Ben knew this could be a big fire. A fire officer calling for a "second alarm" meant the blaze was beyond the control of the rigs he already had on scene. He was asking dispatch to double the number of fire trucks and firefighters at the motor bike shop. Ben soon swung his van out into the night. He loved these night fires. Many hundreds of times he'd driven through almost deserted streets at night, his heart pounding with anticipation. Would he be disappointed and find the fire department had knocked the fire down, leaving charred debris and steam rising, meaning he was too late? Or would flames be licking into the night sky, and would he have new material to convert into another fire video at $14.95 a pop? Approaching from 20 blocks away he started scanning the horizon, hoping for a smoke pall, a glow, any clue. Getting nearer, he started worrying about how far away from the fire would the police have shut the roads. Then he rounded a bend and there were the first flashing lights, fire trucks littering the side streets, well away from the fire, linked to hydrants by hoses snaking across the road. He pulled in, parked, stuffed his coat pockets with his three two-hour batteries, grabbed his video, and set off walking the last two blocks.

His heart sank. It was smoking, grey smoke, not a lot, but coming out of everywhere. The fire department had obviously knocked down the flames, and this must be mopping up time, when they deal with the final hot-spots, and the remaining smoke would get greyer and whiter, turning to steam, then it would fade away, and that would be the end.

"Hiya Ben," said Tony, a freelance photographer with long hair pulled back into a pony-tail, who spent all his night hours out with cops, living off the scanner, coming up with great action shots of night-time arrests, fatal crashes, and anything else the Mail missed during the seven hours a night it was switched off from the world.

"Hiya Tony, what's it doing?" asked Ben.

"Nothing much, it's been smoking like this for ages. They got enough rigs here to wash the building into the Bow River. Nothing's going to happen, I'm just leaving."

"Okay, mate. I'm just going to see Russell, and then I'll probably do the same," said Ben.

Russell was Fire Captain Mick Russell, the public information officer for the fire department, whose job—unofficially, as far as Ben could see—was to attend big fires and keep the media out of the way of all other firefighters. His purpose—officially, as the department described it—was to keep reporters updated about what was going on.

"You winning the battle?" asked Ben when he found Russell's distinctive blue fire helmet among the small army of yellow, red and white helmets of the active firefighters.

"Well, we've withdrawn the firefighters out of there, there's gasoline in all the bike tanks, drums of gasoline, and the place is full of dangerous and explosive materials," said Russell.

Ben's hopes rose.

And now he came to think about it, the smoke wasn't dying away, it was getting thicker. Across the road from the front door, Ben set himself up, and videoed thick smoke pouring out from under the eaves. High above the roof, a floodlight from a fire department snorkel cage played through the smoke, which was billowing in dense clouds high into the night sky.

This fire was getting worse. The dark grey smoke curling out from the doorway in front of Ben started pushing out under pressure, jetting out, thick and black, thicker and blacker by the minute. The "Marcel's Motor-Bikes" sign Ben had filmed through the hazy grey smoke at first, was now obliterated by a solid wall of black smoke. Suddenly Ben heard the shattering of glass and flames burst out from the top of the door, curling up over the roof. More glass burst and more flames roared out. Ben never saw any of this in color, only in black and white through the view-finder. The real essence of a big fire is the sound. You can hear a really big fire—muffled explosions, the crashing down of wood and structures inside the building, the splintering of glass, and the deafening roar of fire truck pumps. This one had all of that and more. Now flames were bursting out all along the eaves. The whole place was erupting in flame. Another huge crash and the volume of black smoke pouring out through the roof turned to a column of spiraling fire as the roof caved in. With most of the blaze now venting through the roof, the flames in Ben's doorway died down. It was time to find a new vantage point.

He walked round to the rear, where doorways and windows were illuminated by roaring flames. Ben filmed until all three of his batteries which always lost power quickly on cold nights were almost dead. He rotated them anxiously—take off the dead one, put it in a pocket to warm up, attach a warm one, film for a few minutes until it died, take it off, put it in a pocket. Eventually, the ferocity of the flames died down and the sheer weight of water pouring into the building started turning the battle. The firefighters had won a hollow victory. True, no one had been injured and the fire hadn't spread to any other structures, but Marcel's Motor-Bikes was destroyed. Bull-dozers later levelled the charred and blackened shell. It was a $1-million loss to the city.

It was a good solid $14.95 worth of video for Ben.

A big blaze like this one was good for copy for two or three days, and Ben was kept busy interviewing the owner, and the displaced mechanics at the shop, and writing about their plans for rebuilding for the future. So it was days later before he could arrange a meet with his contact to discuss these peculiar homicides. This time he drove across the city to the M. E.'s office armed with all four of his files, and some ideas in his head about what it might all mean. His contact must have meant business this time. He offered coffee—a Styrofoam cup, white powder "coffee mate" and a stir stick. Ben always thought there was something horribly tasteless about office coffee, but he accepted it readily. It promised to be a long session.

Ben's main contribution was to point out that the chronological sequence of these four murders seemed to be important, so that's where they started. That wasn't how they'd looked at them before. They'd looked at them first time round in the sequence they'd arisen. It all started when Ben had taken the phone call from Ron Lincoln this year. He was the murderer convicted of the torture slaying of Gillian Warnoski in Red Deer in January 1992. Some similarities had reminded Ben of the case of Darren Sunderland who'd murdered the Calgary waitress Jill Bereson and dumped her on the golf course in November 1990, and between them they'd surmised Lincoln had produced a copy-cat killing of Sunderland's *modus operandi*.

"If you remember, you then turned up the third one we looked at, because you thought that might be a copy-cat," said Ben.

"That was Paul Andres who murdered Angela Braithwaite, the librarian at Pincher Creek in February 1991, after torturing her with his whip."

"Lastly, you had us look at the religious nose-bleed nutcase, the Rev. Jacob Broadbent who murdered Angel Shepherd in Taber in July 1991," said Ben, again relapsing into his irreverent mode when he got agitated.

"Now," said Ben, sounding rather like his old math master at the English grammar school where he was taught, "I did some work on the dates, and look what happens if you put them in chronological order," and he slid out from one of his files one sheet of paper where he'd prepared the list.

"First—November 5, 1990—Darren Sunderland murders Jill Bereson and dumps the body on the golf course in Calgary."

February 25, 1991—Sunderland charged with the murder.

Second—February 28, 1991—Paul Andres murders Angela Braithwaite at Pincher Creek.

June 29, 1991—Andres charged with the murder.

Third—July 4, 1991—The Rev. Jacob Broadbent murders Angel Shepherd at Taber.

July 11, 1991—Broadbent charged with the murder.

"Fourth—January 20, 1992—Ron Lincoln murders Gillian Warnoski at Red Deer."

"I don't know what it means but look at the pattern," said Ben.

"There's the first murder, and when that murderer gets charged, there's a three day gap then another murder, somewhere else. Then when that murderer gets charged, there's a five day gap before another murder somewhere else again. The pattern seems to get broken after that because there's a six month gap before the last murder, but do you think this pattern might have anything to do with it?"

"Well, I can't see it yet. Are you trying to say murders in Calgary, then 250 km south in Pincher Creek, then 300 km southeast in Taber and then 150 km to the north in Red Deer are in a pattern because each one happens a few days after the murderer of the previous one is caught? I don't think so. That's just coincidence, I reckon. What else have you got?" asked the contact.

"Well," said Ben, fearing what he was going to say next might make him look stupid, "all the victims seemed to have the name "Jill" one way or another."

"The first one was straight forward Jill Bereson."

"Then there was Angela Braithwaite, who was known to everyone as Jill. That was the name on her name-tag at Pincher Creek library."

"Then there was Angel in Taber, who called herself Jill because she thought the name Angel was too holy."

"And lastly there was straight-forward Jill—Gillian Warnoski at Red Deer."

Ben shrugged his shoulders and raised his eye-brows, waiting to be pilloried for this burst of trivia.

"Where did you get all that from?" asked his contact. "In my files, I have a Jill, an Angela, and Angel and a Gillian. But you've turned them up as all four Jills. That could be something to work on. Are you sure?"

"Yea, positive," said Ben, surprised his contact wasn't deriding him for sounding like something out of an Agatha Christie thriller. "All that's in my files. I got it from their families and friends and it must be right, we ran it in the Calgary Mail."

That did make his contact laugh, just for a moment.

And then, to Ben's shock, he came out with it.

"I think we've got a serial killer here," he said.

A maelstrom of thoughts crowded into Ben's brain in a split-second—front-page headlines for days on end, exclusive stories every day, a book, film rights, fame, even riches. "What? Yea, good goon, you got me there for a moment. I thought you were serious," he said.

"I am serious," said the contact, and Ben could see he was.

"It's the only explanation. I've been looking again at the four sets of mutilations. They're far too similar to each other to be done by four different people. It's the same hand at work. And once you put them in the right chronological order, the slayings get progressively more sadistic, which is what you'd expect with a serial killer."

The contact had put the four albums of pictures together.

"Fuck me rigid," said Ben, seeing instantly what his contact was driving at. If you didn't know differently, you'd say these were all pictures of the same single victim with the same wounds. Alongside each other, the pictures told an unmistakable story. And there was a progression. A bite mark on the breast of Bereson, the first victim, one nipple bitten off the second victim, Braithwaite, and from the fourth victim, Warnoski, the killer had bitten off both nipples.

"I can't explain how it could be possible. Not yet, anyway. It's just a theory. I know four different men are in prison and have been for years, and each one is in there convicted on rock-solid evidence."

"I can't find any common links between the victims, apart from the wounds—nothing. The victims were a waitress, a librarian, a photo studio assistant and a bank teller. There's usually something linking the victims of a serial killer, but I couldn't find it. You coming up with four Jills is the first tiny possibility. What we need is a whole lot more."

"You do realize what an impossible task we've got ahead, don't you. Somehow, we've got to find better proof all these murders were the work of a serial killer. A theory's no good. We've got to be able to prove we're right. Then, we've got to take our proof to the police and convince them—and remember that's four different police forces hundreds of miles apart—that they each convicted the wrong man. The whole of the justice system will go ballistic. If we're right, there will be provincial and probably federal inquiries into how four men were each wrongly convicted. Then, if we're right, it means there's still a serial killer out there today. He's still got to be caught."

"Fuck my old boots," said Ben, the enormity of it slowly sinking in. "Now you're going to tell me this is all off the record and I can't have it on tomorrow's front page, aren't you."

"You know we can't go public with it yet," said his contact. "To safeguard my career, and yours, we better make sure we're right before we say anything to anyone. No one else is going to get anything from this office, so it'll be your scoop when it goes down, just be patient."

Ben hated that. Many times he'd sat on stories, waiting for the time to be right for his various contacts to have all their ducks in a row when the story broke. In those anxious days between knowing the inside story and being able to break it, Ben would scan the rival's paper and watch every television newscast, dreading to see if his scoop had been snatched away from him. It never had been, but that didn't lessen the nervous tension of those days.

Playing this nerve-wracking cat-and-mouse game with inside and secret contacts had brought him at least one great exclusive.

When he was in England, there had been a serial rapist, a sexual athlete who would have sex with his girl-friend, ejaculating four or five times in a couple of hours. He'd film most of this wild boisterous sex on home-video. Then he'd go out into the night, drag a victim off the streets and rape her, always twice in a few minutes. Ben's paper ran front page stories about the fear he struck in the city for days. And then, when the rapes stopped for a while, Ben's closest contacts in the specially-formed rape task force, drawn up to catch this monster, called him in.

"We now know who this guy is," Ben was told. "And we know for sure he's in France. But we don't want a word of that in the paper, or his friends here will get word to him, and he'll never come back."

A deal was struck. Ben would continue writing stories about "fear in the city" so it appeared the rape-squad was still hunting the monster there, so the suspect would suspect nothing. In return, the squad would make sure Ben and a photographer were at the ferry for their scoop when the rapist returned from France and was arrested. For eight nail bitingdays and nights, Ben sat on the story. But it was worth it. Blissfully unaware the rape squad had any ideas about him, the suspect caught a ferry back to England, and was pounced on by detectives the second his foot touched dry land. The moment was captured by Ben's photographer, and Ben's eye-witness account of the international arrest of a monster serial-rapist filled the front page. No other media was in sight.

Ben had visions of today's cat-and-mouse game becoming a lot more complex and nerve-wracking. If he and his contact had stumbled on a serial-killer that no one knew existed, the very act of them alerting police forces in at least four different cities conjured up nightmares for Ben. Naturally, the federal justice department would get to hear of it. All across Canada, crime reporters had contacts better than Ben's. It only needed one cop or lawyer somewhere to breathe word of a serial killer on the loose, and it would spread through the media like wildfire. Ben knew one legacy of the lightning fast advances in modern communications was that the old-fashioned days of a good scoop were almost gone. If one hint of a leaked story got out nowadays, the word was blasted into cyber-space where a million news-hungry keyboard-punching Internet enthusiasts would find it and read it. One man's scoop would last a fraction of a second before it became every man's knowledge. Ben wasn't even going to mention it in his own office. Reporters were bloody notorious gossips among themselves.

"So what we gonna do?" he asked.

"God knows," said his contact. "Every time I look at these photographs I know these wounds are the work of the same hand. I know it's a serial killer. Then every time I think of the perfectly sound conviction of each of those four men, I know they must be guilty. Hell, one of them pleaded guilty. I need to be more convinced in my own mind before we do anything else. Tell you what, you go back through your files, and reread everything keeping in mind the murder being done not by the suspect, but by our theoretical serial killer. See if that throws up anything different."

"I'll go through these autopsy reports again, and I'll see what I can find."

And that's how they left it.

Ben drove away, with his heart beating harder. This could be so big. He didn't pull into his usual spot and write up any notes. This had gone beyond writing notes. He got back into the office and pulled out the four files—Bereson, Braithwaite, Shepherd and Warnoski. He pulled two new hanging folders from his cache in his bottom drawer and housed the four bulky files inside, creating a new file. He called it the "Theo" file—volumes one and two, "Theo" for "theoretical serial killer," so no one would have any clue what it was. He did so enjoy working with these files. He went back into his "murder list" index and amended all four separate files to indicate they were now to be found in "Drawer 8, the 'Theo' file."

"Don't suppose you've got any copy for today, have you?" asked Frank half-hoping, half-sarcastically, "You've been gone long enough."

"Not for today. But one of these days I'll have a doosie," said Ben, already inwardly dreaming of the day he'd break the story, the four-pager, no six-pager, no probably the eight-pager they'd need for him to relate the entire scoop.

"Great. Well, in the meantime, bash out a couple of shorts on these. We have got a paper to get out for tomorrow, you know," said Frank. He threw Ben a couple of press releases on a new bandit who'd been robbing stores disguised as a blind man complete with white stick, and a fatal road crash on the Trans-Canada Highway where a car driver had rear-ended and gone under a semi-trailer truck. The RCMP believed one factor was the car driver's inattention to the road, as he was on his cell-phone at the time of the collision.

Chapter 6

Two nights later, absolutely in the middle of the night, in bed, in that half dream-like half wishful-thinking state when he always landed his biggest fish, and saw himself filming his biggest infernos, Ben suddenly saw the whole serial-killer shocker in his mind. The whole, total, complete, diabolical, mind-blowing answer came in a flash.

He got out of bed, naked, went into the living room, still naked, sat down on the cold wooden chair, still naked, and drew four pictures. And he knew he had it. He was going to get Ron Lincoln out of prison, and Darren Sunderland with him, and Paul Andres too, and even the stupid Rev. Jacob Broadbent, who Ben now knew had confessed to a murder he never did.

"Fucking right on. Fucking magic," said Ben out loud to himself.

And not having any idea how he'd get through the next few hours of the night before he could take his findings to his contact, he went back to bed, still naked, and tried fitfully to sleep, as best as he could with his mind exploding with excitement.

At 8:01 a. m., knowing his contact was punctually at work at 8 o'clock every day, Ben called him.

"I've got to come and see you right now—right now. I've got what we need. I'm on my way," he blurted out.

"Wait a minute, calm down, first, what have you got?" said his contact quietly.

"I can't tell you over the phone, I'm coming right now."

"It won't do you any good coming over right now. There are bodies over here that need attending to, this is a medical examiner's office, you know. The earliest I can be free is half past nine. Be here then, okay."

"Right, right, right on," said Ben, inwardly groaning.

It took at least 24 hours for the next 90 minutes to pass with Ben driving over to the medical examiner's building and eventually being called into his contact's inner office. He had sat for ages in the foyer with the picturesque fountain giving him the urge to take a piss. Running water had that effect on him, and then, finally he was ushered in, clutching his two volumes of the "Theo" file and the four pictures he'd drawn, naked in the night.

"Look at this," said Ben, waving at his contact to sit down in his own office, while Ben prepared his evidence.

"You remember you first showed me the photographs of Warnoski up in Red Deer, with all those wounds, including a group of three slashes shaped like, well, a mountain top with straight line clouds off the peak in both directions," he began.

"Well, yes, I remember," said his contact, "but I don't know about a mountain peak, that's pretty fanciful, they could be just haphazard frenzied slashes, too, you know."

"Hang on," said Ben. "You remember next we looked at the photos of Bereson on the golf course in Calgary, and she had some small slashes shaped like a wooden chair, sort of standing upright."

"Ummm, I do," said his contact, fearing this was drifting off into outer space somewhere when he was hoping for something down to earth.

Ben was in full cry.

"You remember, third, we looked at Braithwaite, you know, down in Pincher Creek, with the whip lashes, but with that strange sort of human eye shape carved on her buttock that was almost sliced off." Ben glanced up to make sure his contact was nodding in acknowledgement, and went on. "Lastly, we looked at Shepherd, where the killer had underscored the shape of her breast with a curved arc."

"Okay, I remember all those," said his contact. "I don't see what you're driving at yet, because they could just be random slashes, not these exotic shapes of yours."

"Wait a minute, wait a minute, I haven't started yet," said Ben.

"First we have to put the shapes in the right chronological order of the murders—Bereson, Braithwaite, Shepherd, and Warnoski—okay.

That is 'upright wooden chair', 'sideways human eye', 'underscored breast', and 'mountain top with straight line clouds."

Ben was absolutely bursting with excitement, his hands were shaking, and his ear lobes were flushing red.

"Turn the upright wooden chair on its side," he said, rotating his middle-of-the-night drawing on his contact's table. "What do you see?"

"Well, it could be the letter 'J'," said his contact, haltingly.

"Now, turn the sideways human eye to face downward," said Ben, rotating his next drawing downward.

"That's a letter 'A'," said his contact, "I can see that."

"Turn the underscored breast on its side," he said, rotating his third drawing, like a magician producing the ace of spades from a pack of 52 cards right on cue.

"Christ, that's the letter 'C'," said his contact, hardly believing his own eyes.

"And then, turn the mountain top and clouds on its side," said Ben, rotating his fourth drawing.

"It's the letter 'K'," said his contact. "J-A-C-K." "Oh my God, the killer carved his name into his victims and we didn't see it."

Ben's contact leaped up, cracking his knee on the corner of the table, and grabbed the four murder autopsy files, spilling them in a heap on his table, burying Ben's drawing, as he pulled out the four photograph albums.

"I've got to see this on the photographs," he said.

He took the four best shots of the four shapes and rotated them each the right way up, and there was the name "J-A-C-K" staring at him. Now it could be seen, they clearly were not random frenzied slashes. All the other mutilations on the bodies were large and deep, and these were uniformly smaller, four little signatures—one letter for each body.

"I haven't finished yet," said Ben, his knees tingling with anticipation.

"I don't know everything about serial killers but I've read books by serial killer profilers, and I know they say these killers love the publicity they generate. Usually when they're failures in other walks of life, they love to be remembered for their prowess in their new gruesome field."

"Well, I don't think this guy's name is Jack. I think he's laying the preparation work for his notoriety when his crimes eventually come to light," said Ben.

"What do you mean?" asked his contact.

"Well, all his victims are Jills. All four of them, you remember. See, JACK and JILL. He's going to be known forever as the JACK and JILL killer, the media's going to immortalize him, they'll write books, and they'll make films. He'll be more famous than the Son of Sam, or the Green River killer."

The two men stared at each other.

"Unbelievable," said Ben's contact.

"Fucking right on," said Ben.

Once again, the sheer enormity of what they'd stumbled on appalled them. Four innocent men were in jail right now. Each had been convicted of an horrific murder in different corners of the province, put there by the careful work of four different police forces backed up by four different teams of forensic scientists. All had been convicted on irrefutable DNA evidence, and all went through four different courts, and not one of them should be inside. Ben and his contact could prove these four murders were the work of one killer, one serial killer, not these four different men. It didn't mean they could shed any light on who the killer was, they could only shine a floodlight on the injustice which had wronged these four innocents.

It took them a week to put their remarkable discovery in some sort of understandable and logical argument. Ben often used to take fanciful theories to Stone in his homicide office about some unsolved murder. Stone would look over his glasses, shake his head and dismiss him, saying, "Ben, Ben, Ben." But this time, Ben was going to be bringing Stone the most fanciful story the staff sergeant would have ever heard. And he was taking his contact with him, a professional who he knew Stone respected, to present his evidence. They decided to break the news first to Stone in Calgary, as they knew him best. The RCMP could come later. As well, the first of the four murders, the slaying of Jill Bereson on the golf course near Sikome Lake, was Stone's case.

Ben enjoyed being in Stone's office. He'd helped scramble around on the floor under the two desks shifting cables and wires when Stone chose to move his computer around. He wanted to be able to work on line, and see through the Venetian blinded window into the main homicide office at the same time. What's more, hanging on his walls he had oil paintings of a Super Sabre and an F-18 Tomcat bursting through the clouds and diving on the enemy. Right on!

Setting up this meet, Ben had told Stone it was about the Bereson murder, the one Darren Sunderland had been convicted of, the torture case. As Ben and his contact sat down, Ben saw Stone had an old cardboard box at his desk side, curled and torn along the top edge with Bereson, 1990, written along the side.

Ben had his "Theo" file at his side.

"Darren Sunderland didn't do it," said Ben.

"Ben, Ben, Ben," said Stone, taking his glasses off altogether and dropping his chin onto his chest.

"Listen, we can prove it," said Ben, and once he'd started he was surprised how simple it sounded. It was so straight-forward.

"The killer who tortured and mutilated Jill Bereson on the golf course carved the letter 'J' into her body," said Ben.

Stone interrupted, lifting his head up suddenly and raising one hand, "I never heard anything about that, don't you think if that was the case we'd have been told," he said.

"Wait a minute. Listen. We'll tell you about that in a minute. We've got the photographs to prove all this. Take it from me the killer carved the letter 'J' into her body with his knife."

"A year later, in Pincher Creek, this same killer murdered another woman, mutilated her and this time he carved the letter 'A' into her body."

"Ben, Ben, Ben," Stone started shaking his head.

"We've got the photographs. You haven't heard a fraction of it yet," said Ben.

"Later that same year in Taber the serial killer responsible for all these murders struck again, murdering another woman, mutilating her, and this time he carved the letter 'C' into the body."

"And in 1992, the same serial killer murdered his fourth victim in Red Deer, and this time he carved the letter 'K' into her body. He carved the name J-A-C-K into the four women, there's no doubt about it, look."

Stone put his glasses back on. He wasn't dismissing Ben this time, he was listening. That didn't mean he believed it, but he was listening.

Ben's contact leaned down into his briefcase and brought out the four familiar manila files he and Ben had pored over so carefully for so long.

"Here's Jill Bereson," said the contact, putting down and carefully rotating the vital photograph so the letter "J" hit Stone in the face.

"I see that, yes," said Stone. "Why didn't we see that before?"

"Keen was the chief medical examiner in 1990, it was his case, and I think these slashes were simply taken as part of the general mutilation," said Ben's contact, defending his office. He put the other Bereson photographs in front of Stone, showing the mass of slashes and slices and burns which had so hideously disfigured the victim's corpse. Stone recalled the photographs. He recalled seeing the mutilations on the body itself. Seen in context with the rest of the corpse the three little slashes didn't stand out at all. No wonder they weren't noticed.

"Let me see the others," he said, realizing he had to concede that this photograph did appear to show what Ben had described.

Ben's contact brought out the relevant close-up photographs of the "A" carved into Angela Braithwaite's mutilated body in Pincher Creek, the "C" curving under the breast of Angel Shepherd's body in Taber, and the "K" carved into Gillian Warnoski's body in Red Deer.

"My God," said Stone, and this time his whole body slumped in his chair.

"There's just a little more," said Ben. "This next bit isn't as definite as the pictures, but I think this is right. All the four victims were called Jill. Yours was Jill Bereson, the two women in Pincher Creek and Taber had 'Jill' as their nicknames, and the Red Deer victim was Gillian. We think this guy wanted to be known as the 'Jack and Jill' serial killer so he'd be famous. It kind of ties all the ends together."

Ben had spent many hours listening carefully to Stone's philosophy of solving murders, how nothing made sense until every tiny detail fitted exactly into the whole picture. If nearly everything built neatly into a theory but one detail wouldn't fit, then the theory was wrong. Start again. Here was the theory. One serial killer, picking out four women called Jill, and carving "J-A-C-K" one by one into their corpses—fine. Except Ben had to concede there was a tiny detail that didn't yet exactly fit the picture. Four other men had been convicted of the murders, three on rock-solid DNA evidence, and one on his own confession, and were in jail serving their time even as Stone, Ben and his contact were sitting, speaking.

Stone must have been reading Ben's mind.

"We've got a guy convicted for ours, what about the other three?" he asked.

"Yes, three others convicted, including one who pleaded guilty," said Ben's contact.

Not for the first time, Stone looked at Ben with that deep thoughtful stare that looked through him, like there was a chart to be studied somewhere behind his head and the only access was through Ben's eyes, and in a quieter tone he said again, "Ben, Ben, Ben."

Stone removed his glasses again. He'd listened. He still didn't necessarily believe, but, if nothing else, there was now this one detail in the conviction of Darren Sunderland, the man his team had put behind bars, that didn't fit his original whole picture. Sunderland's victim, Jill Bereson, the White Spot Restaurant waitress, had the initial "J" carved into her abdomen, clearly one of this series of four initials carved by the same killer. Yet Sunderland was arrested and in the Remand Centre awaiting trial at the time the other women were murdered. Either Sunderland was one of two conspiring murderers running around at the same time carving strange initials in women's bodies—nah—or he was innocent. Stone was thinking of his own golden rule. If one detail doesn't fit the theory, find a new theory. This case was becoming a bastard. The first theory had already landed a guy inside for life. Now Stone might have to start looking at a new theory—Sunderland may have been innocent. His mind was in turmoil.

He was a methodical man. A lot would have to happen before he'd even think about approaching other police jurisdictions about their homicides. He must sort out his own case first—that was the top priority. He would call in the team who worked on it. He'd run this lot past them, and study every detail again. So far, nothing about all this made sense. Stone's instincts were usually good. Alarm bells sounded early for him if his men were chasing wrong leads. He hadn't had so much as a single inkling anything was wrong with this one back in November 1990. Even without consulting a file, he remembered it clearly. There was Sunderland's DNA on the cigarette butt in the victim's vagina. There was the victim's blood in Sunderland's truck. Sunderland's golf club established forensically as the murder weapon. Sunderland with his background of rape, knew the victim from her restaurant, and he was comfortable with the golf course where the body was dumped. Open and shut. Every detail fitted the picture. In fact, Ben remembered Stone had only recently used this murder in one of his renowned homicide seminars for the media. Ben had been to everyone.

At one of them, Stone had passed round the room at the police training academy where the media had been summoned, a sheet of paper on which was a picture of a house brick.

"I want every one of you to suggest some way of using a house brick in a crime," he said.

All 30 reporters jotted down their thoughts, and Stone went round the room, gathering the answers.

"Hit someone over the head with it," was a winner. "Throw it through a window for a smash-and-grab," was another. But further down the list were some far more obscure suggestions. "Use it to weigh down the body when you put it in the river," read one, and "get it red hot in a fireplace then put in on a sofa to start a big blaze," was another.

Stone was triumphant.

He filled his blackboard with the answers, like a keen first year student teacher, then showed the media what he was driving at.

"I do this with homicides," he said.

"If the two main investigators have a set of circumstances to work with, and they interpret them to discover what happened, they come up with a maximum of two possibilities."

"If I throw the problem out to the entire unit of say eight guys, I'll get eight possible answers. You've just proved it. Each one of you came up with only one answer. Collectively we came up with 30 possibilities. It works."

The seminars were eye-openers for reporters, even those who reckoned they'd seen it all. Stone used crime scene photographs, gory body shots, and explicit close-ups. All the time he was teaching reporters to understand what homicide investigators are confronted with, with the aim of helping reporters ask sensible questions. These seminars were supposed to last three hours, and always, as the three hour mark passed, Stone would still be referring to new photographs, and reporters would be still sitting, enthralled.

And so it was that the case of Jill Bereson, murdered by Darren Sunderland, became seminar material. Stone had used its classic qualities to teach his audience the true value of what might appear at first to be routine investigative techniques. In this case, he had one team check the records of the restaurant where the victim was a waitress, and came up with a list of regulars. It was boring, but necessary. Then he had another team draw up a list of all the members of the golf course where the victim's body was dumped. That was equally boring, but equally necessary.

When the two lists threw up a name in common, one Darren Sunderland, it was a start. When forensic science and DNA proved he was the killer, the true value of the boring routine investigative techniques was immediately self-evident.

One day, thought Ben, this Bereson-Sunderland homicide might end up in a very different seminar, illustrating a very different point.

Stone sensed Ben and his contact had come to the end of the case for the prosecution.

"Look, leave this with me, and I'll get back to you," he said.

But he couldn't resist one last jibe, his mind still squirming uncomfortably that these two had come into his world and clearly enjoyed dropping their potential bombshell.

"Now you reckon we convicted the wrong guy, and you reckon you know for sure some serial killer murdered our woman and a bunch of others," he said, staring for effect over the top of his glasses, "I suppose, you're going to give me the name of the killer as a throwaway afterthought on your way out the door, eh?"

"Nah, I'm saving that for my story in tomorrow's paper," said Ben.

"Get out, you little bastard," said Stone.

The wheels had been set in motion.

Chapter 7

Ben and his contact left, not really knowing what would happen next. Before the elevator at police headquarters had deposited them at the ground floor lobby, Ben felt the first gnawing fear in his gut that whatever actions Stone was about to initiate might tip some other alert reporter out there that something big was in the air.

Ben's visit sparked some busy weeks for Stone. Though the other three murders handled by the RCMP were at different detachments, at Pincher Creek, at Taber and at Red Deer, the set up with the Mounties meant detectives from the major crimes unit based in Calgary dealt with all three. Stone started there.

It was difficult situations like the one Stone was facing here that had prematurely caused his hair to grey and recede rapidly, though he consoled himself with the fact it really only looked like he had a high forehead, which foretold wisdom, so it was said.

He met with Sgt. Max Novak, who headed up the RCMP major crimes unit in his office in an anonymous brick building in northeast Calgary. Between a pair of extremely bland insurance offices on the ground floor, and a seldom visited acupuncture center and herbal plant consultant's office on the third floor, you'd hardly know the nerve-center of the RCMP criminal unit for all southern Alberta took up the second floor. Stone and Novak crossed the main open plan office, went into Novak's private room and closed the plain brown door. Novak fitted in perfectly with his dull grey office surroundings. Younger than Stone, thinner than Stone, still with a head of black hair neatly combed, of course, he sat down, at once looking guarded and defensive, as is the RCMP's perpetual disposition.

Stone had come with a strategy which he launched once the two heads of homicide had exchanged social pleasantries.

"Okay, so what brings you up here to the northeast?" asked Novak, genuinely surprised to see Stone, when no ongoing case was occupying both forces jointly at the moment.

"You have got a problem," said Stone. Up went Novak's black eyebrows, and his mouth opened to speak, but Stone beat him to it.

"You've got a problem, and we've got a problem. You're not gonna like it, just listen. I'll let you in on our problem first."

"It seems there's a good chance, well, more than a good chance we probably convicted an innocent man in one of our homicides."

Inwardly, Stone decided there and then the only way to make all this work was to stop all this careful pussy-footing around and come right out with it.

"Shit. Let me tell you. We did. We convicted the wrong guy."

Novak's mind raced. First Stone said the RCMP had a problem. Now it was clear the city cops had the problem, and here was Stone obviously looking for RCMP help to get them off the hook.

"Yep, you sure do got a problem, how the fuck did you manage that?" he asked, just a touch of smugness in his voice when it was clear Stone was wriggling over this obvious city problem.

"Hang on," said Stone, taking off his glasses and stroking his clean-shaven pointed chin, "I haven't started yet."

"Look, we got this one wrong, but I think, I don't know for sure, but I think you guys may have got three wrong."

Novak was up out of his chair. His eyebrows were up, he was up, his anger was up, smugness gone. He started pacing behind his chair.

"What the fuck is this? So you guys cocked one up and you're throwing mud at everyone so yours won't look so bad, no way." Novak had instantly gone into the well-practiced RCMP total defensive mode—deny everything and attack everyone else.

"Sit down Max, calm down and listen," said Stone, now stroking his high, wise forehead.

"As part of our inquiry into our one that's definitely wrong, we're trying to confirm some suspicions we've got, but I need to see the files on three of yours, the three I think may be wrong as well."

Novak sat, his grey suit, white shirt and dull tie fading into the room, but with his eyes glaring.

"Which ones? Which three? This is fucking crazy. I don't believe this."

"Okay," said Stone, pulling out his notebook.

"Angela Braithwaite, Pincher Creek, February 1991; Angel Shepherd, Taber, July 1991 and Gillian Warnoski, Red Deer, January 1992."

"No way, no, no, no, you've got it wrong. I know those three cases. They're good. Okay, I'll get the files right now, I know I'm right. The files will prove me right. You might have a problem, but we don't have any problem, not with those three. Wait here," and he was up and going for the door.

Stone sat, shaking his head, listening to Novak dragging open cabinet drawers and slamming them shut in the main office. He was back quickly, three thick files under his arm.

"Here you go. Braithwaite. We got Paul Andres convicted, serving life. It was a no-brainer once we found the whip he used to strangle her. You're wrong there, Ed, sorry, you're plain wrong."

He shoved his file to one side, slapping it with his hand in an air of finality, like they wouldn't have to worry about that one again.

"Okay, Shepherd. Fuck Ed, the Reverend Jacob Broadbent confessed to that one—pleaded guilty, guilty to first-degree murder. You're out in left field with that one. And Warnoski, no way, Ronnie Lincoln did her. Fuck, we got his DNA. Hey, Ed, we got DNA in both these two. There's no way…"

Stone persisted. A ton of work needed to be done and it had to start with this meeting. He had to convince Novak.

"I know, I know," said Stone. "I've been through all this with ours. We had DNA, we had matching blood, we had solid forensic on the vehicle used, we could put the victim with the killer, the killer with the dump site, but I'm worried we still got the wrong guy in the slammer. He's still doing time today."

"I think, we think, we've been at this for some time, we think the four murders we're talking about, ours plus your three, we think they were all the work of the same serial killer. We put one innocent guy in jail and we think you may have put three away, and they could all be innocent."

As Stone talked, Novak studied the three files desperately seeking a way of showing Stone how wrong he was.

"Look Ed, you can't be right. Look at this. We had our guy charged in that first one in Pincher Creek before the second one you're talking about even happened in Taber. We had the first guy charged, for Christ's sake. And then

Broadbent had confessed to the second one even before the Red Deer murder happened. You got it wrong, Ed."

"Well, humor me. I need to know, with your three, did the same detectives catch all three? I'm just wondering if they saw any similarities."

Shaking his head, Novak checked the three files. No help there. As in every homicide unit, the primary detectives were assigned to homicides in rotation, and when these three murders came in each was picked up by a different team.

"Sorry Ed. Three different teams, Christ, they were 11 months apart."

Novak was astounded to hear all this from the head of city homicide. If Stone was prepared to admit they were wrong, perhaps he ought to listen. But it didn't make any sense. He didn't believe. He didn't want to believe, but he could see Stone wasn't going to leave it alone.

"Well, what's next?" asked Novak.

"I want to pull together my team that worked on our one with your three teams who worked on your three, plus you and me, a joint task force, and let's start again at the beginning," said Stone. "And we've got to keep the whole damn thing quiet."

"You're not fucking joking," said Novak, hardly daring to imagine the effect if Stone was right and the shit hit the fan over this lot.

And so, before Stone left Novak's office that day, plans for the "Operation Whiskey Foxtrot" task force were put in place, "W F" being much preferred instead of "Wrong Four."

Stone and Novak's very first joint decision was that the task force couldn't meet either at the city police homicide office nor the RCMP's anonymous domain. A sudden gathering of detectives at either location would excite too much interest. But the city police training center, a nondescript gathering of buildings set in their own grounds behind a screen of trees in southwest Calgary was ideal. Officers on fairly obscure courses were sent there and seemingly disappeared off the face of the earth for weeks on end. Few people ever saw the trickle of cars occasionally disappearing into the facility's long driveway, and even fewer cared.

On the first day of "Whiskey Foxtrot" operations, the dozen or so detectives from the RCMP and city homicide units had no clue why they had been summoned to the training center. Their few cars turned into the long driveway of this pleasantly green facility and they left their cars dotted haphazardly in the spacious parking lot. Most of them had never seen this building before. What the hell was going on?

Inside, it was like being back at school with school-like corridors and school-like classrooms off to either side. A cryptic "WF" and an arrow on a poster-sized sheet of card guided them into their classroom for the day.

After the first 20 minutes of that first meeting, every hardened detective in the room, each seasoned, cynical veteran knew exactly what the hell was going on. Ed Stone had shocked them with his bombshell. He blacked out the room and threw up a slide of long parallel slashes on the body of Jill Bereson found on a golf course in Calgary. Click—blackness—click, a slide of long parallel slashes on the body of Angela Braithwaite near Highway 3 in Pincher Creek. Click—blackness—click, a slide of long parallel slashes on the body of Angel Shepherd, found near an oil installation at Taber. Click—blackness,—click, a slide of long parallel slashes on the body of Gillian Warnoski, found on a traffic island at Red Deer. The four separate teams of detectives, who'd each seen their own victim's wounds in the morgue, couldn't believe their eyes. And Stone was only 10 minutes into this introduction.

"This is Bereson," he said. Click—a slide of bloody mutilation on her body, as a large letter "J" filled the screen.

"This is Braithwaite." Click—a slide of mutilation on her body as a large letter "A" filled the screen.

"This is Shepherd." Click—a slide of mutilation on her body as a large letter "C" filled the screen.

"And this is Warnoski." Click—a slide of mutilation on her body as a large letter "K" filled the screen.

Stone had one last slide. Click—He'd arranged the last four slides in a line, so every man in the room could read the hideous "JACK" in bloody, ragged letters carved into the victims' bodies.

Stone switched the lights on. There was a stunned silence, and then everybody spoke at once. Despite what they had just seen, each detective individually and each team collectively knew they hadn't been wrong. It was bad luck for Stone to have picked their particular murder, because of all the cases they had solved in recent years, these were their most cast-iron. So they thought. Stone had destroyed all that with nine clicks of his projector. Every man in the room could see this was the work of the same man, the signature of a serial killer, taunting them with his "JACK," like he was already as notorious and infamous as Jack the Ripper. But he was cleverer. He had four innocent men all behind bars, all serving life for the crimes he had committed. He'd used these professionals in this room, the elite in their field, to do his work for him. Where had they gone wrong? What kind of outcry would there be when the outside world discovered? Who the hell was Jack? Had he killed any more they didn't know about? What about the four poor bastards still inside, and their families? Stone let the clamor rise until the initial shock had passed, then took command of the room again.

"Here's the game plan," he said, dropping the white plastic projector screen, and turning to his blackboard, where his four-point plan was already written in white chalk.

1) Understand and admit we convicted four wrong men.

2) Study everything about each case, to see what wrong assumptions we made.

3) Realize we are hunting a single serial killer.

4) Identify and arrest him.

It had taken Stone 20 minutes to complete the first enormous phase, and now he launched the teams into phase two. His plan was simple. Each team which had worked on one of the homicides would now review one of the other team's investigations. It was pointless to have men check their own work. If mistakes had been made, they'd hardly find their own.

At the end of the day, these detectives went away carrying the files of murders they hadn't worked before with a strange mission—trying to pick holes in what fellow colleagues had done. Stone had covered that. He told each man not to feel uncomfortable at finding mistakes in another detective's work, after all someone was looking to find his mistakes at the same time. And when the full weight of this scandal blew, the only saving grace would be that by then, the men in this task force would have corrected the injustice and would have found the right killer.

Months of work followed. It was a period of hard slogging for the Whiskey Foxtrot teams, and a nerve-racking period of strain for Ben. He could only guess how many teams of detectives were at work all over the province, and if any one detective let slip what he was working on, and it reached the long antenna of any media, Ben would be screwed.

Ben threw himself into his own work. Luckily, a string of half decent stories broke, including two crackers. Seattle experienced an earthquake. And a band of incredible modern-day warriors took on the power of the government of the United States of America in Montana. Both times, Ben's exuberance when the stories broke persuaded Frank to let him go—even though they were in the States and it would cost money. Both times, Ben paired up with Kenny Wright, the "Mr. Dependable" of the Mail's photographers. Ben enjoyed working with Kenny. He was big-built, many thought bordering on being tubby, but Ben knew it was all muscle. Kenny worked out regularly and always seemed to be carrying far more equipment than any other photographer. Once he'd asked Ben to lift his pack and gear into his SUV. Ben struggled to lift it. Kenny carried the whole lot round on his shoulders all day. Most of the time, Kenny was a smooth guy, making friends easily with women he met on stories. But when he was angry, watch out. Ben remembered one day when a cop car-chase had ended with the drug dealer driver crashing into a southwest Calgary median and cops were piling in to arrest him. Kenny had stayed with the chase. Now he abandoned his SUV in the middle of the road and was running the final yards to capture the arrest on film. At that moment, the uniformed duty inspector, who happened to be on scene, ordered whoever this annoying member of the public was to get back in his SUV, and move it out of the road—NOW! Kenny did so, and missed the picture. It had been his bad luck to run into Duty Inspector Conrad Golding, the scourge of media in Calgary. Golding didn't like the media, he didn't help the media, he was short-tempered and plain nasty with media, some he even hated—which was a real bastard as one of the ingredients of his job-description was media liaison! A few minutes later Ben arrived at the scene and soon learned what Golding had done. Thinking maybe Golding hadn't realized this "annoying member of the public" was a veteran Mail photographer, Ben stood there in the road and formally introduced Kenny to Golding. Realizing he'd been wrong in his hasty action, Golding stepped forward right there in the road and in front of everyone extended his hand for a handshake of apology.

Kenny took a step back, folded his arms resolutely across his powerful chest, refusing the handshake, stared hard at Golding, then turned and walked away to his SUV. Forever afterward in Ben's eyes, Kenny was the man who had "out-nastied" Golding. Right on!

Ben always thought Kenny would have made a decent reporter. On any assignment, Kenny always chatted to everyone on the scene, and often found witnesses who had good copy to add to the story. He would sidle over to Ben, give him the nod, and Ben would always follow up, getting more useful nuggets from Kenny's witness.

Getting to the Seattle earthquake was half the battle in the first place. The plan was for the pair to fly from Calgary to Seattle, hire a car and do the business. That was until Ben discovered Seattle international airport had been knocked out by the earthquake. It seemed pilots weren't too happy landing and taking off on a runway with a damn great split running the length of it.

Ben and Kenny switched to "Plan B." They flew from Calgary to Vancouver, hired a car at Vancouver International and drove to Seattle. Ben was happy. This would be his first ever earthquake. He'd covered most natural disasters—even a rare tornado. He was there at the major tornado which killed 12 campers alongside an Alberta lake. In the midst of that terrible tragedy, Ben had two memories. He'd found a house-owner living at the far edge of the lake with the most incredible story. The tornado had picked up a boat in the lake, whirled it into the sky with its anchor swinging beneath it on the end of its anchor rope. As the boat flew completely over the man's house, the trailing anchor, far below, crashed through his upstairs bedroom window and embedded itself in the opposite bedroom wall. Ben used this tiny detail to illustrate the full power of a killer tornado. On the same day, Ben shocked his whole office. Everyone knew Ben's tunnel vision excluded anything political. He knew everything about death and destruction, but nothing about politics, political parties or politicians. That world never even existed or registered in his mind. So, in the middle of the devastation at the tornado, when rescuers were still pulling bodies from the wreckage around him, Ben saw a helicopter fly in and land. Out stepped a man Ben thought he vaguely recognized. Yes, he did. He interviewed the man, and sent back his copy. Ben had only recognized and interviewed Mr. Stockwell Day, leader of the Canadian Alliance Party. Stunned staff in the newsroom simply couldn't believe their Ben Ludlow, the most politically ignorant man in the industry, had pulled off this scoop.

In other natural disasters, Ben had waded through one of the mighty Red River floods in Manitoba which sank half the province; he'd been to more deadly avalanches than he could remember; a catastrophic mudslide in the B.C. interior; wind-storms, hail-storms, snow-storms, and forest wildfires in England, Canada and the States—but never an earthquake. He had visions of what they'd find—collapsed buildings, survivors trapped under tons of rubble with rescue teams searching for them, roads split open, half the population destitute out in the streets with their homes in ruins, and who knows what kind of death toll?

They arrived at night. Next morning things started badly and got worse. Kenny threw them into an international crisis. As they pulled into a store to get Kenny's first coffee of the day, he left the engine running, locked the hire car and—oh shit! They were locked out of the vehicle.

"You know, Kenny, here we are in the United States of America, locked out of a vehicle we hired in Canada," said Ben, idly musing whether it could be a tricky problem.

Fine start, that was. Things deteriorated. Ben discovered Seattle had survived the earthquake perfectly well. Very occasionally, here and there, he found a few bricks scattered across a sidewalk, neatly cordoned off with barriers. He found an industrial site with a flooded parking lot where underground water pipes had burst, but that was about it. He did get invited into the basement of a store where the floor was bulging upward several feet as if a huge volcano underneath it was bursting to get out, but Ben didn't stay in there very long. He couldn't see any point in risking his life for a story. That was one of his golden rules.

By using all his experience of journalistic license, which Kenny reckoned was one third imagination, one third exaggeration and one third plain bullshit, Ben succeeded in sending back tons of copy. They'd worked well as a team, and Kenny transmitted back a bunch of pictures, nearly all of which related to the incidents Ben had so enthusiastically described. It was a good "earthquake package" for the Mail. It was a big disappointment for Ben—he hadn't found a single fatality, and not even one grieving family.

But a week later he was up to his neck in copy with the Freemen of Montana, which was a great story. It had all the ingredients. Militiamen armed to the teeth with an arsenal of weaponry, the FBI and police SWAT teams, helicopters overhead, directives from the President of the Unites States, and all the hype of every USA media outlet camped out on a hilltop overlooking the valley of action. It was much like being on the set of a Hollywood movie.

For the Mail, there was one God-send. One of the Freemen was a former Alberta resident, which made the whole story completely valid for a Calgary newspaper. Basically, this bunch of strong-willed characters had set themselves up in a Montana valley, which they declared was their own "sovereign territory" outside the federal laws or jurisdiction of the United States. For the authorities, this was a nuisance, but acceptable until the Freemen decided the US monetary system didn't exist, and invented their own. They flooded the nation with millions of dollars' worth of very unusual cheques. That brought the FBI down on the backs with warrants for arrests for fraud and related charges. All that was left now was for the FBI to go into the "sovereign territory" and arrest them.

So began the siege of the Freemen. The FBI didn't want to go in with guns blazing, and have bloodshed on their hands, so they surrounded the valley, and sealed it off. From day one, the US media laid siege to a hilltop overlooking the valley where they could observe the FBI laying siege to the Freemen.

This had gone on for 80 days when the ranks of the media on the hilltop were swelled by two more men—Ben and Kenny. Ben had received a tip that this was the day the FBI, the SWAT teams, and maybe even the US military, were going to get the Freemen out. The Mail reckoned it couldn't afford the great expense of flying Ben and Kenny to the scene. They'd have to drive in Kenny's SUV. No problem there, they could share the driving and after all, it was only several hundred kilometers. Timing was a problem. They had to be on scene before the epic FBI operation was launched. Speed was essential— the very point that Ben and Kenny were now trying hard to explain to the border guard at the Canada-United States border.

After he'd asked the usual routine questions, he then stared at Kenny, and told him to drive to the side of the border crossing building. Kenny and Ben showed the guard their media accreditation, all their documents, copies of the wire-stories about the Freemen which proved that was where they were headed, but to no avail. This guard was convinced Kenny was no media photographer, but instead was a crooked camera dealer smuggling a ton of camera equipment over the border to sell in the States without paying the applicable duty. Kenny was given two alternatives. Either he could forfeit all the camera gear in the vehicle, or list it, every piece, serial number by serial number, and leave the list at the border. That way, when he returned in a few days, the guards could check the gear in the vehicle with the list to make sure he hadn't sold any of it south of the border. Only when Kenny started listing his gear, did Ben start to understand what a mass of equipment photographers had to carry. His cases held a bunch of different camera bodies, each with a bunch of different lenses, and filters, and light meters and tripods and lights and specialist containers to pack them in—and all with their own serial numbers. And all the time they sat listing serial numbers, Ben had visions of SWAT teams swooping on the Freemen with helicopter gun-ships overhead and tanks rolling, and every other media in on the action except him and Kenny.

It took more than an hour. When they finally drove on into the States, the guard shouted after them, "Have a nice day."

"Bastard," muttered Ben under his breath, not being brave enough to say it out loud.

They got to "Media Hill" in time. It was an incredible sight. Row upon row of photographers, each with his camera perched atop a tripod stuck into the hilltop, surrounded by cases of extra lenses and equipment. Those who had been there the longest had little camps constructed, with food supplies, and vital coolers with cold drinks to combat the scorching heat. Some had been sweltering there all 80 days. Many had support teams in a fleet of huge vehicles not far away. It was a giant media army. Kenny picked a rare spot of available grass on the hilltop and planted his tripod proudly to stand with the rest. He placed his silver metal chest alongside it which contained all his recently checked and immaculately documented equipment. He fitted in perfectly, looking every bit the professional he was. You would never know he hadn't been there for 80 days like the photographers on either side of him—except his legs in his shorts were white-skinned and all the others were darkly tanned.

Ben sweltered. It was frying hot on that hill. Some of the 80-day guys had constructed heavy-duty awnings and were standing alongside their tripods in the shade. Everyone was in short-sleeve shirts. Ben's was unbuttoned down to his navel. Ben wore a baseball cap to protect his bald spot from sunburn. Every camera lens, mostly at least a yard long it seemed to Ben, was pointed down into the valley. Every few moments, a photographer would lean, one eye closed, against his camera and peer through the lens into the sun to see if there was any movement beneath them. Ben trained his binoculars in the same direction. And so the day progressed. Peer, strain eyes, wait, get hotter, get thirstier, peer some more, wait some more…it was a pain after the first 80 minutes. Pity these guys who'd been here 80 days!

And then, it happened.

The movement, when it came, wasn't from down in the valley at all. It was far off to the right, along the road which led from civilization to "Media Hill."

A bright yellow Schwarz ice-cream van drove toward the hill. A reporter from the Washington Post reacted first. He couldn't have acted faster if it was one of the Freemen escaping from the siege. In a flash, he had bounded down Media Hill, out into the road, and was standing there waving his arms up and down. The ice-cream van pulled to a stop short of the Washington Post.

"I want ice-creams for every person on the hill," said Washington, gesturing with a dramatic sweep of his arm up the hill to the row upon row of cameras. The ice-cream man, delighted, couldn't believe his ears. Every reporter and photographer on the hill was elated. Soon the hill was awash with ice-cream—welcome, cooling, smooth, cold, delicious ice-cream. It was the highlight of the year for the Washington Post. Every reporter worth his salt that day wrote about the ice-cream, and credited the Washington Post. However bad it looked on that guy's expenses sheet "ice-cream while on location…$210" the paper reaped the rewards in good press across North America. It was the biggest ice-cream scoop of all time.

Next to that, the end of the siege was rather ordinary. The Freemen surrendered, the FBI arrested them all, not a shot was fired, and the waiting media was treated to a convoy of vehicles emerging out of the valley toward "Media Hill" each with triumphant cops and angry-looking Freemen visible through the windows.

Now Ben and Kenny's work really started. The Freemen—including the former Alberta man—were making their first court appearances hundreds of kilometers away in Billings, Montana, first thing in the morning.

To be there, Ben and Kenny had to drive through the night. But they had just driven through the previous night to get to "Media Hill," spent all day being roasted in the heat-wave without sleep, and now had to set out, dog-tired, on this next journey. Kenny drove until his eye-lids were dropping. They stopped, switched drivers, and Ben drove until his eye-lids were dropping. Now, alongside some deserted Montana highway, they pulled off the road onto the grass verge, and tried to sleep. The heat of the day had turned into a hot-sweltering night which sparked an almighty thunderstorm. They slept fitfully, watching the blackness being rent by vertical bolts of lightning and occasional horizontal crackles of jagged blue light, with rumbling thunder reverberating around them.

They got to the court on time. Ben sent back reams of copy. Kenny sent back tons of pictures, and they pulled out of there. All that remained was the several hundred kilometer drive to get back to the office.

As it happened, on the way home, while Ben was driving, he noticed a road sign indicating there was no maximum speed limit on Montana's open rural roads. Kenny was dozing, and Ben was quite enjoying the apparent untapped power in this SUV engine. Montana has some wonderful long straight open rural roads with nothing to clutter them like towns, or even much traffic. Ben found they were on one such road with a very gentle downward slope. Almost without pushing on the pedal he was doing 100, and the needle was hardly halfway round the dial. Ben glanced across at Kenny. He was asleep now. Ben pushed his right foot down a little more. Now the needle touched 150—still a quarter of the dial to go. The road stretched straight in front as far as the horizon. Ben took a breath and pushed the pedal right down. The needle went as far as 175—the highest reading on the dial—then it continued, off the dial until it bumped against the little rubber stopper at the end. The needle was completely horizontal, off the dial. Kenny woke, glanced over and saw it. Ben lifted his foot and the needle started rising until it was back on the dial, moving left from 175, ever left to 150, 120, 100, and Ben held it there.

"This thing of yours doesn't half go," said Ben. "The needle was right against the rubber stopper, you know." Kenny didn't say a lot, he seemed to be in shock. And it wasn't long after that that the Montana authorities put speed limits back on all the roads in the State.

It wasn't many weeks later, in October, when Ben was suffering one of his rare quiet days in the office that he saw the potential for another sudden trip to the States. These rare quiet office days were a pain for Ben. Usually it was on the day he was imprisoned in the newsroom writing his hated "Crime in the Community" column. Every week, as he plodded through the lengthening columns of grey type, he prayed for salvation in the form of activity on the scanner. He would inwardly invoke the patron saint of crime reporters to give him a big fire or some mighty pile-up on the Deerfoot Trail, or best of all, a homicide. It never really crossed his mind that he was wishing some terrible catastrophe of death and destruction on unsuspecting innocent people just so he'd have a chance to escape from the newsroom. Today, the scanner was cruelly quiet with spells of near silence spasmodically punctuated only by the most routine of chatter. Perhaps there wasn't a patron saint of crime reporters at all.

He finished yet another weary crime prevention warning from police to shoppers at the Chinook Mall not to leave valuables on view in their cars, but to lock everything away in the trunk. He decided to give himself a break by closing down the dreary pages of type and start flicking through the day's international wire stories instead. Hell, even Ben deserved a break from the drudgery of "Crime in the Community." And there it was. Second item down.

"Arrest in the Spokane serial killer case."

Ben did have a patron saint after all, and he'd thrown Ben a lifeline just when it was most needed. Ben read the details avidly. He'd need to be armed with every fact before he approached the city desk with his argument that he had to go back to Spokane to follow up this story. After all, his first sortie down there among Spokane's hookers—sorry, prostitutes—sorry, street workers—had produced a great Sunday read, and this one could be even better if he played it right.

Associated Press reporters had pieced the wire story together. A man called Alexander Lewis was the suspected killer. He'd been caught red-handed with a hooker's corpse in his car as he was driving it toward his usual dumping ground. Ben knew exactly where that was. Hell, Ben had probably driven the very same road, and had probably driven over the exact spot where the arrest went down. No one seemed to know much about this guy. Neighbors told reporters he'd been living in Spokane about eight years. He was a loner who kept himself to himself in a small detached run-down cabin at the end of a cul-de-sac. No one ever saw him have visitors. Everyone was shocked. He seemed such a quiet unassuming man. They thought he was about retirement age.

At a press conference, covered by AP, the Spokane serial killer task force added the usual bland details. Alexander Lewis, 66, a resident of Spokane, had been charged with the murder of one woman. He had been arrested during a routine check-stop aimed at snagging drunk drivers in the early hours after the last bars had turned out.

"As a result of incriminating evidence discovered by officers at the scene, Mr. Lewis was taken to the Task Force headquarters. His car was impounded by the Task Force. Further inquiries are continuing into other possibly related matters. For investigative reasons, no photographs of Mr. Lewis are being released."

Ben laughed out loud. Homicide cops find a fresh corpse in the trunk of a suspected serial killer's vehicle and, no doubt with serious, dead-pan faces they tell a crowded press conference they had found "incriminating evidence" at the scene. Right on!

From the look of it, this Mr. Lewis really had been a reclusive guy as no media outfits had found any pictures of him, nor had anyone found any of his relatives to interview.

But at least the Spokane media had seen through some of the smoke screen laid down by the police. They had discovered the task force had been watching Lewis for several days, and the "routine" check-stop wasn't manned by traffic officers but by serial killer task force detectives—and it wasn't randomly located. It was on a route where the task force expected Lewis to be driving. Their only real regret was not being far enough ahead of the game to save the latest victim.

Ben yelled across to Frank on the city desk. "Spokane serial killer nabbed" he shouted out, phrasing the whole story in a headline. "We ought to be there, Frank. I'm on my way." Frank already had a damn good Sunday read lined up for the coming weekend and didn't need another one. He was in a "win-win" situation. He could tell Ben "No way" and tell his editorial bosses he'd saved them a bunch of needless expense by his decision. Ben knew he was on a loser. There never really was a local angle in this story and they had already engineered one good Sunday read out of it. It was just a Spokane story now. Though Ben was disgruntled, the Mail was content to run the wire story on page three.

Every week in the Whiskey Foxtrot Operation, Stone had the teams re-assemble on the tenth floor of the police headquarters building to share information. But they were getting nowhere. Where Stone and Novak hoped their teams would come up with the mistakes that must have been made, none did. Every time new eyes looked over the work carried out by the earlier teams, they found themselves checking what they thought were relevant facts—only to discover the earlier team had checked those facts. And both came up with the same answers. No errors there. If just one of the new teams could come up with just one different answer, or find one alley to go down the others hadn't ventured to check, it would be a start. But not even one surfaced in several months of solid study.

Stone applied a new strategy. After several weeks, he rotated the teams again, and a few weeks after that he rotated them again, so each team now got to cover each of the other three murders. At the end of that exercise, all the lead detectives who had initially worked these four murders in isolation, totally unaware at the time of any possible links with any other killings, had spent months pounding the shit out of all four cases until they knew them inside out. And still they couldn't see it.

Chapter 8

But across the city, unknown to them, a possible break in the case was surfacing. They wouldn't hear about it for quite a while yet, but it was on its way to them through a tortuous route. The first clue turned up in Ben's office. Not so many people wrote letters to crime reporters. Ben's little wooden mail slot two rows down and two across in the alphabetically arranged shelving on the newsroom wall was always empty. Decent people wrote letters and sent literature and brochures and packages to travel editors and political columnists and other reporters, so their mail slots were always crammed full, likely to spill out at any minute. Putting pen to paper never crossed the minds of the kind of people Ben crossed. But today, a letter lay jutting out of his mail slot. It was postmarked from the States. Ben thought it could finally be the pink underwear he was expecting! It must be. The only letter Ben could think of coming from the States might contain pink underwear from the Arizona desert! It was a little snippet on the international wire that had sent Ben down to Arizona on the whim of the boss for one of those Sunday features that would make a damn good read. In the Arizona desert near Phoenix, so the story ran, was the meanest, toughest son-of-a-bitch sheriff, Sheriff Joe Arpaio. It was reckoned he kept 1,400 prisoners locked up in tents to fry by day and freeze by night out in the desert. Now, he was humiliating the prisoners by installing cameras to film their every action—even taking a piss—and making the home-videos available on the Internet for all to see.

"Go down there, live in the tents for a day or two and interview the sheriff. That'll be a good read," said Frank, coming out of one of the never-ending editorial planning meetings. Ben set it up, and flew down there.

It was better copy than anyone dreamed.

Sheriff Joe was a newspaper reporter's delight. Every nasty thing said about him was right. He was mean. The week Ben got there, when the daytime temperature in the tents hit 104 F, Sheriff Joe had just cut out coffee for inmates.

"Why should they get coffee?" he asked Ben. "They can drink water. It saves me $250,000 a year."

Proudly, he told Ben he spent 60 cents a day on food for each inmate, and $1.25 a day on food for the guard dogs.

Out in the tents, Ben heard the growling and grumblings from inmates, irked by this detail of their miserable lives that the dogs got fed better than they did.

"If they don't like it, they can eat the dog food, I don't care," said the bad Sheriff, when Ben raised the matter.

The day Ben interviewed Sheriff Joe in his plush office the wicked Sheriff had embarked on turning the screw a little tighter on the inmates. They had been complaining they had no facilities for physical exercise, no gymnasium, no weight training, nothing. Sheriff Joe listened—and acted.

"I'm bringing in exercise bikes, about a dozen of them," he said.

"I'm having them all rigged up to a generator, and they can pedal all day and all night to provide power for the tents."

"If they don't cycle, they'll have no heating or lights, it'll save me millions on electricity bills."

Out in the desert, Ben saw where Sheriff Joe had started putting the latest plan into action. He'd seen the first two exercise bikes, bolted to a concrete pad where there was a space big enough for a generator to be installed. Sheriff Joe never joked. If he said he was doing something, it was done.

He'd brought back old-fashioned chain-gangs. He had every prisoner dressed in a baggy uniform bearing horizontal broad black and white stripes, had them shackled to each other, and paraded them out there in Phoenix, where the whole population could see them, painting curb-stones, and picking up litter, a general picture of abject humiliation.

Women too slogged in the heat in the unflattering black and white stripes, shackled into chain gangs, 12 to a chain. When Ben was out in the tents, he was once surrounded by about 30 black and white clad angry women inmates, all yelling their abuse of Sheriff Joe at once, urging him to put that in his paper—which he did.

"Women as well as men, oh yes, I run an equal-opportunity jail," Sheriff Joe told Ben.

Humiliation was very big on Sheriff Joe's agenda.

After all, as he very simply stated, if you didn't want to be in his jail and suffer the humiliation, you didn't have to be.

Sheriff Joe had every inmate, especially every man, wear pink underwear.

It suited the sheriff's philosophy to further humiliate the men just a little more, but, in fact, as he explained, there was a practical reason for the pink frillies.

"They were stealing $100,000 worth of white towels and socks a year out of here," he told Ben.

"So I had all the underwear, shorts, socks and towels dyed pink, so if we ever see anyone leaving this place with anything pink on them, we know it's stolen."

But the humiliation factor was enormous. In the tents, Ben saw big-built bastards, tattooed and surly, the kind you'd shrink from in some back alley at night, looking stupid in little pink socks, little pink shorts, with a pink towel over their muscular hairy powerful shoulders.

It all made Ben a great feature. He took his own pictures and the feature ran to four pages one Sunday—a damn good read. It was a shocking eye-opener to many Canadians. They shuddered at the thought of how many prisoners' rights were probably being infringed in this barbaric setting. To Ben, Sheriff Joe was a hero. The world needed more jailors like him.

Ben came back to Calgary, bubbling about him. In the newsroom, the pink underwear was the cruncher. Reporters couldn't really believe 1,400 bad-ass criminals were skipping about in jail in the desert in pink underwear. So Ben e-mailed the sergeant in charge of one shift at the jail, the sergeant who'd been his guide through the tents, and asked him to send a set of pink underwear up to Calgary, so skeptical reporters could see Ben hadn't invented this incredible detail.

And here was a package from the States—but no, it wasn't pink underwear at all.

Wouldn't you know it—in the top left corner was a heavily inked hand-stamp announcing "Inmate Mail," just in case any of Ben's colleagues might think he'd actually received a letter from some decent sector of society. What the hell, thought Ben. Inwardly he wore this as a kind of badge of honor. The mayor and aldermen wrote to the paper's political pundits, connoisseurs of

Chablis and Burgundy wrote to the wine columnist, and "lowlifes" in prison wrote to Ben.

This one was different. It was from the States, postmarked April 20, 2001, from Spokane. Ben had spent a week there working on that Spokane serial killer who'd terrorized hooker's through the late 1990s. He'd found the families of murdered hookers and turned the serial killer's victims into women with personalities and lives. It had made another good Sunday read, a solid four-pager. But he hadn't made any contacts inside the Spokane pen. This was a mystery. He sat at his desk, raised the height of his adjustable chair, vowing as he did every day, to discover who religiously, every night, lowered it just to annoy him, and opened the letter. At first, Ben thought it was the latest ramblings from one regular nut-case who bombarded most reporters in the office with giant tomes of type-written papers and photo-copied pages from newspapers, as he ranted at the government, politicians, the police, the establishment, newspapers in general, the Mail in particular, and even Ben in person sometimes. It usually took about five seconds to recognize one of his parcels and another five seconds to file it under "G" for garbage.

But this wasn't one of his.

The hand-writing looked a bit familiar. Ben glanced at the last page and saw the signature "Alex." He didn't know anyone called Alex. But now he looked more closely he saw that hand-writing wasn't just a bit familiar. Ben was certain. This was the scrawl of foul-mouthed Garry, old "Deep Throat" himself. It had been eight years since Ben had heard from him, since the time he'd disappeared into the RCMP's witness protection program, so that one day he could spill the beans about the oil plane bombing. Once in those good old days when Garry was suing the cops he claimed had wrongfully imprisoned him on murders he hadn't committed, he'd sent Ben a pile of hand-written letters and paperwork so Ben would write a story. But Ben hadn't. And when Garry took on the Workers Compensation Board when he reckoned they were short-changing him over a back problem, he'd sent Ben another pile of hand-written papers for another story. But Ben hadn't written that one either. And Ben recalled that day in a plush hotel foyer, must have been ten years earlier, when Garry had unloaded pages of scribble on him to "prove" his oil plane bombing theory. Here was the same scribble, same horrible spelling mistakes, and same foul language. No doubt. It had been years since Ben last heard from Garry, last heard that rasping, cancerous voice on the phone. Sometimes Ben had idly wondered if he'd been killed. Ben knew, even if Garry's continued smoking aggravated his throat cancer, he wouldn't just die. Garry's life style meant he'd have to be killed in some sordid burst of violence, in some back alley among garbage cans and dumpsters somewhere in the world, be it Colombia or Calgary, where the tentacles of crime had penetrated the RCMP's witness protection program. But it looked like whatever had happened to him, he'd wound up in the U. S. federal penitentiary in Spokane. And now he was calling himself "Alex."

It was a short scribble, and it didn't make much sense.

"Ben, You better read this. When you've read it, I won't care what you do with it. By the time you get it, I'll be fucking dead. No one's going to fuck me over any more. This has gone on long enough. It's been more than ten years. The cocksuckers fucked me over, but they didn't know I was the wrong man to mess with. They cops think they sorted me, but they'll be eating shit when they find out how I fucked them over."

"That's one way to get someone's attention," thought Ben.

"Red three, red five, station 22, station 27, we have a standby at Gate 10 at the airport, an Airbus A320 coming in with landing gear problems, 305 souls on board about nine minutes out," crackled the scanner.

Ben swept the letter into his drawer with one hand and grabbed the scanner, radio, tape-recorder, notebook and pens in the usual flurry of controlled panic.

"We got a plane crash coming," he yelled as he took off across the newsroom.

Ben hated and loved these nine minute dashes to the airport fence, where, if he was lucky he'd arrive, get his video camera out, have it focused on the end of the runway, and still have twenty seconds to see the airliner coming up from the south for what was threatening to be a crash landing.

But between Ben's chair in the office, and the stretch of airport fence where he would best see and film the impending plane crash, were an unbelievable bunch of built-in delays. On one "crash alert," his van was blocked in by a semi-trailer truck delivering newsprint to the Mail, and he never got out of the parking lot before the plane was down safely. Most often, there would be a string of traffic in the road outside the parking lot at the very second he wanted to turn out. He'd have to wait another ten seconds for those cars to pass. At every junction on the way, there would be traffic with another ten second wait at every turn. Of course, it was decreed by God himself that every traffic light on the route had to be at red for Ben. And every meticulously careful and slow driver would be in front of him. And courteous drivers would stop in front of him to allow motorists from side streets to pull out ahead of them. This was the part Ben hated. But finally, he'd swing onto the final approach road to Gate 10, park up outside the gate, and be ready to film in seconds. Sometimes he'd feel smug to see a convoy of fire trucks and ambulances still wailing their way up the final approach road toward the gate, way behind him. And always, always, the plane would land safely. Ben often felt guilty about this. While 99% of his whole being was relieved for the passengers and crew, there was an evil, sick 1% which was disappointed he hadn't captured a crash in glorious Technicolor right in his view-finder. He felt in his heart that one day, when he would be flying, his aircraft would crash-land at Calgary with no undercarriage. God would add all those 1% disappointments up for him, and present them to him in one big fireball, with him in the middle.

Today was an average run. The lights were red against him, naturally, but the traffic wasn't too bad, and he was there at the fence, video in hand at the ready as the majestic white Airbus swept in over the perimeter fence and executed the most perfect landing right in the center of his view-finder. Fire trucks followed the monster airliner down the runway as it slowed to a stop, and the scanner in Ben's van confirmed it.

"Red Two to dispatch, this plane's down safely, return all apparatus."

Ben radioed the office to call off the photographers who were still on their way.

"The bloody thing didn't crash," said Ben into the radio, and the office could hear a lot more than 1% of disappointment in his voice.

"You're one sick puppy," said Frank.

And as the convoy of fire trucks and ambulances, now without sirens and lights, swung out of the gate and set off back down the approach road, Ben pulled his van into the convoy and drove back to the office.

He took Alex's letter, well, Garry's letter, back out of the drawer. Where was he?

"When you get this, I won't fucking care no more what you do with it. Heads are going to fucking roll, but where I am, I ain't even going to know.

All my life they screwed me over, you know what they done to me. Shit, I'm getting my own back on the lot of them. It's took me fucking years. I had my pleshur doing it. I've seen things hardly no one's seen, I heard things no one's heard, lovely sounds, and now where I am, it's nearly all done. Fuck everybody is what the world taught me, and that's what I have done and what I am doing."

Ben had noticed before when truly wild paranoid characters ranted, they always repeated themselves. So that's twice now Garry had spelled it out.

"You know I never bullshitted you. Never. And I ain't bullshitting you now. You always wanted a story. You'll get one. It's all ready for you. You go to the Bow River, on the Deerfoot Trail side, between the Calf Rope Bridge and that black railway bridge further down, where them trees are. There's a bunch, about a dozen big trees between the railway bridge and where that shitty little creek runs in. If you look careful, you'll see there's five in a straight line, like they was planted. Go to the one in the middle. Take a fucking big shovel with you, and dig as close to the trunk as you can get. I left something there for you. You'll know what to do with it. I hope you fucking enjoy your story. One day when you get to right it, I reckon you'll be fucking thinking of me. I'm fucking sure you will."

"Don't bover righting back. You'll be wasting your time. Alex."

"Fuck me rigid," said Ben out loud.

"Oh, you're disgusting," said Liz, passing by to her desk down the newsroom.

"Sorry, sorry," said Ben, who'd been so absorbed in this apparently crazed lunatic letter he hadn't noticed her passing by. Ben knew he had a bad mouth on him when he occasionally got excited. He firmly believed women who'd chosen newspaper reporting as a way of life had to live with a newspaper office life, with its stress, noise, and day-to-day dealing with all things foul, like murders, blood and gore and death and destruction. But he didn't think it was right women should be subject to gratuitous foul language from colleagues. Ben believed you wouldn't use foul language in front of your mother or sister or wife. Women didn't need to hear it in the office—hence his apology. Of course, he'd heard Liz sounding off a few times when she was wound up, and she could make your ear lobes buzz when she wanted to, so he didn't feel too bad. Liz used to get most loquacious when her car broke down—as it always did. She was kind of scatty about cars, which were one of life's great mysteries to her. If she wasn't taking it to the garage to be fixed, she was looking for a lift to get to the garage to fetch it back out. But having it back on the road wouldn't last long before it would break down again—and would need towing to the garage. And Liz would dig into her rich well-practiced vocabulary of profanities at each step in this perpetual rotation. No, Ben didn't feel too bad about his momentary lapse into the vernacular.

Ben's first thought was this letter might have been an office goon. The office had its prize pair of "gooners." Alf Twiddy, who with a name like that just had to get his own back on everyone all the time and Cooper Shaw across the room in sports, who delved into in-depth complicated goons, often involving a team of conspirators around him to pull it off.

Gooning came as second nature to someone like Alf Twiddy with his carefully nurtured dubious background. A heavy round-faced beer-drinker with a proudly-sported beer belly, Alf let it be believed that he may have been a jailbird in his wild early days—might even have mixed with the biker crowd back east. No one in the office, least of all Ben, ever knew whether to believe him or not. And that was a perfect foundation for playing "goons" on people. Alf could look you right in the eye and tell you something you knew was on the level—until you found out later he'd been winding you up all the time. In the serious world, it meant he was a polished liar. In the world of "goons," it meant he was brilliant. Usually it was newcomers who suffered. Many a new reporter found himself calling one of the local funeral homes for some supposedly important story, asking "Is Myra Maynes there?" The funeral homes always wore the joke with great patience. And the girls on the switchboard at Calgary Zoo always knew when a new reporter had landed in the Mail's newsroom when they got a call saying "I'm just returning a call, is Mr. G. Raffe there, please?"

Sometimes Twiddy or Shaw would take on one of the old-stagers like Ben, getting a deal more satisfaction of pulling a goon on a cynical seen-it-all-before old hack rather than a green cub reporter. One day, Ben was a few minutes away from leaving the office for the funeral of a three-year-old baby Chinese girl, murdered by her baby-sitter. For a week, Ben had battled with the devastated Chinese family before getting a picture out of them, even using their

Chinese church vicar as a back door ruse to get at them, until there was no love lost between grieving family and persistent reporter.

Ben just knew he was going to get a call from the father, who had a basic control of a few words of English, warning him to stay away from the funeral. Sure enough, the moment he answered the phone, there was that dreaded accent and the expected warning.

"You no come te aah foonrul," said the father's voice. "We no wanyu dare, you got it."

Ben took a deep breath, and was about to launch into his usual explanation to overcome this problem he faced quite routinely with grieving families, when some alarm bell embedded in his cynical reporter's consciousness sounded, and he clapped his hand over the mouthpiece.

"Where's that bastard Twiddy," he shouted, looking round the newsroom. In a split second, he saw the give-away smirk on Frank's face on city desk, and knew his instinct was right.

He'd been gooned. This wasn't the Chinese father at all. But it wasn't Twiddy either. It was the other bastard, Shaw, thin, wiry, and always quick with a snide remark, over in sports. Ben dropped the receiver back on the phone like it was burning his hand. It was the classic operation of the "goon" gang working in the office. It was no good pulling the goon unless one of the conspirators was on hand to watch the victim swallow the hook. This time Frank was the conspirator who just couldn't keep the smirk of his face as he watched Ben take the fake Chinese call.

And now here's this letter, out of the blue, telling Ben to take a shovel and go digging under trees alongside the Bow River. Yea, right. And if he did, how many gooners and conspirators would be hiding behind trees with cameras at the ready, he wondered. But Twiddy and Shaw combined weren't that good. Not even they could concoct a letter on U. S. Federal Penitentiary stationery, and neither of them could replicate Garry's scrawl, or his spelling or foul vocabulary. Ben knew this was from Garry, whatever it meant.

Next morning Ben was trudging through deep snow along the foot of the railway embankment leading to the Bow River. It was just Ben's luck. A crazy May blizzard had dumped deep snow on Calgary the night before. Ben recalled one year when he was writing a crazy snow dump story in Calgary in July! What a city for weather! It was really strange Garry should mention this stretch of the Bow, as Ben knew it well. One of his top fishing holes was along here.

Ben had found a long deep pool where whitefish gathered in hungry shoals in the winter when you could still fish it before plummeting temperatures froze your fly line after only two casts. You could also catch them there in the early spring when the deep freeze let up enough to encourage keen fly fishermen to shake off winter's lethargy. Ben once took five whitefish in five successive casts there, and had one three-day spell when he took 65 whitefish. The regulations entitled Ben to keep five each day, but he released them all, simply enjoying the thrill of the catch. Today, he felt silly, carrying a shovel where he usually carried rod and landing net. His big winter boots ploughed through the deep snow, scattering the powder like speed-boats pushing bow waves. He crossed a set of tracks made by a coyote. He'd seen and heard the coyotes there a few times, and occasionally found the remains of a duck, just one ripped-off wing or even just a scattered heap of feathers and blood. He rounded the embankment so now he could see the stretch of river bank between Garry's "shitty little creek" and the black railway bridge.

Just a sheet of uneven snow, trampled in a couple of places where dog-walkers had been, and interrupted here and there by clumps of grass, bowed under the weight of snow, but still visible. But this was all flat snow. No trees. No clump of trees. No five trees in a straight line. Not a single tree. Ben cursed. He quickly spun on his heels to make sure no one was watching. No. No gooners smirking at him. At least, he was relieved about that. And he started the long hike back through the snow, made more uncomfortable this time as he was now facing the wind, the wind chill burning his cheeks and his nose. He reached almost back to his van, well, back to the coyote tracks when it struck him. What an idiot he was. The coyote tracks did it. As soon as he saw them, he thought of the coyotes, then all the wildlife he saw alongside the river—the Canada geese, occasionally the pelicans, more rarely a bald eagle, and the beavers that sometimes swam past him as he stood waist deep casting his fly.

The beavers. Of course, the beavers. They'd been really busy along that stretch of the river. There had been a stand of trees along that bank. It might have been four or five years ago the beavers had toppled them one by one— huge trees with trunks two feet across. Ben had often wondered why God would put beavers on earth to wastefully fell a whole copse of trees they couldn't possibly use for their dams. But when Garry was around before he disappeared, back in the early 90s, the beavers hadn't even started. All those trees were standing then. Ben turned round again, glad to get his face out of the biting wind, and ploughed through the snow back toward the river. He rounded the embankment, plodded toward the "shitty little creek" and was soon among the long-dead tree stumps left by the beavers, each one shaped to a pointed cone with a picturesque touch of snow on top. Some of the biggest trunks still lay, mostly under the snow, pointing toward the river where they'd been felled. Ben saw the five stumps right away, looking, as Garry said, for all the world like they'd been planted by a forester. He was excited now, the adrenaline warming him instantly. He went to the middle trunk, cleared away the snow and started digging. He was glad this sudden May snowstorm hadn't had time to freeze the ground like concrete, and the shovel cut the earth easily. He quickly hit metal, it wasn't more than a few inches down, and in ten minutes he had a tin box out of its grave. Ben had no idea if the tin box itself had any significance. It was old and rusty and had once contained Walkers assorted pure butter shortbread—a product of Scotland. Through the thin film of rust on the outside lid, Ben could make out a faded painting of Flora MacDonald bidding farewell to Bonnie Prince Charlie in 1746. If that was a clue, it must be pretty damn cryptic—and too obscure for Ben to fathom. The tin itself had never had a lock, but it was wrapped in a small chain and that did have a padlock. The key was in it, frozen solid and jammed with soil. Under his toque even in this freezing wind Ben felt his ears glowing hot like they always did when he was excited. But he couldn't get the tin open. He'd have to take it back home. With great self-control, he stayed just a few minutes more to fill in the hole he'd made, then, with Bonnie Prince Charlie and Flora MacDonald under his arm, he walked back into the wind and back to his van.

As it happened, he didn't have time to go home, it was time to start his shift at the Mail, so he took the tin box with him, and once the lock had thawed out, the key turned, he removed the chain and took off the lid. Now he could see his treasure. Inside was a fat brown-paper envelope, bursting at the seams.

The moment Ben opened the bulky package, crumpled at the edges from being crushed into the metal box, and saw the hand-writing he knew this was more vintage Garry.

A bundle of papers, all covered in crawly hand-writing, some bound by a rubber band, and a larger exercise book, the kind children used in school, tumbled out, adding to the mess on his desk. Pages and pages of scratchy writing were stuffed inside, all loose, some flat, some folded, two or three here paper-clipped together, and some folded in clumps of half-a-dozen sheets obviously connected. Buried in this pile of paper was a spiral-ring notebook crammed with the same hand-writing, all over the pages, in the margins, never on the lines. Beneath that was an exercise book, bigger, floppier, its feeble spine broken, so, although the pages were still packed inside, there was nothing to stop them spilling out. Both sides of every sheet of paper were covered in this same barely legible scrawl. It must have taken years to write this lot. It was going to take years to read it. What the hell was it all about?

Ben cleared a space on his desk, pushed aside the pile of murder files, topped today by Polanski, a truly evil bastard who'd taken his own two kids out into the badlands around Drumheller northeast of the city and murdered them just to spite his estranged wife. He figured this was the way to cause her maximum anguish. He turned the screw by not revealing where the bodies were, leaving her imagination to complete her agony by picturing their corpses perhaps being eaten by wild animals. The file was out because Canada's horribly lenient laws were allowing Polanski the right to start applying for parole, and he'd only been inside 15 years. Hanging him would have stopped all that. Ben was a firm believer in hanging murderers. He wasn't stupid about it. They'd have to be convicted first, and then hanged—quickly. None of this waiting for 20 years crap as in the States while damn nearly every court in the land examined and re-examined the case, while the best witnesses died of old age, and evidence got lost, and cases weakened.

Polanski was pushed to one side, and what looked like Garry's lifetime's scribblings covered Ben's desk instead. None of it seemed to be dated or numbered in any order. Of course the pages in the notebooks were consecutive to each other, and the clutches of pages folded inside each other were probably consecutive, but if there was an order to it all, it wasn't yet obvious to Ben. Wait a minute. The loose pages were written one way with the reverse apparently upside down. No. Ben saw it now. Garry had written down a page, and then instead of turning it over like the page of a book, he'd turned it over top to bottom and written down the back. Now that Ben looked more closely there were numbers on one side in the top left corner. Where was page one then? He tried the bigger notebook, which seemed to start at page 241. No good. But the little spiral ring notebook, with many of the pages dog-eared and crumpled, half torn off the metal spiral, looked a better bet. Page 1 was hanging on by about six turns of the metal spiral, and as on all the loose-leaf pages,

Garry had written all down it, then turned the page up and written down the back.

"T. The guy in the corner's good. It'll be him. And I know which one he's going down for. They don't stand a fucking chance."

That's just great, thought Ben. No introduction, no clue as to what this is all about. No explanation. No "hello Ben." Just scribble.

"Did some basic stuff tonight. Followed him out. Big car. Ford Taurus. License AAP 424. It'll be good. Fucking big trunk. He has no idea. Waited in the parking lot after he'd gone. She came out with two other staff. Has her own Honda. Leave that til later. Don't need that yet."

Was this some prank, some joke? If Ben read a page, or 10 pages or 100 pages would there be an answer? The first two lines meant nothing.

"W. S. again. Same corner. Easy. Followed the Taurus to his home. Has a garage but parked it in the driveway. Better."
"At this more than a week. He's busy. Various feeding holes but W. S. three times. Used the washroom last thing before leaving. Then lights up outside each time just before driving off. Golf this weekend. Not very good. Parked it in the driveway every night. Decided he does live on his own. Never seen a woman come home with him. No lights ever on in there. Busy man."
"Hasn't taken long. Nearly ready. Three times he's been to the airport and flown out. Back next day each time. Left the Taurus in the Park N' Jet each time. Played the same golf course each weekend. Different partners. Always men. Very busy man. That won't last."
"S. Found the right place today. Gravel track out of Fish Creek Park backs onto the rough ground off part of the golf course. Drive there, short walk, do the business."

Bemused, Ben still hadn't picked up any of this. Who was "S" and who was "T?" What was going on? When was it going on? So far, all Ben could see was that this page hadn't all been written at the same time. Sentences were being added separately at different times. Like a journal, clearly with different pens being used, the way a diary always looks like a disjointed succession of different days, though it's the same person writing it. Except this damn diary didn't have any dates, or daily separations.

"Leave T. for now. He's ready. V will be easy. Most nights this one comes out with the same friends. But have seen her three successive Fridays leave a bit later on her own. A Friday would be right. Say, two weeks."

Ben noticed the next passage was longer and did appear to be written all at the same time, whatever it meant.

"It's started. Feels good. Waited til T was away on his overnight flight. Did his house. Streets full of kids on Halloween. In easy, hardly touched the place. He won't know he's been done over til his next golf game. Then he'll know. Cigarette ends easy. Worked good. Waited til T was finished meal. Made sure I was at a table nearer to the door than him. When he got up, I was on my way. He lit up, smoked, threw away the butt. I had it and no one saw a thing. Can't wait for Friday. The cocksuckers won't know what's hit them."

Ben gave up trying this section which was mad, disjointed, and half in code, and looked for something more intelligible. He flicked half way through the smaller notepad, and what he found this time was at least clearly intelligible.

"Enjoyed the ripping sound when I sliced open her other thigh. Thought it would have bled more, but it didn't. Looked in there. Saw her thigh bone. Bones are always shining white and icy smooth when they're still inside. Why should pathologists have all the fun. The slit I made, made her slit look little. And I made three, just to hear that sound again and again. Think next time I'll run a tape-recorder up close, so I can play it over and over. Perhaps I'll send it to a radio station, and they could have a competition to see who can recognize this unusual household sound. Course, no one will ever know except me. Done my carving again. Polaroid a bit dark, good though. What about the sounds on the radio, and the photos on the television? Nah, don't reckon."

"Fuck me rigid," said Ben out loud.

"What's your problem?" asked Frank, "didn't you hear that on the scanner—zero-one, rollover, person trapped. What's up, you losing it or something?"

"No, sorry, missed it, hang on, I'll check an address for you," said Ben, quickly closing the little notepad, picking up the phone and finding the address where a pickup truck had rolled, trapping its driver inside.

It became very clear to Ben he couldn't study this lot in the office, where he'd get called away from his desk every two minutes, leaving all this to the inquisitive eyes of guys in the newsroom. He shoveled it all up and piled it back in its crumpled envelope and stuck it in his bottom drawer, and locked the drawer. He was confident no one else had even seen it. He dropped the chain and padlock inside the old tin and put that on the floor under his desk out of the way.

It might have been out of sight, but it wasn't out of his mind. If this lot was on the level, not some sick joke, and was maybe Garry's memoirs, it was fucking scary. Any other day Ben would enjoy a "rollover, person trapped." Well, not enjoy exactly, but welcome the chance to turn it into a fully-fledged drama, which would probably command some prominent position in the up-front news pages of the paper. This time, he half-heartedly covered it by telephone from in the office. Competent, professional, all the necessary facts, adequate for the next day's paper, but not the top job he could have done if he'd gone to the scene. His mind was inside that crumpled envelope.

By the end of the day's shift, Ben was ready to stay on. The newsroom emptied out, some leaving at 6 p. m., some at 8 p. m., till just the lone night guy and Ben remained, and Ben could switch off his brain to the scanner and leave it to Allan, who was on nights for the week.

Ben pulled out the envelope, anticipation high like some teenaged boy alone in his room who can't wait to retrieve his girlie magazine from its hiding place. He spilled the contents across his desk, the two notebooks sliding out first and being buried under the loose sheets of handwriting. Garry's favorite obscenity caught his eye on the top sheet.

"*The cocksuckers haven't paid enough yet.*" In Garry's eyes, most people he crossed, especially most cops, were "cocksuckers."

"*They'll fucking know when I've finished with them. Heads will roll. The shit will be hitting the fan long after I'm gone. I paid for what they did. They are going to pay. A lot of them. Cops, lawyers, the whole fucking system. I don't care I won't be here to see it. I know what's going down. They won't never forget what I've done."*

Ben cringed at the double negative. Whenever he saw a double negative he remembered instantly the appalling line in a country and western hit song about a lovesick fool who'd burned his bridges. It ran "Ain't No way he can't never go home." A quadruple negative!

What could Garry have done that was going to cause this much trauma to cops and lawyers—well, all levels of the justice system, by the sound of it? And what could continue to have heads rolling long after Garry was dead and gone? The answer must lie in all this mound of paper.

The next moment brought the first real ray of light. And it wasn't any of the sheets of paper. Halfway buried in the pile were sheets of paper folded square to form a bulky little pouch. And when Ben opened it, he was looking at six little squares of fabric, roughly torn, delicate but dirty, uneven in size, four in one piece of paper and two more in a separate piece of paper. They looked like—Ben knew they couldn't be—but they looked like pieces of women's panties. Ben instantly covered them over, looking quickly at Allan to make sure he hadn't seen them. He hadn't. Ben lifted the sheet of paper off them again, hardly daring to look. This time he was sure. These were sections half-torn, half-cut from the crotches of women's panties.

Quite ridiculously, Ben knew immediately why he recognized them.

When he was a teenager in England, green to the world and impressionable, he'd traveled round the southern counties covering one of his local team's rugby union matches for the local paper's Saturday sports edition.

This was before Ben was even employed by his first newspaper. In fact, it was his stepping stone into journalism. While in the upper sixth in his grammar school, his English teacher rounded off an afternoon's lesson by asking whether anyone fancied writing sports stories for the local paper. While the class en bloc ignored this strange request and scrambled for the exit door, it being the end of the day, Ben stopped and asked for details. It turned out the English teacher's husband was the president of the local rugby union club who needed his team's exploits covered for the local paper every week for the coming season. Where better to find a potential writer than among his wife's budding literary stars? Ben was taken on—not exactly a glamorous assignment but one which gave him an insight into how one aspect of newspaper reporting worked. Every week, as the coach spilled out his team's players and they found their dressing rooms in exotic locations like Farnborough, or Chichester or Guildford, Ben would hunt the sports field and its surroundings, searching for a working telephone kiosk. His task for the day was all in the timing. Making notes during the game, he would position himself as near the phone box as possible just as the half-time whistle would sound. He would make his "reverse charge" call to the newspaper, get put through to one of the bank of copy-takers sitting under their headphones in the typing pool and dictate his 90 words plus the half-time score. This was the first skill he learned, to condense the entire first half of a rugby union game into 90 coherent words, and send it in on time.

"In a scrappy first half ruined by a blustery gale, neither team was able to produce much constructive rugby," he'd write for a game which had ground to a 0-0 score line by half-time. It was a simple formula. He'd repeat the phone box visit at the end of the game, with 50 words for the second half, making sure any try scorer's names had to be in capital letters, and then give the final score. All done. He well knew that all over southern England, guys like him were in telephone kiosks like his, phoning in their reports from every other game that day, all vying to get to the copy-takers before the lines were busy, so for Ben, getting in first was vital—his second skill learned.

Then, after the game, after the rugby team had sunk the required number of pints of beer per man in the nearest pub, and their decibel levels had risen to the required level to produce annoyance to all around them, they'd be poured back into the coach transporting them all home. It was on the coach, in this noisy, raucous, drunken environment where Ben learned most of the worldliest lessons of life he ever encountered. Two things stood out in Ben's memory about the team's infamous hooker, Harry, who did his best work in the set scrums. This guy, with a meticulously curled handlebar moustache, was some kind of martial arts demon. Often, the scrum, a whirling crush of 16 big bruisers including Harry would collapse on the ground but only 15 would drag themselves up to carry on playing. No one had eyes quick enough to see it, but Harry the hooker would have used his lethal edge-of-the-hand chop across the throat under the huge melee, and each time one of the opponents would be carried off for treatment.

But it was Ben's other memory of Harry that he was recalling now. On the coach driving home, Harry had once pulled from his rugby bag a pillow, set it against the headrest of his coach seat and rocked himself into a drunken slumber as the coach rumbled back toward the south coast. Production of the pillow produced enormous cheering, jeering, and yelling from everyone on board, as if it was a highlight of the day, which mystified Ben.

"What's that all about?" he asked the full-back giant squeezed into the seat alongside him.

"You don't know? That's Harry's pillow," slurred the full-back, seemingly pleased to have found someone who didn't know the story, and proud to be the one to relate it.

"Harry fucks women. Tall women, short women, fat women—if they've got a cunt, Harry fucks 'em," he said, in an embarrassingly booming voice, so everyone on the coach knew Ben was hearing the story for the first time.

"And when he's fucked 'em, he cuts out the crotches of their knickers and sews 'em into his pillow. The whole pillow's made up of 'undreds of them. The more soiled the better."

"And every week, the pillow's thicker and fatter than it was the week before. 'undreds an' 'undreds of 'em, he's got, and you should just smell it!"

It was another of those little insights into life for Ben—a virgin at the time—which would stick in his mind forever. Ben had no idea what the crotch piece of a pair of women's knickers would smell like. Not knowing that sort of thing was all part of being a virgin, after all. Hardly believing this account, he craned his neck and looked up the coach, where he could see the pillow billowing round Harry's head. And he could see the separate little squares. It was true. And however it smelled it didn't seem to put Harry off. He was unconscious with his nose buried in the pillow, so only half his handlebar moustache was visible.

On later rugby runs, Ben made sure he looked more carefully at Harry's pillow, so he'd know what the crotch pieces of women's knickers looked like if ever he saw one in real life. And now, here were six of them, on his desk. The two sheets of paper folded round them had no words on them. He folded them back inside their separate papers, and put them back in the crumpled envelope. The light suddenly started to dawn on Ben. As the possible meaning of this jumbled heap on his desk began taking shape, he remembered a detail from his "Theo File." It was already on his desk in the pile of files pushed to one side, and he lifted it out. It took him longer than he expected to find what he was looking for. He started looking in the wrong murder. But he found it in his background for the Gillian Warnoski murder in Red Deer in 1992.

In his notes of what his contact in the medical examiner's office had said to him, he'd written this, quoting his contact:

"This is strange. As you could see in those first pictures the killer left her panties on, at least that's what it looked like at first, but when the autopsy started, and we took her panties off, the center crotch piece had been cut out, probably with the double-edged knife, quite carefully, so he had access to her vagina, but there was no sign of rape, in fact, no sign of sexual intercourse at all."

"Fuck me rigid," said Ben out loud—again.

"No thank you," said Allan. Ben was so absorbed he'd forgotten Allan was there.

"Very funny," said Ben.

He read it again. "The center crotch piece had been cut out."

Ben's mind raced, not through the details he knew about the Warnoski murder, but about the tiny details he realized he didn't know. When his contact had mentioned the mysterious hole in the panties, Ben hadn't asked questions, just noted down the comments. Now he needed to know what color were the panties and what fabric were they made of, and where were they now, and could a forensic expert match a piece of fabric and say for sure it was the missing piece? And if it was, and Ben had it, and knew where it came from, and who gave it to him, did it mean he knew who the serial killer was? And if Ben had six pieces altogether, did that mean the killer had struck six times? And if so, who were all the victims? Ben's mind raced and whirled. This was no longer a little ray of light. This was perhaps a blinding revelation. Say Garry was a serial killer and this was his journal, his diary of death, what then? If it was all this, it was a God-send for Ben. He'd have scoop stories for weeks. Christ, he'd have enough to write a book. At some stage, he'd have to turn the whole lot over to the cops in Red Deer where Warnoski had been butchered. But that was down the line. Ben had been through this moral dilemma before. If this was the journal of a serial killer, he'd use it all first. Get the story first, be a responsible citizen second.

It had been the course he followed years earlier when a young mother murdered her two babies, dumped one down the garbage chute in her apartment block, and then left the other to starve to death abandoned in its room.

Neighbors heard it crying in hunger for hours on end, before the crying grew weaker. Eventually there was a deathly silence. Ben's digging around through the mother's background meant he came into possession of her personal diary and hundreds of her photographs capturing her lifestyle. Her loving the baby showed up first, followed by fewer pictures of the baby and more pictures of her partying and boozing with a bunch of guys. Next came brazen pictures of them all snorting cocaine. Ben had her love letters to the babies' dad. He had her letters home asking for ever more money from her parents to support her parties. Ben even had her passport and personal documents. Ben's stories were scoops day after day for so long, other reporters from television and radio told him they dreaded opening the next day's editions of his paper for fear of finding out what new scoop they were missing. It was the happiest of times for Ben. But when he'd finally milked it for all it was worth, he eventually did the decent thing, and handed everything over, lock, stock and barrel to the homicide detectives on the case. He was even good enough to guide them to the right pages in the diary and letters where they'd find the most self-incriminating passages.

Ben decided to plunge back into Garry's writings in the bigger of the notebooks.

"Got 'im. Got 'im. Easy. Got 'im leaving church. T walked his usual route out of the church, past the 7-Eleven. I could see him through the slats in the fence, like I'd seen him three times in a row. Came up behind him, hit him with a swinging right hand right on the nose. Best fucking nosebleed I ever saw. He went down. Crumpled. Bled good. Nearly went bad. Using the syringe was easy. Noses bleed good. Fucking car came by, lit me up in its headlights, but it probably looked like I was helping him. Left real quick in case the car came back. Had what I needed. Never had so much blood to play with. He didn't know what hit him. They still won't know what's hit them. None of them will know. Cocksuckers."

Ben tried to fit this into the puzzle. This was the second notebook, presumably a different time, but whoever "T" was he was still on the scene. And this passage cast doubt on Ben's supposed overall understanding of what it all meant. Ben reckoned this might be the journal of a serial killer preying on women. Yet here he was attacking some man and seemingly injecting him with something. It made no sense.

"Well, that's me done for the night," said Allan, breaking in on Ben's thoughts.

"See you tomorrow, Ben. What the hell are you doing here so late, anyway? If you're going to be here regularly this late at night, you can do my late shifts, eh?"

"Piss off," said Ben. "See ya."

And Allan went out leaving Ben alone in the newsroom, with the scanner talking to itself, competing with the television Allan had left on.

Ben prepared for his day off the next day. He put the notebook back with all Garry's writings, piled the whole lot back into the crumpled envelope, stacked it on top of both of the "Theo files" and scooped it all up under his arm. He'd be reading it all day at home tomorrow.

Chapter 9

Next day, sunk in his armchair with Garry's writings spread across two folding-leg tray tables, Ben decided dipping into odd snippets here and there wasn't the way to sort this. Instead he planned to read one long section until he understood it. He picked up the bunch of loose pages folded together, half-a-dozen pages, obviously consecutive, written on both sides, and plunged in.

"Costs good money just to waste time talking with these hookers. Girl near the French Maid pointed out Chili for me for packet of smokes. High cowboy boots. Black mini-skirt. Arse-cheeks showing. Went back two nights later. She got straight in. Wanted to see my cock to show I wasn't a cop. Said she'd been busted before. I know that's right. Got the newspaper cutting to prove it. She was scared before we reached my place. Made sure she could see my knife and my razor-sharp screwdriver all the way. Better when they're scared shitless. She was dreading a bum fuck when I laid her on her face. Never even imagined the screwdriver coming. So quick. In that pretty ear, and most of the way through. Took another smack to get it out the other side. Hard bone. Very short, very high-pitched shriek. Very sudden. Then worked with my knife. Lean girl, not so much fat. Life on the street, I guess. Don't waste hard-earned money on food when you need another fix. Knife hit some ribs on the way down. Long way down. Carved "A." "Artist, I am. Something about seeing that come up on Polaroid made me smile. That special sound again. Tiny panties. Red, thong. Cut out my piece. Hardly enough left to put back on her. Shame about using my best screwdriver after I spent so much time filing it sharp. They got to find it one day. One day they'll find two. Kept to timetable. She was little. Easy to stuff in trunk, wrapped up. 2 a. m., Drove straight to S. Burnco sign shows up at night, thank God. Threw her over top strand of barbed wire. No trouble. Kick-rolled her down the hill. Not a problem. She was rolling faster than I could keep up, carrying tools. Found bushes at bottom of hill just before

it flattens out. Fucking deer scared me in the dark. Worked for one hour digging. Put her in. Nearly pulled my screwdriver out. Shame to lose it. Must stick to plan. Left it through her head. Filled her in. Put back in plants I'd dug out. Still more earth left over. Spent long time spreading extra earth under the bushes at the bottom of slope. Fucking climb up that hill hard work. Stopped, several times, wheezing. Getting too old for this. Back at my car 10 to 5. Ten minutes to spare. Out of there. Never saw no one."

This time the double negative hardly registered. Ben was numbed—and confused again and much more scared than before. If Garry was a serial killer relating with obvious relish every minute of his actions, the killings were too close to Ben. One phrase scared Ben to death.

"Carved 'A'." "Artist I am."

Ben recalled only too clearly where he'd seen the letter "A" carved in a murder victim's body. It was Angela Braithwaite down in Pincher Creek. He'd seen the pathologist's photograph of the "A," which he'd first taken to be a human eye with its prominent eye-lashes. But this didn't really make sense. Braithwaite's body was found right away, in an open field. So it couldn't have been her. How many more woman had he killed and carved? Why was there another "A?" Christ, hope he hadn't gone right through the alphabet and started again. And so much for "Jack and Jill," that must have been wrong.

Much more frightening for Ben was the realization he recognized the location where this body was supposedly buried. He himself had regularly slid on his backside down that very hill, on his way to a productive fishing spot. And he'd wheezed, too, going back up when it seemed more like a mountain. And Ben's fishing location was reached when you turned off the 22X highway at the Burnco sign. Ben calmed his rising panic here when he applied some reasoned thinking to his racing fears. No buried body had ever been discovered there. Whatever else all the rest of this package was, this piece here was obviously a sick and morbid joke by Garry, knowing he'd throw Ben into a panic. Ben felt sweat across his forehead and at the back of his neck.

The first of this bunch of folded pages was numbered 260. Nothing was dated but if the numbers were strictly chronological, then at least Ben could put all the different accounts in the right order. He worked all day at home on the task. It became both a revelation and the start of a nightmare. His conclusion after 16 hours studying the pages of scribble shocked him. Garry was not only a serial killer, he was THE serial killer of the four women in Ben's "Theo File." It suddenly became obvious to Ben. This killer hadn't been satisfied at killing four women. It wasn't anything to do with murdering them. The killer had worked equally as hard, no, harder, at framing innocent men, who were still in prison right now. That's what this was all about. And Garry was the sick bastard. Ben's underworld contact, a man who'd almost brought a veneer of glamour to Ben's job a few years back, was the monster Ben was about to expose. Until Ben started working with his contact in the medical examiner's office, no one knew a serial killer even existed. Ben had already managed to make the cops understand they'd convicted four innocent men, and missed the real killer. But they were still searching for their first clue. They had no idea who the real killer was.

Now Ben reckoned he knew.

Before he'd do anything about it, he'd run through everything in this hated package again. He'd better be right before he took his next step. When Ben started matching Garry's previously incomprehensible scribblings with the facts he knew about at least four of the murders, it was suddenly easy. It was terrifying, sickening, but not difficult to follow at all.

On one of the two tables in front of him, Ben opened the "Theo File" to the first murder. Jill Bereson, the White Spot restaurant waitress murdered in Calgary, head caved in with a golf club, mutilated, dumped on a golf course, with Darren Sunderland successfully framed, tried, convicted and sentenced. Ben now felt confident he understood in his own mind what had gone on sufficiently to change the classification of Sunderland from simply "convicted" to "framed and wrongly convicted."

On the other table, he placed Garry's first spiral bound ragged notebook, opened it at page 1, and worked as carefully as possible, seeing what he could match with his "Theo files."

Those very first phrases, so baffling only 24 hours earlier when he read them in the office, made sense right away.

"T. The guy in the corner's good. It'll be him. And I know which one he's going down for. They don't stand a fucking chance."

"Did some basic stuff tonight. Followed him out. Big car. Ford Taurus. License AAP 424. It'll be good. Fucking big trunk. He has no idea. Waited in the parking lot after he'd gone. She came out with two other staff. Has her own Honda. Leave that til later. Don't need that yet."

"W. S. again. Same corner. Easy. Followed the Taurus to his home. Has a garage but parked it in the driveway. Better."

"At this more than a week. He's busy. Various feeding holes but W. S. three times. Used the washroom last thing before leaving. Then lights up outside each time just before driving off. Golf this weekend. Not very good. Parked it in the driveway every night. Decided he does live on his own. Never seen a woman come home with him. No lights ever on in there. Busy man."

"Hasn't taken long. Nearly ready. Three times he's been to the airport and flown out. Back next day each time. Left the Taurus in the Park N' Jet each time. Played the same golf course each weekend. Different partners. Always men. Very busy man. That won't last."

"S. Found the right place today. Gravel track out of Fish Creek Park backs onto the rough ground off part of the golf course. Drive there, short walk, do the business."

This was Garry, stalking someone, but not the woman victim at all. This was him stalking the man he'd earmarked to be the poor bastard who was going down for the murder. Garry was stalking Darren Sunderland by day and by night, so he could frame him. It made Ben's forehead and neck sweat again to think of Garry sitting in the White Spot restaurant—*"W. S. three times"*—watching Sunderland, learning how he entertained business contacts there, probably watching how he seemed attracted to one waitress in particular, Jill Bereson. Garry would be skulking in the shadows of the parking lot, watching Sunderland go to his car, even noting such grisly details as *"fucking big trunk,"* knowing full well what he'd be stuffing in there later on. He'd obviously been watching Sunderland a long time, following him home and studying his lifestyle, before starting the journal. Garry already knew in these opening pages that his unsuspecting victim lived alone, regularly played golf and frequently flew out of Calgary International on business trips.

Mostly everything was falling into place. From his Bereson murder file, Ben checked and confirmed the discarded golf club used to murder the woman had been found thrown into deep undergrowth where Fish Creek Park abutted the golf course. As Garry put it,

"Found the right place today. Gravel track out of Fish Creek Park backs onto the rough ground off part of the golf course. Drive there, short walk, do the business."

Some small references in Garry's writings still didn't yet make complete sense. It seemed to Ben he'd used as few words as possible, hadn't wasted any, and hadn't included any detail he didn't need to. So why he was so interested in Sunderland's lighting up a smoke outside the restaurant wasn't at all clear. But Ben realized one of the next passages in Garry's deadly journal contained a time reference, the first one, giving him a chance to do some cross checking with his notes in the Theo files.

"Waited til T was away on his overnight flight. Did his house. Streets full of kids on Halloween. In easy, hardly touched the place," Garry had written. Ben turned to his Bereson murder file, now gaining confidence with every move, pretty sure he knew what he'd find. And there it was. Among the notes of his long telephone interview with Sunderland he found it.

Sunderland was angry and frustrated, yea, yea.

Sunderland had told Ben a bunch of bad things had happened to him around that bewildering time (the time of the murder, November 5, 1990), yea, yea.

Here it was.

"On Halloween Night that year, a few days before the murder, someone under the guise of trick-or-treat had broken into his home in Calgary—on Halloween Night."

Garry had broken into Sunderland's home Halloween Night, making his final preparations for murdering the waitress and framing the restaurant customer. Sunderland, mystified by everything happening to him at that time, put it down to bad luck. He thought it was trivial and only mentioned it in passing. If only Sunderland knew it, this was a vital step in the events that shattered his life. Ben knew it. He had Garry's word on it.

Now everything was matching so easily, Ben couldn't believe he hadn't seen it all straight away, except it was so mind-numbing.

This was in his notes from Sunderland.

"Whoever broke in had stolen one of his most expensive golf clubs. His whole set of clubs were available, but the thief had chosen one and left the rest, though the others were damn expensive, too."

And this was in Garry's hand.

"It's started. Feels good. He won't know he's been done over til his next golf game. Then he'll know."

Garry had broken in without trashing the place, so Sunderland would hardly notice. He'd probably take his golf bag to his next game, and only when he went for his No. 7 iron, would he find it missing. Sunderland's No. 7 iron—the murder weapon.

Ben stopped his headlong rush through all this. It was suddenly dawning on him how thoroughly this had been planned. It was inconceivable you could murder someone and frame someone else so perfectly they would stand no chance of being acquitted. You'd have to make every morsel of forensic evidence fit. You'd have to make every circumstantial fact fit. You'd have to mold the murder to the killer's life-style. The victim would have to be a part of the murderer's life for their paths to cross. It would have to be a fantastic endeavor. You'd have to devote your life to studying your two victims, your target for the framing and your victim for the murder itself.

"That's it," said Ben out loud, with no one to hear. He'd just solved one of the few remaining pieces of the puzzle. At first, Ben couldn't work out who "T" was in Garry's narrative, and certainly couldn't understand when "T" turned up again in what seemed to be the wrong murder in the wrong year. Garry hadn't bothered with naming names. In each murder, 'T' was the target." It didn't much matter to Garry who they were, as long as they fit in his frame. And "V" wasn't any particular woman, just a victim. Ben supposed Garry must have actually found out the names of his targets and victims doing his research on them, but was it possible he could have killed one, and ruined the life of the other, without even knowing their names? Was there any bottom to this pit of cold, evil malice?

The phone rang.

"Yo, Ben Ludlow."

"Pack a bag, Ben, you're going driving through the night," said the instantly familiar voice of the office.

"What's up?"

"You know those tunnels in the Rogers Pass in BC, well, some semi's demolished a tour bus inside a tunnel and they're already talking about six dead."

That was about par for the course. Ben had noticed a story just a day or two earlier about this crazy May weather with ice and snow in the interior of BC, and he'd travelled through the Rogers Pass enough times to know when weather was bad in BC it was a bastard in the Pass. And now he'd have to drive, probably out there in snow, with ice on the ground, through the night, most likely on the same black ice that no doubt caused this crash, without crashing, to get the story.

"I'll be there," he said, putting the phone down, inwardly annoyed at having to leave his murders when he was making real headway, but pleased at least he'd be working on what would be tomorrow's front page story.

He packed a bag, hit the office, grabbed a laptop and a cell phone and turned his old Chevy van across the parking lot, seeing out there on the western horizon beyond the illuminated "Calgary Mail" sign, the snow-capped mountains where he knew he'd eventually wind up in some hours' time, in their least glamorous setting, inside a tunnel of death.

He listened to radio bulletins on the half-hour all the way out there. These confirmed there were six dead, there was black ice, and these were German tourists in a tour bus. Ben mentally noted to himself that would mean language problems, little to no chance of pick-up pictures of the victims, and all in the land of the RCMP.

He knew his life would be made hell by the Mounties' enthusiasm at following the code of their profession to be as obstructive to media as possible, a skill they'd honed to perfection over generations of practice. Ben recalled the day a small float plane crashed in some tiny remote lake in the far-flung northern reaches of BC, where the one-man RCMP detachment probably never had contact with any humans for weeks on end. Word was the pilot was from Calgary. When Ben asked the one man on duty for some basic details, he was stone-walled with the classic Mountie first line of obstruction, "I'm not authorized to talk to the media." Well-versed, the guy followed it up with the second line "you'll have to check with the media liaison officer tomorrow." And showing his complete understanding of how to handle the media, he put the phone down. To this day, Ben was still amazed that the deeply inbred doctrine of media dislike had permeated so far north to such a remote and tiny outpost of the RCMP. So Ben totally circumvented this temporary obstruction as he always did. He soon discovered the name of the one bar in the tiny community, the "Lakeside Lodge," rang it and talked to the barman.

"That's damn funny you calling from Calgary," said the barman who was also the owner. "Guess what, the pilot was from Calgary as well." What a start to an interview.

Ben reached Golden, the last stop before the Rogers Pass, when Golden was in a state of siege. The Mounties had shut the Trans-Canada Highway, the only way to the west immediately it became obvious nothing was going to get through the Pass until the carnage of whatever was inside that tunnel had been removed. That meant first rescuing survivors; then the careful body removal of however many didn't survive; then meticulous vehicle and road measurements and examination by traffic analysts for the pending court cases which were bound to follow; and then the removal of the wreckage, no easy task when it involved an intertwined semi-trailer tractor and a tour bus. It had clearly taken hours already and from what Ben could see around him even more clearly wasn't yet complete. The only part of Golden the motorist sees driving through is the ribbon development alongside the Trans-Canada Highway. Tonight the ribbon through Golden was the world's biggest parking lot for semis. First one lane of the road had filled nose-to-tail with parked semis for the entire length of Golden's Trans Canada stretch. Then, the inside lane filled up with a parallel line-up of semis, all with radiator grills to back fenders. Then a full line-up of hopefuls who'd tried to sneak through on the inside hard-shoulder formed the third parallel row, which blocked every available west-bound space. And as hundreds more semis poured westward into Golden, they overflowed into the parking lots of motels and restaurants, like a dammed river bursting its banks and spreading sideways into its flood plain.

Denied any hope of parking on asphalt, Ben found a tiny island of grass and squeezed his Chevy onto it. As he'd done so many times before, he walked up to the Mountie standing resolutely in the middle of the highway, knowing he was about to get nowhere, and at least asked the question.

"Ben Ludlow, Calgary Mail, can I get through to the crash scene?" he asked, not wasting his breath on niceties when he already knew the answer.

"Wait one," said the Mountie, pulling her radio from under her top coat.

"Golden to dispatch, I got one more media here, can I let him through, it's one red Chevy van," she said, and waited.

She received word in her earpiece, and motioned Ben nearer.

"Yea, it's the second to last tunnel before Revelstoke. Watch out for the black ice, and report to the command post at the tunnel," she said.

Hardly believing his luck, Ben hurried back to his grass island before someone in high command changed his mind. He drove his van along the grass median, over the grassed section of Tim Horton's forecourt, and the wrong way along a slip road, reached the Mountie, looked anxiously at her, fearing perhaps he'd misunderstood everything she'd said, and swept by onto the Trans-Canada Highway heading westward. Ben felt the glares of hatred from several hundred truckers, all of whom just had to get onto that roadway and head west, as they watched him disappear into the night, where they could not go.

It was an eerie journey, being the only vehicle driving through the night on the Trans Canada which was usually alive with semi-trailer trucks. For nearly an hour, Ben drove, the cones of light from his headlamps never illuminating another vehicle. It would probably be like this on the day after a nuclear bomb had wiped out all mankind—just Ben and the darkness, and no one. Ben always felt he'd be the one spared. After all, there would always have to be a reporter left to write about it for posterity. He overcame the urge to speed, reminding himself over and over he was probably driving on black ice. And then he saw lights up ahead. This must be it—a recovery crane in the center of the road. The ugly underside of a semi, all wheels and axles was jammed across three lanes, with the cab section dangling off the road, hanging over the parapet of a bridge at some grotesque angle, like a fish's head held on by a slither of skin during gutting. A workman waving a sizzling flare in the darkness motioned Ben to the one narrow lane still open.

"Go easy, it's all black ice through here," cautioned the workman.

"I thought the crash was supposed to be in a tunnel?" Ben shouted at the flare-bearer.

"No, that one's about a mile up the road, this one happened hours before that one," said the man.

"Anyone killed in this one?" asked Ben, always hopeful of finding some little "meanwhile" to add to his main story. Ben loved the "meanwhile" adds to his death and destruction articles.

He'd write about some fresh murder where some teenager would have been knifed to death in some parking lot outside a night club. And he'd be able to neatly finish off the story with "meanwhile, city homicide detectives are still investigating last week's night club stabbing which left one man dead and two others in hospital with stab wounds."

If and when he ever reached this road carnage in the tunnel of death, somewhere up there in the darkness, he could already see his story of multiple deaths among the tourists ending with "meanwhile in a separate crash a few hundred yards east of the tunnel, a semi-trailer rolled off the Trans-Canada Highway, killing its driver."

But Ben was to be disappointed.

"No, it was a miracle, the driver climbed out and called us on his cell-phone," said the man.

"Cheers, then," said Ben, robbed of his "meanwhile." When you're writing about death and destruction, miracle escapes aren't worth a "meanwhile." He drove on with the little oasis of light round the crash scene growing ever smaller in his rear-view mirror as he headed further westward.

As it happened, the tour bus and the tractor trailer unit that met head-on in the tunnel had been towed into Revelstoke before Ben reached it. He found the wreckage in a breaker's yard in the town. Six tourists had been killed outright when the tractor unit, mercifully without the additional weight of its trailer, had sliced away half the bus and everyone sitting on that side.

Next day was going to be a nightmare. Where to start? Where was Ben going to find relatives of the dead who were all German visitors? Where would he find survivors? And if he found them, what were the chances of them speaking English? And where would he get photographs of the horror crash? And what were the chances of doing all this in time for deadline? Ben soon discovered the patron saint of "death and destruction" reporters—whoever he is—was shining on him that day. By the end of it, Ben felt like he'd won the lottery. He'd interviewed survivors, he'd talked to relatives of the dead, overcome the language barrier, and he had a handful of satisfyingly gory and graphic photographs of the crash scene inside the tunnel of death, and everything was back to the office in time for deadline! Of course Ben let the office believe his personal brilliance had overcome all these obstacles to produce the goods on time. He didn't let them know the first people he ran into that morning were a Swiss television crew out of Los Angeles, who had raced from the Los Angeles earthquake of a few days back to get to the tunnel of death in the Rocky Mountains. They were ahead of Ben by having a German interpreter on their team. In the whirlwind day that unfolded, Ben made sure he was at the interpreter's elbow every time she interviewed a German relative arriving at the police station in Revelstoke. He soon had a notebook full of survivor stories and grieving relative tributes to the dead.

And as for the photographs—this was where Ben's patron saint worked overtime. Suddenly, the RCMP called a press conference, which Ben, with his ear to the ground, heard about just in time. Helpful Mounties, a paradoxical phrase if ever Ben had heard one, gave their detailed and really useful information against a backcloth of a montage of photographs taken inside the tunnel during the rescue operation. And they had a set of the photographs available for the media to take away. It was above and beyond helpful. It was everything a reporter could wish for—and more. In future, whenever Ben lapsed into cursing all Mounties for their obstinate hatred of media, he vowed always to add "with the exception of Revelstoke."

It was on that trip, driving a deserted road in the dead of night on black ice with no human contact around him, not knowing when he'd reach the action that Ben went through the "deadline mathematical calculations" he always needed on these panic jobs. How long will it take me to get there? How long will it take to get the story? How long will I have to get to civilization to find a phone link to get the story in? Deadline was this mysterious newspaper word that most people took as an abstract nebulous almost meaningless phrase that reporters used. In fact, if only people knew it, it was the whole exact, precise, clearly-defined structure on which the newspaper was based. Ben found it easiest to explain it to people by looking at the whole process backward.

In those days in England, many people started their days by picking up their newspaper at 6 a. m. promptly from their corner newsagent's shop. It was just there, like magic. But for that to work, the newsagent had to have the bundle of papers in his hand by 5:30 a. m. That would only work if the delivery van bringing the papers was at his door precisely on time at 5:29 a. m. This meant the van had to be loaded and leaving the newspaper office halfway across the city at 5 a. m. at the latest. So the presses had to be running hours before that so that all 100,000 copies of the latest edition would be ready on time. And the guy in the press room couldn't push the start button until all the pages were in place on the press. Those pages couldn't be prepared until the sub-editors had finished with them, and they had to have the last one away by an exact minute, say midnight. And for the sub-editors to have any time to work on the story, it had to be in their hands by say 11:30 p. m. Which is where Ben came in. It was very simple. He must have finished getting his story in by 11:30 p. m. It didn't matter how icy the road was, how far he had to drive, how brilliant his story was, how hard he had worked to get it, if it reached the office at 11:35 p. m. it was too damn late and would never see the light of day. Hence his "deadline mathematical calculations" which governed his every move. He'd got it all right again that time. He was getting quite good at it.

It was several days before Ben could get back to Garry's hand-written odyssey, two days in which the headline "HORROR IN TUNNEL OF DEATH" took its rightful place on the wall behind the city desk. As well, a memo from the boss commending Ben for his professional work took its rightful place in Ben's file of similar memos being saved for the day when the Mail might sack him, and he'd try suing for wrongful dismissal, waving the memos as evidence of how good he was—like it would help!

He knew exactly where he wanted to plunge back into the hand-written scrawl. An idea had crossed his mind out on the eerie stretch of the Trans-Canada alone in the dark. He'd had plenty of time to think after passing the Golden obstacle and before reaching the golden aura of light illuminating the first crash scene. Thinking while at the wheel is a feature of driving in remote western Canada—a luxury denied drivers in traffic-crammed cities elsewhere. Roads are predominantly straight, sparsely used, and you can think, well almost daydream, having only to devote a relatively small portion of your brain to concentrating on the road. Not like in Britain, where every nerve, muscle and ounce of fiber and concentration has to be razor sharp every second, as you drive on the edge, inches away from tons of hurtling metal racing in front of you, behind you, and coming at you, in a non-stop blur of motion. And on that night in particular, of course, Ben was the only vehicle for miles in either direction. It wasn't surprising his thoughts strayed back to Garry and the murders. In the darkness that night, he'd had a vague idea linking Garry's reference to the guy he intended to frame for the first murder as lighting up a smoke, and the fact Ben recalled that a cigarette end had been found in the murder victim's body. Out on the road, Ben couldn't match it all up exactly, but mentally noted he needed to check it out whenever he got back to Calgary.

It didn't take long for him to find the reference he needed. Here it was in Garry's small spiral wire-bound notebook.

"Cigarette ends easy. Worked good. Waited til T was finished meal. Made sure I was at a table nearer to the door than him. When he got up, I was on my way. He lit up, smoked, threw away the butt. I had it and no one saw a thing. Can't wait for Friday. The cocksuckers won't know what's hit them."

Okay, thought Ben, trying to marry together the theory he'd concocted out on the Trans-Canada Highway in the dark, with the crazy hand-writing in front of him. Ben reckoned the vital words were *"He lit up, smoked, threw away the butt. I had it and no one saw a thing."* Ben turned to the relevant page on the notes in his file on the murder of Jill Bereson.

His contact had shown him these notes from Keen, the medical examiner at the time.

"Removed from inside the vagina, one cigarette end entirely unseen from exterior. Sent for laboratory analysis and DNA testing." The later notes showed forensic laboratory analysis indicated the cigarette end bore DNA evidence, and more detailed DNA analysis showed it to match Sunderland's DNA.

Then Ben switched back to Garry's scrawl. Complete confirmation. Here was the next section, in really scribbled hand, like he had been especially hurried, or excited. *"It's all done. Club went almost thru skull. Had trouble pulling it out. Like that sound when knife's going thru the skin. Done it over and over. Only burned her once. Was real careful where I put butt. Been looking after that one like it was a diamond ring. Remembered to do all the happies. Carving, panties, Polaroid. The lot. Work of art."*

There it was in hand-written black and white. *"Was real careful where I put butt. Been looking after that one like it was a diamond ring."* Before, that passage probably wouldn't have meant a thing to Ben. Now it was crystal clear. Sunderland's cigarette butt had been carefully placed precisely where Keen's diligence had found it.

Ben went back to his notes of his interview with Sunderland. In one of his most frustrated moments, Sunderland said he didn't argue with the prosecution's findings that it was his DNA on the cigarette end inside this woman. He simply said it was impossible.

Ben suddenly knew how the impossible had been achieved. It was almost unthinkable. It was incredible. Only some mad, tormented mind could conceive it, and God only knew how Ben would ever get anyone to believe him if he ever tried to explain it. But here, surrounded by all this evidence, it was obvious.

Garry had concocted a scheme to obtain a cigarette end which Sunderland had smoked, which had Sunderland's saliva on it, and which meant it had Sunderland's DNA on it. When Garry murdered his victim, he placed the butt inside her vagina, providing the final clinching detail of forensic evidence from which Sunderland could never escape. And it would explain why she was wearing her panties. He'd carefully replaced them as a second line of defense to ensure the precious cigarette end stayed inside her. Ben knew the crotch-piece of the panties had been cut out. Shit, Ben knew he almost certainly had it in the bunch of panty remnants he'd found in the package, but an explanation for that too fell into place. Ben had been to enough of Stone's seminars to know a classic hallmark of the sexual serial killer was for him to keep a trophy of each victim, which he'd often use to help him revisit the murder in his erotic fantasies. The delicate part of a victim's panties which had nestled closest to the lips of her vagina would do very nicely.

Now that Ben felt he'd cracked Garry's cryptic code and almost knew what he was looking for in advance, he plunged quickly on. A few mysteries still remained, like Garry's apparent reference to six victims, and Ben only knowing of four, which meant Ben didn't know what order they came in. But applying what he knew, he calculated Garry's next murder could have been the next one in Ben's sequence of four, the whip torture murder of Angela Braithwaite down in Pincher Creek, back in February 1991. Ben hunted through the scrawl.

"Got out of Calgary right away. Got set up renting shitty trailer on fucking rough piece of land 200 miles away at PC. That's far enough. Mounties down here. They ain't got the sense to suss it out. Perfect. No one can see nothing I'm doing. Remote. Even got pissed at Christmas. Seen a good looking V in the library."

Oh God. Ben was right again. Here's Garry in "PC"—Pincher Creek—around Christmas, a couple of months before Braithwaite was murdered.

"Got my T. Real redneck cowboy, right down to the black fucking cowboy hat. They got something going. He's in most days. I watch 'em together. I'm looking at fucking nudes in the art books. All them shaved bushes. How come these models don't have no fucking pubic hair. Followed T to big ranch, south, turn right along gravel track, lots of horse boxes in his yard. Must be fucking rich. No matter. When this lot fucking lands on him, all his money ain't gonna help him."

Ben saw a break in the writing. What came next was clearly written sometime later.

"Easy this being a real cowboy. Got my own fucking black cowboy hat. Timed my walk to T's place, went through his barn. Never touched nothing. Just looked. He's a whip freak. He's got 'em lying all over. He'll fucking wish he'd never seen a whip when I've finished."

Captivated, almost mesmerized, knowing what was coming next, Ben read on, feeling like he was looking into the future and knowing a tragedy was going to happen, and being unable to prevent it. He noticed another break, another section written later.

"Fucking cocksuckers finally got it. Halle-fucking-luya. They finally nicked the bastard. Calgary's gone down. Finally. Spoon feed it to 'em and they finally swallow it. Took the fuckers long enough. What's their problem? It never took 'em that long to nick me, and I never done nothing. That bastard will be sweating now. Ask him where his fucking No. 7 iron is? That'll fuck him. Time for me to go to work again. Friday will be good. Gives me three days. His rich rancher buddies fetch him every Friday. I seen 'em. His nightmare's coming down."

Ben puzzled a bit over that lot. But he remembered talking to his contact in the medical examiner's office about the timings of the murders when they were first trying to unravel the mystery. Ben had found a pattern. He'd noticed each of the four murders happened a few days after the suspect in the previous murder had been arrested. Ben had no idea what the possible pattern meant, and his contact had dismissed it altogether as coincidence, and they'd ignored it. Ben checked again in his "Theo" file for the Calgary killing. Sunderland was arrested and charged February 24, and it was reported in the media next day, February 25. Braithwaite had been murdered in Pincher Creek on Friday, February 28, three days later. Now it became all too perfectly obvious. Garry had to wait for one suspect to be arrested before he committed the next murder, so there would be absolutely no link between them. Each would be a completely separate murder, neatly wrapped up by one police department before another unrelated murder would land on another police department. It was brilliant and it worked.

"Getting her's easy. He drives to V's house, parks in same place outside. She looks out window. He raises cowboy hat. She runs out to get in. Same every time I seen it."

Ben shuddered. He had this vision of Garry, always skulking in the shadows, one day watching his target's place, seeing his friends picking him up, learning his social curriculum, and another day, following the target to the victim's home. How many times, Ben wondered, had the pair met at her home, perfectly innocently, unaware a man with staring eyes was hidden out there somewhere, watching them with murder in his heart.

A long passage followed next, clearly written after the murder had taken place. It was very detailed, blow-by-blow, save for any account of sexual gratification. Maybe there was something in this sadistic sexual deviant which he liked to keep private, maybe his most personal erotic fantasies to be shared with no one.

"Walked there, wearing my black cowboy hat after watching ranchers pick him up. They fucked up snow in the gravel yard lovely, so my footprints hidden. Went to barn, chose old whip thrown in corner. Remembered exactly shape it was in. Went to his truck, drove it to her place, parked outside in exact spot, watched her in the window, raised my cowboy hat. She came running out to me. Fucking easy, easy. She was in the truck before she knew she was in fucking trouble. Drove her to my trailer. Time to play. No one to hear her begging, screaming. Surprised how much fucking blood came from the whipping. Liked the sound of the swishing whip on skin. Wrapped that whip round her neck so tight it left a crisscross pattern. Some clever cocksucking

cop will match that good. But you gotta make sure. So I bust off the end of the whip for later. Played with my knife, making them nice sounds I like. Did the panties and my artistic thing. Took its Polaroid picture. Bit bloody this time, but you can make it out. Threw her in the back of T's pickup. Fucker had a pile of hay bales in there, but there was enough blood to soak through to the metal. Smeared her around in there, getting blood on the metal, then drove her to where she'd soon be found, up by Highway 3 near wooden cut-out cowboys. Put my busted off end of whip on the ground and laid her on top. Even fucking stupid cops could put that together. Drove back to his place. Deserted just like my time plan knew it would be. Put that whip back in the barn exactly in the shape I found it, two rings and a letter 'S', and parked T's truck exactly in the same spot I found it. Walked back to trailer."

Ben noted throughout this entire section, Garry had referred to this couple only as "T" and "V," never once by their names. It was chilling. And, as before, Garry seemed to have taken more delight in framing the man than he did in the murder, torture and blood-letting of his victim, which he kept mostly to himself. It was as if his anger directed at these unknown male targets whose names he didn't even use meant more to him than his sadistic sexual pleasure from torturing and murdering these women.

Ben wondered what the reference was to Polaroid pictures. He hadn't found any in the tin box. Perhaps they were so powerful an erotic stimulus for Garry that he'd kept them. There was still a lot Ben didn't know.

With two murders accounted for Ben was now looking for clues in the scrawl to show that Garry's next episode had begun. If Ben's interpretation of all this was right, he should be able to find some sign of the action shifting to Taber. He should find some reference connected to a murder by a vicar in the Taber Tabernacle Church there of a woman in his flock, the third in the series of four. Ben just needed to check a date. Knowing exactly what pattern he expected to find, he pulled out his "Theo" file on Angela Braithwaite again to check when her killer Paul Andres had been charged. He found it. Andres was charged in Pincher Creek on June 29, with the story saying so in the next day's paper. So, from June 30 onward, Garry would have read it, probably avidly. It would be completely safe for him to move on to his third murder. He could be smug in the knowledge that brilliant detective work in Pincher Creek had already solved his second murder, and his second innocent target was already in the slammer, bewildered, confused, and scared shitless.

Ben was right. As usual, Garry quoted no dates, but it wasn't difficult now for Ben to interpret Garry's odd code that had seemed so baffling before.

"Picked a church in Tab. They won't fucking believe this one. Me, in church, that's funny. Picked the North Tab. Anglican. Been there so much they think I'm part of the congregation. Why not? I'm living in Tab. Fucking horrible place. South of railway tracks. Renting this place with tons of crap in back yard. That'll be good when I gotta do what I gotta do. No one can see in through all that garbage."

It looked to Ben like it was all falling into place again.

Garry made no reference to time but at least according to the sequence of the pages, he'd moved again. He'd gone from renting some acreage at Pincher Creek near where the last murder happened, to Taber where Ben knew exactly what was developing here. But Garry was in the wrong church. Ben turned Garry's page, bottom to top and started reading down the next page. Oh good God, Garry was trolling all the churches in Taber, stalking vicars, looking for a candidate to be the next "T."

"Three times now I been to the Mormons. Stick out like a fucking sore thumb there. Not good. Been to the United. At least, no one noticed me there. Been to church more times in the past few weeks than all my life put together. Bet I don't get fucking redeemed though."

Reading this section, Ben shuddered again at the thought of this force of evil mixing with the good God-fearing people of Taber. These were people who had probably been welcoming him with genuine love and affection, while he'd been planning the probable destruction of all their faith with his every move. Ben read on. Here was another of those sections, clearly written after a break from the one above—this time in red ink.

"Hellafuckingluya. A fucking sign from heaven. Right in the middle of the sermon, right in the church, this fucker, this preacher has a nose bleed. I can use him right away. United fucking church it is. Stop looking. Like any good

Christian, ha ha, I rushed out to help him mop it up. You bet I did. Others got there before me. He's always doing it, they said. They're used to mopping up his blood. Even finished his sermon with plug stuffed up his nose. We are on our fucking way."

The red ink stopped. Ben stopped. Here it was again, a serial killer of innocent defenseless women spending all this enormous effort to stalk a man target he was about to frame. So far Garry hadn't even mentioned finding a "V." No thought of that, yet he already had an innocent man targeted as the killer—and a perfectly respectable honorable man of the cloth, at that.

He was back to black ink.

"T lives nearby the church. Seen him lots of nights leave his station wagon at the church and walk home. He's gonna be a fucking pushover. Busy work this. One woman at UC spends a lot of time there with him. She'll probably do. Works in photo shop. Seen her there. This fucking lot's coming down on this town. It's the cops fault. You watch. Fucking heads'll roll over this fucking lot. They'll wish they were never born. Any day I reckon. Just waiting."

Ben still had difficulty trying to understand the ramblings driving Garry's thoughts. Maybe there was a motive, maybe a philosophy, a reason for all this, but it never really made sense. Who was Garry really aiming at? Serial killers were usually driven by a power complex of having total domination over their victim. They enjoyed controlling how much violence they wanted to unleash on them. They relished having the victim vulnerable to their every sexual fantasy. Above all, they reveled at being in the position of playing God—to be able to choose the moment when they would decide when this person would die. Where was any of this in Garry's ramblings? Ben hadn't seen a single word. The times when Garry had his victims at his mercy, when they were clearly being physically tortured and sexually butchered, when he was demonstrably wielding his power, none of these were referred to here. Stalking these women clearly provided some element of enjoyment for Garry. But stalking a male target to be the suspect brought him even more enjoyment. But far above all this, the driving force seemed to be his ranting about every cop having to pay for the injustices heaped on him. Ben turned the page.

"PC has gone down. The fuckers fell for it again. Need to get busy. Got V in view. The photo girl's gonna have her photo in the paper, but she won't see it."

There was another break in the writing. The next section was written in particularly scribbly text. Rushed? Excited even? Ben struggled to make it out.

"Got 'im. Got 'im. Easy. Got 'im leaving church. T walked his usual route out of the church, past the 7-Eleven. I could see him through the slats in the fence, like I'd seen him three times in a row. Came up behind him, hit him with a swinging hand right on the nose. Best fucking nosebleed I ever saw. He went down. Crumpled. Bled good. Nearly went bad...Using the syringe was easy. Noses bleed good. Fucking car came by, lit me up in its headlights, but it probably looked like I was helping him. Left real quick in case the car came back. Had what I needed. Never had so much fucking blood to play with. He is going down. Fucking God Almighty won't save him when I'm done. He's going down and taking all them fuckers with him. He didn't know what hit him. They still won't know what's hit them. None of them will know. Cocksuckers."

Ben winced again at the awful juxtaposition of the deity and the obscenity, so seldom seen other than in Garry's preposterous prose. Well, Ron Lincoln actually did it once. It must be something about the people Ben knew.

The phone interrupted him again.

"Ben Ludlow."

"It's another big one, Ben, it's a pickup truck into a Greyhound bus, big explosion and fire, four or five dead. Get on the road as soon as you can, it's up on Highway 43 well north about five hours."

"On my way," said Ben, inwardly cursing; after all, it wasn't many days ago he was driving through the Rockies on the tour bus crash. What was it— open season on buses? It was rare for Ben to go far north. The Mail's chain of newspapers had its own office and paper in Edmonton to cover the northern half of the province. Occasionally, when Calgary's editorial hierarchy wanted a thing doing properly it would send north, never being too impressed with Edmonton's performance.

Ben left straight from home, not looking forward to the drive north which was a boring drag. Driving west for buses and trucks colliding in snow tunnels was interesting, with panoramic mountain views round every bend, mountainous hairpins, long descents into fir-tree lined valleys, never a dull moment really. But driving north was a drag—three hours of nothing much to reach Edmonton, a slog through the always-congested city, and two more hours ever northward. It wasn't as bad as the mercilessly flat and featureless bore when heading east, where the greatest danger was falling asleep at the wheel, but it was bad enough. Once on the road, it struck Ben he would be lucky to find much of a scene left on the highway after five hours, but those in the office who decided such things must know best.

As it happened, Ben was right. Five hours later, as he reached the stretch of Highway 43 where a Greyhound bus had become a fiery tomb for a bunch of passengers and where 30 others had suffered burns and injuries, nothing much remained. A large black patch of melted asphalt and burned grass marked the fatal spot.

He was too late. How late? One grieving family had already had time to erect a roadside memorial to their loved one lost in the fiery encounter. Their small flag and flowers, signaling their grief, made Ben groan. He wasn't often this far behind the action. Still, he read the message on the little memorial, gleaned names and information and turned it into a sidebar for his story after he's pursued it with a few telephone calls. With nothing else to see at the scene, Ben scouted out the nearest hospital where some of the 30 survivors must be. He decided to camp out in the parking lot outside the main door.

As he drove up, a family group was leaving. He intercepted them and was straight into copy for his story. They'd been visiting mother who was on the bus. All her possessions were burned in the inferno. She'd been soaked in fuel but luckily didn't catch fire. She'd been dragged out through a window by some unknown hero and, to make Ben's day, she was from Calgary. Ben filed his story, a good read, pleased to have salvaged the day after arriving so late. He was looking forward now to a well-earned rest after his five hour drag north.

"Hang on," said Phil back at the office, who'd just endured the pain-in-the-butt imposition of having to take Ben's copy over the phone, "Frank wants a word."

Ben listened to ten seconds of the Mail's promo recording everybody had to suffer while being transferred from one extension to the next, and was onto Frank.

"Where are you exactly?" asked Frank.

"Highway 43, where do you think I am," said Ben. "Why?"

"Good," said Frank. "You're on your way again. It's not far. Peace River. Massive flooding. They say the whole town's under water. You'll be there in no time."

"Thank you, Frank," said Ben, as his thoughts of relaxing went out the window. Ben looked at the map. What the hell was Frank talking about? "You'll be there in no time"—it was about four hours' drive further north—four hours at least.

In fact, it was nearer five hours. And when Ben pulled into Peace River, he did find a large section of the town cordoned off. This wasn't down to flood water, but because the entire place was under six feet of clinging, oozing, smelly, brown mud. He was late again. Ben discovered the cause had been a huge ice-jam of piled up icebergs wedged at one stage under the town's main bridge over the Peace River. Completely dammed at the bridge, the river swelled until it burst into the town.

Of course, by the time Ben had driven the extra five hours to get there, the ice-jam had cleared itself and the river was flowing normally again. The flood water had receded and all that remained was a deep clogging blanket of mud. True, 4,000 people had been evacuated, $50-million damage had been wreaked, and Ben found plenty of survivor tales, enough to fill two pages of good-reading copy, but he was late again.

Four days he was away, and when he got back, he was rueful. Yes, he'd produced a raft of copy, pages of it, no trouble. But thinking about the trip, he could only see it as a five-hour drive for a fatal road crash where he never saw a single vehicle, followed by five more hours driving to a major flood where he never saw a drop of water. What a glamorous life he led!

As it happened, Ben had been well taught early in his career never to fail to turn in the story no matter how disappointing the details. In the first weeks of joining his first newspaper, he was sent out to cover a report of a penguin seen on a beach on the south coast of England. Yes, a penguin on Southsea beach! He inquired of everyone he could find on the beach, and, not surprisingly, no one knew what he was talking about. He returned to the office, sat down, and got on with his day.

"Where the hell's that story," shouted the news editor.

"Oh, there was no story. No one had seen a penguin," said Ben, and turned back to his desk.

"Come here and watch," the news editor ordered.

Ben stood at his elbow as the old veteran wound a sheet of copy paper into his typewriter and began typing, fast and furious.

"Holiday-makers were amazed yesterday to hear a report that a penguin had been seen waddling up Southsea beach," he wrote. There followed a light-hearted account of all those people who had heard the report but hadn't seen the penguin. It was short, snappy and entertaining and appeared in the paper's social gossip column next day.

"Learn, Ben," said the city editor. "There's always a story. Never come back without it." Ben took it to heart.

As usual, after every away trip, Ben was given a couple of days off, and now he looked forward to settling in with Garry's notebook. First he had to remind himself exactly where he was in the foul-mouthed narrative. If Ben was reading this right, Garry was now living in Taber in the summer of 1991. He appeared to have stalked and chosen his "T" as the vicar from the Tabernacle Church, who, presumably, was about to murder his "V," the church-going receptionist at the photo shop. Garry had already obtained himself a useful quantity of the T's blood, which was no doubt going to convict the man. Ben had marked the last passage he'd read.

"Fucking God Almighty won't save him when I'm done. He's going down and taking all them fuckers with him."

Even though Ben pretty well knew what to expect, it still shocked him when he came to passages where it was clear Garry was recounting actual murders. What had Garry written about torturing Angela Braithwaite in Pincher Creek?

"Time to play. No one to hear her begging, screaming. Surprised how much fucking blood came from the whipping. Liked the sound of the swishing whip on skin,"

Inwardly Ben was relieved Garry kept most of his sadistic sexual pleasures buried in his tortured sub-conscious and didn't commit everything to paper.

Now, Ben was on track again, knowing he was about to see Garry's sick account of murdering Jill the photo shop receptionist in Taber.

When he found it, Ben recalled he'd stumbled on this murderous description before. That day when he'd first spread all these pages across his desk at the office and plunged into the spidery writing in bewilderment, he'd come across this passage,

"Enjoyed the ripping sound when I sliced open her other thigh. Thought it would have bled more, but it didn't. Looked in there. Saw her thigh bone. Bones are always shining white and icy smooth when they're still inside. Why should pathologists have all the fun. The slit I made, made her slit look little. And I made three, just to hear that sound again and again. Think next time I'll run a tape-recorder up close, so I can play it over and over. Perhaps I'll send it to a radio station, and they could have a competition to see who can recognize this unusual household sound. Course, no one will ever know except me."

Of course, it was so much nonsense then. Now that Ben could place it in its chronological sequence, he could recognize it as part of Garry's own lustful memory of the butchering and mutilation of Jill Shepherd. It closed the Taber episode.

There came a break in the writing in the large notebook. Hell, it even looked as if Garry had turned to a new page. If Ben was reading this right, the action should all be leaving Taber now and heading for Red Deer, and this whole thing was about to turn full circle.

It had all started when Ron Lincoln made that first phone-call in the office. If Ben was reading this right, he was about to discover exactly what had landed on Ron in Red Deer. Ben had a good idea that Ron, who had no idea what had hit him, had been framed. Ben was pretty sure how it had been done, and, more pertinently, by whom. Ron, still rotting in his jail cell, had no clue about any of it. The police didn't even know. Ben felt sure he was about to find out the exact details.

"Here we go," he said out loud, as he started reading.

"Glad to get out of that fucking crap-heap dump down south. Been south long enough. Some brain-laden cop might put PC and Tab together and look

around. Going north's good. Biker I once worked with had a place I could use. Good place. Big grounds. No one to hear nothing. Strange fucker, that one. He got religion. Was gonna start a church. Least that's what he reckoned. My place? Half-way house I called it. Better than that hole in Tab. Fucking horrible rent. That's bikers for you."

There came a break in the scrawl. Ben was guessing. No mention of Red Deer yet. But "north" was the right direction. Why Garry called his place "half-way house" Ben didn't know. Was it half way between Calgary and Edmonton perhaps? Maybe Garry considered his rotten "hole" in Taber to be like a prison and this was a step up the ladder. Ben had long given up hope of understanding everything he read here.

It was obvious some weeks had passed before the next entry.

"Finding a T in HWH was a real pain. One guy looks good. Been working on him for weeks. He looks good, lives on his own, rough bastard, runs an old Ford truck wreck. Run down to his house a few times, some little place south of HWH. Regular habits. Drinks in the same rowdy Irish bar all the time. Better still, he banks regular. He's the T in the TD. Comic, I am. Every time I follow him in the bank he uses the same woman. She'll do for the V. Worry about her later. Ain't never fucked with the cops this far north before. They'll suffer like the rest. They all deserve to suffer. Every last one of 'em."

You bastard, thought Ben. Once again, he had this picture in mind of Garry sneaking around in the shadows tailing his "T." This time, Ron Lincoln, who had no idea he was being watched. Why should he? He'd never done anything to warrant anyone studying his every move. How could he have known the simple habits of his routine lifestyle fitted perfectly the twisted plans of an evil madman, who'd singled him out as an ideal target? This time Ben was confident he could put together an exact picture of how this murder was going to go down. He could match Ron's account—the whole case through the eyes of the target—with Garry's account which he was sure covered the next few pages of scrawl in front of him. He pulled out his "Theo" file on the Lincoln case, and turned to his interview notes from that day he'd met Ron in Drumheller prison. He placed the notes alongside Garry's scrawl, and set to work.

Here in Ben's notes was Ron describing the year he got arrested as being just one disaster after another.

"My fucking house in Penhold got broken into, though whoever done it didn't get my money, and didn't hardly make any mess."

Ben ran his hand down Garry's rotten writing. Yes!

"Here we go. Turned his place over. Early hours. He was in there asleep. I was in, did what I had to do and no more, Took the impression off his truck key. Even resisted taking the cash out of his wallet, then back out again. Fucking shit hot. Great start to the new year. Don't think he ever knew."

Well, Ron did know. But he misunderstood what was going on. There he was relieved this obviously amateur burglar had missed his money, when in fact the break-in was the work of the most sophisticated of criminals plotting not to steal his money but to wreck his whole life.

Ben turned back to his interview notes.

"A couple of weeks later my truck got dinged by some fucking hit-and-run merchant and I had to put a new wing on it. I got that out of the 'pick-your-part' yard up there in Red Deer."

It was clear Ron dismissed this as a separate stroke of rotten luck. There was no logical reason why he should think they were linked. Ben expected the next passage of Garry's writing would prove otherwise.

Yes! Right again! Here it was.

"Two weeks since I did his pad. His fucking nightmare's soon starting. Busy night. Stole a beater in Red Deer, ran it down to his place in the night, stove in his front fender on his truck. Fucking great mess. Noisy as fuck, enough to wake up the whole street. I was long gone. When he gets that fixed, all shiny new against the rest of that rust, it'll look just right. He's gonna wish he was never born. Then, they'll all wish they were never born. Fuck the lot of them,"

Garry had written. And it was obvious he'd followed up his fender-bender raid on Ron's truck with another visit to Penhold. There was a break in the scrawl, followed by another passage.

"Some fucker's on my side. Went past his place again. He must have put a new wing on himself. A completely different fucking color. Looks rough, but it's gonna work a treat, better than I planned."

Ben knew he could match this exact detail into the picture. He went further back through his Lincoln file and there was the police reference to the witnesses who'd seen a suspicious vehicle near the site where Gillian Warnoski had been dumped at the bottom of Gasoline Alley.

"They issued a description of a rust-bucket pale blue Ford truck with the offside front wing a distinctive dark blue that didn't match," was the record he had.

Ben marveled at the depth of detail in Garry's planning. Red Deer cops must have praised God when they discovered the murderer had used such a distinctive truck, one they could trace so easily—a give-away. Who could ever dream it had been engineered by a sick calculating mind pointing the finger at the innocent owner of the truck. All he had done was no more than repair a dinged front wing the cheapest way he knew how. Just imagine if Ron had been able to find a pale blue fender in the "pick-your-part" yard, it might have made all the difference.

Ben turned to the next page in Garry's murderous ramblings, and discovered a passage he understood perfectly, which was amazing, because, at first glance to anyone else reading it, it would look unintelligible.

"It's on now," Garry wrote. *"Must be getting good doing this cigarette butt thing. It worked the same as the first time. Better this time. Got two to choose from. They don't have a clue what's coming down, none of them. They'll know when it's too late, then they'll all be fucked, careers down the drain, no pensions, whining they'll be, cock-sucking whiners."*

If Ben had read this passage on that first day when he'd tipped Garry's writings over his desk in the office, it would have seemed like an unbreakable code. Now, Ben's mind translated it as he went along. He was beginning to get instant understanding. Rather like the consummate skill of the linguist who reads the written French and understands in English.

This was where Garry had probably spent another evening in the Irish pub watching Ron like a hawk, with Ron having no idea he was there. And at the right moment, when Ron got up to leave, Garry would have timed his leaving to ensure he was hidden in the shadows in the parking lot. Seconds after Ron's butt dropped, he'd be there to pick it up and transfer it into his polythene bag, to provide the perfect DNA sample for placing inside his next victim's vagina to frame Ron. If Ben didn't know differently, he would have dismissed all this as incredible fantasy. But he knew it was right. Garry had pulled this identical stunt once before and it had worked like a dream. Hell, Darren Sunderland was still in prison to that day, convicted of a murder in Calgary, proving how well it had worked last time Garry had tried it.

Ben moved on to Garry's next section, one of the longest single unbroken passages in the whole package, clearly the full account of the Warnoski murder.

"Learned something new with this one. Different knife blades make different sounds. I could be a scientist. If they wanted to know the different sounds of a ripper knife and a sharp blade going through human flesh, I could be the world's expert. It was a lovely noisy one. Best yet. Started off noisy when I tied her up and she started screaming. Didn't do her no good. I ain't got no neighbors to hear her. Bit her. You can hear your teeth going through skin, you know. I heard it once before. Heard it twice this time. No good her whining. Burning her skin didn't make no noise. Apart from her screaming, of course. Smelled funny. Do anything you want, she was saying, but don't kill her. I was doing anything I wanted anyway. And I killed her anyway. They make a noise strangling. I heard it with the whip strangling down south in PC. Sounded louder like this with my hands. Her face was right there. There ain't much neck. When they're tied up, they can't fight much. Wanted her dead so's I could do my thing with the knives without her squirming around. Did fucking tons with both knives. Left the special letter on her left thigh. Real artist. Polaroid was a beauty. Then I stopped all that good stuff. Really got to fuck 'em up this time. Went through the plan. Cut out the panties I needed. Did the cigarette end trick. Put it right in there, put what was left of the panties on her. More careful this time. Tied her legs tight together holding it in there. It all went like fucking clockwork. Drove to near the T's house, parked up, walked to his rustbucket truck. Started it up with my magic key. Drove his truck to my place, dumped her in it. Sorry about the blood everywhere. Yea right. Wonder if the fucking cocksucker cops will find it. They better. Drove out to Gasoline Alley,

pretended to be taking a piss in the bushes, but dumped her body there. Took one minute to make sure her legs were still tied together and up a bit, so nothing fell out. Sure some people saw me. What a shame. And they probably saw my rusty old truck. Fucking dreadful. With its wrong-color repair. How fucking terrible. Drove his wreck back to his place. Only 14 minutes down the highway to the turn off, five minutes more, parked it up careful like, where I found it, walked to my car, and was back home. Easy like clockwork. Plan it careful, it's a fucking piece of cake on the night. They'll have him. Then I'll have them. When they think they've got you, they get stupid. They don't fucking check things they should check which could clear you. They don't fucking want to find the truth about it. They just want the stuff against you. If it don't match what they want to find, they don't find it. Well, fuck 'em all. This time, they'll want this guy so bad. They'll find everything they want. I ain't left nothing out. They'll rush it all into court. Fuck, it must be right, it's fucking evidence. Can't argue with that. And this bastard who ain't got no clue the sky's just fell in on his head's gonna end up in the slammer all the rest of his life. And them cocky bastard cops are gonna think they're so fucking clever. Then when I pick the time, they'll all go down so bad. Every stinking cop involved is gonna go down, and no cop will be able to hold his head up in this province ever again. It's gonna be the biggest cop screw-up the world's ever seen. Serve the fuckers right, every dog shit cocksucking one of them."

Wow! There was that venom again at the end. Something very powerful was driving Garry, and it didn't seem to be just the sexual thrill of the killing of helpless women, or the power trip over dominating and controlling the victims. It was as if they were the collateral damage in his main thrust, this fanatical hatred of police everywhere, against whom he was venting his life's anger.

Ben had noticed another detail in this passage which he could match up with what he knew of Ron Lincoln. He flicked back to his notes of the Lincoln interview.

"I know every night I park it at home. I park it on a slight angle to the wall at the back of my yard. That following morning it was square to the wall, but I suppose that night I'd parked it straighter than usual," Ron had told Ben in the prison.

Not so, Ron, thought Ben. It wasn't you who parked it up squarely that night, it was Garry who put it back square to the wall, after he'd carried out the murder.

"parked it up careful like, where I found it," was how Garry had just described it.

And then there was Ron's bewilderment on discovering a murdered woman's blood in his truck. Ben recalled how suspiciously he'd listened to Ron in that prison visitors' room, when, like a whiner, he was conceding it was the murdered woman's blood, but he had no idea how it got there. Ben remembered how he was convinced at that time the blood was in Ron's truck because Ron was the killer.

How had Ron put it?

"You park your truck at the back of your house tonight and in a week's time cops find blood in the trunk from somebody what's been whacked. You can't argue about whose blood it is, but you don't know how it got there. How can you, if you didn't have nothing to do with it?"

Here was the true answer, in Garry's account.

"Drove his truck to my place, dumped her in it. Sorry about the blood everywhere. Yea right. Wonder if the fucking cocksucker cops will find it. They better."

They did! And they made the obvious link, as Garry had planned, fiendish and effective.

That made four out of four. Ben was confident he now knew exactly what had happened. He knew beyond any doubt all four of these women were murdered and mutilated by a serial killer. He knew even more certainly Garry was the serial killer. He felt he knew pretty well what the motive was, but here he was a little less confident, after all, it seemed so incredible—a revenge vendetta to destroy as many cops as he could, that's what it looked like.

Ben put down Garry's writings and the Theo Files, and went over in his mind again all those outbursts of anger against cops Garry had talked about with that growling cancerous sore throat of his. Could his feelings really amount to a hatred of cops eating away at his guts so badly, they'd drive him to these extremes? In those years when Garry used to call almost daily Ben recalled how at first he'd recognized the tell-tale signs of the reporter's nightmare caller. Every reporter had one, sometimes more than one. He was always the nutcase-bordering-on-the-mentally-ill who'd call in over and over with some grudge. Sane people faced the same grudges every day, dealt with them, moved on and probably never thought of them again. Nightmare callers found their private grudge to be a topic worth battling against for their whole lives. They'd call day after day, always repeating the same injustice they'd suffered, seeming to have no recollection they'd explained it all the day before, and the day before that. And each one would progress to the dreaded second stage of the reporter's nightmare, when they'd insist on visiting the office and bringing in their paperwork, their proof. It would be in the form of hundreds of letters they'd written to other poor long-suffering victims, who all had one thing in common. None had any hope of influencing the nightmare writer's original problem any more than the reporter could.

"Oh God, I've inherited another nutcase," Ben would sing out in the office after putting the phone down. Every other reporter knew exactly what Ben had just gone through, each being secretly relieved they hadn't taken the call.

To his surprise Ben discovered that these crazy eccentrics weren't confined to Canada. He recalled encountering them in his early days on his paper in England. One day, being the most junior cub reporter in the newsroom, he'd been sent down to the foyer when a receptionist recognized this strange guy who'd turned up, needed the attention of a reporter.

"Come outside with me," said this guy dressed in all black leather motorcycle gear. Ben followed. The man sat on his custom-modified motorbike which had two wooden platforms attached to where his feet would usually sit on foot rests.

"I go along tap-dancing on these platforms as I ride," said the guy, proudly. "And watch this." He pulled from his pocket a beer bottle. In a flash, he opened his mouth and stuck the beer bottle, large bottom end first in his mouth. Taking it out again, he said, "Bet you haven't seen anything like that."

Ben had experienced his first nut-case.

Garry's early calls to Ben had started off sounding frighteningly like the beginning of the odyssey of a new "nutcase" caller. Always it was the injustice heaped on him by cops. Every move they ever made against him prompted a call to Ben. In the very first days, the calls lifted themselves out of the "nutcase" category because they were made from some none-too-private telephone in a drafty corridor in prison when Garry was facing murder charges.

That alone made them potentially newsworthy. No "nutcase" call ever stood a snowball's chance in hell of becoming a news story. First, Garry hated the cops for the way they arrested him. They didn't pick him up in his car, or ask him to attend the station, or even arrest him at work. No. They came to his home, right there, in front of his children. He often told Ben how he could still see the look of shock on his children's faces as they played in the front yard while four officers grabbed their dad. The cops had escorted him past them, in handcuffs, proclaiming in a voice loud enough to please all nosy neighbors that he was being arrested for murder. From that moment on, he hated those four, and the officers who had sent them. All the details flooded back through Ben's mind. Garry had been beside himself with rage when he discovered the cops hadn't even bothered to check his cast-iron alibi. He told them he had his employer's paperwork proving he wasn't even in the right province on the day of the murder. Years later, after Garry had been charged with the murder and been locked up waiting for trial for 19 months the alibi was checked and found to be true. The charges were dropped like a hot potato. Garry hated the cops involved in that fiasco worse than those who'd arrested him in front of his kids. There were more cops to hate. After two other "trumped-up" murder charges had similarly been thrown out, so no murder conviction stained his record at all, cops never removed the references to murder from the paperwork attached to his name.

It meant every time he was stopped for speeding, or pulled over for a broken tail light, the same thing would happen. Each cop would run his name and suddenly discover through the records that he was dealing with a guy charged with a murder here and a murder there. This man must clearly be an ongoing potentially violent danger to society. That usually led to a thorough search of his vehicle every time, where each new cop seemed disappointed not to find an AK-47 or a blood-stained machete in the trunk. Garry hated the cops who never pulled the wrongful murder references from his records.

He went after all these cops the best way he knew how. He went through the right channels. He found out how to lay an official complaint against police. He discovered, to his eventual disappointment but not his surprise, his complaints were later officially classified as "unfounded" and no action was taken against any one of those cops. That fueled his rage. So he sued them—the whole damn lot of them, from the chief of police right down through the ranking officers who had ordered what he considered wrongful action against him, to the officers who carried out the "wrongful" orders. This brought even greater disappointment. After his legal aid, lawyers seemingly dragged their feet for weeks before acting on his instructions, the courts decreed his lawsuit against the police was simply out of time. Not only did the courts fail to find on his behalf, no courtroom ever heard a single word of his case. It never even reached first base, which all compounded his frustration.

Ben tried to struggle with the possibility that Garry's years of perceived injustice at the hands of individual police officers, multiplied by the impenetrability of the legal system, had spawned in him the intense hatred which had turned him into a serial killer. Hell, it was a plausible motive in a field where logical motives almost never existed. Psychopaths don't usually need a reason to kill to satisfy their sadistic cravings.

Ben expected to have the complete picture at this point. He'd matched all four murders—dates, times, victims, and innocent men framed and convicted—and was feeling pretty smug that his impeccable files and notes on the murders had tied in with Garry's accounts so exactly.

So what the hell was this? There were still two bundles of paper-sheets covered in the hated scrawl which he hadn't looked at yet.

The next passage was the one Ben had started reading at random before he decided to methodically study Garry's stuff from page one onward.

"Costs good money just to waste time talking with these hookers. Girl near the French Maid pointed out Chili for me for packet of smokes. High cowboy boots. Black mini-skirt. Arse-cheeks showing."

Ben remembered. This was the passage dealing with an extra "A" which troubled him, and the supposed location of a body near one of his favorite fishing holes. He checked Garry's page numbering. This was referring presumably to a fifth murder, committed after Gillian Warnoski in Red Deer, and one presumably where nobody had yet been found.

Ben was back in uncharted waters. This time he had no corresponding murder in any "Theo File" to guide him. Although he could construct for himself a blow-by-blow account of how this "supposed fifth" murder went down thanks to Garry's graphic account, this was all a mystery. Ben didn't know who the female victim was or why she was chosen. If there was to be male "target" this time, as per the pattern, Ben didn't know who he was, nor whether he was linked to the victim, nor if he'd been successfully framed, nor if he was already in jail.

He studied the hated scrawl again looking for clues.

Now he read it more carefully, he saw an odd phrase right away. Garry had got one prostitute to point out "Chili" for him, like he was looking for her in particular. If he just wanted a hooker to butcher, why should it matter which one? Why pick out a particular girl he obviously didn't recognize?

"Said she'd been busted before. I know that's right. Got the newspaper cutting to prove it."

What did that mean? It looked like Garry had at least done some research on this special hooker, but why her? More questions, no answers. Ben was none the wiser.

And there were still a few more pages of scribble folded behind these pages, making them consecutive, meaning they must refer to something after the apparent fifth murder.

Fearing what he was about to uncover on these the pages with the highest numbers, Ben read on. This time, as with the fifth murder, Garry didn't seem to stick to his pattern of writing about his murderous activities step-by-step, spread over a period of weeks. No, this time he saved it all up and ran through the whole episode in one long diatribe of blood and gore and bad language.

"You worked out why I needed this one yet? You know I love them noises. That ain't it. Better than that. Wanna clue? This one's the last one here. I'm disappearing then. So, something I done to her I had to do to finish the picture. Pity she had to die for it. But all them cocksucking cops had to pay, and it had to be done. Had to talk to a lot of girls on the stroll before I found this one. But I got her in the end. From a distance she looked good. One of them shirts tied in a big knot over her belly button so you could see her nipples trying to push through the cloth. Long legs all the way up to her shorts. Not so good when she got in. Someone had obviously busted her nose years back. Looked like she'd been through a boxing match with someone. Just like what you wrote in your feature. Remember? For what I needed, a busted nose made no difference. Here's a clue for you. Chris she said her name was. There can't be many Chrises. Making it too easy, ain't I. Being the second one, the same way, no

problem. Knew what I wanted to do and I knew it all worked. Getting to enjoy this too much. Just had to remember the plan. Used my Phillips this time. Much easier to grind to a sharp point. Crunching noise when it went through her skull. Don't remember that from last time. Must add that to my list of favorite sounds. Had to remember when I was ripping her to leave her belly. No problem. Long legs make long slices. Enjoyed them. Then. This is what I needed her for. I carved the letter. Right there where her belly button was the period. 'L'. Simple, but artistic. Polaroid perfect, this one. Nearly forgot one detail of the plan, though. Put her panties back on, but I fucking forgot to cut out the bit I needed. They were soaked in blood by then, but I cut out the crotch, right there, between her legs. If everything's gone to plan, you'll find the really bloody bit I mean. Sorry about that. Wrapped her up like the other one. Waste of a good sleeping bag, but I got my fucking reasons, and it'll be well worth it one day, as you'll find out. She went down the same hill. Fuck, I am ever good. In the dark I knew I was near where the other one went, but I couldn't see where she was buried. I knew she was there, but there ain't no trace. Put this one right close by. Dug her in. Planted the bushes back on top. Took more time, this time. Track covered in hoof-prints nearby there is. That's the last clue you're getting."

Ben noticed another major shift in the tone of this narrative. Instead of being an objective account like the earlier passages, this one, for the first time, appeared to be addressed throughout right at Ben—personally. And there was no doubt. This appeared to be a sixth murder, presumably the second where the body hadn't yet been found. This marked another shift in Garry's pattern of butchery. The first four bodies were deliberately dumped where they'd be found instantly, so the wheels of justice could begin turning immediately. That meant Garry's "targets" would be quickly arrested, charged and convicted. For some reason, Garry obviously hadn't targeted anyone for these last two, hadn't stalked any poor unsuspecting innocent, and hadn't laid out any chain of incriminating evidence to frame anyone. There weren't two whining "killers" in any jail protesting their innocence for these two murders. Hell, the bodies, if they existed, were still undiscovered in the ground. And Ben thought back to the first remarks in that letter from the Spokane prison. Garry had been talking about being dead by the time Ben read it anyway. So what possible satisfaction could Garry get from murdering two hookers and burying them so successfully they were never found all the time he was alive? Ben tried to fit these two murders into his brilliant motive theory that Garry was trying to get back at all cops by having them lock up innocent men for his murders thus creating the worst cop scandal Canada had ever seen. Perhaps, but Ben reckoned this was stretching the theory pretty far. How much worse would it look for the cops who'd already locked up four wrong men for four murders, to discover they had two more murders on their hands they hadn't even recognized, let alone solved?

It could possibly fit. Of course, a far more grisly explanation for these two could be Garry's sadistic sexual pleasure in murdering women and mutilating their naked corpses had taken over and these last two were just for the thrill of it all.

Ben went back to these very last pages, trying to dissect what Garry had written and make sense of it.

"Someone had obviously busted her nose years back. Looked like she'd been through a boxing match with someone. Just like what you wrote in your feature. Remember?"

What the hell did that mean? What busted nose? What feature? Ben didn't remember at all, but read on.

"Then. This is what I needed her for. I carved the letter. Right there where her belly button was the period. 'L'. Simple, but artistic."

Oh shit! One giant piece of the puzzle suddenly dropped into place. Ben went back through the first clues he had picked up when he'd realized the small carved mutilations on the first four women's bodies had spelled out "J-A-C-K." He'd first surmised the killer was elevating himself to the notoriety of Jack the Ripper. Then Ben recalled how he'd later amended his theory after discovering the first four women were all called "Jill" in one form or other, and how he'd decided this killer wanted to go down in history as the "Jack and Jill" killer. Now Ben saw he was wrong all along. It was an understandable mistake. After all, he only had four bodies to work with. He didn't know then he was dealing with six bodies. But he knew now. Number five was carved with an "A," and number six was sliced with an "L." Garry had carved "J-A-

C-K-A-L" on his victims, and even went to the trouble of providing punctuation.

"Right there where her belly button was the period."

It was sickening to think these two lives had been sacrificed in an orgy of brutality just so Garry could complete his one word message to the world.

"This one's the last one here. I'm disappearing then. So, something I done to her I had to do to finish the picture. Pity she had to die for it."

Why Jackal? It rang some bell in Ben's brain. Ben always saved any tape-recordings he reckoned were important. Day to day in the office over the years Ben had made thousands of phone conversations, all inconsequential other than to ensure the quotes he used in his stories were accurate. Ben would use the same tape over and over again obliterating the previous messages. But Ben had an inbuilt alarm system warning him when a conversation was vital. He'd sense the guy at the other end might one day deny making some outrageous statement and claim Ben had misquoted him. Ben would apply the experience of years in the job and save that tape.

The practice had headed off plenty of law-suits on those nerve-wracking days when the boss would wave a lawyer's letter at him saying "this guy says you made it all up, and he's suing us. What the hell have you done now?" This always pissed Ben off. Each time a letter like this arrived, the boss always assumed the writer was right and Ben was wrong before hearing Ben's side of the story. And, pre-armed, Ben would sift through his box of saved tapes, each with some cryptic note scribbled on the side, until he found the right tape. He'd fiddle with the tape recorder, running the tape back and forth until he located the exact sentence.

"Listen to this," he'd tell the boss, and he'd play the tape, and there, in the caller's own voice, would be the very words his lawyer's letter claimed he never said.

"I'll sort this bastard out, leave it to me," the boss would say, doing a miraculous about face, as if he never doubted Ben for a moment.

"City editors," Ben would mutter.

At the beginning of all this, Ben had put every relevant thing in his "Theo file." That included the tapes he'd made of each of the killer's telephone conversations from various prisons, interviews he'd done in person, and Garry's tapes. He soon found Garry's tape, the "oil plane bombing" tape, and found the passage he thought he remembered. *"Who did they think I was, Carlos the Jackal, no way? I might be a bad bastard, but I'm no international terrorist."*

Ben knew he remembered Garry making some reference to Carlos the Jackal. It threw up an answer, but raised a bunch of worrying questions. Ben tried to put it all together. If people were already treating Garry like he was Carlos the Jackal, a murderous psychopath, throwing him in jail for murders he didn't do, then perhaps he'd act the part. In some weird way, this made some sort of lunatic sense. But one glaring fact stared Ben right in the face. Garry's prime objective was bringing down as many police officers and as much of the justice system as possible by having innocent men convicted for his murders, Ben was confident that much was right. And Garry must have some deep degree of sadistic sexual pleasure from the murders themselves, that much was self-evident. But the "Jackal" thing, the carving of J-A-C-K-A-L in the women's bodies, that must have been done just for Ben. As far as Ben knew he was the only person Garry had talked to about being the "Jackal." It wouldn't mean anything to anyone else. The cops were still only working on four bodies. If they never found the last two bodies which Ben believed were out there, they'd never have the word "Jackal" to work on. They would never even be at first base. Garry, whose entire *modus operandi* was spoon-feeding cops what he wanted them to find, clearly never meant them to know about this. So why did he intend Ben to know? Why was so much of this aimed at Ben? Why was Ben finding all the answers? Why was Garry supplying him with so many explanations?

The damn phone rang.

"Ben, we've got some more deaders for your book. Avalanches. Out in B.C. Several dead by the sound of things. Pack a bag, you'll be out there a while, and pack tons of heavy clothing. It's brass monkey weather, right."

It was Frank. It always was. Just when Ben needed to look back over all this Garry information and try to figure out where he fitted into it all, because it sure looked like he did, the office called.

Ben left everything spread out just where it was.

He packed everything he had by way of heavy weather clothing. He even thought of causing a flutter in the office by taking his snow-shoes, but he couldn't be bothered. Every reporter in the place was a skiing expert, especially Dan Cole, the photo editor. Survived an avalanche, he had. Been spread-eagled down a mountain slope with tons of cascading snow and lived to tell the tale. He was beyond downhill skiing now. Heli-skiing was his thing, where a chopper would take him and his fellow suicidal skiers to some impossibly steep high mountain slope, where it was too dangerous to land the helicopter, and drop them off at the peak. To Ben it looked like a recipe for instant death. For Dan, it meant happy memories of "deep powder" and "whiteouts" and other phrases which sent him off on some reverie whenever he spoke about them. Ben, who couldn't even stand up on skis, had, however mastered snow-shoes. It was another of the multitude of little things which made Ben feel he was nearly a generation apart from the guys around him in the office. They could all swish through snow on skis. He could only plod through the snow on snow-shoes. No matter. He enjoyed it just the same. But today he left the snowshoes at home.

By the time Ben reached the office, Frank had mustered a few more details.

"Sounds like we got eight dead in a bunch of avalanches out north of Creston, Ben, check it out," he said.

A few phone calls and Ben had found them, one dead here, two dead there, and five dead in a third avalanche.

"You got it, we got eight dead," he said.

"On your way," said Frank. "See if you can get a flight out there. Anyway, check out the air fare."

Ben checked.

"That's a no go," he told Frank.

"There's a blizzard blowing out there, and all the airports are shut. They're diverting everything to Vancouver, and that's as far away from Creston as we are from here, so that's a waste of time."

Dan, on the photo desk, sat quietly making a few phone calls of his own.

"I got a pilot here who's offering to fly us in, he reckons he can get us into one of the airports they've shut to the airlines," he called out.

"Go for it," said Frank, exhibiting that marvelous cavalier attitude which hallmarked city editors who saw stories first, and potential danger to reporters and photographers second.

Ben imagined a small airport in the mountains, with some horribly narrow valley-approach through the Rockies. He could almost feel the tricky, swirling crosswinds, everything totally enveloped in a whiteout blizzard, and a tiny Cessna being buffeted on its way in. Air traffic control had forbidden all other planes even to approach, but this plane would be battling its way through the white soup, its wings getting heavier by the minute with ice forming on the leading edges.

Ben heard his photo editor calling the photographers on the radio.

"Count me out, fuck that," said Joe Bassetto, and he was a Vietnam War veteran who'd flown through God knows what kind of hell and back, but he wasn't making this flight.

"I don't fly in light planes, you know I don't," said Dennis, picking exactly the right moment to remind Dan of some apparent unwritten clause in his job description.

Ben, who'd just fought a short sharp mental battle, balancing his natural cowardice for flying against his bravado for always getting the best stories, inwardly decided he would go. Hell, he would get the story. He was preparing to tell Dan to count him in, when Dan took another call.

"Forget all that," he called out.

"The pilot's changed his mind. Says it's too bad out there, he's not going."

Ben was inwardly relieved. He loved aircraft, and had watched and filmed endless hours of air displays, but was always uncomfortably nervous about flying in light aircraft. Now he wouldn't be called on to display the bravado he didn't really feel.

"Okay, we'll drive," said Frank, whose cavalier spirit just wouldn't be daunted.

Out there, one of the worst blizzards for years was making driving a treacherous nightmare, but Frank was happily sending out his men, while sitting safely behind his desk.

"Ben, team up with Joe, you're on your way."

Inside an hour, with Joe driving, the pair were beyond Banff, heading west on still dry roads, fast approaching the wall of grey on the western horizon.

And then it started snowing, gently at first, then harder, and it was clear it had been snowing for a long time the further west they drove. For a while, two grooves of asphalt showed through the snow on the ground where vehicles had driven ahead of them, but before long the blizzard filled them in. Now, with the road a sheet of white, and the sky a curtain of white, Joe couldn't see even though he was only crawling ahead, dead slow. Through the murk to the right Ben saw a string of shadowy semi-trailers pulled in to the side of the road. Shit, it looks like it's too bad for professional drivers, he thought.

"What do you think, Joe," Ben asked, mentally calculating they'd have about four hours more of this nail biting blind driving before they got anywhere remotely near Creston.

"We're turning back. I'm not risking my life for the sake of a story," said Joe. He'd already made his decision way back, but hadn't said anything. He would have turned back earlier, but with zero visibility in the whiteout he hadn't been able to pull off.

After they'd taken the off-ramp to the right, then swung left across the overpass, they slithered slowly into Lake Louise, where sodium lights cast an eerie orange glow on the falling snow. Ben marveled at the natural sculptures produced by really deep snowdrifts. The snow here was clearly ten feet deep, way higher than the roof of their car, and had been carved into white-walled canyons by who knows how many snow plows. The sharp vertical walls of yesterday's plowing were topped by beautifully rounded accumulations of today's new snow. No matter how bad the disruption caused by a heavy snowfall, Ben was new enough to Canada, just a newcomer of 15 years, to still stare in awe and appreciate its natural beauty.

"Hey, it's gorgeous, just look at that, Joe," he said.

"You're mad. Shut up about gorgeous. We've still gotta get back to Calgary through all this shit, and it's coming down harder than ever," said Joe. With the professional eye of the photographer, he knew better than anyone about the beauty of snow. His beloved forte was still making photographs in black and white while living in this modern world of color. His breathtaking photographs of snowscapes and natural snow sculptures had graced galleries across western Canada. But today, he didn't appreciate it one bit.

He swung the car back onto the Trans-Canada, cursing as the slightest touch on the accelerator had the back end sliding off line, and where the whiteout was just as blinding even though now they were driving with the snow. Ben enjoyed the mesmerizing effect of really heavy snow seemingly assaulting the windshield from the center and suddenly veering out in all directions at once. It was a strange and dreamy optical illusion as if every snowflake in the heavens was starting in the center of the shield and shooting away over and under and to the sides.

They passed a semi way off to the right where it had skidded out into the ditch, nose-down in deep snow. Ben imagined the driver having to dig out 32 wheels up to their axles in slushy snow.

It took forever, but they eventually caught up with the front blowing ever eastward, came through the heaviest of the snow into the lighter flurries, and as Joe accelerated, they were back in front of the storm, back on a dry Trans-Canada with perfect visibility. It seemed incongruous now to have to tell the office by radio they'd been beaten back by the storm, now that the road was dry and the sky was clear, but it had to be done.

"Ben to city desk, over."

"You there yet?" asked Frank, being clever.

"Yea, right on! We'll be back in the office in less than an hour. The blizzard has shut down the Trans-Canada, and we're stuffed, over," said Ben. What was a little white lie? Why should Frank ever know they'd chickened out and turned back? Hell, Frank was sitting there in the warm office. If he wanted the story so damn badly, let him come out here and drive through this crap.

"Ten four."

The moment Ben arrived back at the office he discovered Frank wasn't one to be beaten by a storm. If the Trans-Canada was closed by the blizzard, Frank would go round it.

"Okay Ben. Dennis has got a 4 x4 with snow tires, so you're going with him down Hwy. 2 and through the Crowsnest Pass, through Sparwood and Fernie and over to Creston, alright."

Ben had to admire Frank's determination. Hell, he'd just sent two guys into the teeth of a blizzard where the world's toughest semi drivers had pulled over, save one who'd braved it and lost it. Now he was sending two more guys back into the blizzard, aiming to outflank it from the southeast. Right on, Frank.

It took more than three hours to get through the Crowsnest Pass, into B.C. before Ben and Dennis ran into the southern edge of the blizzard. It might have been the 4 x4, it might have been the snow tires, but Ben felt the snow wasn't so thick, and the road wasn't as slick down here as earlier in the day. He even filmed the view through the windshield with the falling snow filling the view-finder and a spray of snow spitting out from either side of the semi in front. Ben played back his footage. It looked scary as hell. Filming through a windshield always gives the visual impression everything's hurtling at the camera faster than it is in reality. It looked for all the world like Ben and Dennis were dicing with death at every second. He'd show Frank one day. Show him what reporters and photographers went through to get his stories. Like he'd be interested!

Once they reached Creston, Ben found getting the story was much easier than getting to the scene. Search and rescue teams had a working media operation up and running. Friends who'd survived the avalanches which killed their colleagues were still in town. Luckily for Ben they were still in that early shocked state when they were talking about the tragedy, before the defensive barriers dropped which put a wall of silence between them and reporters. Some family members of the victims had even arrived. It really was Ben's lucky day. Hell, some of the family members even had photographs of their loved ones with them, and were willing to let Dennis copy them. And the sheer remoteness of the place even worked to Ben's advantage. All the vital players in this story of death on the slopes congregated at some time in the day at the hospital, which for most could only be reached by helicopter. Ben and Dennis staked out the landing pad alongside the snow-covered hospital and each chopper to land brought another piece of the story to them. Search and rescue team members flew in, survivors, more friends of the dead, and the helicopter pilots themselves who could describe the scene up there aloft in the cloud-enshrouded peaks. They all filled in accurate details which far improved on Ben's imagined description of the white death. None of these people could reach the hospital's automatically opening front doors without running the gauntlet of Ben's ever-present tape recorder and Dennis's motor-drive camera. Wherever the rest of the reporters were, they weren't here getting this great material.

This was another aspect of the cynical world of the newspaper reporter which Ben felt set him aside from ordinary people. Here, at this immense human tragedy, eight people were dead, eight families were devastated by instant grief, untold rescuers had been forced to cope with the trauma of recovering bodies, and friends had suffered the mental anguish of seeing their colleagues killed before their eyes. While all these people's lives had been torn asunder, probably never to be the same again, Ben's thoughts only flickered between two questions. "Where are the other reporters?" and "When can I get this story back to the office?" Ben had learned always to be aware of the other reporters. If they weren't here at the hospital, were they somewhere better? Were they up in a helicopter at this moment surveying the death scene from an aerial advantage point? Had they somehow sneaked themselves inside the hospital? Were they at a survivor's bedside? Were they getting better interviews than he had? Or were they hopelessly behind, floundering around in Creston trying to find the vital players Ben had already captured on tape?

Ben had perfected the required cynicism of the good reporter. He could look a heart-broken mother in the eye with utter sympathy as she tells of her son's love of the wild snowy mountain peaks, while inwardly gloating this was going to top his story, and no one else was getting it.

Out there in the mountains Ben never knew how well he was doing. When he and Dennis reckoned the helicopters weren't going to bring them any more exclusive interviews, they left, found a hotel, and Ben filed his stories. He sent a main story, outlining the tragedy, and plenty of side-bars. These were separate in-depth pieces on the victims through the eyes of their loved ones; on the knife-edge seconds between life-and-death up there on the mountain as told by the survivors; and on the drama of the rescues by the helicopter pilots. This was enough for a whole page up front and two pages inside, all illustrated fully with enough art to make any editor happy. And only when they returned to Calgary several days later did they know they had done well again. Wherever the other reporters were while Ben and Dennis were lurking in ambush at the hospital, they were missing out.

A yellow "sticky" note was stuck, curling at the edges, on Ben's screen when he returned to the office. "Kicked their ass, Frank," was all it said. It was all Ben needed.

Well, it was all he was going to get nowadays. In the good old days when Ben first joined the Mail, the boss would stick $50 as a bonus in an envelope very occasionally for some work above and beyond the call. Ben earned himself a few of those. His most unusual was on a memorable day when he carried out a one-on-one personal interview on a love seat with Sophia Loren, only one of the world's greatest ever sex-symbols. It turned out Sophia was at Calgary International Airport for a major press conference but some unbelievable blunder meant no media turned up—except Ben and a Mail photographer. Ben remembered Sophia in her black fish-net stockings, recalled unbuttoning his top shirt button to flash his manly chest, getting the interview of his life, and forever cherishing the photo which appeared in the Mail of him with Sophia looking adoringly at him. The paper loved Ben's exclusive brightly-written column which earned him his $50. But since the Mail had been taken over by bigger and bigger media conglomerates with headquarters out east, things changed. Some faceless corporate office lackey with not a drop of newspaper ink running in his veins had ordered the financial purse-strings be tightened on editorial budgets and $50 bonuses disappeared very quickly. Yellow "sticky" notes flourished instead in the newsroom like a field of daffodils. Ben picked his latest daffodil and took it home with him. He also took home with him his photograph of him and Sophia Loren. From time to time, he would take it out of its drawer and place it prominently on the living room book case. And from time to time his wife would take it down and put it back in its drawer.

Chapter 10

Every Friday for ten weeks the task force gathered in the homicide room, making room by shoving aside the cardboard cut-out of the "Maytag" man. He'd been installed there by some comedian detective during a quiet spell when the city once went for 27 months without a single new slaying, and, like the "Maytag" man on the television advertisement, the detectives had almost nothing to do. Each week the "Whiskey Foxtrot" investigators filed in, hoping this would be the day one of the teams would come up with some blunder from the past. On the tenth Friday, the session started off much as those before it, disappointing, not much more than a routine update.

"Ee, gaffer, listen a'this," said Geordie.

Det. Hugh Milburn's broad brogue instantly told every Brit he met he was from Newcastle, and immediately intrigued every Canadian to ask where that dialect came from. Of course, Ben, being a Brit and a Canadian, never needed to ask.

Even though Milburn, thin, wiry, and with a trim moustache, had been in Calgary for years, some Brits still had to concentrate hard to understand him. Of course, no one called him Hugh. With his last name, he had to be "Jackie," after the footballer, Newcastle's most famous and beloved soccer star Jackie Milburn. Just listening to Milburn would set Ben off into a soccer reverie. The original Jackie Milburn was a Geordie demi-God who thrilled home crowds at Newcastle's ground at St. James' Park in the northeast, and the nation's soccer-lovers at Wembley when he turned out for England. He had also played at Wembley in the famous black and white vertical stripes of the Newcastle "Magpies" in their cup final appearances in the early 1950s, when, of course, he scored a string of goals. Hell, they even put up a statue to him. Those were the glorious heydays of soccer when teams played with five forwards, all intent on feeding the ball to the number 9's, the center-forwards, the Jackie Milburns. They could head in goals, and hit shots with equal power with both feet, helping their teams to win matches by scoring four, five or six goals a game. Not like today's sad shadow of the game, mused Ben, where teams were defense-driven, the paramount aim being not to let any goals in, and where scoring goals was an afterthought. Those glorious days were played with a brown leather football—none of this black and white or multi-colored patterned ball of the modern day.

Those wonderful Saturdays used to start for Ben when his dad showed him the art of preparing the football, of taking out the valve from the rubber inner bladder of the ball, pumping it up with a bicycle pump, forcing the valve back inside, then lacing up the leather with infinite care ensuring the thick white laces were lying perfectly flat, then hammering them into perfect alignment with a wooden mallet until the ball was ready for play.

Ben's other soccer memories came when he was working at his first newspaper in England. On some Saturdays, he could get away to become a radio commentator at the prestigious Fratton Park home of the famous Portsmouth Football Club. His match descriptions went out to the local hospital where patients under their headsets could listen to Ben's ball-by-ball account of the game. One day, as Ben was describing Albie McCann cutting into the penalty area, a small kid sitting in front of Ben, turned round and in a loud voice said "That's not McCann, that's Hyron." It was a dilemma. Should Ben shout "shut up kid" or just carry on? Even worse was the day when Ben had been in full flow for the whole of the first half, 45 minutes of his best work. At the half-time interval, it was discovered that just before kick-off Ben had accidentally dislodged the electric lead with his leg, had unplugged the microphone, and patients throughout the hospital had sat in total silence for 45 minutes!

Years later, working on the cop beat for the paper, Ben returned to the same soccer stands for the darkest possible reason—to document soccer hooliganism, soccer "aggro"—well, as he saw it, plain bloody soccer violence. So called local "fans" would pay their hard earned cash to buy tickets for Saturday's match, but never see a ball kicked. Ben discovered they'd be under the wooden stands, probably armed with knives, fighting gang warfare with the similarly armed visiting "fans." Portsmouth's "fans" with their blood-curdling cry of "Pee-orts-muff Animoes" (Portsmouth Animals) were as bad as any in the country. What went on provided sickening copy for Ben's paper. The bloodiest rivalry was with visitors from the nearby city of Southampton, called the Saints. Ben recalled the day a gang of the "Animoes" cornered a lone Saint and carved their initials "PFC (Portsmouth Football Club) in his back with a Stanley knife. He needed 70 stitches. On another even worse day, after Ben's photographer had captured a stabbing on the terraces on film, the visiting gang, knowing they were in his pictures, grabbed him and held him by his ankles over a railway bridge, threatening to drop him under a train until patrolling cops arrived and saved him.

All kinds of such soccer memories would tumble through Ben's mind every time this "Jackie" Milburn spoke.

"It's all too easy, gaffer, that's the problem here. Okay, I've looked at all four of these murders now, and in each one, the answer was handed to us on a plate. And that's what's wrong. It isn't the details being spoon-fed to us we should be looking at it's the fact someone was spoon-feeding them to us. Hear me out."

"Take the first one—our one here in Calgary—Bereson, the waitress. First, the body was left where it would be found immediately. That was our first break."

Where? Right on the golf course where the killer was a member. That was another gift.

How? Beaten to death with a golf club we could instantly trace to the same player. Thank you very much.

"Where do we find her blood? In the trunk of the same bloke's vehicle— and what's inside her? Only the cigarette butt she's been tortured with—a perfect DNA gift. Give me a break. This killer is saying, please catch me, I've left you every possible clue, please come and lock me up for the rest of my life."

Jackie had the attention of everyone in the room.

"Keep all this in mind, and look at the second one, the librarian woman down in Pincher Creek, that the Mounties had. For Christ's sake, here's another killer with the same death-wish. Her body is left on display so it's found instantly. What a wonderful break."

"How is she killed? Strangled with a whip left in the killer's barn with the broken whip end left under her body. Thank you very much. Where's her blood? In the same man's truck."

"Who do witnesses see at the scene? This guy, in his truck, wearing southern Alberta's most distinctive cowboy hat to make sure everyone gets the picture. This isn't careless. A bloke would have to be suicidal to leave that many clues."

"Okay, you're getting the picture?"

A lot of eyes in the room were staring at Jackie. A couple of heads nodded, he was making sense.

"Look at the third one, in Taber. The victim's a member of the church congregation, and where did the Mounties find her blood? Only in the trunk of the vicar's car. Why were they looking in his car in the first place? Because witnesses saw it at the scene of the dump site and it's a rare and distinctive car, one of only a few in the whole province. Thank you very much. And what sealed it? This man is the world's most prolific nose-bleeder, and very helpfully bleeds all over the crime scene, under the body, on the body, in the interview room, even at the bloody trial. The most perfect gift any homicide detective ever had. You think it was bad luck for him he just happened to turn to murder and bleed for the Mounties benefit? More like he was purposely chosen."

"Are you with me?"

Now Jackie had the undivided attention of every detective in the room.

"Number four. This one is ridiculous. This killer makes sure his truck has different colored wings on it so it cannot be confused with any other. Then he makes sure the witnesses actually watch him dumping the body. The blood in the trunk's hardly had time to dry before the Mounties were matching it up. He pulls a copy-cat stunt with the cigarette butt, just like the first one, to make sure we've got his DNA. I mean, what else could he do, apart from walk into the nick and tell 'em he did it?"

"No. Four different killers could never all be so stupid. I'm like you, gaffer, I don't like coincidences and the chance of four separate men all offering themselves up this easy? No way. No. Someone else did all these four and gave us four different men. And we bought it. It was clever. Four different sets of investigators each working separately, each thinking their hard work had cracked their cases, each having no idea about the other cases."

"What I'm driving at is this. We've been looking at these, thinking serial killer—thinking sexually sadistic serial killer. Thinking this bloke's been killing women for the pleasure of mutilating them, the sex thing. I don't think so. This is a bloke whose main thing is sticking innocent men. When I was studying these four, I looked for some detail linking these four guys we nailed to each other, to see if I could see a fifth link, which would be our man. But there's nothing. I can't find any trace of any link between the four killers we've got locked up. So if our guy's got no axe to grind with any of these four guys, and I can't find any, why would he do it?"

"What's the net result of it all? We've screwed up, big time. It was probably the biggest cock-up in police history. We're all going to be famous—infamous—notorious probably. We're not just the cops who put away one wrong killer, who locked up one innocent man, and let a murderer go free, but the cops who did it four times. We're the cops who shattered four innocent men's lives, and still let the killer go free, four times. And he's still free. And those four guys are still in the slammer. There's the motive. Our guy orchestrated the most almighty police fuck-up scandal in living memory. When this shit hits the fan…It doesn't bear thinking about. We're looking for someone who's the worst cop-hater in history, fucking savage, but who's street-wise, and very, very intelligent."

What a speech. The room burst into spontaneous applause. "Nice one Geordie," said a voice from over by the "Maytag" man.

During his homicide seminars Ed Stone would show how information coming into a murder inquiry would channel the line of questioning in a certain direction. He'd draw it on the blackboard. Information in, shown by an arrow, direction of inquiry, shown by another arrow. Then he'd add new information, and illustrate how it would send the inquiry off on a new tack by changing the direction of the second arrow.

Jackie had just changed the direction of the second arrow.

Stone had shown these detectives there was a sadistic sexual serial killer behind all this by showing them his nine photographs. These were blood-lust mutilations on women's bodies and had his men thinking they were looking simply for a sexual deviant. Now, the direction had changed. Now they were looking for a man, certainly capable of murdering and mutilating women, but driven by his hatred of cops—a cop-hater first, a serial killer second. There aren't many serial killers for whom the killing is the secondary pleasure in life. All they had to do now was find such an animal.

Stone went home thinking about this new change of direction. His job as task force commander was to react to new ideas, sift out and discard those false trails leading the team astray and provide impetus and direction for any new moves that might prove rewarding and productive. By the time he came in next day, he'd decided to carve four guys out of his team, with Jackie in charge, with the soul objective of finding likely cop-hater suspects. The "cop-hater squad" was formed. Its job was to draw up a list of the worst known cop-haters in the province, not your average jerk in the street who hated cops because it was the macho image for his buddies, but those with a deep-hatred of authority who wouldn't be averse to using violence, corruption, any tactic to bring a cop down. The squad would throw up suspects fitting the bill, research their recent backgrounds, find out if they were available as viable suspects to fit these four murders, and bring the results of their work back to the table. A lot of bad-ass criminals fitted the bill. Jackie had brought a ton of work down on his back. He was used to that.

But Stone wasn't sinking all his eggs in Jackie's basket. These murders under scrutiny by the Whiskey Foxtrot team may be old, but in Stone's eyes, since he'd inherited this mess, this was a homicide investigation still in its infancy. It sure as hell wasn't at a stage when you could concentrate on one avenue to the exclusion of any others. He looked again at the big picture. He had teams checking all the work carried out by the original detectives, still looking for flaws in their investigations. He had teams checking on known sex offenders and perverts who could have progressed to the status of sexually sadistic serial killers and who were available as viable suspects for these four murders. And now he had the cop-hater squad following up Jackie's very plausible profile of who the killer may be.

Day-to-day life in a homicide unit threw up its own possible suspects as well without Stone hunting for them. Detectives on other forces across Canada and some in the States shared information. Some would send Stone their homicide files when a serial killer connection needed checking out. In the routine life of the office, four or five of these crossed Stone's desk in the next few weeks. He looked at every case now as possibly providing the answer to "Whiskey Foxtrot." He thought at least three of them were worth looking into.

Details of one sexually sadistic serial killer suspect, who could well have fitted the bill, landed right in Stone's lap almost immediately. But typically, this guy had been charged with killing women down in the States, where FBI profilers reckoned at any given time there were probably 30 serial killers stalking victims. Stone knew not to exclude long-shots, no matter how obscure, but this one was quickly buried in the "remotely possible but highly improbable" file. It wasn't discarded. But no one was tasked to follow it up. It was as far down the totem pole as it could get but one day it may be worth looking into. This suspected serial killer who cops reckoned had murdered a string of prostitutes in Spokane had been tracked down and captured—and was now dead.

Stone recalled that media coverage of that arrest had already reached Canada. He'd seen it on the television. A guy had been caught red-handed with a dead hooker's body in his car on the way to his dumping ground. Stone had to chuckle to himself when he recalled how the cops down in the States had phrased the finding of a dead hooker's body in the trunk of the guy's car. He remembered they had officially talked about "incriminating evidence discovered by officers at the scene." The man had been arrested during a routine check-stop aimed at snagging drunk drivers in the early hours after the last bars had turned out, a law enforcement spokeswoman had told the camera crews. But at least the Spokane media had seen through some of this smoke screen laid down by the cops in their city. They had discovered the Spokane serial killer task force had been watching this particular guy for several days, and the "routine" check-stop wasn't manned by traffic officers but by serial killer task force detectives. Neither was it located at random. It was on a road where the task force expected this guy to be driving. Their only real regret was not being able to save the latest victim. The television had reported the man was charged with one murder, but more inquiries were under way—and cops hadn't released his mug-shot for "investigative reasons."

The television said not a lot was known about this guy other than his neighbors said he'd been living in Spokane about eight years. People said he was a loner who kept himself to himself in a small detached cabin at the end of a cul-de-sac. No one ever saw him have visitors. Everyone was shocked. He seemed such a quiet unassuming man. They thought he was middle-aged.

The file now on Stone's desk which came from the Spokane serial killer task force filled in pretty well all the gaps, including the most vital fact of all. Long before the guy got anywhere near a court of law he had topped himself in prison.

Stone looked at the name in the file—Alexander Lewis. It meant nothing to him, which probably meant this man hadn't crossed Stone's path before. Stone had this little library in his brain where names and details were stored. It never failed him. Maybe the knowledge that each of these men in the library had taken a human life was so enormous they were etched into his memory forever. This Spokane file was a little strange. It didn't have a mug-shot. What kind of police force sends a suspect file to another force without a mug? The whole file was pretty thin. Name—Alexander Lewis, date of birth—January 15, 1958, occupation—unemployed, residence—some address in Spokane—prime suspect in the murders of 11 prostitutes in Spokane between 1992 and 2000—committed suicide in his cell April 30, 2001.

It was pretty clear law enforcement officers down there were just tidying up all their files—just routine. They'd noticed Calgary was handling a cold-case serial killer investigation, and thought their man might be worth a look. As Lewis had been a homicide suspect, his Spokane paperwork came in to Stone. True, Stone was looking for a serial killer. But he needed one who killed respectable women and who was probably still very much alive. A fairly routine American serial killer who restricted himself to prostitutes and was dead anyway, wasn't going to help his inquiry. It crossed Stone's mind that it was a sad reflection on life in the States compared to Canada that they had so many serial killers some could be considered "routine." Hell, this "Whiskey Foxtrot" operation was the first confirmed serial killer case ever conducted in Calgary.

Then, in quick succession, two far more promising leads came in which landed higher up the totem pole than the dead guy in Spokane.

One was so important that Stone immediately took two of his detectives out of the "Whiskey Foxtrot" pool and tasked them to track it down. It centered on a convicted killer already behind bars for a murder in Williams Lake, B.C. This killer was serving life with no chance of parole for 25 years after being convicted of first-degree murder for pounding in a 15-year-old girl's head with a rock because she wouldn't have sex with him. The DNA which sealed his fate in the Williams Lake case was now opening up all kinds of earlier chapters in his life. The RCMP elsewhere in B.C. knew he was the last person to see a woman alive who was now listed as missing. They felt sure when her body turned up, they would find his DNA on it. Years earlier, in a celebrated case in Toronto, a convicted killer had spent 23 years behind bars for the strangling murder of a woman in a doughnut shop. Recently, police had applied the latest DNA technology to the case. It had a sensational and stunning result. The 23 year convict was an innocent man after all—like he'd always said he was. Now, the whole of Canada knew about the man whose life was stolen away by a miscarriage of justice. Television documentaries delved into every minute of his life. Books had been written. Even a movie was in the making.

What hardly anyone knew was that the same DNA which exonerated the unfortunate innocent also threw up the real killer. It was none other than the Williams Lake lifer. The wheels of justice were in motion that would one day put him back in the dock charged with the doughnut shop murder. Court documents from Williams Lake showed his violent sexual background stretched far back beyond Toronto. Even people as far east as Newfoundland had learned to fear this man when he brought terror during a string of serial rapes in which he'd attacked four young girls. That landed him inside for a six-year jail term. So why had this man's copious file landed on Stone's desk?

It was simple. During the years in which murders being investigated by the "Whiskey Foxtrot" team were committed, this serial rapist and killer was known to be living in Calgary—right in the center of the catchment area where four women had been slaughtered.

Here was a sadistic serial rapist and killer, the rarest type of criminal in Canada, a man happy to traverse the country from Newfoundland to B.C. venting his psychopathic fury on innocent women, living within easy reach of all four victims in Calgary, Red Deer, Pincher Creek and Taber, and right when the murders were going down. Stone was already preparing to throw more resources into hunting down this lead, if his initial two-man team made the right breakthroughs.

Between the two extremes, the dead Spokane long-shot and the Williams Lake hot favorite lifer, a third suspect was thrown up. This was a bad bastard Calgary police knew well, but until now, not for homicide. He had attacked a woman in a Calgary apartment block years before these four "Whiskey Foxtrot" murders. He'd beaten her to within an inch of her life after cornering her in her apartment. It was so savage an attack it left her with terrible brain damage. The case made history in the city. Neighbors put in 911 calls when they heard the victim's screams and cruisers were soon screeching up to the block. As it happened, Calgary's brand new city police helicopter was airborne on one of its first night flights, and was over the building in seconds. Its observer saw the rear door of the apartment crash open and a man flee to the north as officers reached the front door on the opposite south side of the building. In a split second, the helicopter's high-power spotlight illuminated the sprinting man, and radio messages guided those on the ground to the fugitive. He was on the ground and in handcuffs even before his victim's blood had dried on his knuckles.

He was already on Stone's list of "sex offenders and perverts." He would have been subject to scrutiny when one of his teams reached his name in their routine work. What suddenly elevated him to his own spot midway up the totem pole, to be looked at far more urgently, was a file which landed on Stone's desk from Winnipeg, Manitoba. All these years later this same man had been convicted of murder. He had stabbed and beaten a woman to death in that city and was serving life. He had clearly progressed from sadistically beating women up to murdering them. The question Stone needed answering was whether he had ascended to murder before he left Calgary?

Chapter 11

Surrounded by Garry's writings and his Theo File, Ben quickly put Creston and avalanches and frozen bodies out of his mind and concentrated on the uncomfortable turn this serial killer story was taking. Dropping one subject and instantly immersing himself in another was a skill he'd perfected, mainly out of necessity. He'd once returned from a funeral which had been a particularly poignant affair with a small white coffin bearing a child's teddy bear and flowers. A youngster was being mourned by distraught parents since the father had backed his car over his own son and killed him in the family driveway. Inside a minute of finishing his story Ben was phoning a happy restaurant owner who'd just had his stolen 20-foot high inflatable parrot returned. Some called it callous to write with such sympathy, empathy, and caring thought one minute, and to switch to comedy in the blink of an eye. For Ben, life was like that…pull up in the parking lot of a funeral home, put on his funeral tie accompanied by his somber face, and observe carefully every little point of interest around him to add color to his copy, then leave after the funeral, back into his Chevy van, take off the tie, and get on with the day. He could do it well, but he wasn't the best. After all, he had seen the real experts at work.

Ben had spent two years experiencing first-hand the life of the medical examiner's investigators covering southern Alberta. It had been a delicate operation to be allowed to ride-along with the investigators. Strict parameters had been laid down outside which Ben could not stray. These investigators were dealing with sudden death every day. Basically, every time the close relatives were not at the scene, and every time the case wasn't a homicide, the investigators would page Ben. They'd given him a pager, and they called him, and every time they called, he went. They'd take him to numerous scenes of death so that eventually, when he wrote his two-pager, he could meld all those cases he'd seen together into an anonymous picture of death at work so no individual family would recognize their loved one being highlighted and no one could be offended. The investigators ruled out his arriving at any scene where the relatives were with the body, as respect and consideration to the grieving family was paramount to the investigators. For them, to be responsible for introducing a newspaper reporter into the scene of death to add to the relatives' grief would be unthinkable. He was barred from seeing murdered bodies at crime scenes, as the fallout from him being there as a witness would massively complicate legal proceedings when it all came to trial. But even after removing the cases of homicide and those with relatives present, he saw many deaths, weird and incredible sights and watched how these investigators dealt with the great leveler of mankind.

To Ben's surprise, all four of the investigators were women. The investigators saw, touched, smelled, and handled the most appalling degradation which death in all its forms heaps upon the human body. There was nothing serene or peaceful about any of these deaths. Few people, save professionals in the emergency and medical services, see death like this, up close and dirty. Sights Ben saw were an eye-opener to him, and he reckoned he'd seen most things. In one trailer home, Ben had to ask the investigator exactly what it was he was looking at in this unbearable hot room where a decomposing body was throwing off a cloying stench which took on a physical presence in the back of Ben's throat. This man, in his dying spasms, had rolled off a sofa onto the floor, his last voluntary act being to vomit most of the contents of his insides onto the floor where he then lie face down, suffocating and drowning in it. At the same time, at the moment of death, his bowels involuntarily evacuated everything left inside him, while his bladder emptied into the mess. And while this lonely man lay dead, with no one to turn down the heater in his trailer, decomposition set in. The whole perfectly normal routine of death became more awful to see, though no one saw it, and more pungent to smell, though no one smelled it, for fully two weeks until the investigator and Ben were the first to study the results up close and personal. With clinical accuracy, the investigator pointed out to Ben which was decomposition, which was vomit, which was feces, together with an explanation of why she needed to know, and what each could teach her in piecing together this death. Ben suddenly found he wasn't noticing the grossness of death. He overcame the fleeting urge to throw up himself and became absorbed in the work of the investigator.

Like the true detective she was, she quickly noticed the calendar in the room was still at October 31, though they were now in the second week of November.

"He probably died last month from looking at that," she said.

And in the squalid kitchen, among the smelly and decomposing food she pointed out to Ben the row of brown paper bags on the dirty table, each containing an empty vodka bottle and a receipt.

"He was a heavy drinker, a bottle a day according to these receipts, and they're all here up to the last week in October," she said.

Among the debris in the trailer, she hunted for and found bottles of pills, this sad man's medication, from which, with her lifetime of medical training, the investigator could piece together exactly what had ailed him.

"He was a chronic alcoholic with advanced liver and kidney problems, which almost certainly killed him late last month," she said.

It hadn't taken her long. Presented with a scene of death and decomposition, in working conditions of hot high humidity and appalling stench, her trained eye had ignored the gross surroundings and found the clues, and her skills had interpreted them to reveal to her all this man's secrets. He had probably spent a lifetime concealing his drinking problems from all around him, but death revealed them and death's detective recognized and documented them in an instant.

After her initial work was done, and the body-removers came and removed the corpse, Ben learned how this true professional then put this morning's work to one side and got on with her day. The body-removers had been another eye-opener for Ben. The pair, a guy and a woman, were slightly built, but handled this large and mostly liquid man with ease. Ben inwardly noted the man went to the corpse's feet end which meant he was physically handling the man's shoes. This left the woman to lift the head end which meant plunging her gloved hands into the thickest puddle of appalling liquid matter where the stench of death was fiercest, to find and lift what remained of the head. Once they had left, the investigator was free to get on with her day—which meant lunch. She told Ben she was having a quick lunch as she had business with a funeral director in less than an hour's time. As Ben's Chevy van followed her car out of the trailer park she turned off a few blocks down the road, into the Kentucky Fried Chicken house. Now that was how to put work aside and get on with your day.

No matter which way Ben looked at it, Garry's writings were pointed right at him. Why?

Here was a serial killer who'd successfully got four different innocent men convicted of the murders he'd committed, which was evidently the whole purpose behind the killings, in some warped plan to take revenge on cops he hated. Yet he'd apparently carried out two more murders, for which no one had been convicted. How could that embarrass cops and fit into the plan if the cops didn't even know about them? Ben threw himself out another theory. How about if the killer revealed the last two murders to a newspaper reporter? A newspaper reporter with close ties to the local homicide cops at that? And if the reporter tipped off the cops, wouldn't they look pretty stupid, firstly, not even knowing the murders had taken place on their beat, but worse, for them to have to admit the serial killer in their backyard had murdered six women without them having a clue he was at work. And, if the reporter was worth his salt and revealed the last two murders in an exclusive in his paper, wouldn't it be something for the cops to learn about the murders only when they picked up the newspaper next day?

"Fuck me rigid," said Ben out loud. He was only caught in the middle of Garry's war with the cops. The bastard was only using Ben to stick it to the cops some more. And Ben had no alternative. He'd have to do it.

It was time to walk the tightrope. Ben was going to have to blast murders five and six out in the open on the front page of the Mail. He'd kept Garry's package at home away from prying eyes in the office all this time. Now he was going to produce a major exclusive for the Mail. But at the same time he was going to have to see Stone again and give him the full low-down on these two. The balancing trick was to get these last two murders into the paper without pissing Stone off, without wrecking all the work of the Whiskey Foxtrot task force, and while still keeping the first four murders secret. Ben hatched a plan which if it worked would leave the Mail covered in glory and keep his hard-won contacts intact. He ran over the basics in his mind. First he'd tell them in the office he'd been tipped off where two murdered prostitutes might be buried. He'd need a photographer. They'd have to realize the cops would be in on it. The Mail would be at the scene with exclusive pictures as the cops would discover the bodies. That would be a huge scoop with exclusive art. Ben could write in vague terms about the mysterious killer thought to be responsible for both slayings.

And what about writing follow-up stories for the next few days?

Ben hated doing follow-up stories. His passion was for breaking stories right now. Having the contacts to discover victims' names today, doing his own detective work to find out their secrets and background lives this afternoon, and getting everything in tomorrow's paper. He wasn't interested in elaborating on the reasons behind the story and the in-depth analysis which took up news print on the second and third day. Let the damn columnists do that stuff. By then, Ben liked to be breaking the next day's new story. But city editors, the Franks of this world, wanted their follow-up stories. There was even an edict from Mail editorial management on high which pronounced that today's front page lead story must have a page-lead length follow-up the next day. This took no account of whether Ben had covered every angle the first day, leaving no stone unturned, so there was precious little to follow. So, by the second and third days, whatever was being written was boring and repetitive compared to Ben's original breaking story.

But at least Ben consoled himself that the Mail didn't take this lunacy to the extremes of the Echo down the road. By the second day, for their follow-up stories, they usually turned to some sociology professor at the city's university to expound his view that profound and deep-rooted social reasons were behind a murder. Ben knew the simple truth. Some murderous little crackhead shit in a back alley had stabbed some equally lowly and vulnerable homeless bum, leaving him to drain his AIDS-infected blood into the gravel behind some dumpster, where they'd later find his corpse. Ben's follow-ups, never works of inspiration, would at least be about the price of crack, the profusion of knives, and the deadly dangers of living on the street—something half interesting. Down the road, the Echo's professor would be boring the pants off half the city with a breakdown of criminal trends in certain sociological sub-strata and the influences of inherent poverty upon crime rates. Columns of grey print would flourish, in which never a knife or a drop of blood or a stiffening corpse would appear.

At least, in following up this story one avenue could be explored. For a start, he could find out who the last two victims were. For some reason, Garry seemed to have chosen two hookers Ben had apparently written about. It was a long shot but Ben decided, if he couldn't remember writing particularly about Garry's "Chili" and "Chris," perhaps he might find them somewhere in his "hooker" files. That could wait until he was next in the office. If all this panned out, Frank would have to get a new pack of yellow "stickies." Yet, if Ben was careful, the Mail would be writing a straight-forward story about two new murders, gory and sensational enough, but giving no clue to any links to any earlier slayings.

With his secret still intact and without giving anyone a clue, Ben sat at his machine next day after raising the damn chair again since the phantom overnight chair-tampering maniac had lowered it, and found his "hookers" file—well, files, actually. He had many. There was one on hookers, some on solved hooker murders, and more on unsolved hooker murders, many more. Unsolved hooker murders far outnumbered those solved. It was the same in every big city. Witnesses never come forward when the victim is a prostitute. Like any man with a wife and kids at home is going to voluntarily go public on the things he saw when he was on some hooker's stroll at 3 a. m. In the back alley, you could kick a hooker to death in front of a crowd and no one would see anything. But Ben straight away discounted all the murdered women files. These two he was looking for hadn't been found dead yet, always assuming they had been murdered.

If he'd written about them, they must be in his general file on "hookers." File 4-16 (H1). The murdered women files were H2 to H16. Ben had gone ride-along with the vice squad several times which provided copy for this general file on life on the streets. When prostitutes had been slain, he'd trolled the streets at night getting background from the working girls for follow-up features, just routine "Fear stalks city streets" type material. When city police launched a crackdown on prostitution in a district where vociferous residents had kicked up enough stink to jolt local politicians to do something about it, Ben went ride-along with the crackdown teams. The blitzes would work. In time, the hookers, their Johns and all the accompanying crime would leave the area. Pretty soon vociferous residents in a new district, suddenly blitzed by a mysterious influx of hookers, Johns and accompanying crime would kick up a new stink with their local politicians, and a new crackdown would be launched. And Ben would go ride-along again. All these features on the city's sex-trade and the women peddling their bodies for quick bucks were in his general file.

Ben started reading. Chili and Chris soon surfaced—well Chili and Kris actually. Ben had forgotten this feature. It was after three young prostitutes had been murdered in a period of a few months and all their bodies had been discovered buried in shallow graves west of the city, and talk of a serial killer was rife. Well, rife among the scared women on the stroll, rife among every reporter in the city who could put two and two together, rife throughout the whole city—except among police. Two of the decomposed and skeletonized remains were dug up just outside city limits in the realm of the RCMP, while the killer, not aware of the niceties of city boundaries, dumped the third corpse inside the limit on city ground. As a result two homicide inquiries were run by the RCMP and one by city police. And not a single officer Ben talked to on either side would even contemplate the possibility of using the dreaded "S…K…" words. It clearly was a serial killer, but, Ben mused, some politically motivated edict had obviously been issued from on high among the upper echelons of the top brass forbidding any mention of "serial killer" when talking with the media. Ben could never understand the logic of senior officers who went to great lengths to quash any talk of a serial killer being on the loose. The alternative in this case was that three separate sex-killers were on the loose, having murdered one woman each. That apparently was quite acceptable, but a single serial killer would, in some way, reflect badly on cops.

Ben once pushed the boundaries, finding a cop who went on the record saying at least the possibility of a serial killer was being considered, and blasting it into a front page shocker. The results were electric. The headline in all the Mail sales boxes round the city started with the words "SERIAL KILLER." Most passing drivers only got to read that far as they drove by, and took it a serial killer had been confirmed probably seeking new victims in the city at that very moment. That was the case with the head of the RCMP's major crime unit. The dreaded words he had vowed would never appear in print while he was in charge were there blaring from the front page.

Enraged, he called Ben.

"You've said there's a serial killer on the loose in the city," he yelled.

"No way," argued Ben. "Read the rest of the headline, it says, 'SERIAL KILLER THEORY PROBED', which is completely different and completely accurate."

"People don't read that far down, all they see is 'SERIAL KILLER', what you've done is irresponsible…" and he rattled on about scare-mongering and sensationalism, and all the usual barbs which would bounce off Ben's thick skin during such angry phone-calls.

Next day the RCMP called a press conference, where the head of major crimes himself flatly denied there was a serial killer on the loose, seeming pleased to have shot down Ben's front page story in public in front of the city's assembled media. In fact, Ben took the day as a vindication, as the cops, hotly denying there was a serial killer, did confirm they were looking at the possibility, which is all Ben's story said in the first place. Next day his follow-up story told of the police confirmation of a serial killer theory. It meant "SERIAL KILLER" appeared in another headline. Right on!

One of Ben's features which followed, so the Mail could keep its serial killer genie active now it was out of the bottle, was to discover to what extent worried sex-trade workers feared they might become the next victim.

Two of the hookers he interviewed were Kris and Chili. In his file, he had their real names—Stephanie Gurdey and Elaine Wattler—but in his feature he used their street names. It gave more flavor to their sordid lives on the stroll. It was soon clear that so many rotten, degrading, often violent ordeals were heaped on them that the threat of a serial killer was just another painful fact of life. No real big deal to them.

And then Ben had a shock. Here was a detail he didn't remember writing.

To illustrate how Kris, a 21-year-old woman, could end up as potential fodder for a serial killer he ran through the downward spiral which led to how he found her that day. She was leaning against the outside vent of a downtown building, so the hot air would warm up her body thinly wrapped in its transparent blouse and spandex pants, waiting for the next trick. She'd had a baby at 16 years old, when she was heavily into parties and booze, which was just the start. She became a severe alcoholic, prone to binge sessions lasting days. She was into drugs, and somewhere down this slope, social services officials came and took away her baby.

"I've had the crap beaten out of me plenty of times," Ben quoted her in the feature.

"Once a guy used me as a punch bag. He bust my left arm and my nose, as you can tell."

And Ben described her crooked nose.

Now he looked again at Garry's scrawl in the loose pages with the highest numbers, apparently the last murder.

"Someone had obviously busted her nose years back. Looked like she'd been through a boxing match with someone. Just like what you wrote in your story. Remember?"

"Shit a brick," muttered Ben out loud. It looked like Garry had taken to picking his victims out of Ben's stories.

Could it be coincidence that Garry had chosen Chili, too? Chili, whose slide downhill to the street was another classic demise featured in this same article. Chili's real father had died when she was a kid, and her trouble in life could be traced back to when her uncle moved in with her mom, who'd taken to booze to help her get through widowhood. As Chili blossomed into a pretty teenager, the uncle took it upon himself to introduce her to the pleasures of sex which awaited her in life. That's how he put it. Chili took it to be rape, and ran away from home to escape his pawing hands and the dreaded visits to her bedroom in the middle of the night when Mom was passed out. The route which led her to the streets had been well trodden by many girls. The rest of the journey was so predictable, it was almost compulsory. She met some guy who seemed to care for her, who let her enjoy his drugs at his expense until she was hooked, but who then had to pay dearly for every fix. When Ben met her, she was a coke addict, the entrance fee to her body being just enough to pay for the next high. She went by "Chili" because she said she was hot stuff. It was her little joke—very little. There was next to no humor in her life. She'd been busted by the vice unit so many times she was scared every John was a detective out to trap her. But the need for that next fix was greater than the risk of being busted, so that never stopped her. More importantly for Ben's feature, the fear of the next John being not a detective but a serial killer still didn't override the need for the next 60 bucks.

Were Kris and Chili a coincidence? Not fucking likely. Ben went back to the scribble in the folded bundle of pages where Chili appeared.

"She got straight in. Wanted to see my cock to show I wasn't a cop. Said she'd been busted before. I know that's right. Got the newspaper cutting to prove it."

Yea, thought Ben. You mean my cutting, my article. Why?

Just as he was taking his hooker feature and adding it to his "Theo File" for future reference, his phone rang.

"You shouldn't be there," said a voice Ben recognized as a contact from down in the deep south of the province, "you should be in Milk River, well, a few miles further south on a farm really, there's two kids dead, it's all very strange."

"Good man," said Ben.

"Hey Frank, we've got a double death down near Milk River, I don't know yet but I'm reliably informed it'll be worth me going. The deaders are both kids," he called across the newsroom.

"On your way. Let me know as soon as you can what it is, eh," said Frank.

Ben winced like he always did when city editors told him to do the absolutely obvious. Like Ben was going to discover what this one was all about and then not tell the office, so they wouldn't know whether it was for the front page or page ten, like it would be Ben's little secret.

The drive to Milk River reminded Ben of the first time he'd travelled one of these long straight southern Alberta roads. He'd only just stepped off the boat from England and on the third day of his new career at the Mail they'd told him to drive to the Alberta/Saskatchewan border near Moose Jaw and interview some hero guy called Rick Hansen who had wheel-chaired round the world and was about to re-enter Alberta. On day two of Ben's new career, he'd bought a beater of a car, a ratty old Ford Maverick with a rapidly worsening oil problem, and now it would be tested, grinding out the 400 km to the border and back. Ben bought pots of oil and punctuated his day by stopping to tip ever more oil into the thirsty engine. It was a day of vivid memories. For the first time, Ben saw the vista of wide-open space that is southern Alberta. For a Brit used to England's crowded cities, heavy traffic, and thickly hedged roads, the unbroken view from horizon to horizon, from the curvature of the earth in the east to the splendor of the Rockies in the west was awesome. Every time he stopped to pour in more oil, the field of wheat alongside him would look the same as at the previous stop. Was it all one damn big field all the way from Calgary to the border? Ben got there, interviewed the man, marveling at what kind of inner strength could drive someone to tackle and complete so daunting an endeavor, and set off back to Calgary.

He hadn't gone a kilometer when nasty knocking noises reminded him it was time for the next oil fill. So he pulled over, lifted the hood and was pouring oil when Hansen and his entourage passed by, heading ever further westward. It was humiliating when Ben thought about it. Here was this new hot-shot reporter on the third day of his new glamorous career being overtaken by a guy in a wheelchair.

But Ben had his revenge in a few minutes. With another liter of oil inside it, the Maverick's engine burst into life, sounding smoother, and Ben pulled back onto the road, quickly overhauling and passing Hansen in his wheelchair. Ben glanced back in his mirror just in time to see the wheelchair, Hansen, and a couple of his followers all disappearing in a giant cloud of oily blue smoke. Right on!

Now, years later, Ben still enjoyed the sense of space he felt out on this road, where he saw many more cattle than humans, and where only an occasional vehicle would disturb his day-dreaming driving. Just after Milk River he turned south until away on his right, in the driveway to a farm, he saw the RCMP cruisers and a gaggle of pickup trucks to guide him into this scene, whatever it was.

It was a new one for Ben.

"Hey Frank," he called in as soon as he knew what had happened, following the instructions of his master's voice, "you're gonna love this one."

"These four kids are out chasing gophers in this wheat field. Lying in the field are those long hollow pipes they use for irrigation, you know, those pipes attached to huge wheels which they rotate around the field. Well, this gopher runs into one of these pipes, so two of the kids lift up one end, so the gopher will tip out the other. Just when the pipe is nearly vertical and the gopher's just about to drop out, the pipe hits an overhead power cable and the two kids get zapped. That's 750,000 volts or 750 million volts, something like that. It's a shocker." He just couldn't resist another sick joke, even one that obvious. "Anyway, I'm just going to find the families and do the business. I'll let you know if I get the boys' mug-shots."

Ben got the photographs, interviewed the families, and the other boys who were in the field, and the little community in mourning, and the whole package made the front page and page three.

Chapter 12

Jackie Milburn and his "cop-hater" team started off knowing all criminals hated all cops. It was all a matter of perspective. On the one hand, a cop using a sleazy grass would learn secrets the criminal never want revealed—that was just being a good cop. On the other hand, that same criminal, being ratted on hated both the cop—for being devious and underhand—and the rat he was using.

Similarly, any detective worth his salt had an uncanny sense of where to look for evidence and usually found it. Every old lag would swear blind that the cop must have planted it, and hated him. Hatred of cops became inbred in career criminals. But few would take it so far as to be violent. The dump of shit that would land on their own heads would far outweigh any satisfaction they'd get from smacking the cop they hated.

Jackie's men were sifting through the few violent exceptions. Like Tony Widgeon who drove a stolen car at his hated cop in a northwest Calgary shopping mall parking lot, shattering the officer's knee, putting him in rehabilitation for six months and a wheelchair for a year. But Widgeon had done his time, was out again and had gone back east to Newfoundland. Not their man. Some bad asses, the worst, had even shot cops, shot at cops, even been shot themselves during gun battles, but these were all still inside. Jackie checked them personally. He wanted to ensure they really were still in prison. Too many times the records showed these guys were "inside" when they were really out on parole or day-release or on "supervised leave." Jackie only discounted them when he was satisfied they were still inside.

The "cop-hater" team was working to a plan. First, they'd searched through the criminals who'd been convicted of murdering police, attempting to murder police or assaulting police.

They didn't find the answer there. Now they were looking at the files of people who'd put in complaints against police. Some were regulars. If police arrested some violent drunk in a scrap at a bar, the complaint would come in they'd used "excessive force." If they didn't arrest anyone because the evidence didn't warrant it, complaints would come in they that were "negligent in their duties." Some citizens, usually with a personal grudge against one cop, made a practice of raising complaints against all police all the time. And every time a complaint was deemed "unfounded" the complainant hated the system, and cops, a little more. Jackie hoped the cop-hater driven to the extremes of the man they were hunting, might be found among the ranks of these people harboring long-term grudges. This work was slow, but necessary.

In contrast to this unyielding slog, the next two major breaks in the case were sudden and dramatic. They came on consecutive days in Stone's mail. He never guessed from its routine look that the large brown envelope from Spokane police which came in on the first day would be a bombshell.

It was another strange file relating to Alexander Lewis, the suspect arrested for their serial killings, who'd topped himself in his cell. It was a secret report marked "for information only" with bright red "confidential" and "for police eyes only" hand-stamps across it. It was like nothing Stone had ever seen before.

Spokane police had mistaken the identity of the man they had arrested. He had been booked in under the name of "Alexander Lewis." He had died as "Alexander Lewis" and had been buried in that name, with not a single relative having been found. "Alexander Lewis" was engraved on the small plain tombstone on his grave. But despite every piece of identity discovered on his body and at his residence in Spokane proving he was "Alexander Lewis," that was not his name.

Stone read on.

"As a result of further inquiries by members of the Spokane homicide unit, in conjunction with the RCMP in British Columbia, it has been established that 'Alexander Lewis' was a false identity provided to this individual by the RCMP when he was placed into a witness protection program nine years ago in 1992. We are, of course, not at liberty to reveal why he was in the witness protection program, and were not aware of that fact when he was arrested and taken into custody in connection with our homicide inquiry."

"His real identity is Garry Chartreuse, date of birth, January 15, 1958, a resident of Spokane. These facts have been forwarded to you for information as we now understand this individual did have links with Calgary prior to his taking up residence in Spokane. As such, we felt this may possibly have a bearing on your ongoing homicide inquiry."

Now that name was in Stone's secret internal library in his brain. He would have to pull the man's files to confirm it, but Stone seemed to recall this was a guy who'd been charged with a murder and acquitted. As Stone remembered, it hadn't been a woman, so it still may not mean too much to the "Whiskey Foxtrot" operation. But it certainly meant one thing. "Alexander Lewis" who had been at the bottom of the suspect totem pole for being a suspected Spokane killer of prostitutes, had now been resurrected. Now, he had climbed to a much higher priority as Garry Chartreuse, one-time Calgarian suspected killer of prostitutes. Pity he was dead already.

Stone called the entire "Whiskey Foxtrot" task force together next morning. Half the guys reckoned they were going to get blasted for failing to come up with anything new. The others reckoned it must be something big. It was the first time the whole task force had been recalled since being broken up into their separate teams.

"Okay," said Stone, bringing quiet to the babble.

"You will all know that for about the past eight years a serial killer has been taking out prostitutes in Spokane. You all know that a suspect was arrested, and he topped himself in their jail."

Cheers broke out spontaneously round the room. "Way to go," said a voice at the back.

"Okay," said Stone, bringing order.

"Some of you will know this suspect, Alexander Lewis, was a Spokane resident who we hadn't yet looked at because he had no links with Calgary or southern Alberta for that matter. His name was just on file."

Some of the more astute detectives now listened intently. Stone was about to tell them something they didn't know.

"We now know their suspect was living under a false identity. He was really Garry Chartreuse, formerly of Calgary, who some of you know was once on a murder rap here, but he beat it."

Now, a new animated babble suddenly ran round the room until a voice stilled it.

It wasn't Stone. It was Jackie Milburn.

"Gaffer. He's on our list. He's on our cop-hater list. You know he did nearly two bloody years inside on a couple of murder raps that he beat. He reckons he never did either of them. He reckons he was framed, and he's hated cops ever since. He went the whole nine yards. He put in official complaints against police and he even tried to sue the force—fat lot of good that did him."

"What? Shit," said Stone recognizing instantly this was a potential major breakthrough.

His Whiskey Foxtrot operation was about to take off in a new direction. The cock-up over the identity of the Spokane serial killer had kept his team in the dark a little longer, but maybe now the light was breaking through. Right there, Stone acted. He decided to form another new team inside the task force. This was the "Spokane serial killer" team. Once again, Jackie Milburn would lead it, together with the guys from his "cop-hater" team who'd already looked at Garry Chartreuse. They were the nucleus. Stone picked out four more detectives to strengthen the new team.

"We don't know where this is going yet, so I want everything else to stay the same," he said. Garry Chartreuse might now be sitting atop the suspect totem pole, but Stone still wanted the "Williams Lake man" chased down, and the "Winnipeg killer" followed up, and the sex perverts investigated. He still wanted to keep a lot of eggs in a lot of baskets. The meeting split up. Stone went back to his office, where today's mail sat on his desk.

One envelope looked anything but routine and dull. It was edged with the bright red and blue flashes of an airmail envelope and was festooned with stamps Stone had never seen before. From Colombia they were, each stamp showed a pair of dolphins cavorting in front of a majestic sailing ship. Stone knew no one in Colombia. It was addressed to the "Head of Homicide, Calgary city police, Downtown Headquarters, Calgary, Canada."

He opened it carefully. Four Polaroid pictures tumbled out onto his desk. They were in color—predominantly red and flesh-tinted. Stone had seen images similar to these before. They showed the four hideous wounds on the four women's bodies—the four series of slashes which spelled out J-A-C-K. Momentarily shocked, Stone was about to pick them up when his inbred professionalism took over. Stop. Call in the scenes-of-crime guys. These were evidence. These were almost certainly taken by the killer Stone was hunting. Just maybe his finger-prints were all over them. Stone left them exactly where they were and went out into the main homicide office to use a phone to call in the forensic experts.

Chapter 13

Planning how he was going to reveal that he knew where two corpses were, was one thing for Ben. Executing the plan was something else. Sitting at his desk for a long time with the scanner chatter drifting in and out of his brain, Ben was really concentrating on all the disasters he feared could blow up in his face once he started. Finally he took a deep breath and took the fateful step.

"Frank, we need to talk—everybody, you, me, the photo editor and the boss. First, though, I need to talk to you on your own," he said.

They checked the editorial boardroom was available, and the pair of them disappeared inside. It was a room of nasty secrets. Usually, when something bad had happened, was happening or was about to happen, people went into the editorial boardroom. Reporters were usually summoned in there. Usually to have some shit unloaded on their shoulders. Ben had been called in there enough times to hate the damn room, with its heavy mahogany table and Venetian blinds. When Ben was in serious shit, the boss would always drop the blinds so no one could see in, and Ben couldn't see out. It was a psychological thing, like Ben was cut off from any possible help from the outside world.

One of Ben's best attributes was his ability to get grieving people to part with precious photographs of their loved ones so recently and usually so violently taken from them. One of his worst failings was in returning the photographs back to the families. They'd phone him. He'd promise to send them back, he'd suddenly get called out of the office on some blaze or crash or murder, and he'd forget the photos. Days would pass. Then the family would phone again…it was a nightmare circle. After some time, the pile of files, papers, books and general office crap that heaped up on Ben's desk would swallow up the family's treasured photos and they would just disappear— irretrievably lost. Ben used to dread the next phone call. By now, the family, fed up with Ben's pathetic excuses and idle promises, would phone again—

only this time, they'd call the city editor who'd drop on Ben like a ton of bricks. Sometimes, the worst times, when this still failed to produce the photos, the next call would go in to the boss, the editor or managing editor or some similar high strata of editorial management with immediate access to the editorial boardroom. Then Ben would get a summons to attend. The managing editor would storm into the hated room with Ben sheepishly in tow. It was always a bad sign when the blinds would be dropped—and they always were. Ben was on his own. People got fired in this room. Ben was threatened with the sack several times in this cursed room. During one stinking day at the mahogany table he was fired twice—in the morning and again in the afternoon—over a foul-up with a cop story that happened the day before when he was on a day off, fly-fishing on the Bow River. He had had nothing to do with it!

This day was the first time Ben ever strode into the editorial boardroom first with anyone in tow behind him, let alone the city editor.

Ben dropped the Venetian blinds. He'd always wanted to do that. Frank flinched as the blinds crashed down.

"Christ Ben, this must be serious. You leaving us or got a job down at the Echo, or something," said Frank.

"No, just listen," said Ben, trying, even at this late stage to mentally convince himself what he was about to do was the right way to approach all this. "Look, what I'm about to tell you stays inside these four walls, okay. Don't go blabbing it to any other reporters or anyone just yet. Otherwise we'll all be in the shit."

"You got my word," said Frank, who was now listening very carefully.

Ben drew in an exaggerated deep breath and blew the words out all in one long sentence. "I know where two murder victims are buried, and the cops don't know about them yet because only I know," he said.

"Oh fuck, what have you done?" asked Frank, immediately putting two and two together and making five, and realizing the Mail was going to be blasted across every other media outlet when it became known its crime reporter was a multiple murderer.

"No, you stupid bastard, I haven't killed anyone. You know some of the stuff I've been working on in the office that pissed you off because it didn't produce copy? Well, this is it, and it's going to produce copy soon enough."

Now he'd started, Ben was intent on spelling out how this was all to go down his way before interfering editors and bosses changed the sequence of events which would foul everything up royally.

"This is how it's got to happen. When we're ready, we'll go—a photog and me—with the homicide cops to the scene. They'll have to organize the search however they want, and the digging up of the bodies, but we'll be there for the photos—just us, exclusively, our scoop."

Ben was putting in all the words he knew Frank would need to hear—"exclusive," "Mail only," "good art." "I can produce a big feature in advance, ready, so when we go, we'll be miles ahead of anyone else," he said.

Then he shut up. He sat waiting for some crazy response. He half expected some crackpot suggestion from Frank that the Mail should go and dig up the bodies themselves and tell the cops the next day. Frank drew in a deep breath then blew it out as if exhaling non-existent cigarette smoke.

"Yea, you're right, we better go get some higher advice," he said. This was way beyond the scope of a decision on the spot from him. This was going to take higher management, probably even the lawyers.

"When you thinking of doing this?" he asked. "Tell you what, let's do it Saturday, so we can run the whole lot with a feature on Sunday."

Fuck me rigid, thought Ben. Here was probably the biggest local story the Mail ever had, and Frank was still seeing it as no more than good fodder for his precious Sunday read.

"Suits me," said Ben. Frank raised the Venetian blinds, the accepted signal the meeting was over. They both walked back into the newsroom, conspiratorially. One of the greatest sports in the newsroom was trying to be the first to find out what went on in any secret session behind the Venetian blinds in the editorial boardroom. Usually, whenever the boss and the poor unfortunate reporter left the boardroom, other reporters would sidle up to the victim and ask what it was all about. They'd hope for some revelation or scandal—someone sacked, someone discovered pregnant, or getting someone pregnant, someone reprimanded for some cock-up in the paper, arrested for assault, caught drink driving, or some other shameful episode.

Once obtained, the "scandal" would be passed in secret to the next reporter, who'd pass it in secret to another, each promising never to tell a soul, until the entire newsroom knew. Ben was hopeless at this sport. Half the time he was out of the office anyway and missed it. He wasn't in anyone's clique, and word seldom reached him until days later. He was happy to be outside the circle of internal office politics, scandals and gossip.

This time the scandalmongers sidled up to him and asked, "What's it all about?" They were hoping to be the first with the lowdown on whether Ben had been fired, arrested, or got someone pregnant, or whatever.

"Ah, nothing, just a story idea," said Ben. Nothing was quite as boring to one reporter as some other reporter's idea for a big story. The sidle-uppers soon slunk away disappointed.

The more astute among them knew this must be some bloody good story idea when an hour later Ben and Frank went back into the boardroom with the managing editor herself, Sarah Langdon, in tow. On the way in before anyone even sat down, Langdon exercised her rightful seniority and dropped the blinds.

"Frank's told me something of what it's about. Now, you tell me exactly what's going on," said Langdon, shaking her head left and right, flicking her long black hair back from her face. Langdon had come through the ranks to reach where she was. She had put her years in as a reporter, made a name for herself as a fearless columnist, blasting any public figure who deserved criticism, and now she planned the editorial strategy that guided the paper. She knew only too well that story ideas often became swallowed up in their own "spin" before they reached her desk. She wanted to hear this from the reporter on the ground, where her own roots were, where she knew the story wouldn't yet be embellished or complicated by internal politics. Ben felt like a prime suspect, who's already told the cop at the scene what happened, then repeated it to some lowly detective, and was now having to repeat the same story higher and higher up the line, each higher rank presumably unable to trust what his lower minion had discovered.

"I've been working on something for weeks now and I'm sure I know where two murder bodies are buried," said Ben. "I've done a ton of work on it and I know who the victims are and where they're buried. I've only discovered all the details in the last two days. I've got to go to the cops about it, but I wanted us to be as far ahead of the game as we can be before I do that," he said.

"You're certain you're not involved in this, aren't you," said Langdon, her eyes staring hard into Ben's face, scared to death she might be about to linking the good name of the Mail with some sordid murder plot involving an employee.

"Thanks very much," said Ben indignantly.

"Next question," said Langdon, ignoring Ben's comment. As always, she was forthright and straight to the point. "If you know where the bodies are, you must have been told by someone, so you must know who killed them. So, it looks like the Mail is shielding a killer if we haven't told the cops yet, doesn't it? What are we playing at here?" asked Langdon, giving Ben another piercing glance. As managing editor, she needed to comprehend the overall picture as well as just understanding the details. Ben wasn't enjoying this cross-examination one bit.

"I think the killer's dead, so that's not going to come back on us," he said, hoping he'd correctly interpreted some of the more cryptic clues in the scrawny handwriting. Frank, who'd brought the matter to the managing editor's attention with some pride that his staff had come up with such a scoop, raised his eye-brows. Smugly, he thought he knew all about the story. Perhaps he didn't.

"So, how come you've got all this and no-one else has?" asked Langdon, flicking her hair again. She sounded a little incredulous that the Mail seemed to be miles ahead on a cop story. Major cop stories usually broke over the scanner, so all alert media were starting off on a level playing field.

"It's just a contact I have," said Ben. Langdon knew better than to ask about her crime reporter's contacts. Once a psychopathic mass murderer invited a bunch of friends to a drinking party at his home then murdered them all by shooting them dead and slitting their throats. Then he phoned Ben during the trial to complain the prosecution was painting him in a bad light—and could Ben get the Mail to print something righting the wrong. If psychopathic killers like that rang up her crime reporter for favors, Langdon didn't really want to know what else went on behind the scenes.

"Okay, next question," said Langdon. "If there are two bodies, how come we haven't been running stories about two missing persons?"

"They were both hookers," said Ben. Frank's eyebrows flinched.

"Figures," said Langdon. Women disappeared off the streets all the time and the Mail never knew about them, and probably wouldn't have cared if they had known. Ben, his managing editor and hookers were a touchy, complicated subject. Ben once came back from a meeting of the Police Commission, the political wing of the force, with a great story idea. The commission wanted to publish in the local media the names of all Johns arrested in "hooker stings" on the stroll. The contentious part of the plan was to announce in advance this was going to be the new strategy. The admirable intention behind this move was that potential Johns would read of the plan and be afraid of using hookers on the stroll in case they were caught in a sting and exposed in the press. Just imagine—their names in the Mail next day! Instead, they would stay off the stroll, putting at least a dent in the city's hooker problem. What's more, the public-spiritedness of the Mail would have been a big factor in pulling it off. Ben brought the idea back to the office, where it was instantly crushed by Langdon. It had been a topic sufficiently sensitive and delicate to warrant Ben being summoned to the editorial boardroom again, where the Venetian blinds were dropped even more quickly than on Ben's story idea.

Langdon explained the official reason why the Mail couldn't entertain such an idea was because arrested Johns on a sting hadn't yet been convicted of anything. It would be legally impossible for the Mail to name these men as they could eventually be cleared of any criminal charge, which would leave the Mail open to numerous expensive libel law suits. Oh dear me no!

Ben reckoned there was another reason. Some large percentage of the paper's advertising revenue came from the hundreds of escort agency ads it ran in its classified section. Everyone knew, though everyone denied, the ads were the engine driving the city's sex trade. How blatantly hypocritical would it look for the Mail to condemn evil men on page three for getting caught using the city's sex trade workers, while the Mail itself was making thousands of dollars a day off these same women by advertising their wares on pages 60-64 in the classified columns. Oh dear me, no, no, no!

Langdon would have been more delighted if Ben was going to come up with a story "Calgary Mail Solves Two Murders" with all the accompanying praise and rightful recognition for community service. It was tarnished a little to have the headline "Calgary Mail Finds Bodies of Hookers," as the bottom line. Such was life.

"Next question," said Langdon. "How much space are we going to need for all this?"

Ben relaxed. It was clearly a go.

"An up-front news story and a two-page feature inside," he offered, "all exclusive with exclusive art."

It was a done deal. "Right on," said Ben. Frank glowed. All three stood up. Langdon and Frank left Ben behind to raise the blinds, as they left together, pleased with themselves.

Chapter 14

When things fall into place in a homicide investigation, events can happen so fast it can take your breath away. After weeks or months of methodical work when it seems no progress is being made, the sudden breakthrough can be electrifying. Stone was having an electrifying day.

"Jackie" Milburn started it off. His "cop-hater" team had already put in a bunch of hours on this Chartreuse guy even before Stone had re-assembled them and made them the "Spokane Serial Killer" team. The "cop-hater" team was working on Chartreuse, using his correct name when he'd been living in Calgary and hating cops, long before anyone knew he was the Spokane killer. Now Milburn went into Stone's inner office with some startling new results. Stone knew something big was coming. Milburn usually worked away on his own, hardly ever communicating with the gaffer unless he had something important to say.

"Chartreuse didn't only live in Calgary," said Milburn. "Do you want to hear some remarkable coincidences?"

"When that woman was killed on the Calgary golf course in November 1990, Chartreuse was living in Calgary."

"But when that second victim was strangled with the whip in Pincher Creek four months later, Chartreuse had moved and was living in a dump of a trailer not a mile away, in Pincher Creek as well."

What! Stone could hardly believe his ears. But Milburn hadn't finished yet.

"And guess where the bastard was living in July that year when that third woman, the photo shop girl from Taber was killed? He was renting a run-down place in Taber, I kid you not."

Stone was shaking his head in disbelief. He stared at Milburn as if he was a miracle-worker. "Where did you get this all?" he asked incredulously.

"Wait a minute. There's one last surprise," said Milburn. "You know that last one, at Red Deer in January 1992. Chartreuse had moved again. He was living on a remote rural hunk of land he'd rented from a Hell's Angels biker on the outskirts of Red Deer, not far from where the body was dumped."

"You see, we first thought Chartreuse lived in Calgary all the time. He was definitely living here in November 1990, and he was here in the summer of 1992, as well. We just took it from granted he was here all the time. Well, you would wouldn't you?"

"So I had the guys check to make sure—and all this lot came up."

Stone stared at Milburn, and then roared with delight. His main man had only cracked it. Stone never believed in coincidences—and well Milburn knew it. Stone leaped up from his chair, pumped the air and howled like a wolf. Milburn had never seen such a show of emotion from the gaffer.

"You fucking genius. Fucking genius," yelled Stone as he war-danced round his little office, his face red with exertion. It was unusual for Stone to use such language, him being a deeply religious man, as he certainly was. The phone rang. Milburn chose the moment to escape Stone's office, fearing at any moment the gaffer might suddenly hug him or kiss him, or something equally as horrible.

"Yea, Stone," yelled Stone into the phone, still euphoric.

It was Calgary's scenes-of-crime boss who ran the fingerprint section. He sounded pretty up-beat on the phone himself.

"We got a print off those Polaroids of yours," he said. "We got a hit. Some guy called Chartreuse—Garry Chartreuse. I've got all his full details here if you need them. I'll send them along. Hello, Stone? Are you there?"

Stone stared at the phone as if in disbelief. "Yes, sorry, yes, send them along, brilliant," he stammered.

A few minutes later a scenes-of-crime guy brought the envelope containing the Polaroids to Stone's office. It was the next bombshell.

"Don't forget to look at the back of 'em, remember, the fingerprint was on the back, in the glue," sang out the detective as he left, smiling.

Stone hadn't looked at the back of them before, he had hardly touched them, and had no clue what the detective meant. First he looked at the bloody picture of the letter "J" which had been carved into the first Calgary victim on the golf course. He turned it over, knowing nothing could have been written there, as the back side of any Polaroid is a surface which won't take ink. There, glued on the reverse were two little pieces of newsprint. One was the word "Sunderland." The other was the word "wrong." Both cut carefully from a newspaper. Stone saw instantly this was the killer mocking him. He himself led the team which had convicted Darren Sunderland of this woman's murder.

He turned to the second Polaroid, with its horrific letter "A" carved into the flesh of the whipping victim from Pincher Creek. Almost knowing what he'd find, Stone turned the picture over. On the back were the words cut from the newspaper and glued in place—"Paul Andres" and further down "wrong again." Andres was still in jail serving his life sentence, put there by the RCMP.

"Oh God!" thought Stone. The realization hit him that the Polaroid pictures weren't taken just as a sexual thrill by the killer. This was his ultimate revenge on all the cops he'd grown to hate. This was his personal way of mocking the cops, of spelling out to them exactly how they had cocked everything up.

He took the third picture, with the letter "C" carved into poor Angel Shepherd's body in Taber. On the back were the dreaded pieces of newsprint. "The Rev. Jacob Broadbent" was one piece. Four separate words obviously cut from different parts of the newspaper spelled out "Will—You—Never—Learn."

Stunned, Stone looked sadly at the fourth picture, with the letter "K" slashed with three strokes into the Red Deer victim's body. On the back after "Ronald Lincoln" on one piece of newsprint were glued a series of bits of paper, reading "You-Still-don't-get-it-do-you."

It had all happened in 30 minutes. When Stone walked into his office that morning, he had nothing. Now, he had his serial killer, he had cast-iron evidence, and he had this terrible motive. It was a bitter-sweet triumph. He called Milburn back inside his office.

"Gather up the whole Whiskey Foxtrot team, everybody, get them all in, and make sure you're here with them," he said.

It took an hour, but when the entire team was assembled, crammed into the homicide room, Stone told them.

"We have him," he said. "It was one guy, Garry Chartreuse. He murdered all four of these women. I'm certain the motive was revenge against us. He worked it so four innocent men would get convicted. And they were. All four are in jail right now—but they'll soon be getting out. All of you know how much shit is going to land on us when this gets out. That's what he wanted. He reckoned cops fitted him up for murders he didn't do. He spent 19 months in the slammer, and this was his revenge. All of us are about to experience his revenge when the public learns we convicted and locked up an innocent man, and we did it not just once but four times."

"You guys have worked your bollocks off. I'm proud of you. Any one of you teams could have hit the right answer. As it happened Jackie Milburn's team came up with the breakthrough. Put it on the board, Jackie."

Milburn walked over to the wall board running the length of the room. It was covered in notations all in black, the names of the victims, the names of various suspects, important dates, team assignments, in fact the whole story of the Whiskey Foxtrot operation. Now, Milburn went to the board, and in the space rather blandly left under "accused" he wrote in the name, Garry Chartreuse, in red. Knowing Chartreuse was already dead Milburn took the liberty of crossing out "accused" and wrote "killer" instead in red.

Some pretty wild celebrations were still in full swing in the homicide room when Stone heard his phone ringing in his office. He went in and closed the door.

"Stone here," he said. It was Ben on the other end. Stone shook his head. How the hell could he possibly have found out what had just happened. No one outside the homicide room knew they'd cracked the case literally within the last hour. Hell, half the detectives in homicide itself didn't know they'd cracked the case until the last 10 minutes.

"I really have to see you right now," said Ben. Stone considered it was better to have Ben here in his office where he'd have him under some control, rather than out there on the loose where the wrong publicity at this delicate time could be disastrous.

"Okay. Come to the downstairs lobby and buzz up. I'll send someone down for you," said Stone. He was being careful. This way he could get Ben led into his room without him wandering into the homicide room where there were three words in red ink on the wall he didn't want him to see.

Ben drove across Calgary, mentally preparing himself for what he saw as a frightening ordeal ahead. How should a newspaper reporter break the news to the head of the city's homicide unit that he knows where two murder victims are buried? And how does he tell the top cop he's going to have his paper's photographers at the scene when the bodies are dug up? And how could he convince Stone that when Stone breaks the news of these two bodies to the press, he doesn't make any mention of four earlier murders that are linked? And that was hardly the beginning. How was he supposed to tell Stone he's known for quite a while who the killer of all these women was, but hadn't mentioned it before? And how would be contain his excitement over this last revelation? How many reporters ever get the chance to solve a murder, let alone solve a string of serial killings?

If any one of those steps went wrong, Ben would be fired, for sure. He'd probably be locked up if he got it all very wrong. He arrived at the spacious lobby at the downtown police headquarters with its highly-polished floors and bank of elevators and with its concierge sitting behind his grandiose mahogany consul.

"Ben Ludlow for Staff Sergeant Stone in homicide," he announced, handing over his picture identification, which had to be surrendered to the concierge while he, in return, gave Ben a visitor's tag to clip to his lapel. Ben waited, nervously rehearsing in his brain everything he was about to unload on Stone. Excitement at solving a murder, and fear of what was about to unfold were a strange mixture of emotions. An elevator arrived, and two homicide detectives beckoned Ben over. The doors closed and they went up to the tenth floor, the cops making their usual cheery banter about busty Mail pin-up girls, making sure they weren't talking about anything that had taken place in the homicide room that morning.

They ushered Ben quickly into Stone's inner sanctum, where Ben noticed right away that his Venetian blinds were down, so he couldn't see out into the main homicide room. It reminded him of the editorial boardroom on a bad day.

"So, what's up, Ben," said Stone, in control of the situation, with Ben safely tucked is his office where he could do no harm.

"Look, I'm pretty sure I know the name of the guy who murdered those four women, you know, the four unmentionables we mentioned before," he started, the excitement at his moment of triumph bubbling through his voice.

"Oh, do you," said Stone, just a little uncomfortable at the thought that the name had only gone up in red on the board in the secret inner-most temple of the homicide unit less than two hours ago. "Well, go on then, surprise me."

"I think it's a guy called Garry Chartreuse," said Ben. Seeing no flicker of emotion on Stone's poker-still face, he rushed on with his explanation. This part of the ordeal would only work as long as Ben didn't reveal any time table of when this information had come to him.

"I know this because I've got some letters and a sort of diary which Chartreuse sent to me. It's a kind of blow-by-blow confession of how he did the murders. They cover a couple of years, and they explain why he did it and how he did each one. Everything's there in graphic detail. There are just a couple of things I don't quite understand but I'm certain he killed those four women."

Now Ben was under way, he hardly stopped to draw breath.

"I know quite a lot about Chartreuse. He was a mercenary gun-runner in South Africa at one time. He traveled to Bogota, Colombia. That was probably for drugs or guns or both. He got locked up for murders he reckoned he didn't do. He was supposed to be some major witness in the oil plane bombing trial. And I think he may be dead, now."

"Go on," said Stone, realizing with great relief that Ben had no idea what had gone on in the homicide room that morning. Stone didn't have any nasty moles in his outfit who'd tipped Ben off. All this stuff was down to Ben's own inquiries.

"Yes, there's more. When he sent me the letters and stuff, there was a little package inside it. I think in the package are bits of the crotches from the panties of some of the victims. You can have it all of course,—the letters, the diaries, the package of panties, everything, but there is one mystery."

"The diaries make lots of references to Polaroid photographs. They weren't in the letters. I'm not sure where they fit in, but somewhere there should be some Polaroid pictures, I'm guessing of the victims."

Stone's stoic features revealed nothing to Ben. Inwardly, Stone was smirking. He already had the four Polaroids with their vital fingerprint. Perhaps Ben's torrent of information including Chartreuse having links with Colombia might explain the envelope in which they came. More and more of the gaps were being filled in as this electric day unfolded.

Ben seemed to have stopped to draw breath.

"Come with me," said Stone, supremely confident, getting up from his chair and leading Ben to the door of the homicide room. Not knowing what to expect, Ben followed. Stone led him through the homicide room to the far end. "Look up there," Stone ordered, totally in command of the situation. Ben looked at the wall, at the only words written in red. "Killer—Garry Chartreuse."

"Well, shit, you knew all along. You let me prattle on in there, and you knew all the time," said Ben. He felt deflated. This was his big moment when he was going to solve Calgary's only serial killer case, and the cops were miles ahead of him.

"You know there were six, don't you," said Ben, realizing if the cops knew who the killer was, they obviously knew the whole story, even though only four cases seemed to be written up on the wall.

"Nice one Ben, you joker, you can't throw me," said Stone, enjoying Ben's attempted counter-attack to knock him off balance.

"No, I'm serious, there are six. There are two more that aren't up here on the wall. It's all in the letters," said Ben. Stone stared at Ben. If he was trying to fool around, he was taking it pretty far. And then he saw in Ben's eyes just a flash of fear.

"Christ, you're serious, aren't you? Come back in my room," he snapped. On Stone's electric day, Ben had just blown all the fuses. Stone stomped back into his room, and after Ben trooped in behind him, Stone slammed the door shut.

"Okay, this is what I know from the letters," said Ben, knowing he was now taking the first steps into a minefield. "I think he killed two more women in Calgary. They were both prostitutes. I think he killed them both in June 1992, after he'd killed the other four. I know their names. I even interviewed them both at some time when they were working. In his letters, he says he killed them by kicking screwdrivers through their heads. In the letters, he says where he's buried them, so I can show you that."

Ben was taking this all very slowly, step by step, expecting at any second some mine would explode underneath him. Stone hadn't said a word. He was glaring at Ben. "How long have you known all this?" he growled in a voice Ben hadn't heard before.

"Wait a minute, there's more yet," said Ben, intent on getting everything off his chest in one session.

"You remember when all this started when I came with my contact from the M. E.'s office. You remember we showed you the letters he'd carved into the victim's bodies. You remember 'J-A-C-K' and 'Jack and Jill' and all that. Well, that was all wrong. In these letters he says he carved the letters 'A' and 'L' in the last two bodies, so he was spelling out 'J-A-C-K-A-L'. It was all part of him being pissed off because cops were treating him like 'Carlos the Jackal', you know, the terrorist. I don't exactly understand it all, but it's something like that."

Stone was furious. "Stay here and don't move," he snapped, getting up from his chair.

"Wait a minute," said Ben, who was now so far in over his head, there was no point in not going on. "You remember when I first came to you, we made a deal so you wouldn't release what I knew to other media, and I wouldn't write about it. Well, that's worked great so far. Now, my boss at the paper wants us to have photographers there when you go to check on these other two bodies. They want us to be there exclusively—just us."

"What!" shrieked Stone, going red in the face for the second time in one day.

Ben could sense the mines exploding around him but ignored them, and plunged on. "And when you release the news about these two new ones, could you not mention the first four—not yet anyway, not until we're ready. That's it, I'm finished." The minute he'd said the last words, he wished he hadn't used that particular phrase.

"Do not move," said Stone, who got up, strode out of the room, slammed the door shut and stomped out of the homicide unit. Ben sat wondering what would happen next. Stone went straight to his immediate boss—the inspector in charge of the major crimes section, of which homicide was just one unit.

Whichever way Stone explained it, it sounded incredible. The Mail's crime reporter knew where two murdered bodies were buried, and he was willing to take police to the scene, provided the Mail could photograph the scene, exclusively, and police wouldn't tell any other media what was going on!

Stone's version was self-serving, painting the Mail as black as possible. He didn't mention how the Mail had spent months sitting on the time-bomb that cops had locked up four innocent men for murders they hadn't committed. To admit that would mean Stone would have to reveal he was party to the deal. Neither did he mention the Mail had steered the cops toward the guilty man.

With so little to go on, the inspector could hardly advise Stone what to do—and he left it to Stone to decide how to proceed. Delegating difficult decisions to lower ranks was one of the perks of the higher ranks. Storming to his boss's office and walking back to his own had given Stone a few minutes to recover from his initial shock. The vital over-riding fact in this case that made it different from all the others was that the killer was already dead. That alone took some of the pressure off Stone in making his decision. Whatever happened with these next two bodies, if they were there, couldn't influence any legal procedures or court cases. He re-entered his office and slammed the door again. It looked to him as if Ben had sat petrified without moving a muscle since he'd left.

"Look you bastard," he said. Ben waited for the whole minefield to explode in his face. "The boss says we can probably make it happen. I wouldn't have done it, but he says it's a go."

Ben exhaled a long breath. It seemed to him he'd been holding his breath since Stone left the room. To his surprise Ben found he was still alive.

So he produced his final shocker.

"Look, if you find these bodies when you go looking, and if it all goes to plan, I've already written the basic article we want to use. I've got it here," he said, producing a sheaf of papers from his pocket like a magician with his rabbit. "Any chance you could run through it now, so that in the panic when everything happens, you already know what's coming, and I can safely run it, knowing we're all on the same page?"

"Christ!" said Stone, snatching the pages out of Ben's hands.

If Stone did but know it, Ben was putting his head in a noose here. If Ben's bosses knew he was letting a cop see a story in advance, with an unspoken understanding he could change things, they'd go ballistic. Every Venetian blind in the boardroom would crash down at once. He'd be fired on the spot.

This news story and feature of Ben's was as polished a piece of tight-rope walking as Ben had ever written, a piece of which he was inwardly quite proud. It heaped an underlying layer of unwritten praise on the Mail itself for revealing two murders to the police, who otherwise wouldn't know about them. It left the reader understanding homicide cops had reacted swiftly to the revelation and had instantly put a large team to work on the double murder. Most importantly for Ben's working contacts, it made no reference, no hint, not even the slightest suggestion, that there were four more murders the Mail knew about which it wasn't mentioning. And most importantly for Ben's bosses, there were numerous references to this being an exclusive Mail scoop. No other media in the city had the slightest knowledge about any of this.

Ben had excelled himself. Stone, who'd feared what revelations Ben could have made at this delicate stage, was relieved it didn't yet contain any bombshells for him.

"Yes, I can live with that," he said, giving it back to Ben, who hid it away very quickly.

"Now listen," said Stone. "You come in here at 7 a. m. sharp, and you can take us to where you reckon these bodies are. We'll be ready. Now sod off, you've done enough damage for one day," he said, ushering Ben out.

Ben rode silently down in the elevator, quietly gave back his "visitor's tag" to the concierge, took back his driver's license, walked slowly out into the sunlight, then punched the air in excitement. It was all going to work. Now, there were only about a thousand things left that could go wrong.

Chapter 15

Ben was up early. It's not every day you get to show police officers where two murdered bodies are buried. Feeling nervous, he drove into the downtown core, parked up as near to the police headquarters building as he could get, and walked inside the two pairs of double swing doors. He found Stone waiting for him at the concierge's desk.

"Okay, everybody I need is waiting outside," he told Ben. "This is how we're going to play it. You're going to show us where we've got to look. Your guy can take all the photos he needs of us digging and working, whatever. But if we find anything, he's got to back off. Okay."

Ben nodded, as if this was a huge concession he was making to Stone. In fact, Ben knew it was the policy of the Mail never to show any body shots, anyway. In bygone years, the Mail used to show body shots. Many a murder victim's feet were shown protruding from the end of a hastily thrown plastic sheet on the Mail's front pages years ago. But, in an effort to lose its "sleazy, gutter-press" image and prove it was a responsible newspaper, body shots were banned. Even long-range shots showing yellow plastic sheets lying at the scene were banned, as the paper's upper hierarchy knew its readers would instinctively recognize what was lying beneath the tell-tale sheet and be offended. The strange fact was that the rival Echo paper down the road—reputedly the city's responsible newspaper—still ran body shots. What was even more amazing was that all Calgarians remembered the Mail used to run graphic photographs, and still branded it with its "sleazy, gutter-press" reputation, even after the policy change. On the first murder case Ben ever covered at the Mail, the shooting dead of an RCMP officer, the Echo ran really graphic photographs of the officer's body lying in the gravel. The Mail adhered to its new policy and ran no such shot. Yet, days later, it was the Mail's photo editor who took phone-calls from irate readers, blasting the paper for running such a disgusting photograph on its front page—yet it was the Echo which ran the picture! Later today, if Sam Reef the photographer took 50 shots of skeletons and corpses which Stone might unearth, the Mail wouldn't run a single one. But still Ben nodded, appearing suitably disappointed.

So the convoy set off, Ben in his van, Sam following in his well-worn mud-splattered truck, and a various bunch of police vehicles tagging on behind. It was strange for Ben to be leading Sam to the southern-most outskirts of the city, out to the south-east, to the Burnco turn-off, and further south toward the Bow River. It was Sam, probably the best fly-fisherman in Alberta, who had once led Ben along this very road, for a fishing trip to this stretch of the river charmingly known by all as "Must-Be-Nice." That first trip had been a great success for Ben. He had actually caught one rainbow trout. Mostly he had watched in awe as Sam landed one after another. It had reminded him of another fly-fishing effort on the Bow when Sam, Ben, and a guide had float-boated down the Bow after trout. How could it be when three men fly-fished with the same flies from the same boat that two of them could catch fish all day, and Ben couldn't? Sam had taken 22 trout that day. Cast, hook a trout, pull the boat into the bank, step out, land the fish, push the boat back out into the river, drift a few yards, cast, hook another trout, pull into the bank, over and over again. Each time Ben would cast, no hit, and wait while Sam was landing his next trout, then push off, cast, no hit, and wait for Sam to unhook his next fish. Ben didn't think it could get worse, but it did. At one point, they stopped the boat on a sandbank in the river. Sam had another trout bending his rod almost double. He'd handed Ben the rod while he quickly loaded a new film into his camera. In the few seconds Sam's dexterous and experienced fingers flicked the new film into place and he turned to take back his rod, Ben had lost the fish. Not only had he scored a total blank for the day, he'd even lost what would have been Sam's best fish of the day.

Ben had another memory of Sam, his fly-fishing mentor. There had come a day when both Ben and Sam had won awards for professional work done. Ben had won an internal Mail corporation annual award for the best story of the year across all the chain's newspapers. Sam was receiving a top accolade for a series of nature photographs he'd produced which were so spectacular the paper turned them into a calendar and made pots of money off Sam's brilliance.

This was a best suit and tie affair, attire entirely out of keeping with this pair, and as the start of the proceedings had been delayed, they each strolled down to an ornamental lake set in the grounds of the grand and voluminous venue. They both saw the opportunity at the same moment. Each had his fly-rod in his vehicle and in minutes they had their rods tackled up. Years before, Sam had perfected the most difficult fly-fishing cast known to man, the roll-cast with no back lift. Patiently he began illustrating it to Ben, with Ben trying to emulate the skill. Every fly-fisherman suffers the day when a wall of trees stands at his back and there's no way to cast except by flexing his arms while simultaneously flicking his wrist so his fly line rolls out in front of him across the water, landing his fly right under the nose of his target trout. Sam rolled perfect casts across the ornamental lake, while Ben's casts staggered out, but getting better with each attempt. At this moment, another of the Mail's photographers, sent to record the prestigious award ceremony, captured the moment. While the Mail eventually did get pictures of these two award-winning professionals shaking hands with the enormously important top executives of the whole corporation in the plush surroundings of the very expensive location, Ben only saved the other photograph. It showed this pair, together, immaculately dressed in suit-and-tie (probably for the first and only time in their lives) standing at a lakeside, fly-fishing rods in hand with two beautiful roll-casts spiraling out toward the camera.

This wasn't the only time Ben saved a strictly unofficial record of what was a prestigious affair in the eyes of the upper echelons of executives. The time came when Ben was awarded a "lifetime achievement award" for years of work at the Mail. It came in the form of an etched glass trophy which found a place in Ben's trophy cabinet after he retired. But above it was Ben's most cherished memento of the same day. The guys in the newsroom presented him with a plaque inscribed "never before in the annals of history have so many died so thoughtfully just so one man could enjoy such a successful career." Now that just appealed to Ben.

Ben's convoy pulled in at the little pull off on the top of the hill, with the Bow River and "Must-Be-Nice" spread out beneath them, about 300 feet below. Everyone parked up and piled out. The wind was shrieking at the top of the hill. One by one they followed Ben, through the gap he'd made in the barbed wire fence and down the ridiculously steep slope. It was easy enough for Ben, he wasn't carrying anything. Usually going down this slope he was trying to carry his fly-fishing rod, and some kind of food basket for a day's fishing. Mostly, he sat on his bum and slid down, holding his rod and basket aloft as he progressed down the near vertical slope. Today, the others behind

Ben were slipping and sliding, trying to carry shovels and tarpaulins and boxes of equipment, and large black body-bags. Ben couldn't decide if the body-bags were to be interpreted as good news, a sign of confidence in him, or seen as bad news, signaling the finality of death. As the group slowly reached the base of the grassy slope, they ran into a belt of thick bushes beyond which was a large grassy flat meadow. The Bow River gurgled along beyond that.

Ben stopped at the bushes. He knew exactly where in the foliage he usually took a slightly worn track to get through to the meadow. He reckoned Chartreuse would have put these bodies exactly where Ben had been, after all that's what all this was about. Ben saw some bushes which looked rougher and more straggly than the others. Could it be they had been disturbed in the past?

"I think they are around here, probably under those bushes, around here," said Ben, pointing Stone toward the saddest looking undergrowth.

"Okay, let's do it," shouted Stone. A police photographer took pictures of the area which was about to be dug-up. And Sam took pictures of the action, as the first bushes were ripped up and the pick-axes and shovels glinted in the early morning sun.

It was a pain for Sam to have to take straight-forward news pictures, getting all the ingredients into a single shot so that it told a complete story. Here, he must position himself so the inevitable yellow police "do not cross" tape was in the foreground, the officers digging so that their overalls emblazoned with "Crime Scene Unit" logos were clearly visible, and a background of bushes showed this was a remote area on the city outskirts. His love was photographing nature. He was thrilled to be in this beautiful place soon after the crack of dawn when the light was at its most atmospheric.

Many hundreds of times Sam had been out at dawn, just like today, making pictures of southern Alberta's glorious natural scenery. He had no need of a home and a bed and such mortal trappings. He was at his happiest sleeping rough in his truck out under the stars, so that he would be perfectly positioned at dawn for some breath-taking glory of nature. His photographs were famous throughout the province. Every year without fail his most spectacular scenic pictures won major awards when they appeared in the Mail. Sam didn't care much for awards and accolades. He mostly loved being there with the environment, capturing these moments when he was at one with nature for himself. Ben recalled a time when he and Sam had been sent into the interior of British Columbia to cover some story where an armed robber had shot a cop and taken a pregnant woman hostage in her farmstead home deep in a long valley. All western Canada's media was there. Banks of photographers lined the only road out of the valley, waiting for the moment the cops would disarm the criminal, save the mom-to-be and bring her out safely. Every long-lens camera was trained down the valley—save one. Ben looked round to find, to his amazement, that Sam was lying on his back facing away from the valley partially under a fence lining the road. Staring incredulously, Ben looked at what Sam was doing. He was utterly engrossed in a tiny blue bird which was nest-building in a tiny wooden box attached to a fence-post above Sam's head. Undeterred by this giant lying statue-still beneath it, the bird made numerous short flights into and out of the box, carrying wisps of grass and fluff and short sticks for the nest. Sam was a study of a man in love with nature. But he was also the complete professional. When the action broke later in the day, he was where he had to be, and his action photograph ran across the front page as the pregnant woman was saved from disaster.

It was the same today. Sam would ideally have loved to be fly-fishing in the Bow he could hear behind him babbling even above the sound of the wind. He would even prefer to be photographing the red-winged blackbirds he could hear not far away. Instead, he worked at composing the necessary news pictures showing cops digging for corpses in remote countryside.

It really didn't take long. The second bush attacked by the police almost fell out of the ground where its roots were so weak. In a few moments, Ben's perception of the scene changed dramatically. He was no longer an important part of the operation, leading police to the scene. Now he was strictly "media" and was ushered well back, together with Sam, so that whatever had been unearthed wasn't for their eyes.

Ben had laughed to himself when they'd arrived at the base of the vertical grass hill, when one of the officers brought out the "yellow tape" and strung it through a few trees as his first priority. This was a remote section of countryside visited very rarely by a few very select fly-fishermen who knew it was there. Even to get there, the rare few had to trespass through the barbed wire at the top, and fewer still were prepared to do that. Many weeks would pass without a single human foot treading this way. Yet still the dutiful officer had to put up the ubiquitous "yellow tape" to keep back some inquisitive crowd of onlookers he expected would soon come pouring down the hill. Now, Ben and Sam—the only two civilians probably in a 20 mile radius—were sent back behind the tape.

While everything had started quickly, it now stalled as far as Ben was concerned. Ben discovered that exhuming a murdered body, if that was what had been found, was not a procedure to be hurried. Every tiny step was photographed by police. The excavation of the body became akin to an archaeological dig, where precious evidence was exposed inch by inch.

Hours passed. It was clear to Ben and Sam from their slightly distant vantage point that two sites had been unearthed. Two distinct teams were beavering away at two spots a few yards apart. More reinforcements arrived during the morning. Representatives from the medical examiner's office came slithering down the grassy slope. Men carried more equipment down. Eventually a large white tent was erected and now Ben and Sam really couldn't see what was happening. But it was a bonus for Sam. Nothing looks more sinister and portentous of murderous revelations than a crowd of police officers huddled round a white tent in a remote location. That could be the front page picture right there.

Ben's first clue that this would take far longer than he ever expected came when some heavy trucks started appearing from across the meadow. What Ben didn't know was that the meadow belonged to a farmer whose farm track several kilometers to the west gave motorized access to the remote area. It was this farmer whose barbed wire had been breached at the top of the hill. He gave police permission he would never give to fly-fishermen to drive along the track to get their vehicles to the site. One contained heavy-duty floodlights. The work was clearly going to last through the night.

Late in the day Ben sought out Stone.

"Look, I'll get all those letters and the other stuff to you tomorrow or whenever you've finished here, if that's okay," said Ben.

"Make sure you do," said Stone.

"And how's it going here?" Ben asked, nodding toward the tent and fishing for confirmation that Stone had found everything, when it was pretty obvious he must have done.

"We're going to be here all night and into tomorrow. We'll know exactly what we've got by then and we'll have everything removed from here that we need," he said.

"Well, have you found them?" asked Ben, not getting the confirmation he wanted.

"We'll know what we've got by tomorrow," said Stone, staring at Ben and carefully repeating his message. Ben understood. Stone wouldn't have these teams working through the night under floodlights on an operation that was going to last at least two days unless he had found what he was expected to discover. Of course, he'd found them. Ben felt almost stupid asking the question. He was reminded of a more outrageous moment of media stupidity which Stone had faced, which, thank God, wasn't down to him.

Stone, who enjoyed working very closely with the media, once called a press conference after arresting and charging a suspect in a murder case. Reporters quickly gathered, and the usual forest of microphones and tape-recorders were thrust under his chin as he made his announcement.

"Today, officers of the homicide unit charged a 27-year-old man with first-degree murder in the stabbing death of a south-east store-owner," said Stone in a somber voice, as was his usual way, quietly expressing respect for the family of the deceased man.

In a flash, one of the young girl radio reporters spoke the immortal words:-
"Would you call that a breakthrough in the case, sir," she asked.

In the total silence which followed the question, Stone stood with his face perfectly still, then, unable to contain himself for another second, he exploded into uproarious laughter, totally unable to find any answer to the ludicrous question.

Now, leaving Stone and his small army with their floodlights and their large tent at the bottom of the hill, Ben and Sam left "Must Be Nice" the hard way. Unlike the police, they had no permission to use the farm track to the west. They struggled up the vertical grassy slope, Ben puffing and wheezing hard by the time he reached the top and half collapsed through the barbed wire strands.

Next day, Stone's meticulous work at "Must-Be-Nice" concluded after shifts of men had worked through the night, and everything which could be construed as evidence had been photographed, recovered, bagged and removed.

Anxious hours followed for Ben sitting at his desk, with his scoop story hanging in limbo. Frank was a poor buffer between him and the editorial hierarchy above, who wanted to know right now whether they could go ahead with the Mail's mighty exclusive next day. Editorial heads were putting the heat on Frank. Frank took some of the weight, but transferred most of the anxiety down onto Ben's shoulders.

"When the hell are you going to know?" Frank asked Ben for the hundredth time. Frank felt it was this bastard Ben who'd placed him in this terrifying position. The entire Mail newsroom, no, face it, the entire Mail newspaper was waiting for Frank, the city editor, to tell them they could go ahead with tomorrow's paper. But Frank couldn't say one way or the other until he got the green light from Ben. And Ben couldn't give that until he got the word— probably in some secret code only he could understand—from some God forsaken cop, who was probably drinking beer in some bar right now and couldn't be reached. Every time Frank pressured Ben, Ben called Stone's office. Finally, late in the day, Stone answered.

"Am I ever glad you're there?" said Ben. "I know you can't tell me what you found, but can you tell me this?" he asked, playing by the unwritten rules of engagement he and Stone had devised between them over the years. "If we run with my feature tomorrow, the one I showed you, will we be on the money?"

"You wouldn't be wrong," said Stone, sounding non-committal. He hadn't told Ben a single thing. He hadn't revealed what had been found. He hadn't even revealed if anything had been found. If he was ever questioned in future, Stone could honestly tell superiors he hadn't divulged anything to the Mail. But Ben knew his scoop was complete. The two men had understood each other perfectly.

"It's a go, Frank, it's a go," shouted Ben across the newsroom.

"Thank fuck for that," said Frank, leaping up and relaying the good news to all the important editorial masters he served, making sure they understood it was his persistence that had forced the green light to flash on.

Ben left the office. They already had his feature to work on in there—after all they'd been sitting on it all day. He went to the nearest Swiss Chalet and had his favorite meal—double chicken legs and fries with a chocolate super sundae—to give him strength for what he knew would be a long night ahead.

Whenever Ben was working really late on a Saturday night in the office, it meant he had a major story or feature or both appearing in Sunday's paper. Most reporters produced the copy then went home. Ben had a nasty fear of last minute glitches getting into his copy as the editors worked on it. A long-standing mental war raged between reporters and "rim-pigs" as the writers called the editors tasked with handling their copy. "Rim pigs" really couldn't win. Every day they found mistakes in reporters' copy, quietly corrected them, so the version in each edition of the paper was perfect. The reporter, of course, never remembered making the original mistake. When he read his fine words in the next edition, he remembered that was how he wrote them. "Silent saviors" they were really, these "rim-pigs." But no reporter would ever concede he'd been saved by a "rim-pig." But if these editors changed words and meanings, most often to make the copy more concisely fit the space on the page, and reporters noticed it, they hated the changes. "Butchers" they called them, these "rim-pigs." Ben found one way to avoid seeing unexpected changes in his story next day. He used to nurse his story through the "rim-pig" stage the night before. It took years to form a working rapport with the people he'd call "rim-pigs" to their faces. So as he waited late into the night, they'd take the trouble to pull him a proof of the page they'd just finished. What's more, if he found an error had slipped through, they'd have time to correct it. It was a diplomatic tightrope he walked of enlisting the help of the "rim-pigs" without making them feel it was their mistakes he was putting straight.

He was there that Saturday night. His two-page murder scoop feature for the inside pages was worked on first. One damn problem with providing all the exclusive photos the paper could handle, was that the Mail loved to use them. And that meant there was less space for his precious copy. When he first saw the two-page spread allocated to his feature, he was aghast at the huge white boxes drawn across the pages. These were for the photos. It was always a heart-breaker for Ben to go through these late nights. First each page had expanses denied to him because of the advertisements. These had top priority. It was written in stone. The entire newspaper started with the advertisements. When some advertising rep from the floor below drew boxes on the page allocating space to advertisements, they were inviolate. The entire editorial floor, reporters, editors, even high-ranking managerial editors all played second fiddle. Editorial began with the remnants of the pages which advertising hadn't used. And, if that wasn't bad enough, the paper was keen on its photographs. They took more great chunks of the page away. Ben and the other reporters had what was left. Luckily, Ben's stories were always about death, destruction, calamity and mayhem, so they were nearly always given top priority for the remaining spaces. Other reporters suffered the pain of filling the smaller spaces Ben's daily disasters didn't fill.

But there was one exception to the space rule. On Sundays, a two-page space was allocated for Frank's "good Sunday read" and advertising representatives couldn't touch it. So Ben was hoping for great things that Saturday night. Except that he'd provided the opportunity for such great art. One giant box dominated one page where Sam's huge color photograph of the corpse-digging scene would sit. And three smaller boxes spread themselves across the pages where detailed photographs would land. Ben's feature could only fill the spaces between. Still, there had been communication. Ben had been told to write to a length, and he'd crammed everything he knew into the right number of words. Better that, than write too much and let a "rim-pig" choose which literary gems to exclude. In the end, Ben had to admit, it looked damn good.

He stayed long enough to look over his up-front exclusive of how the Mail had literally uncovered two murdered women. That story was the last thing to leave the rim that night. That too looked striking. It was midnight before he left, feeling he was negotiating this whole minefield like a veteran. The up-front story and the feature only talked about two murders. There was no clue about four more. No suggestion of any serial killer. Ben calculated he'd still have contacts among the homicide cops when the paper was out on the street next day.

Next morning Ben was back in the office, reading the feature again. It looked even better now the glorious color photographs were splashed across the front page and the inside spread. Grudgingly, he knew he had to admit the Mail's strategy of playing exclusive photographs big had its value, even if it did chop down the space for his stories. The whole package was an eye-catcher.

Something else caught his eye, too. He ran to one of the panoramic windows of the newsroom. A thick black pall of smoke was rising out of the southwest. Nearly every new reporter on the paper at some time or other had rushed into the newsroom to report a huge pall of oily black smoke rising in the northeast of the city. "Yea, yea, yea," he'd tell them. "Calm down, it's just the airport." Every month, Calgary firefighters tested their ability to knock down a "blazing" aircraft fire. They would fill a huge open-topped tank with oil and gasoline, flash it all up until a ferocious inferno was roaring then put it out with foam. Each time an impressive and dramatic pall of oily smoke would dominate the skyline, and new reporters would go running for the newsroom.

But this pall was in the southwest.

"I'm on my way, send a photographer," yelled Ben as he ran out of the newsroom, grabbing mobile scanner, radio, notebook, tape recorder and pen, knowing that his trusty video-camera was in the van, loaded with film and ready to roll.

Other reporters filtered over to the newsroom window. Ben was right, it was an impressive plume of smoke, already rising vertically until the top billows reached some high-level wind stream and bent off to the west.

Ben heard all the right messages on the scanner as he drove toward the smoke. Before he was halfway there going south, firefighters were calling for a "second alarm" and as he made the final dogleg to the west they called in a "third alarm." That meant there would be more than a dozen rigs on the way, some ahead of him, some behind him.

Driving on one of the main elevated east-west highways across the city Ben found himself looking down on the blazing factory, below and to the left. He'd be in heaven just to stop right here on the overpass, in the middle of six lanes of traffic and start filming. Some hopes. Traffic was sweeping over the overpass. Ben glimpsed flames roaring from one corner of the factory roof, and dense black smoke belching out from under the eaves along its entire length. Then he was past and heading downhill ready for the left turn into the industrial park now dwarfed by the giant mushroom cloud of smoke. In the distance, he could hear the approaching sirens of the fire rigs he'd beaten in, and luckily, this early in the blaze, the police hadn't yet marshalled their little army of road-blockers and yellow-tape stringers. South of the factory was an alley and a large abandoned storage shed, the perfect fire barrier between him and the blaze. He parked on the far side of the storage shed, stuffed all his pockets with equipment and his three two-hour batteries for his video camera, and set off on foot for a better vantage point. Upwind, an opening left him with a direct sight of where the collapsed roof end was spewing flames high into the sky.

"Okay, let's have you back out of there."

It was a constable. Young, probably a rookie on probably one of the first really big fires he'd ever seen. The cop's training kicked in. First—move the damn media back. Second, move everybody back. Further. However far back is safe—move them all further back. If he only stopped for a second, he'd see the fire is very nearly out of sight, it's so far away. And the smoke is blowing in the opposite direction. But he has his training, and he has the power of his uniform. And everybody—especially this guy from the media, will go back as far as he orders.

Ben remembered the worst case he'd ever seen when a power-crazy cop exercised his media training. It was in downtown Calgary at lunch-time when a truck driver had pulled his rig across the LRT lines and a C-Train took out his flat-bed trailer and was derailed. When Ben arrived, police were evacuating shaken passengers off the train, traffic chaos was fast spreading through the downtown core, and a swelling crowd of onlookers were pressing forward to see such excitement as they munched their lunches. The Mail's photographer, Max Greywood had been downtown on another assignment, and was among the first there. He'd captured commuters being led off the train, and had taken the truck-train wreck from every angle.

Later, behind the onlookers, another police car, sirens wailing, screeched to a stop, well after most of the action was over. This officer ran from behind the crowd, which included Max, through the throng to the front and launched into page one of his training manual.

"Everybody back. Come on, everybody back," he yelled.

This was a quiet, curious crowd which had been standing watching for maybe 20 minutes, getting in no one's way, hindering none of the emergency services, and in no possible danger from anything. With some amusement, they watched this agitated officer now running back and forth across in front of them, yelling ever louder. And they dutifully moved back—including Max. And when they had all obeyed his orders, instead of being satisfied, he redoubled his efforts, obviously, now on page two of the manual.

"Further back, further back," he yelled, the veins in his neck standing out as he strained to scream louder than ever.

And the crowd moved back once more—including Max.

And then it happened. The screaming officer suddenly saw the cameras hanging round Max's neck, and the pack of camera gear on his back, and knew he was dreaded media. He was straight on to page three of the manual.

"You, get back further, didn't you hear me," he screamed in Max's face. Max stepped back two paces, now standing further back than the crowd of spectators. It was already ridiculous. Twenty minutes ago, Max had been at the doors of the C-Train with the first police officers when the passengers were escaping. Now, here, 20 minutes later, when he was further away from the scene than spectators, this purple-faced officer was screaming for him to get even further back.

Those nearest in the crowd watched in fascination at the very moment when Max's patience snapped. As he took another step backward, obeying the officer again, Max looked the man straight in the eye.

"You douche bag," he said, quite quietly. But the officer heard it. Many in the immediate crowd heard it. And it provoked an immediate leap into a different chapter in the manual altogether.

"You're under arrest," yelled the officer. And in a flash Max was in handcuffs and being led away, much further back than the crowd. All the way back to the cruiser, and all the way back to police headquarters.

Ben recalled the sequel. Amazingly, Max Greywood was charged with "inciting a riot." He pleaded not guilty, and when it went to court, several of the crowd who'd been nearest to the action, gave testimony. To a man, they described how Max had been a paragon of patience, obeying every command, until he uttered his fateful two words. They also described, how, if anyone had been inciting a riot at the scene it was the temper-driven officer. Case dismissed. Funny thing, Ben recalled, the officer's name was also Greywood.

Now Ben had his own version of "Officer Greywood" at this fire. He simply shook his head in wonder. He'd been to hundreds more fires than this rookie. He knew how close was too close, and how far away was safe. And he was so far away now the fire would be a distant blur even at full zoom in his camcorder. But he moved back as ordered. Well, he moved right away, to the end of the block, turned south, went along another block and came back up toward the fire from two blocks away, where no rookie cops were flexing their muscles.

On the fire scanner, Ben heard them calling for "Hazmat"—the firefighters' hazardous material specialists. This factory was full of chemicals, and that billowing cloud of smoke towering across the city was laden with toxic fumes. What's more, the officers in fire control had passed on some bad news to the incident commander in charge at the factory. The wind was forecast to change any minute now. That toxic cloud could be expected to swing back south of the blazing factory pretty soon.

That might suddenly explain why a fleet of ambulances was pulling up at a building in front of Ben two blocks away from the fire and to the south. It was a seniors' home housing dozens of elderly folk whose lungs and breathing capabilities were bad enough already. The last thing they needed was a dose of toxic gas. It was a mass evacuation of the whole building. Ben took one look and decided he could do with some help here. He seldom did that. It was a matter of professional pride that he could handle any story single-handed. But even he knew he couldn't be at a blazing factory, cover a spreading toxic cloud settling on the city, and handle the stories to be found in a mass evacuation of dozens of frightened old folk, all on his own. To start with, with all these story angles flying around, how could he concentrate on getting his beloved fire video? He radioed city desk, and other reporters were soon headed for the seniors. Ben grabbed two quick interviews with two elderly women in wheelchairs with tubes from their arms to overhead gantries attached to their chairs before paramedics shunted him out of the way. Then he left the old folk to the reporters he knew were coming.

Ben hurried along a road parallel to where the rookie cop was set up, calculated when he was level with the factory, and cut into the front garden of a house, down the side alley into the back yard. Right on! All that was left of the roofless factory was now under a massive fireball roaring into the sky. When the roof caved in, it took one wall in with it, and pushed out the other side wall across the alley into an abandoned storage shed. In seconds, Ben's camera was rolling. This was the vantage point he should have had the whole time. It was spectacular. From deep inside the factory, volatile drums of chemicals were exploding, shooting flaming fireballs into the sky. Even the abandoned storage shed was becoming engulfed. Thick black smoke was pouring out from under its eaves and through its windows Ben filmed a dull orange glow inside. Then, a shattering sound as one window blew out. Instantly, every window in the shed blew out, each belching a blowtorch of flame, accompanied by a mixture of crashing, roaring sounds as the whole shed flashed over. This shed wasn't built solidly like the factory. It was consumed in a few minutes, the thick black smoke turning to deep red boiling flame, and the structure collapsing in a welter of crashing timbers and a cloud of sparks. This was rare footage even for Ben's extensive library. It wasn't every day Ben found himself exactly at the right place at the right time as a really huge fire unfolded before him. Against a backdrop of the blazing factory, here was a large storage shed being consumed by flames right in his view-finder, and even now it wasn't finished. In the foreground, here were two parked vehicles, partially buried under the collapsed outside wall of the shed, now catching fire. One Ben could see had been a pickup truck, its shape still visible through the oily black smoke rising from it, but the other was nothing but a ball of fire. It often amazed Ben how much smoke and flame a burning vehicle could produce, and this one was roaring.

It suddenly hit Ben like a sledge-hammer.

He'd been all over the place on this fire. Backed down one street by a keen cop, looking for better view-points two blocks away, seen a seniors' home being evacuated, dodged through a guy's yard to get here. Now, he realized where he was in relation to where he'd started.

That fireball was his fucking van.

It had to be. He remembered the pickup being parked next to him. Now, through the smoke and flames he could see his roof rack. Right now, as firefighters brought another jet of water to play on the two vehicles, his van became visible through the cascading water and thinning smoke. His beloved Chevy van was now just a blackened skeleton sitting on metal rims where its tires had burned away, its roof stove in by the collapsed building. It gave Ben a shaky feeling to think he'd filmed this great fire without realizing in the heat of the moment he was recording the destruction of his own van.

Now he knew what Jessica Sewell, another of the Mail's photographers had felt like when Ben had filmed the whole of her building, an entire apartment block, going up in flames. The fire had started in Jessica's apartment, spread into the attic, and swept through the roof, dropping blazing ceilings into all the other apartments until they too burned out. Ben remembered that fire for the dramatic footage of a firefighter hot-footing it down an aerial ladder through a storm of blazing embers as the roof finally collapsed and the inferno in the attic was released into the sky. Ben had also captured Jessica on film at the scene, bravely taking photographs for the Mail of her own home being destroyed. He'd wondered then what Jessica must have felt, capturing her own home going up in flames. Now, in a small way, he knew. Ben's Chevy van was an important part of his life. There was nothing left. He'd left his fly-fishing rod in there and his fly-fishing jacket with pockets loaded with flies and leaders and lead shot. Come to think of it, his chest waders and felt boots were in there too. Everything was gone.

He radioed the office. He just knew they'd think it was hilarious. They'd be polite and make the right apologetic clucking noises to his face. But behind his back they'd never be able to stop laughing.

"Ben to city desk, over," he started.

"Go ahead."

"Ben to city desk. I've got a spot of bother down at this fire, over," he said.

"You haven't been arrested, have you?" It was Frank, fearing immediately he was going to be short of copy on this major fire if Ben was in the slammer.

"No. My van's been destroyed in the fire. I parked it two buildings away, and the fire still reached it. It's gone. Toast. You got a reporter who can get me back to the office?"

"God Almighty, Ben," said Frank, making the first of the right apologetic clucking noises, "sorry to hear that. Yes, where are you? I'll get Allan to pick you up."

Ben waited. Now the fire was rapidly coming under control. There was a moment at every big fire, when the flames seemed suddenly to die down, when the smoke ceased to boil black, when Ben would become aware of more firefighting jets of water pounding the building from more angles, and when more white steam started to rise.

Ben switched off his camera, walked back through to the front yard of the property and met Allan. They drove back to the office, Ben swearing most of the way, and Allan managing not to laugh out loud. Just.

It wasn't until Ben was back at his desk, where his good-looking two-page murder spread was looking up at him from on his desk where he'd thrown it, that he suddenly remembered. It had completely slipped his mind in all the turmoil of the fire. Now, the murder spread reminded him. All Garry's fucking material, all his original scrawled letters and notebooks, the whole lot, had been in the van, in the glove compartment, ready to show Stone.

"Fuck me rigid," Ben said out loud. He'd never made himself a copy of it all, there was too much of it. Now, unless he was damn lucky, there would be nothing left. He needed to know as soon as he could get away from the office. He pounded the computer keys like a demon, hammering out the fire story. The devastation, collapsing walls, lucky-to-be-alive employees who escaped, the battling firefighters, the toxic fumes, the environmental scare, evacuated seniors, anxious neighbors, the dollar loss—$2-million—all these essential aspects of the story leaving no space for any mention of burned out vehicles.

He spell-checked it, so the computer would iron out any obvious, careless spelling mistakes. Stupid computer. As always, it threw out the word "Calgarians" to the great annoyance of Ben and every other reporter who used the word in very nearly every story.

"Frank, you've got the fire story. Have you got someone who can run me back to the fire, so I can find out what's happening to my van?" he asked.

"Why, you got some burning reason to get back there," said Frank. "Oh, sorry, Ben, I forgot," he said, lying and smirking at his clever joke at the same time. "Yea, there's a presser down there in half-an-hour, Allan'll take you."

When they got there, Allan went to the front of the charred factory for the presser while Ben skirted the building, walked past the blackened shell of the storage shed and found firefighters and two police officers looking at the two burned out vehicles.

"Get back," said one of the uniform cops almost as a reflex action.

"That's my van," said Ben.

"Ah, we've been looking for the owner. Why did you park it here, sir? Had business in there, did you?"

"No, I'm from the Calgary Mail. I was covering the fire and parked it here when the fire was only over there in the factory. I thought it would be safe here. You don't know if they saved any papers out of the glove compartment, do you?"

"No way," said one of the firefighters. "Look, come and see for yourself, there is no glove compartment left, there's no dashboard left come to that. It's right back to the metal. Sorry."

Ben started sorting out all the necessary arrangements with the cop like getting the hulk towed to a scrap yard, insurance paperwork, and witness statement as to why his van came to be part of Calgary's biggest fire of the year. But his mind was most occupied with his real loss—Garry's papers. It was a disaster.

And now Frank was on his case again, on the radio.

"Ben, get yourself down to police headquarters. They got a presser in an hour about the bodies. Get Allan to take you when he's finished there. And you better get yourself a new vehicle pretty damn quick. You're no good to me without transport, over."

"Up yours, you miserable bastard," Ben thought silently to himself. "Right on Frank, over," he said politely into the radio.

It was a nervously exciting press conference for Ben for two reasons. Half the media there eyed him suspiciously, copies of his scoop tucked under their arms, wanting to know how come he had been so far ahead. Which cop had tipped him insider information and more to the point had shat all over them? What more did he have that they did not? Mostly they just glared at him. It had been a truly monumental exclusive for Ben, and he basked smugly in the accumulated limelight of the glares.

What worried him was the possibility of what Stone might reveal. Ben had kept his end of the deal. His feature hadn't mentioned a word about the four other murders. Would Stone protect him? Stone started by revealing the details of what his team had found at "Must-Be-Nice." They had located the bodies of two murdered women. He released a great deal of new information which hadn't been in Ben's story. The bodies had been reduced to skeletons. They'd probably been there anything up to 10 years. Homicide detectives had established how they had died, but he could not reveal the method used. His officers believed both were killed by the same person. Police had preliminary information to suggest who the women were, but names would not be released until positive identification had been made, and relatives informed.

Then, he stopped to invite questions. Ben, watching him silently and nervously, began to breathe more easily—so far, so good. But in a room full of professional reporters, the obvious question was bound to be asked.

"Did you find anything to link these two murders with any others?" came the question Ben was dreading. He held his breath. Ben knew Stone never lied to the media. He might bend the truth, omit things he knew, and cover up information by explaining why he couldn't release certain facts, but he wouldn't lie—it was one of his personal unwritten rules.

"There was nothing found at the scene at 'Must-Be-Nice' to link these two murders with any other," he said. Ben knew that was very strictly true. Stone had told the truth and evaded the truth both at the same time. Ben's secret was still safe for now—but for how long?

Chapter 16

In the next few weeks through the late summer months of 2001, Stone had a team of detectives working the two new murders as a separate pair, not related to the "Whiskey Foxtrot" operation. It would have been simpler to take it for granted they were two more victims of his suspected serial killer, Garry Chartreuse, as they obviously must be, but Stone didn't like taking anything for granted where murder was concerned.

He wanted them investigated from scratch as new homicides. If the results confirmed they were two more down to the serial killer, then that would be for the future. Until then, they were unsolved homicides. And until he was certain one way or the other, he wasn't making any public references to any serial killer possibilities.

He was reading again the autopsy results that had just come in on the two skeletons when the phone rang. It was Ben needing to see him. He too needed to see Ben. Where were those letters and diaries?

In half an hour, Ben was there, visitor tag on his lapel, and a rusty old tin box under his arm.

"Look, you're not going to believe this, but I don't have the letters or the diaries anymore," said Ben, who'd been dreading this moment for some days. "They were all destroyed. The whole lot got wiped out when my van was gutted during that big chemical factory fire the other day. I had all his stuff in an envelope to bring to you, and it was all destroyed."

"Christ, that's fucking ridiculous," snapped Stone. Irreligiously. "Didn't you make copies of it all? You must have done."

"No. There was tons of it. I was just going to hand it all over to you," said Ben. "But I do still have these, I'd kept them separately at home," he said, opening his tin box with its package of panty crotches still wrapped in paper, hoping this vital evidence might save the day.

"This is exactly how they were in the tin—four bits of cloth together in a bunch in that bit of paper, and the other two wrapped up separately in that bit," said Ben, pointing to them in the tin, without touching them.

Stone was a lot more careful than Ben. Without even touching the tin, he left it on his desk and called in one of his detectives.

"Bring gloves and an evidence bag," he sang out on the phone. A homicide detective wearing white rubber gloves put the tin box with its contents in a transparent evidence bag, sealed it, and wrote on it.

"It's part of the Whiskey Foxtrot evidence. Get it to the lab, will you?" said Stone, and the tin box was gone.

"Tell me again, how did you come to get that lot?" asked Stone.

Ben related the whole story in detail. Garry's letter coming apparently from a prison in Spokane, the instructions of where Ben should dig alongside the Bow River, unearthing the tin box, reading all the details of six murders, references to Polaroid pictures, bundles with bits of cloth inside, everything he could remember.

"A likely tale, I've never heard such rubbish. I don't believe a word," said Stone. "Still, if that's the best you can do, I'll have to work with it. Now, bugger off, I've got work to do," and he ushered Ben out of the office.

Ben went down in the elevator, relieved to have survived this latest ordeal. He knew when Stone was joking, and it looked as if the homicide guys now had enough to put the whole lot together. It would just be a matter of time before he'd get the okay to go ahead with the "serial killer murdered six women" scoop, and the whole story would be complete.

But several more weeks passed, and nothing new came out of the homicide unit. It was a frantic time for Ben. Stories were breaking in all directions. For the first time in his career, he covered a fatal cougar mauling. He had to drive all the way into the interior of British Columbia where this unfortunate family lived in a homestead remote from neighbors and away from civilization. They liked it like that. Ben could appreciate their choice of location as the scenery he passed was glorious in its autumnal splendor with splashes of gold, red and yellow interspersed among the evergreens. On the day it happened, the mom and two of her young kids were riding on the family horses, where, unseen, a cougar was stalking them. The first they knew it was when the cougar pulled the young lad off his horse. With incredible bravery, the mother snatched her boy from the jaws of the cougar, and sent the two kids away to fetch help, while she fought the wild animal. By the time the kids returned with help, it was all too late. Their mom had been mauled to death by the cougar.

The story wrote itself. "MOTHER LAYS DOWN LIFE FOR SON" was the front page headline. It would have said "Mother sacrifices life for son" but "sacrifices" is too long a word for tabloid headlines. Other family members paid tributes to the hero mother, and the family photographs of happier times even with the family riding on horseback together made it a poignant package. Experts even embellished it with opinions that it could only have been a freak attack. Apparently cougars wouldn't attack three humans together, and certainly wouldn't attack a human on horseback, but this one did. That provided the headline for the inside page story—"FREAK COUGAR ATTACK KILLS HERO MOM." Hunters went out the next day, and found and shot the offending animal. Ben was there in the nearest town when it was brought in splayed out across the back of a pick-up truck. Ben couldn't believe how huge it was—but then, what could you expect from a city slicker from Calgary, and a Brit at that?

For Ben, the story was a straight-forward quick hit—a two-day wonder. Go there, hit every angle, and back to the office. In a way, it was a sad commentary on the necessary perspective a crime reporter had to maintain on life as he saw it. For him, it would be the only time he'd ever see that place. In another few days, it would be an almost forgotten episode, just another violent fatality to add to the list. Never mind that for the family involved and their friends and everyone who knew them this was a shattering disaster, leaving children without a mother, a distraught husband without his loved one, a personal human tragedy changing all those lives forever. It had one distinction for Ben—it was the first time in his death book he'd recorded "cougar mauling" as the cause of death.

Then Ben was sent to rural Saskatchewan for a sex scandal that was exactly the opposite of any "two-day wonder." It was a scandal which took weeks to unfold. At its heart, it had outrageous allegations against all kind of respected people in a community that they'd been molesting and sexually abusing little children. Added overtones of "ritual satanic cult" behavior were the next bombshell. Then, it was rumored the very police officers investigating the scandal were among the evil-doers. Ben went to Saskatchewan time after time. And every time he drove there Ben was left with one lasting impression of Saskatchewan. Its roads were appalling. Driving east on the main drag from

Drumheller through Oyen in Alberta toward Kimberley and the rural plains of Saskatchewan, Ben always knew when he's crossed the border. The beautiful smooth tarmac of Alberta's roads had the tires on his new Dodge caravan purring almost silently. Moments later, some rough road surface, pitted with potholes and bumpy repairs, had his whole van lurching and bouncing and rattling. Good morning, Saskatchewan!

Homicide detectives, meanwhile, were making fast progress in the case of the "Must-Be-Nice" skeletons. They were still viewing it with completely open minds, but always with the shadow of Garry Chartreuse in the background. Stone was happy to keep it that way. He was a master of hiding his innermost thoughts while throwing out a smokescreen to cover them.

Ben had even seen this at work on the most trivial of levels. They'd be walking across downtown to Stone's nearest coffee shop. Ben would be asking him about some current murder and Stone would say something non-committal. Putting his arm round Ben's shoulder, which in itself was disconcerting as Stone fully intended it to be, he would interrupt himself to suddenly ask about fly-fishing, a topic in which they shared a common interest. Stone would ask a pertinent question about a spot on the river or a fly or a technique, knowing Ben could furnish him with the answer, and Ben would do so. Soon they'd be deep into the advantages of a bead-head Prince's nymph over a San Juan worm during the cold months of winter when the whitefish and the rainbows schooled in deep pools along the Bow River. Only when the coffee was ordered and half-drunk would Ben finally realize how neatly Stone had hidden his thoughts about the current murder under the smokescreen of fly-fishing, and warded off his prying questions.

In a way, this was exactly what Stone was doing with this "Must-Be-Nice" investigation now. Something truly dramatic had happened. Stone's smokescreen was to have the whole team looking at all the routine possibilities, of course with Chartreuse at the top of their suspect list. But, all the time, in his mind Stone had a new personal theory—a niggling innermost thought gnawing at him. One vital report which he'd just received from the crime laboratory had set this new theory in motion. It came as a complete shock to him. The two pieces of material in the separate piece of paper in the tin which Ben had brought him were blood-stained sections of women's panties as Ben had suggested they would be. Forensic analysis confirmed these pieces of fabric had been cut from the panties found in the graves with the two skeletons at "Must-Be-Nice." Stone had expected that much.

The astounding result of the DNA analysis on them was that the blood on them was that of Ben Ludlow!

Stone could hardly believe his eyes. He was surprised as well to find police had Ludlow's DNA on file in the first place. Apparently, it was related to some feature Ben had written years earlier. He had no option but to consider the almost unthinkable very seriously. What if these latest two murders weren't the work of Garry Chartreuse at all? What if Ben Ludlow was the killer?

Working late in his office, when the day's activity in the homicide room had died down and he was alone, Stone brought all the "Must-Be-Nice" files into his room to study this new possibility in detail, including these most recent shocking files from the crime laboratory.

First, he went over again the known basic facts. The first of these two skeletons had been positively identified through dental records as being Elaine Wattler, date-of-birth July 20, 1970, making her aged 21 when she apparently disappeared in the spring of 1992. Wattler was a prostitute who went by the street name of Chili.

Detectives had established her father died when she was a child and her uncle had moved in with her mother. Other girls working the street told detectives Chili had run away from the home as the uncle was sexually abusing her. She was turning tricks to support her coke habit.

She'd been buried in quite a deep grave at "Must-Be-Nice," which hadn't been disturbed by animals. The medical examiner's office calculated the bones had likely been in the grave between seven and ten years. The pathologist's report concluded she had been buried naked apart from panties, the remnants of which were in place with the bones. While the panties were fragile and badly deteriorated with time, the pathologist concluded they were not intact—a part of the crotch area appeared to have been removed.

The cause of death had been massive brain injury caused by a screw-driver being forced in one ear, through the brain and shattering the skull at the other ear. The screwdriver was still in place with the skull. It appeared the screwdriver point had been sharpened for the purpose.

Stone turned to the details of the second victim. Dental records established she was Stephanie Gurdey, date of birth December 3, 1971, making her aged 20 when she was reported missing early in 1992. Detectives had compiled her life history which was one downward spiral of disasters. She had a baby at 16 years which apparently had no effect in slowing down her descent into alcoholism. She continued to be a wild party animal, binge-drinker and drug addict. Social Services had taken away her baby, and she was a regular out on the downtown stroll. Among her numerous brushes with the law, when she was the offender—mostly for minor offences—she was once recorded as the victim of a crime. She'd been put in hospital with a broken nose and arm during a brutal assault which was never solved.

She too had been buried in a separate grave at "Must-Be-Nice," sufficiently deep to have escaped the attention of animals. Her report from the medical examiner's office was almost identical to that of Elaine Wattler. She too had been killed by having a sharpened screwdriver forced through her head from ear to ear. The murder weapon was still in situ in the skull. She was also naked apart from partially disintegrated panties. It was possible but not so definite in her case that a section of the panties might have been missing. Her skeleton had been in the ground from seven to ten years.

It was impossible for the pathologist to say whether either victim had been sexually assaulted or mutilated before or after death as no soft tissue remained. He could say for certain there were no signs of damage to any of the bones other than the damage to the skulls from the screwdrivers.

Stone started to assemble what else he knew, inserting Ludlow into the picture as the killer—to see whether this new possibility would even fly.

Top of the list was the forensically established fact that Ludlow's DNA in the form of his blood was on the remnants of the panties which Stone could prove forensically had come from these two murder victims. This alone must indicate Ludlow was the killer.

Ludlow had taken police to the precise location where both bodies were buried, almost a decade after the murders. Strike two against Ludlow.

Ludlow knew exactly how both victims had been murdered, describing the method of death, which had been confirmed as accurate by the medical examiner's report. Strike three against Ludlow.

These were the basic unquestionable facts which could not be disputed. True, Stone had Ludlow's story that he had been in possession of letters and diaries written by Garry Chartreuse, and that's how he learned all this information. But, what a surprise, when it came time for Ludlow to present this most vital evidence to Stone, it had all been destroyed in a rather convenient fire. Stone didn't like surprises like that. It was a classic fabrication, the like of which Stone had been dealing with all his life. Ludlow had been thorough. He really had lost his van in a fire. Stone had checked it out. It had been parked in the path of a fast-moving factory blaze and was destroyed, no question. And Ludlow could say anything had been inside it at the time. As yet, Stone had no proof the letters and diaries ever existed in the first place, save Ludlow's word for it. He certainly had no proof any letters were inside the blazing van. And then, consider the likelihood that Ludlow would have parked his van where he did, just by chance. Stone knew that Ludlow was probably the most experienced fire reporter in the province. Many times Ludlow had told him of the thousands of fires he had attended in England and Canada. In England, the fire department had even furnished him with his own helmet and had taken him inside blazing buildings, helping to ensure his reports were more accurate. Yet, on this day when all this crucial evidence to a double murder was in his van, Ludlow parks it in the path of a roaring fire by accident, and it's all lost. Did he think Stone was a complete idiot?

In addition, if Stone had to consider the possibility that these last two murders were committed either by Chartreuse or Ludlow, there was circumstantial evidence leaning away from Chartreuse and toward Ludlow.

Stone considered the "M. O." used by Chartreuse in the first four murders which Stone had established to his own satisfaction that Chartreuse had committed.

In all four cases, Chartreuse had engineered it so the victims were discovered quickly, if not immediately. In all four cases, vital evidence leading police to a "suspect" was left to be discovered, which was Chartreuse's sole intent to ensure police convicted the wrong man. Finally, in all four cases, Chartreuse had used different methods of killing his victims. One was manually strangled, one was beaten to death, one was stabbed to death and the fourth strangled with a whip ligature.

With these last two murders, nothing even remotely resembled Chartreuse's "M. O." Neither had been discovered quickly. Quite the opposite, they were buried and never found for nearly ten years. This obviously meant no evidence had been left to implicate any innocent "suspect." In fact, Stone knew that Chartreuse had taken his own life before these two bodies were even found. It was totally impossible for these two murders to have any bearing on Chartreuse's motive for the other killings. These two led to no wrongful conviction by police. It made no sense for Chartreuse to have killed these two. And finally they were both killed in the same way—and Chartreuse never used repetition.

So, with these arguments leaning strongly away from Chartreuse and toward Ludlow as the killer, what could be Ludlow's motive? One stood out immediately. It was very obvious. These killings could provide Ludlow with probably the greatest exclusive in the annals of Canadian crime reporting. Stone just allowed his imagination to take over. Here would be Ludlow the crime reporter leading cops to two murder bodies they didn't even know existed. Then, Ludlow the crime reporter would solve the two murders for them. In doing that, he would solve a serial killer mystery, handing the cops the serial killer on a plate for six slayings they had no clue he had done. And most incredible of all, here would be Ludlow the crime reporter getting four innocent men freed from prison, where they had been given life sentences for murders they didn't commit. All Canada would know him for that. Ludlow and the "four innocent men" in Canada would be more famous than Woodward and Berstein in the States for bringing down President Nixon in the Watergate scandal. And on top of all this public glory, Ludlow would have the secret knowledge that he'd got away with two perfect murders.

Stone's theory about Ludlow was definitely flying. Hell, when he tried to pick holes in it, he couldn't. There was still more circumstantial evidence against Ludlow. Serial killer profilers always quoted that a basic building block of profiling was to look for a suspect who tried to interject himself into a homicide inquiry. Yes, thought Stone, it could be said Ludlow had done that, at every turn, over and over again.

For Ludlow's motive in these last two killings to work, he would have to try throwing suspicion on Chartreuse as the killer. Stone asked himself if Ludlow had done that. Of course he had. He'd invented the whole story about the letters and diaries supposedly containing Chartreuse's confessions. That was all.

Stone was now satisfied he had enough real suspicion about Ludlow to set up a team of detectives to investigate him. There were many more facts Stone wanted checked out. He brought in two of the newer guys more recently seconded to the homicide unit, outlined his suspicions, and drew up a list of information he wanted researched about Ludlow's background.

All this time, Ben was busy with this developing sex scandal in Saskatchewan, spending more time across the prairies than in Calgary. That suited the homicide detectives admirably as they made seemingly idle inquiries about him whenever they encountered Ben's fellow reporters. One of the team spent many hours in Calgary's public library archive section studying back issues of the Calgary Mail going back more than a dozen years.

Every few days the team reported back to Stone with snippets they had discovered, never really knowing where their little nuggets of information fit into the big picture, if at all.

First, they discovered that throughout the late spring and into June of 1992, the period when it was thought these two women were probably murdered, stories appeared nearly every day with Ludlow's by-line on them in the Mail. There was no doubt Ludlow was working in Calgary throughout that period. He hadn't been sent away on any stories. It was a small building block for Stone. Ludlow was in Calgary and therefore could have had opportunity to carry out these two murders.

Research into earlier cuttings from the Mail in the library helped Stone put another piece of the puzzle together. And this one was a real shocker. Way back in 1987, Chartreuse was wrongly accused of a murder for which he spent 19 months behind bars before being freed. This was the spark for his fanatical hatred of cops which supposedly led to all this. Stone knew all that. But the cuttings showed Ludlow had covered the original murder for the Mail. His by-line was on the story on the very day it was revealed that the cause of death for the victim who'd been found in the trunk of his own car, was a screw-driver through the brain.

These cuttings showed that Ludlow knew Chartreuse had been charged with murdering someone by forcing a screwdriver through their brain. Of course, it was all a frame-up and Chartreuse had done no such thing, and had never been convicted. But Ludlow knew police records would show the link between Chartreuse and the screwdriver "M. O." Of all the methods of killing these two women which Ludlow could have employed, which did he use? He used the only one which he knew for certain would be linked with Chartreuse, and would throw suspicion on him. These cuttings proved to Stone that Ludlow, the killer, had cunningly and deliberately tried to frame Chartreuse, who, remarkably in these two particular killings, was beginning to look more and more innocent. It was the ultimate beautiful irony. Here was a four-time killer who had framed four innocent men for murders they didn't commit, being framed by someone else for two murders he actually hadn't done.

The next bombshell came in Stone's mail—another envelope from Colombia, this time the pictorial dolphin stamps being replaced by stamps showing world cup soccer scenes. He'd been half expecting it, and knowing what it must contain, Stone again had it handled carefully by a scenes-of-crimes officer. When the forensic scientists had finished with it, the contents came back to Stone. As expected, here were the last two Polaroid pictures. Stone studied the first picture. It showed a bloodied letter "A" carved in flesh. The second picture, also of mutilated human skin showed a bloody letter "L" and nearby was a human belly-button, looking exactly like a period. He had never seen these particular wounds before. They were very similar to the carved flesh he'd seen on the previous Polaroids. Of course, he had no way of knowing which wound came from which victim.

They were exactly as Ludlow had predicted they would be. Ludlow had described these wounds in perfect detail—right down to the belly button. He could only have known this minute detail if he was the killer.

Stone turned over the picture with the bloody "A" and saw the expected newsprint words on the back. This time they said "Ben Ludlow" and "You"—"Got"—"the"—"Picture"—"Now?" with the words separately cut from some newspaper. On the back of the "L" picture were the words "Ben Ludlow" and "Don't"—"Get"—"it"—"Wrong"—"Again."

All this time, Stone hadn't wanted to believe Ludlow was the killer. But now he saw, with these two Polaroids, the devious depths to which Ludlow had sunk to pull off his perfect double murder. These two Polaroids, which Ludlow had obviously produced after his two murders, were a double bluff. By putting his own name on the back of both, he was trying to make it appear Chartreuse had prepared them to frame him. Stone saw through the ruse right away. He was convinced now this was Ludlow trying to throw him off the scent.

Well, it wasn't working. Stone was growing daily more confident he almost had enough evidence to charge Ludlow with these last two homicides. More reports were coming in from the team checking on Ludlow's background. No reporters in the Mail office had ever seen Ludlow with a tin box at his desk. No reporters had ever seen him digging up any tins at the river bank. No one had ever heard him talk about digging up tins at the river bank.

None had ever seen anything they could recognize as "letters and diaries" on his desk, but there was usually so much crap on his desk anyway, that wasn't surprising. Negative findings were often as important as positive findings in homicide cases. Stone still had no independent corroboration that Ludlow's supposed "letters and diaries" existed, even though his detectives were trying to find such proof.

Then the researches in the library threw up another interesting piece of circumstantial evidence against Ludlow. A detective found a feature Ludlow had written in the early 1990s which featured both the latest two murder victims. Of all the prostitutes in Calgary, Ludlow had a prior association with both these murdered women. On its own, it didn't mean much, but it was another brick in the wall Stone was building against him.

Detectives discreetly checking on Ludlow's private life discovered he had probably the most extensive library of murder documentary books in the entire province. His home was crammed full of just about every true-life murder book ever published. Being well-read for his profession was one thing—but this was almost like a shrine to murder. It would make another half-brick in the wall.

And then there was this strange Colombia thing. Why on earth did the Polaroid pictures come to Stone through Colombia? Stone had his detectives check on Ludlow's well publicized interest in stamp collecting. Hell, Ludlow had even won national literary awards for writing knowledgeable features about stamps. Did he have links with any Colombian stamp collectors? It was a long shot, but it brought a result. Detectives found Ludlow did have connections in exactly the right place in Colombia—in the Bogota post office. It would have been no problem for him to organize the link through Colombia. But why would he do so? It only made sense when Stone remembered Ludlow had told him Chartreuse had been to Colombia, probably drug-smuggling or gun-running. Why would Ludlow have told Stone this seemingly useless piece of information. Now it was obvious. It was Ludlow linking Chartreuse's name with Colombia where only Ludlow knew the tell-tale Polaroids would come from. It was another straight-forward attempt by Ludlow to frame Chartreuse for these last two murders.

Stone was now surprised to find himself convinced that Ludlow was the killer of these last two women. Applying his own golden rule that every detail must fit for a murder to be solved, he was troubled to find every detail did fit.

It was time to share everything he had found with the rest of the team. He called the whole team working on the last two murders together.

He was well known in the homicide unit for outlandish presentations always aimed at making his detectives think outside the box. This time, as the team arrived in the homicide office, they discovered the seats in the room arranged in two rows of six, one row behind the other. They sat awaiting his arrival. He surprised them by sweeping into the room wearing an English barrister's white curly wig and flowing black gown and armed with a gavel. When the cheering and laughter had died down, Stone stood behind a single desk standing in the center of the room facing the two rows of officers.

"Gentlemen of the jury," said Stone, clutching the lapels of his gown in the stance of bewigged barristers he had seen in English plays on television, "you are here today to listen to the case against Ben Ludlow for the dastardly murders of two women, whose skeletons were recovered from their burial spot on the southern outskirts of the city."

The assembled homicide detectives immediately listened carefully. They knew this was no joke. Stone instantly had their attention. He presented his case as carefully as any prosecuting attorney. He was fair. He filled in the background that Garry Chartreuse had been responsible for four earlier murders, and could be considered a suspect for these two. But he outlined his solid reasons why the evidence pointed to Ludlow, leaving no room for any reasonable doubt.

In Stone's "court," his jury members now had a chance to question the "prosecutor" directly face-to-face.

"If Ludlow was the killer, and had successfully evaded detection for nearly ten years, why would he suddenly reveal the whereabouts of the bodies to police, and bring this prosecution down on his head?" asked a veteran detective in the back row of the jury who clearly saw this as a reasonable doubt.

"Ah," said Stone, relishing the chance to answer this vital point. "This goes to his motive," and he explained in the greatest detail how Ludlow could only pull off the greatest exclusive in newspaper history by revealing these murders to police—and framing Chartreuse for them. "It's all a matter of glory. Ludlow is a reporter who has been in the business for 30-odd years. This was his last chance to pull off probably the biggest newspaper scoop ever. He couldn't resist it." The juryman in the back row nodded and raised his eye-brows in one movement, satisfied with the explanation.

Another member of the jury in the front row had a question. "It seems the strongest evidence against Ludlow is his blood and DNA on the remnants of the panties. Why the hell would he personally hand this damning evidence to police? That makes no sense."

"Good question," said Stone, pleased his detectives were putting his theory to stringent examination. "The answer is three-fold. In the first place, I think he was careless in getting his blood on the panties. The quantities were small and I believe he may not even have realized he'd done it. Secondly, when he brought these things to me he knew the murders had taken place nearly ten years earlier. I doubt he realized we could still trace the DNA. And thirdly, I am sure he had been told and believed all those years back when his DNA was taken for some news feature that it was going to be destroyed. He had no idea we had his DNA, so it couldn't possibly put him at risk."

Stone took off his wig and gown and threw them on the desk. The detectives turned the room back into its normal state. "That's a fucking shocker," said the veteran who'd been in the back row. "I've known Ludlow for years. Who'd have thought it? Just shows you can't discount anyone as a suspect in this game. When we are we going to lift him?"

"I'm going to get him tomorrow in his office at the Mail. You'll be with me." Stone beckoned another of the more experienced detectives over. "Us three will do it tomorrow," he said. He just had some paperwork to complete with the prosecutor's office and the stage was set. The rest of the homicide unit dispersed, and the three old hands prepared themselves for what was coming tomorrow. It was going to be a real stunner.

Chapter 17

An entire television crew was crowded in the Mail newsroom as Ben arrived next day. Newspaper reporters usually had strong views about television crews. Ben had strong views. Mostly they pissed him off. It wasn't the individuals. Ben got on pretty well with most of them individually. It was the way the "television crew" acted collectively. Worse still, it was the way most of the world reacted to having a television crew in its midst. Ben had wasted much of his life waiting at press conferences for some cursed television crew to turn up. They would roll in late. And, most infuriating of all, some senior police officer would patiently wait for them, keeping a room full of mere newspaper reporters and photographers waiting. This would be this uniformed guy's chance to have his face on television. There would be little point in starting without the television cameras. The late-comers would arrive, pushing their bulky equipment, tripods, cameras, cables, and fluffy-covered microphones to the front, scattering other reporters' microphones to one side. And instantly the press conference would begin.

Ben chuckled as a thought crossed his mind. He imagined a room full of television crews lined up for a press conference, and senior police officers lined up waiting to get their faces on the 6 o'clock news. And the word would go out "Hang on, Ben Ludlow's not here. We gotta wait until he gets here." And the whole room would wait until Ben would make his grand entry! Right on! In your dreams, Ben Ludlow.

Ben pushed through the throng to get to his desk. He knew what the cameras were here for, it was always the same. Ben's ferreting around on murder stories often meant he came up with the vital mug shot of the murder victim that no one else could get. The Mail loved to blast any such picture right across the front page under a giant headline "Schoolgirl Slain" or "Young Bride Murdered." It would be the only picture available. No other family members would yield any more photographs to any other media outlet. The

Mail would have another exclusive scoop. Ben would probably pick up another "daffodil" for the day's work. And next day, a high-ranking executive from one of the television news programs would call the Mail's city editor or the photographic editor. The actual conversation would be straight forward and unemotional. Could the executive send over a camera crew to copy the Mail's exclusive photograph for use on the news that night? It wouldn't take a minute. The news cast would credit the Mail for the picture, of course, so everyone in the city would know the Mail had kicked their butts. And if the Mail ever needed a favor in the future, well…

In fact, it would be a call charged with emotion. It was the ultimate admission that Ben had kicked ass when the boss of a television company with mighty resources behind him had to come cap-in-hand to the Mail asking to copy the picture the paper had featured the day before. The executive was eating humble pie and he knew it. The Mail's city editor and photo editor glowed and gloated inwardly. They always said yes. Magnanimous, they were. It was one of the brightest moments of their day.

Ben didn't like them doing it. Too often, the city editor was conned by the silver-tongued television executive. After all, that's why he was an executive. He'd promise the credit line would go to the Mail. But it seldom appeared. The Mail's city editor would play the game. He'd watch the television news at 6 p.m. He'd see the Mail's exclusive photo with no credit line for the Mail. Everyone thought the television crew had used their wiles to get their own photograph. Then the city editor would call the television station, yelling about the missing credit, and what the hell was going on. And he'd be placated, "I told them to put it on there. Didn't they do it? Heads will roll, you mark my words." But heads never rolled. Ben imagined the television executive sitting back in his deep leather-bound armchair, smirking that he'd pulled the wool over the Mail again.

"What's that all about?" Ben asked Frank, nodding toward the camera crew. Frank allowed his voice to be loud enough to be heard beyond only Ben's hearing.

"They're just here to copy our front page picture from yesterday," said Frank, glowing with pride. He'd already made the deal. The television would put the Mail's credit line on the photo when it appeared. And the television company was in Frank's pocket. They owed him big. "Yea, right on," thought Ben.

It was another exclusive photo which Ben had wheedled out of a family. In fact, this one was easy—almost a giveaway. This young mom had been missing for a day and Ben had simply urged the family to give him a photograph, so the Mail could help find her. By the time the picture could be used, the woman's murdered body had been found. The Mail's exclusive photo ran, as usual, across the whole front page, under the headline "Mom's Body Found."

It was one of Ben's unwritten golden rules—when a family needs help with a missing relative, grab every available photograph of the lost soul. Then, down the line, no matter how much later, when the case turned to murder on the day the corpse was discovered, Ben would be one step ahead with the photograph. The added bonus was, if Ben got in first and scooped up all the available photographs, other media outlets would be left with nothing. It had worked again this time.

"You should have told them 'no'," said Ben.

"No, it's good for us," said Frank, basking in the knowledge of the deal he'd cut with the executive, and knowing the Mail would be credited for all to see when the television used the picture. It was another of those battles with the boss that Ben never won, but he felt better for having grumbled about it.

Suddenly, all hell broke loose.

Just as the television crew were pinning the photograph on the corkboard alongside the picture desk to copy it, just as Frank was admiring the fruits of his deal with the television company, just as half the newsroom was idly watching these glamour-guys of the media industry with their mighty cameras, coils of cable, and clapper-board assistants, there was a stir at the corridor leading into the newsroom. Most of the reporters noticed the two uniformed cops first. Ben glanced up and saw Stone first. Strange he hadn't called ahead to say he was coming, Ben thought. Probably wants to check something in my files, he's consulted them before. But he didn't usually come straight over. Then Ben saw behind Stone and the two uniforms were two more guys from the homicide unit. A whole deputation! Ben started to rise to greet Stone. Just as he got to his feet and pushed his chair back, the two uniformed officers pushed past Stone and each grabbed one of Ben's arms.

"What the fuck?" said Ben. The officers were grabbing for Ben's hands. Ben's natural reaction was to try to keep his hands free. As usual, a tall pile of files littered Ben's desk, and as he whirled trying to free himself, the files went crashing to the ground, scattering a small cloud of papers across the floor. The officers quickly had Ben's hands trapped—handcuffed. Ben was so preoccupied with the two officers he hardly noticed that Stone had stepped right in front of him.

"Ben Ludlow, I am arresting you for the murders of Elaine Wattler and Stephanie Gurdey. You have the right to retain and instruct counsel without delay. That means that you may call your own lawyer or get free legal advice from duty counsel. If you do not have a lawyer, I can provide you with a 1-800 number for free and immediate advice. Do you understand? Do you want to call a lawyer?" said Stone, staring right into Ben's eyes.

"Fuck me rigid," said Ben. "What are you talking about?" For a split second, neither of the names meant anything to him. Elaine who? And Stephanie what? In the next split-second, he remembered—Chili and Kris, the two hookers. Oh no!

"You got it all wrong," he shouted. "No, I don't need a lawyer."

A lot of things happened in those next shocking seconds. The television cameraman reacted quicker than anybody. His camera was already rolling, copying yesterday's photograph. He swung it onto Ben and captured the moment Ben was captured. He caught the moment the cuffs clicked shut right there on film—in close-up.

No matter how bad this was for Ben, this was Frank's worst nightmare. Panicking, he grabbed the phone and called Sarah Langdon. "Get out here right away—right now. Christ knows what's going on," he shouted.

Frank guessed instantly it must be connected to the two dead hookers. He'd dreaded this happening right from the first moment Ben talked about this story. Frank had helped sell the story to Langdon. It would turn out to be his fault. The shit would land on his shoulders. How could Ben do it to him? The lying bastard, he'd promised Frank it was all above board.

Sarah Langdon hurried out from her executive editorial office. What she saw was a blur. Her top crime reporter was there, his arms pinioned behind his back by two uniformed cops. He was surrounded by three guys in suits. Langdon recognized Stone. She'd met him once at a banquet at city hall, together with the publisher and the chief constable. She couldn't take it all in—the head of homicide?—and a television crew? What the hell were they doing here? By now the Mail's photographer Jessica Sewell had appeared. Frank had called her in from the photo studio along the corridor the second after calling

Langdon in from her office. Sewell was up on a chair, taking pictures of the television crew filming Ben being arrested for murder.

Most reporters in the room, especially those over there in the life-styles section, whose worlds revolved around the sophisticated, cultured, sedate, artistic, and peaceful elements of life, were stunned. It looked like the two cops were man-handling Ben rather roughly. Police brutality was something they saw only in films as they watched from their free media seats during film previews. Cops really were like that, now they saw them in the flesh. They'd knocked Ben's files all over the floor, and just grabbed him, wrestled with him. It was shocking. They crowded nearer to see what would happen next.

Langdon tried to bring managerial order to the scene. First—get that damn television crew out of here. Whatever this was all about, it had to be hushed up. The Mail didn't want any of this on the television news. What the hell was Frank doing, allowing a television crew to be in the newsroom in the first place?

"I'm afraid I must ask you guys to leave," said Langdon to the film crew. The very fact they agreed should have confirmed her worst fears. They already had every detail they needed on film. Now, they were doing the gentlemanly thing and leaving. Langdon strode purposely over to Stone.

"What's going on?" she demanded.

"Just stand back, ma'am," said Stone. "We're just doing our job, please don't interfere."

Langdon decided the next priority was to distance the Mail from whatever personal disasters Ludlow had brought upon his own head. She picked up the nearest phone and called the Mail's lawyers. Ben might not think he needed a lawyer. Langdon needed legal advice on behalf of the Mail right now. Were the police officers trespassing? Did they have the legal right to come into her newsroom, uninvited, and arrest her staff willy-nilly? But the Mail's lawyers weren't available right now. They would call back later in the day. Langdon slammed the phone down with a crash. Frank heard it and winced. This was turning very nasty. Langdon shouted at Jessica Sewell.

"Take pictures of everything the police are doing," she ordered, hoping the photographs would show the police breaching some technicality which would enable to Mail to have recourse to sue them. Of course, Jessica was a long way ahead of Langdon. She had already taken pictures of everything that happened.

Why did management always have to try to tell their top professionals how to do their jobs, even in times of crisis?

Now there was movement. The little knot of men in the center of the crowd began shuffling away from Ben's desk. It was like a mini-parade. The two homicide detectives walked in front of Ben, who walked with his arms handcuffed behind him, where the two uniformed officers held him one to each arm, with Stone behind them. Jessica pushed past the little group and moved backward ahead of them, snapping photographs every few seconds, demonstrating that uncanny skill which professional photographers have of walking backward, taking pictures, yet not tripping over obstacles behind them. At the top of the stairs, Jessica leaned on the heavy red metal rail, still taking pictures, as the police and the murder suspect went downstairs. It was one of the first times Jessica realized with a grin that Ben was completely bald on top. The arrest team went across the foyer and out the front door.

The television crew was waiting in ambush. They'd left the newsroom when requested. No one said anything about not waiting in the parking lot. They filmed as Ben was led by the officers across to a waiting cruiser, where he was pushed into the back seat, one of the officers pressing down on Ben's head as he got in, so he wouldn't hit it on the door frame. The police didn't want bloody head injuries to occur which anyone could misconstrue as police brutality.

One of the uniformed officers sat beside Ben in the back seat. The other got into the driver's seat. Stone stood at the cruiser window.

"Just wait here until I come out," he said, peering in and staring coldly at Ludlow in the back, before he walked away, back into the Mail building.

Ben's mind was in turmoil. Firstly, he was scared. He felt nauseous. A thousand thoughts crowded through his mind. He saw himself spending years in prison for a crime—well, two crimes—he didn't commit. He knew such things happened. Look at the four men in prison right now.

It suddenly dawned on him. He was going to be the fifth man. Garry's fifth fucking victim. He had done it again. Even from beyond the grave. How? Oh Christ! Ben suddenly remembered the day he'd cut his finger in Garry's stretched limo. Garry had his blood. Garry had obviously prepared the seatbelt buckle, knowing Ben would cut his finger. Somehow Garry must have used the blood to give police Ben's DNA. Oh God, on the knicker crotches. That's where he must have put it. And Ben had given them to Stone, presented

Stone with the very evidence Garry wanted him to have. Ben's mind raced. What else? Oh my God! Ben had given Stone every detail of the two murdered hookers before they'd dug up the bodies. Only the killer could have known those details. Stone obviously didn't believe Ben that there had been any letters from Garry in the first place. He didn't believe they'd been destroyed in the fire. He only had Ben's word for that. The only alternative for Stone to believe was that Ben was the killer.

Ben was scared. Why? Why would Garry want Ben behind bars? Ben groaned at the answer. It wasn't anything to do with Ben. Garry had engineered it now so that the cops were about to put a fifth innocent man in jail for a murder he didn't commit. It was going to be the fifth giant cock-up to embarrass the police. Ben just happened to be a convenient victim—just the like the four before him.

Sitting there, hunched down, broken, Ben's terrified imagination ran riot.

What about when he got in there, in prison, what about all the murderers he'd featured in his articles, all those psychos who hated him, they'd get to him for sure. Guards would find him one day stabbed to death in a shower room, probably mutilated after death, or worse still, tortured before death. Ben knew he was hopeless at withstanding pain. Oh God! How could the cops have got it so wrong—again? Before, Ben had this blind faith in cops. They didn't arrest anyone until they knew they had the right man. But they'd already got it wrong four times in a row. Now it was five. But no one knew that—except Ben. People would think the cops wouldn't have arrested Ben unless he was guilty. And now he desperately wanted to take a piss. Ben guessed fright must be a physical thing that pressed on your bladder.

"Oh God, oh fuck me rigid," he groaned.

"Did you say something?" asked the cop in front.

"No, nothing," said Ben, and distraught and stunned, he let his head slump down lower.

Chapter 18

All you could hear in the newsroom was laughter. Shrieks of laughter, and hand-shaking, back-slapping, and the greatest party atmosphere the newsroom had ever known. In the center, around Ben's desk, was a new knot of men. Stone was there, together with his two homicide detectives. Sarah Langdon was there, Frank was there, Jessica Sewell was there, and every other reporter in the room crowded in to be as near the scene of triumph as possible. It had been the greatest goon the newsroom had ever seen. Maybe the most sensational goon the Mail had ever known. Probably the finest goon the newspaper industry had ever experienced, anywhere in Canada.

Ben Ludlow was sitting in handcuffs out in the parking lot in the back of a police cruiser, believing he'd been arrested for a double murder—and it was all a goon!

It had the unlikeliest of beginnings at that city hall banquet when Langdon had met Stone. During the quiet after-dinner mingling session when the cigars come out and the guards go down, and the formal dinner-time smiles and polite banter give way to real conversations, Stone, the head of homicide, and Langdon, the newspaper executive, bumped into each other.

The only topic Langdon could think of to talk to Stone about was the double murder scoop they'd had just a short while before. Stone had rubbed his chin thoughtfully when Langdon raised the matter.

"You know, at one time I had your man Ludlow down as a good suspect for those two killings," he said. "He knew a hell of a lot about the killings long before we did. He knew details about how those women were killed that only the killer could have known."

"God, I didn't know any of that," said Langdon, making sure she was distancing the Mail from anything to do with Ludlow and any murders.

"Yea, Ludlow came to me with information. I had to decide if he was coming forward just to be helpful, or was he coming forward as a giant bluff, because all the time he was the killer," said Stone.

"Ah," said Langdon, flicking her head to throw the hair out of her face again. She suddenly realized that all this could easily have rebounded on the Mail rather badly.

"In the end, we chased down every word Ludlow had told us, and when we matched it all with the other evidence we had, we knew he hadn't done the murders. And do you know, Ludlow never even knew we were looking at him for having done them in the first place. He had no idea."

"Does he know now?" asked Langdon.

"No, not a clue," said Stone.

"Look," said Langdon, drawing Stone nearer her conspiratorially, "what about arresting him for the murders anyway—you know, a spoof. I'll set it up in the newsroom, and you guys come and arrest him. I can get television cameras there and everything."

Langdon had known newsroom gooning all her career. Hell, she'd been a victim as a reporter herself. This was too good a chance to let go begging. And so the diabolical plan was hatched.

Now, the perpetrators were enjoying their moment of triumph, already reliving every second. Everyone had acted their roles brilliantly. Stone kept his dead-pan face all through the moment of arrest, every sinew in his body straining not to burst into laughter. The police officers had really used quite some strength to get the handcuffs on—assured by Stone there could be no repercussions on them whatever happened. One even enjoyed the moment he knocked all the newspaper files off the desk all over the floor to add to the confusion. Frank played his panicky part beautifully—well, it was almost natural for him—calling in Langdon and Jessica Sewell, who were both, of course, sitting at their phones, awaiting their cues. Langdon found it no big deal to act out "anger" during the scene. Her "lawyer" phone-call, of course, with no one on the other end, was masterfully done. And her dismissing the television crew was done with authority, it being she who had invited them along in the first place to copy a photograph their office already had anyway. The newsroom had been particularly packed, because word had leaked out something was going to happen that no one should miss.

"Did you see his face?"

"I thought he was going to burst into tears."

"He was really struggling."

You couldn't hear half the banter for the laughter. Now, all that was left was to be there when they broke the news to Ben out in the parking lot. All the actors had their final instructions. They were all to crowd around the car looking serious, after all, it wasn't every day they got a chance to see a "killer" in a police car, let alone a "double-killer."

The cruiser was parked facing away from the front door of the Mail. As the posse walked through the front door led by Stone and Langdon, the driver, expecting them, saw them in his rear view mirror and started the engine. Ben felt a new fear, a new surge of nausea rising and a new urgent need to take a piss. He was in for one last humiliation as he became aware most of the newsroom was out there crowding around as he was about to be driven away.

On the back seat, there was room for one more person. The uniformed cop was to the left, Ben was in the center, and now the right hand door opened as Stone leaned in, obviously to sit there for the ride down to homicide.

"Ludlow, face away from me," said Stone in that same cold voice Ben had heard inside. Cowed, Ben did as he was told. In a second, Stone had the handcuffs unlocked and Ben's hands were free.

"Look at me, Ludlow," said Stone. Ben turned round. Stone's face was a picture. Roaring with laughter, he said, "you've been gooned, Ben, you've been had," and he half lifted Ben out of the cruiser to the cheers of the reporters who were laughing and high-fiving each other.

It slowly dawned on Ben.

"Bastards," he said, "I can't believe it." Every face he saw had been in on it. Frank was laughing, Sarah Langdon was shrieking with laughter, Jessica was laughing, and the television crew was giving him the thumbs up—still filming the look on his face. Stone put his arm around him and one of the uniformed cops shook his hand. Ben just kept repeating it. "Bastards," he said, over and over.

Ben invited the arrest team, and anyone who wanted to come to the nearest northeast Calgary bar for a drink. There was a lot he needed to talk to Stone about. And he badly needed a piss.

Chapter 19

It was a hell of a drinking session at the Top Brass bar, which was quite an eye-opener for most of Ben's office colleagues. They seldom saw him drinking. There was a very boring reason why he usually didn't join them. He was diabetic. Some medical specialist told him he had two choices. Carry on boozing and have to live with insulin injections every day, or cut out the booze and live a normal life. Ben, ever the coward with needles, cut out the booze.

But that night he had a few. He couldn't keep up with those around him, but he had enough to need a cab to get home. He did remember the last thing Stone told him before he left was to be sure to get to the homicide office next morning—really early, 6 a. m. at the latest.

He got there on time, exchanged his picture identification for a visitor's tag in the lobby and went to the 10th floor homicide office. Stone took him into the homicide room where it looked like the whole of the Whiskey Foxtrot team, city detectives and RCMP officers, was gathered. It was packed even at this ungodly hour in the morning. A few of the city detectives Ben had worked with for years put down their Styrofoam coffee cups and shook his hand.

"Okay, let's run through the whole thing," said Stone. "We know for certain that Garry Chartreuse killed all six of our victims in Alberta. He succeeded in tricking city cops and RCMP officers into arresting, charging and convicting four innocent men. It looked as if his final act of hatred against police was to get us to convict a fifth innocent man, you Ben, even from beyond the grave."

"First, we knew you couldn't possibly have done it the way it played out. We knew you obviously had received the letters and diaries you said you'd received, which accounted for how you knew all the details you did know. We believed the diaries were destroyed accidentally in the fire, like you said they were. We knew you were telling the truth both times."

"But the clincher was the last two Polaroids."

"You couldn't possibly have been responsible for the last two Polaroids from Colombia, because you didn't know anything about any Polaroids until after you'd read Garry Chartreuse's diaries earlier this year. Yet those Polaroids were taken at the time of the murders back in 1992."

"I had checks made in Colombia by a drugs-squad detective. He tracked down the guy over there who had sent the two packages of Polaroid pictures. This Colombian once had dealings with Chartreuse years back. Earlier this year he'd recently received the two packages from Chartreuse with instructions to send the larger package by post at a certain time, and the smaller package by post some weeks later. He got paid well for doing next to nothing. So we knew the Polaroids had nothing to do with you."

"Looking at how Chartreuse had stitched up those first four suspects with DNA it was obvious he'd done the same to you with the blood on the panties. I doubt you even realized you'd given him a lovely sample of your blood until it was too late."

"Yea, I know," said Ben, remembering the ride in the stretched limo.

"So here's where we stand. You kept your word all this time about not mentioning the four disasters that we've got to face. Now, I'm keeping my word. Tomorrow you can go ahead with doing what you've got to do. Run with everything. You'll have a one day start."

"On the day after tomorrow, there will be a press conference like no one has ever seen. For us, it's going to be a horror job. The police chief, the head of the major crimes unit and I will be there from the city, together with the superintendent in charge of the Alberta division of the RCMP and his senior detective officers—more top brass in one room than you've ever seen."

"Basically, this is what the most senior officers are going to say. First they will reveal that a serial killer had been at work in Alberta in the early 1990s who murdered six women in Calgary, Pincher Creek, Taber and Red Deer. He had then moved to Spokane where he murdered another 11 women before being caught. While he was in custody in Spokane awaiting trial, he committed suicide," said Stone.

"They'll be revealing that the first knowledge we had that these six Alberta homicides were the work of a serial killer came from Ben Ludlow, crime reporter of the Calgary Mail."

Cheering broke out in the room. Ben actually felt himself blushing.

"They'll reveal that confirmation of the identity of the serial killer and the most damning evidence which would have convicted him had he lived to stand trial was brought to police by Ben Ludlow and the Mail."

"My hero," shouted a voice from the back.

"Piss off," said Ben.

"Finally, and most important of all, they'll say that four innocent men who were convicted in error by police in Alberta in connection with the first four of these murders committed by the serial killer, are being released immediately, and all four will be receiving pardons. The senior officers will be sure to say that these men getting their freedom and the righting of a huge injustice is all down to Ben Ludlow and the Calgary Mail," said Stone.

"Satisfied?"

When it was all put together like that, even Ben could hardly believe it. It would be the major story of the year probably across the whole of Canada. Innocent men spending years in prison for murders they didn't commit was a major talking point across Canada even before this case. It would have massive ramifications for years to come.

"Right on," said Ben. "I'm on my way. Do you know how much work you've just landed me with?"

Back at the office, still ridiculously early in the morning, Ben grabbed Frank and told him they really needed to use the editorial boardroom right now. And he'd better call everybody in. This was bigger than anything he'd ever imagined. "I promise you you're going to end up smelling of roses," said Ben.

Frank made a flurry of phone calls. The upper echelons of the Calgary Mail editorial ranks weren't used to "early morning" as a concept. Finally, when all the Mail hierarchy was assembled in the dreaded room and the Venetian blinds had been dropped, Ben ran through everything Stone had said. The Calgary Mail was going to get the sole credit for unearthing a serial killer who murdered six women, for identifying the killer for police, and most importantly of all for freeing four innocent men who had been serving life sentences for murders they didn't commit. The most senior police officers in the province were going to stand before a battery of microphones and cameras the next day and tell the whole world all this was accomplished by the Calgary Mail.

There was more. The Mail could run with the whole story tomorrow and have it out on the streets as the biggest exclusive in the paper's history just before the press conference would begin.

Ben had two final pieces of good news. He had tons of the background already written up—pieces on the four innocent men, another on the serial killer, other pieces on the six victims, and his blow-by-blow account of how he—sorry, the Calgary Mail—the medical examiner's office and the homicide unit had smashed the case wide open. And he had a large file of photographs of all the major players. They were well ahead of the game. Tomorrow's paper was going to be a wonder to behold.

It was still early morning, well before noon, when the Venetian blinds were raised, and the euphoric editorial hierarchy bounced out of the room, bubbling with the colossal coup their brilliant newspaper had achieved. This was going to stick it to those guys down the road. This would elevate the Mail above all other media in the city. This could make the Mail the most prestigious newspaper in all Canada. Tomorrow's Calgary Mail was going to be the greatest self-advertisement the newspaper industry had ever experienced. And every word would be thoroughly well deserved. To a man, they could hardly wait to see the final product.

As Frank returned buoyantly to the city desk, he glanced up out of habit at the television monitor above the desk. What the hell was that? That looked dramatic. It looked like one of the towers of the World Trade Centre in New York was badly on fire.

"Look at that," he shouted, and most reporters in the room gathered at his desk to watch. Suddenly, on the screen, out of a clear blue sky they watched in disbelief as a giant jet airliner drove deliberately straight into the other tower, with a fantastic fireball erupting from the far side. Frank turned up the sound. The commentator, seemingly a little confused, was saying that two airliners had hit the twin towers of the World Trade Centre. Word was coming in that another airliner had slammed into the Pentagon in Washington turning it into a giant fireball.

This was the morning of September 11, 2001. It seemed that suddenly America was at war. As far as newspapers were concerned all over the globe nothing else happened in the world that day. Ben recalled a day long ago in the medical examiner's office when he imagined he'd have story, a doosie, covering four pages, no, six pages, no eight pages, and at last that day had come. But it wasn't Ben's story at all. Now it was the World Trade Centre story. On this one day of all historic days, nothing else ever made it into print.

Not even in the Calgary Mail!

Epilogue

In time, Ben did get his eight-page exclusive revealing his part in exposing a serial killer into the Calgary Mail with all its accompanying fanfares. And not much later, in fact surprisingly quickly considering the obstacles thrown up by the bureaucracy of any federal government department like corrections or justice, the four innocent men were released from prison and each was pardoned. The Calgary Mail could finally revel in every aspect of its hard-earned scoop.

Ron Lincoln, who'd started the ball rolling all those years before, used the million-dollar compensation paid him by the government to set up a major used-car dealership in Red Deer. His celebrity status as one of Canada's "Framed Four" massively increased his trading. It was something to buy your used, excuse me, "previously owned," car from such a celebrity.

Darren Sunderland hired a ghost writer and his story became a best-selling book, with even talk of a film in the offing to follow.

Paul Andres was delighted to find that when he came out, he was still young enough to be able to go back to ranching, with enough money behind him to buy new horses and an even bigger spread in southern Alberta.

The only sad story was the demise of the Rev. Jacob Broadbent. His quite extreme view of religion and mankind had the perfect environment in prison through all those years to push his mind beyond sanity. His view of God showing his hand as being the final judge and freeing him, where mankind had made such a glaring error in locking him away, babbled out of him. He was clearly insane when he was committed to a psychiatric hospital.

As for the Calgary Mail, its giant scoop, though delayed by world events, was a major newspaper coup far beyond the wildest dreams of its editorial hierarchy. The vagaries of the federal prison system meant, pleasingly for the Mail, that the four innocent men were released separately from different prisons on four successive days. This meant the Mail had four separate masses of publicity. What was more, throughout those weeks immediately following 9-11, while New York and "Ground Zero" was the lead story every day, the story of "Canada's Framed Four" was always the second lead. For a long time, the world's news was dominated by these dual leads, "9-11 and Canada's Framed Four," and every time that happened, the Calgary Mail was in people's minds again.

Mail executives were ecstatic. This time Ben was ordered to wear nothing less than a bow tie and suit when he was summoned to Toronto, the Mail's corporate headquarters. This was for another award ceremony far more glittering than that happy night years earlier when he'd learned to perform a roll-cast with his fly rod. This time, he received the newspaper's "award of excellence" which they reckoned no-one from Calgary had ever earned before.

The subject of how four men could be wrongly imprisoned for murder in the era of DNA brought intense debate at all levels—from intellectuals and philosophers, through lawyers and forensic scientists, from politicians and law enforcement and civil rights advocates, right down to cops and crooks. DNA—which was the strongest plank in the modern argument for bringing back the death penalty because mistaken convictions could no longer happen—had been the very tool which was used to create the mistakes. Now, it was debated across the nation. And every Canadian who had the topic on his lips inwardly gave thanks that the Calgary Mail had been there to restore justice and save Canada's collective shame.

Ed Stone retired from the city police, with his career reputation as being a sound and successful head of the homicide unit intact, despite being embroiled in the case of the "Framed Four." While it was true a serial killer had operated in his city while he was in charge of homicide, it was Stone who eventually ensured justice was done. It was his driving force which made sure the truth was revealed.

And as for Ben Ludlow, he too retired from the Mail, and from journalism. He had spent 37 years with one ear listening for scanner messages and reacting in seconds to human tragedies unfolding around him. His whole working life had been dictated by deadlines, with pressures from bosses above him, and the mental trauma of interacting with distraught people in the midst of their most terrible grief every day of his life. One thing pleased him most about the "Framed Four" story. He succeeded in keeping secret the identity of his contact in the medical examiner's office, without whom none of the story would have happened.

He left the Mail on a Saturday, and by the Monday he was living on a remote tiny island off the west coast of British Columbia, way beyond those mountain peaks he had gazed at so many times from the parking lot of the Mail.

This was an idyllic "be mellow" existence which he allowed to enfold him from the day he arrived. There was no traffic, hell, there wasn't a single traffic light on his island and damn few vehicles. The silence was dreamlike—no scanners, no telephones ringing, no surrounding babble of voices. He was free to go fishing.

On many days, he would see more seals sunning themselves on rocks and dolphins cleaving the mirror-calm sea surface with their fins, than ever he would see human beings. He was never happier than sitting out there fishing, surrounded by the most gorgeous scenery with uninhabited islands in the foreground and mountain ranges as a backdrop. He'd never had any doubt about what he would name his boat. Other boaters would pass by and see this quiet man happily fishing in his little cabin boat with his boat name emblazoned along the topsides—RIGHT ON!